IT'S NOT ABOUT YOU, WALLY

the traveling memoir

of a

solitary white man

KENT H. ELLIOTT

Wally and the people he meets, the places he goes, the events in which he participates are fiction—either from the author's imagination or are used fictitiously. The author's use of locales and public events, while real on a map or in history, are backdrops and not accurate portrayals. Any resemblance to any actual persons living or dead, places, or occasions is coincidental.

Cover art is from a pastel by the late Arlene Morgan, whose copyrights, where applicable, are held by her daughter, Barbara Morgan Elliott. For information about available Arlene Morgan art, contact the author.

Published by Wheatgrass Publishing,
the personal imprint of Kent H. Elliott

www.wheatgrasspublishing.com

Printing and world distribution through CreateSpace.com

ISBN-10: 069273838X

ISBN-13: 978-0692738382

DEDICATION

For introverts and the extraverts who love them;
for hermits and travelers;
for those who interpret and misinterpret motives;
for all who reach toward a future while trying to understand their past;
for all on life's journey, in trust or in doubt;
for you I imagined Wally and let him tell his story.

Also by Kent Elliott

Novels of old Montana:

I've Seen Dry

The Shallows of Jabbok

Short fiction collection:

The Deerhide Creek Mine Disaster and Other Stories
(includes the novella: *The Bursar's Calculation*)

PART ONE

(1)

"It looks like you can go home now, Wally."

I looked up and saw Hiram Magelsson with a grin that stretched from Lethbridge to Medicine Hat. Putting the wrench down on the engine block, I jumped off the gigantic diesel tractor and looked at Hy in puzzlement. "What did you say?"

"I said you can go home. It's safe now. Look at this. The paper just came with the mail." He grabbed the folded copy of the *Lethbridge Herald,* dated January 23rd, 1977, from the hip pocket of his insulated coveralls and pointed with a gloved finger to the story he'd kept outside the fold.

I wiped the fog and smudges off my glasses and read:

Unconditional Amnesty.

Washington, D.C. On his first day in office US President Jimmy Carter issued an unconditional amnesty to draft resisters."

I read on. I was looking for the exceptions and there were some which didn't apply to me. It was true. I looked back at my kindly employer and mentor who'd kept me on the farm for over five years.

"See? You can go home, see your family. Whadaya think of that, eh?" Hiram waited for me, his hired hand, to show some excitement.

"I am home. This is home and you're more like family than..." I shook my head, pushed overgrown hair from my face, and pulled the stocking cap down over my ears. "Are you firing me? Anyway, I come from Kamloops. I told you that? How does this apply to me?"

"From British Columbia? The hell you say. I never believed that for a minute. You might think so, but you can't hide that Chi-caa-go accent."

3

Hiram exaggerated the broad vowel of Midwestern-American speech almost into a long 'a'.

"If you knew I was lying, why'd you hire me? Why'd you keep me on and treat me like kin."

"Hell, boy, where do you think I'd ever find an honest ranch hand? I let go a drunken liar and took on a drunken liar who beat his wife. I'll keep a simple liar. Except..."

"Except what?"

"Except you ought to go home, eh. Make things right with your folks now that you can do it free. Now you won't get arrested — nothing like that."

"I told you. This is home. I'd rather stay here and work. Nobody bothering me. Nobody getting me to trust them and then, boom. Everybody lets you down, you know."

"God damn, you're making this hard, Mr. Wallace Mitchell Bradford the Third. See, I know more about you than you think. Don't you suppose your rich ma and pa miss you?"

That was enough. I put my insulated gloves back on, climbed up and picked up the wrench. "I got this tractor, two balers and a combine to overhaul, Mr. Magelsson."

"Plenty time, plenty time. Let's go up to the house. It's too damn cold in this shed." He looked up at the heating unit that wasn't making any noise. "You're allowed to have some heat out here?"

"The wind is blowing the heat away before I can feel it. Sorta like you. What's eating you, anyway, Hy?"

"Up to the house. I'll tell you where my nose won't freeze."

***

Prudence had the coffee ready. When she saw us coming through the gate she pulled the caramel rolls out of the oven. She'd been keeping them warm while she watched for us. "What kept you fellas?" she asked as she filled the mugs and we shucked off our heavy winter wear.

"This young man here was bound and determined to get everything ready for planting two months before the ground starts to thaw. He wants to work out there in the cold, eh."

"Did you tell him then, Hy?"

"That his new president says he can go home? You bet I told him." Hiram plopped into his captain's chair at the kitchen table.

"And the rest?"

I stiffened in tension.

"I'm about to. Had to get him in from the cold first, eh. And, like I said, that weren't an easy chore in itself."

Itching to know, I finally broke in, "What's the rest?"

"Cards on the table, eh," Hy said, placing his hands palm down one on each side of the plate in front of him. "Sit down and have a sticky bun while I tell you." He passed the plate of rolls across to the waiting plate beside my coffee mug.

I was coming quickly to the conclusion that whatever the rest was, it was difficult for Hiram to say it, so I took a sip of coffee. Hiram waited until my mug was safely back on the placemat before he spoke another word.

"Okay. Here it is. Pru and me, we're retiring, selling out. We're getting a little place over to Medicine Hat where the daughter is. Be able to watch grandkids grow up; get to more of their games and recitals and what not. I don't think we'll be needing a ranch hand for one dog and a patch of garden. You've been like a son to us, so it's hard, yeah. But you got a real family missing you."

I ignored the real family stuff. "Selling out? You have buyers? I could get them to hire me. I know the operation here. I could be a real help for them."

Hiram shook his head. "Won't work. It's more Hootterites coming, you see. Big families and all, they won't be hiring, eh."

"Have you signed? Made a firm commitment to sell to a Hutterite colony? What if I could make a better offer?"

Hiram looked at Prudence, who stared right back. Then she turned to me and said, "Oh, dear. We never considered any such thing possible. Hiram said you come from money down in Illinois (she pronounced the final letter which made me involuntarily cringe for a second) but we assumed they cut you off, what with you being a draft dodger and all."

I emptied my cup. Pru refilled it and I picked caramel off my plate while I pondered for a long moment. My accent made them suspicious. Okay, but how did they learn my true origin? It had to come from the bank in Taber where we all had accounts. "Oh, Junior probably did disinherit me or whatever. But Senior, my grandfather, keeps his promise with the trust fund. You never know, he might allow me to move the investment from Bradford and Son to Hy-Pru Farm. Didn't your banker friend show you my account balance when he told you where I'm from?" I immediately wished I hadn't asked that. But hell, I can't even trust them to trust my big lie. They let me think they believed it for five years.

Hiram's face reddened, but he stuck to his agenda. "I'm sorry, Wally. It's too late. The new folks'll be the ones planting come spring. Put money down last week, they did. Don't forget, though, your guy Jimmy Carter says you can go home. Give it a try. You've been with us five years and more. Have you talked to your mum in all that time, eh?"

"Of course, um, it has been a couple years, maybe more. Last time I called home, well—where I used to live. Right here is home. Last time Mom hassled me for besmirching the family name. Kept it up so long I hung up. Besmirch. She kept using that word. Who uses a word like that anymore? My Mom, that's who."

Prudence stood up. Hiram and I pushed our coffee mugs a few inches assuming she intended to refill them. Instead, she tugged at my shirt sleeve and said, "Come along. Time to make that call."

"What? Right now? It's international long distance; gonna cost." I called out all the excuses I could muster as she dragged me to the room they used as farm office. "I should call collect, then, eh?"

"Oh no, you'll not reverse charges. You'll call. You'll tell them you're coming for a visit."

Within two minutes I was back at the kitchen table forking into another sticky bun. I had a mouthful when I answered their question, "Busy signal." After I swallowed I added, "I can try again later. Next month."

"You know somebody's home. You will try again in a few minutes, not a few years."

The reprieve allowed Hiram to ask, "Now that you know we know, tell me something. What made you decide to skip the country when you did? A kid like you? You'd've been taken care of. Your rich daddy's got strings he can pull, eh. He could've kept you away from the worst of it."

"What if that's the reason? Pulling strings is just wrong, somehow. But did I even think about that? I don't remember. Ask Junior for a favor?" I shook my head. "It's all in my journals somewhere."

"Ah! Your journals. Always writing in those notebooks. What do you do with that lot anyways, eh?"

"I write. When it's full I put the dates on the cover and drop the notebook onto the pile. That's about it."

"Hmm. I wonder about you, young man. You're saying that coming north wasn't just your own survival? Not just about staying away from the wrong end of a commie gun?"

"Well, sir, it was that for sure. If I'd have relied on Wallace Junior and Rummy, his Congressman friend, to keep me safe, I'd owe him. And pay forever. So, maybe it is only personal. Maybe what got me here was a long hike. Maybe it was college and a mission trip. Maybe it was some short-time friends out of a scary-huge herd of people. For certain it was meeting a guy in Montana that everybody called Cracker. And he wasn't a white bigot, in spite of the nickname."

Hiram scratched his earlobe, started to ask another question, stopped, got up and topped up all the mugs. Then he said, "I'll get a wood fire started while you try that call again. Then we'll sit where it's warm and hear more about you."

The phone was answered this time. My mother didn't use the word 'besmirch' a single time. She cried and said, "Trey, just come and surprise the rest of the family. Come unannounced. Just show up. Let your father see you without warning so he won't have time to prepare a speech."

***

"Let's sit by the fire, young friend," Hiram said, encouragingly. "We'll take a Sabbath day and you can tell us about things that go in those journal notebooks."

"A Sabbath? Today's Tuesday."

"Close enough. Call it a snow day of rest, then. You will have to break bales for the critters later, though."

We sat. We finished our coffee in silence and watched the fire. I waited, expecting Hiram to ask a question or make some leading observation. He didn't. We sat.

Finally I spoke; it was time to say what was on my mind. "I don't like people much, especially in bunches. You might've noticed that. That's where it starts, I guess. It seems like it took me a long time to figure that out. But, damn, I was barely a grown up. I really figured it out settling down in a two room cabin east of the 'Bob'. Even there, my only neighbor proved me right about people. You can't trust 'em. That was the heavy load I put in my backpack; everybody lets you down. That was a nice home in the woods, just me, the trees and critters; and, of course, my notebook and pen.

"Now you're selling the ground out from under me. I'd rather stay here than go anywhere. I know you got every right to your retirement, but it hurts like hell. Yeah, I lied; you knew it and let me get away with it. What can we trust, Mr. Magelsson?"

"It's not about you, Wally." Hiram said it softly in a calm, even voice. "Was it ever, really? About you?"

"It sure seems like it when it's happening. Seeing as how you know that I don't come from Kamloops, I might as well tell you all about it. Then you can tell me what's not about me."

"I wouldn't presume to say…"

(2)

I come from the so-called 'filthy' rich: born, bred, and suburbanized. New Trier High, my alma whatever, is a public school with a prep school base of support. Winnetka, Illinois was still among the richest when I was growing up.

I started dating that one girl midway through our junior year. She was kind of cute, little and blonde; surrounded by a girl group conspiring together. I don't know how it happened, since I was still scared to talk to any of the girls I lusted after. Anyway, we dated whenever she was willing, which was any time she didn't have something better to do. We did whatever I planned and paid for, mostly movies. I liked to go to the movies. Nancy liked hanging out or partying with a crowd. That made me nervous and I didn't have it figured out back then. At a crowded theater I could still be alone once the house lights dimmed and the screen action began.

Nancy wasn't the girl I really wanted to be with, but I could sure be jealous whenever she turned down my invitations. Diane was the girl I desired and couldn't get close to. I'm trying to remember how Nancy and I started. I think she used her friends and arranged to corner me into asking her out. Through most of our senior year we dated only each other, I think. We didn't say we were going steady, but I thought we were.

It's all foggy except for one night I remember clearly. Well, maybe clear to partly cloudy. What I really is the moment she dumped me. High school was over. So was our relationship. Just like that. Oh, she had some grand excuse but all that meant to me was that I wasn't good enough. All I had going for me was family money. So, yeah, it wasn't about me. It was about Junior's money. At the company my father is known as Junior.

***

It was a couple nights after we graduated. I reached Nancy on the phone. "Hey Nance, you want to go to a movie? *A Thousand Clowns* is playing at the Skokie. I hear it's pretty good."

"Oh, hey Trey. I was gonna call you. Let's go to the beach tonight."

"Beaches all lock the gates at night, or they're private and always off limits."

"I know a place."

I was thinking, "Whoa babe. She wants to get past third base." We'd only reached that close one time and she wouldn't speak to me for two weeks after. I had a condom and a single rolled joint of marijuana in my pocket when I picked her up.

***

"I shouldn't be telling you all this, Hiram. Oh well. How do you say 'we got to third base' in a hockey metaphor?"

Hy shrugged and loaded his cheek with another plug of Beech-Nut, so I went on.

***

Nancy guided us half way to Waukegan and a mansion on the lake. I remember saying something, a compliment, about her new auburn hair color on the way. Then I foolishly had to ask, "Which is the real color?" She turned away and didn't answer, just stared out the window, silent until she said, "Turn right at the next street."

All her friends, the whole gang and many more, were there. I'd been tricked into a party. Someone shouted, "Nance is here, guys." He turned to us and added, "About time. We've been looking for you. Oh, hi Trey. Glad you could make it." Nancy started to move into the crowd around the keg. I followed, reluctantly. They were talking about summer fun before college in the fall. The guy who'd met us — Gary, possibly Greg or Gord, the tall, arrogant quarterback — started in about Princeton and how great that'll be. "Where are you headed, Trey? Chevy Tech at the Pure Oil?" He handed me a paper cup of beer.

I had avoided the college subject. I hadn't even told Nancy. Now I was caught off guard by the insulting tone and answered. "Yankton. It's a *college* in South Dakota." I emphasized the word 'college'.

"Yankton?" Nancy was incredulous. "You're going to a little college nobody's heard of? In North Dakota?"

She said it with such scorn it made me want to scream. It was hard to argue the point. She was off to Stanford in the fall. With my academic record and no varsity sports I was lucky to go anywhere. Still, I had to defend my plan. I even told her the truth. "Yankton, *South* Dakota, may be small but I can get a quality education there. My grandmother went there, so I'm probably a legacy admit or some such. I just don't see what the big deal is."

"Just go drink your beer, Wallace." Nancy took the G-named guy's hand and led him through the throng.

I started to do as she said, then reconsidered and stepped in front of them. "Is that it? Are we done, or what? We've been going out for over a year and you're gonna just push me off like none of that mattered?"

"Maybe it didn't. G____ will drive me home."

"Maybe it didn't." Her last words before she skipped off with that Greg/Gary/Gord creep.

I'd been tricked into a party for a break-up. "People. You can't trust people," I murmured my new motto, my life force. I dumped my beer in the sand and left. I probably sat in the car for twenty minutes before I was ready to drive home. I pounded my anger on anything near at hand. Then the great sadness took over until I said out loud to the rearview mirror, "I should be relieved. We were always more convenience than anything else we might have been. Yeah. I should be relieved." After I'd said it, and started almost to believe it, I drove home, crawled in bed and failed to sleep.

***

I remember the rest of that summer as nothing but hassles. I'd been put to work at Bradford & Son corporate headquarters. 'Son' in the company name was my father; 'Bradford' was my grandfather, Wallace Senior; so, of course I, Wallace Mitchell Bradford the Third was called Trey. Junior expected me to become familiar with corporate operation. For three weeks I played office go-fer and obnoxious ass. Other than family, the whole office cheered when I quit. I went to work at the Pure Oil service station that had long been my Saturday hangout. At every opportunity my family made sure to let me know that I was letting them down. My two older sisters fed me endless derision. My kid brother sneered and called me 'Pump Boy'. Dad lectured me. He questioned my character and loyalty. Mom kept silent. She was either unwilling or unable to challenge them. Her silence still hurts.

My excuse, to quiet them, became, "I'm not quite ready for the business world yet." I did not mention that I would never be ready. I'd just mumble nonsense and spend as much time as possible at the garage working on cars that came in needing fresh oil, plugs, tire repair or brake shoes.

Working for Mr. Morrison at the Pure Oil was my island of peace. Mr. M's oldest kid (we called him Buddy) was fifteen and working there, too. I had just turned eighteen and could do any job that Mr. M had taught me and that he trusted me with. I said he taught, but his method was mostly to make sure I was watching carefully and listening intently to the messages from the engine as I handed him tools. He was an intuitive mechanic.

Back at home, when the family was on me with all that Bradford drama, I'd close my eyes and remember what a big Ford V-8 sounded like before the ring job and then the way it purred after Mr. M had worked his magic.

When I bring him to mind now, I realize that Mr. M is kind've like me, or vice versa. He wanted to deal with people one or two at a time; he was happiest alone with an engine to rebuild; and he didn't trust much. An independent businessman in Winnetka, he and Buddy went home every night to their little duplex in Des Plaines. He'd bitch about the rich North Shore bastards who couldn't seem to pay on time. Then, he's apologize to me, saying he forgot I'm a rich kid. Yeah, that garage was my island of escape. And Mr. Morrison paid actual wages, unlike the company internship crap.

Junior, Dad, did his best to keep me upset with his reminders that if he was, by damn, sending me to college, I would, by damn, be at the company next year, by damn, if not sooner.

(3)

Yankton was a welcome change of scene, a different world for this city boy. It didn't take long for me to feel more at home there than in the city where I'd always lived. A small school in a small town with fresh air was nothing like my summer under automobile hoods and oil pans. I missed the work with my hands and tools, but I was ready to make a real effort at college. Professors offered personal help along the way, and then gave me the C-minuses my work deserved. I was assigned a faculty adviser in the English Department, likely because I didn't have any idea what my major would be and I don't have a German surname. Yankton had a lot of German-American religion students. Well, not many, possibly a small plurality; there were only a hundred or so of us in the entire freshman class. It's only a lot to a guy who prefers dealing with people one at a time, or not at all. The small classes made Grandma Charlotte's alma mater a good choice for one such as I.

Dr. Graves, my adviser and Composition 101 prof, took a shine to me and inspired use of phrases like "one such as I." We called her Old Doc Graves, though she was probably not much over fifty. Her gray hair and love of old books made her seem old. She tried mightily with me, but I just couldn't get into those ancient Greek and Roman epics. I'd write a few pages on essay assignments and turn them in unfinished. With her red pen she'd write encouraging words about the good start on the assigned topic and give it back for me to finish. Then I'd turn in more, but still not covering to the whole topic, too late to get a grade. She liked me and wanted me to succeed, so I'd get a C with a warning that the next paper must be complete and on time.

By second semester I somehow managed to move most—well, some; okay, Calculus and Composition—'C' grades up to 'B'. Even so, something was affecting my attitude. I was getting cynical and aloof. Approachable teachers pulled us into discussions to make us think, and

I'd sit in sullen silence until directly called upon. Most profs, not only Old Doc Graves, were always ready to help us. I'd do an assignment, looking always for the key to please a particular teacher, turn it in on time, and still come out with another damn 'C'. When an assistant professor wrote on my test blue book, "Baffling with bullshit won't cut it, Mr. Bradford," I wasn't surprised to be caught. I was surprised by the language at the college affiliated with Gram's pietistic church.

***

I tried, I really did. I made a genuine effort through freshman year. Then sophomore slump came and stayed. Fall term began near the edge and went down to academic probation from there. The small college really wanted to see me—plus Gramp and Gram's big donations—succeed. The school had a philosophy that all students, once accepted, were to be guided to earn degrees that lead them to lives of fruitful service. It was something about their Christian tradition, they said. It didn't convince either Wallace Bradford, Senior or Junior, that the extra money wasn't also necessary. They were intent on buying me a degree and enough smarts to be useful in their company.

I hadn't declared a major and I freely admitted that I'd like to major in 101, that is, in the introductory classes of every field. Surprisingly, the college didn't offer that major. Gramp said I should consider Botany, while Junior urged Accounting. I put off thinking about it.

That fall I bought a pale green VW Karmann Ghia sports coupe that didn't run. As the prairie winter arrived, I was spending more and more solitary time rebuilding two engines in my single room in the old dormitory. I was convincing myself that if I stayed away from people, people couldn't hurt me.

Loneliness hurt, too. But I could trust it and name it solitude. It wasn't that one girl from back home that I missed; it was the company of a girl, any co-ed who might take an interest. Just one female companion to love, that's all I craved. But that required trust and the assumption that betrayal could come at any moment.

There was a certain young woman, a freshman, who especially made my heart skip a beat. She always had such a sweet smile as she served up the entrées in the cafeteria line when I came through. Her hazel eyes sparkled and her blonde hair seemed to be trying to escape the hair net. As I watched her scoop potatoes and vegetables onto my plate, I was struck dumb. I could hardly mumble a "thank you." At times like that I envied the students who needed on-campus jobs. It seemed more honest than Gramp and Gram's alumna gifts intended to assure me special treatment. I envied, but not enough to apply for one of those cafeteria jobs. But that cute freshman — wow. Did she smile like that at everyone? Or was she, maybe, could it be? Was she interested in me?

I found out her name was Carolee Siebert and that she came from somewhere in Pennsylvania. I wanted to ask her out. I thought about it constantly while I tinkered with my spare VW engine or tried to do coursework. I could read a textbook chapter and have no idea what I'd just read. My daydreams had completely taken over my brain. And yet, I choked whenever I started to dial her dorm floor. If she was working the food service line, I smiled back, took my tray and ate a peaceful meal. If I didn't see her, it put me in a sour mood. I'd slink off to eat alone, even if others came and filled the table around me.

***

Sophomore year passed in a silence of incompletion. Incomplete work in my courses. Incomplete progress wordlessly fixated on Carolee. I still hadn't had a conversation with her, much less a date. When spring term ended in 1968 I picked up my grades and went to the consultation Old Doc Graves demanded.

"What's going on, Wally? You're too smart for this mess."

I shrugged in response.

"Love problems, is it?"

"Lack of, maybe."

"Well, young man, it's time for you to declare a major. Do you see where this might be going? What really interests you? You've had half-way decent grades in your math courses." Dr. Graves scanned my transcript again with her red pen in hand.

"If he can do calculus, why can't he pass biology?" She asked this more of the ceiling fan than of the student across the desk from her. "And why is he assigned to an adviser in the English department?"

"Maybe I should be at a trade school. But that would probably kill my grandfather and my father would kill me."

"Well, Mr. Bradford, let me lay it out for you. Are you ready to be drafted into the army? Or enlist?"

"Oh God, no."

"That's reason enough for me. I'll see that we find a way to keep you here with your student draft deferment. But I can only do my part. You have to do yours. Come back in the fall with a major declaration, and work your tail off. Use that fine brain on your shoulders for something more than feeling sorry for yourself."

"I'll try, Doctor Graves. I just don't know what I want. I know what I don't want, though. I don't want to go to Nam. And I don't want to get stuck at Bradford and Son, Inc."

"Very well, Wallace, here's what you're going to do. I am quite aware of your poor record at completing assignments, but I'm giving you another one anyway. Beginning today, you will write in a daily journal. Write whatever is on your mind. You will write every day this summer. When you return in September, you'll bring the journal. We'll sit right here and find out if it tells us anything. You will come prepared to declare a major course of study."

"You'll look at it? What if I write things I don't want anyone else to see?"

"Tear out the page. I can and will keep confidences, however. We'll discuss what you discover from writing it, not what I might discover from reading. I'm not easily shocked, by the way. You are only required to honor the assignment and follow through. You'll write daily for half an hour for one summer."

"I'll do the best I can, Doctor Graves. I mean, what the hell, oh, sorry. It's worth a try, I guess."

"We are agreed, then, that an 'A' looks better on a transcript than it does on a draft card?"

"Oh, yeah."

"Have a good summer, Wally. Just set aside a time, pick up pen and paper and write every day, that's all you're required to do."

I bounced down the granite staircase into the late spring warmth, feeling hopeful. It was intriguing—a writing assignment. Right away I was deciding that this was one that I would actually complete. "Come hell or high water," I said aloud and punched the air.

Looking back at a second story window I saw Dr. Graves watching me go. She gave me a thumbs-up. I guess she saw the new energy in my stride, as if she were reading my "what the hell" comment the way I meant it.

(4)

I nearly bumped into Fred as I waved to Dr. Graves. We were friendly but not exactly friends; he'd been dorm proctor of my floor freshman year. He was always trying to get me to join his prayer meetings, which I avoided with the lamest excuses. I could feel another evangelism attempt about to happen.

"Hey, Wally, I have something you might be interested in."

"Ah well, what now, Fred?"

"No, I'm not gonna preach. Jesus'll get to you in his own time. But, speaking of that, if you had ever given up those dumb excuses: 'I got a study group. I'm this or that.' If you'd ever just said, 'I don't want to,' I think I'd have quit asking. But never mind that. I'm moving out of a really cool apartment in an old house. It's on the main floor and faces the street. If you're moving off campus for junior year, I could recommend you to the landlady."

"Geez, I hadn't thought about where to live next year. Yeah. Do you have time right now?"

"Absolutely. She's inspecting so she can try to keep my cleaning deposit in an hour. You can help me lug a couple heavy items into a U-Haul trailer."

"Aha! A motive. Sure, no problem."

***

With a new place to live secured, I spent the rest of that day packing up, deciding what to store at my new apartment and what to take with me. I wrote journal entry number one and camped in the apartment; I rolled out my sleeping bag on the Murphy bed lowered from its wall cabinet. In the morning I had my own heavy lifting motive to track down my friend Pete. We shared a love of engine mechanics. With his help, I

17

swapped the spare engine into my little VW. The landlady gave her okay and we stored the other engine in the furnace room.

Pete asked for a lift to the bus station. Instead, I drove him to his home. Sac City, Iowa was along the way. We had fun arguing about anything and everything for a few hours. His folks were surprised by his early arrival at the farm. Pete was giddy at being home in his element as he gave me a tour of farm life amidst the corn and soybeans. I could not imagine it, and said so at supper. "How can anyone enjoy such hard work? You never know if there will be anything gained in the end. Everything depends on an uncertain harvest. What makes you love this life, Pete?"

Pete shrugged that off. He must have thought I was trying to start another of our good-natured arguments. "I don't know, Wally. It's life. It's natural." He shrugged again.

I shook my head in disbelief. To me, natural in a barnyard had an awful stink. Little did I know what was ahead for me, eh.

***

I was traveling light and yet my stuff nearly filled the tiny car even without Pete and his bags. On the passenger seat I put the ring binder that contained three sheets covered on both sides with that awkward script I detested but couldn't change. That left ninety-seven blank sheets of lined paper. I wondered if I'd fill them in one summer.

After tagging along with Pete doing morning chores and enjoying a huge, unhurried breakfast, I traveled leisurely via back roads. I could claim it was to go easy on the air cooled engine. The real reason was to delay my arrival as long as possible. Let it take two more days. I had camping gear I'd bought and used at spring break. The weather was warm with many small clouds, causing the road ahead to go back and forth between bright and shadow. Even with the late start I had covered nearly half the distance by mid-afternoon. The drive was so pleasant, and the destination so troublesome that I considered driving right on through Chicago without stopping. "I could just go right on by. Maybe I'll go to Altoona, Pennsylvania. I could get a job there; bump into Carolee Siebert; ask her out; be her lover. Yeah, dream on, fool.

"Is that black cloud an omen? All those fluffy white clouds, I think about running off, and right away a big dark one appears."

A light rain splashed the windshield. I used it as an excuse to stop at a small town café, maybe get a burger. The waitress, a fiftyish woman who served and cleared without a wasted motion, set the chicken-fried steak beside my open notebook. When she apologized for the slow service from the kitchen, I didn't quite know how to respond, so I told the truth.

"The slower the better, ma'am. I'm in no hurry to get where I'm supposed to be. Besides, the wipers on my car are crap. Can I hang around 'til the rain stops?" As soon as I said that, the sky began to clear, the sun shone, and a rainbow appeared.

Through the big picture window we both admired the rainbow. The waitress refilled my coffee and said, "Regardless, you just relax and write in your book there, young fella. I'll keep the coffee coming."

"I appreciate it." I had hated coffee until finals week the previous winter. It wasn't clear whether the benefit I perceived came from caffeine or the mounds of sugar I poured into it. Now I was a dedicated javaholic and drank it black, no sugar, no cream. It must be the caffeine.

The rainbow disappeared and I started to write my doubts about the summer ahead. Working for Bradford & Son, Inc. could only be anticipated with serious foreboding. With a few lines written, I emptied my coffee cup and pulled out the letter I'd tucked into the notebook. I read it again. I had a powerful urge to tear it into tiny scraps; somehow I resisted. On company stationery Dad had hand-written an ultimatum. If I didn't successfully work for and learn the systems of the family business I would be without financial support to continue in college. "Doesn't Dad realize that if I drop out, I'm on my way to Viet Nam?" I wrote that in the notebook. Then I leaned back and took a tongue-scalding sip from the cup that had been refilled when I wasn't paying attention.

"Maybe with the journal I can endure B&S, Inc. without going totally nuts."

"Was there something more you'd like, young sir?"

"Huh? Oh, nothing. Just the check." I must have talking aloud to myself, so I wrote in the journal, keeping my mouth shut, "Maybe I'm already totally nuts."

Still in Iowa, at Joy Springs Park, I rolled out my sleeping bag beside the car. I slept pretty well until thunder and rain moved me inside the car at about four the next morning. That cramped me up.

***

"Where have you been?" Mom caught me pulling a Michelob beer out of the small refrigerator under the basement wet bar. "Go get cleaned up. Everyone's coming for dinner. Your sisters will be here any minute."

I popped the cap off the bottle, poured half the beer down my dry throat and said, "Fancy bottle. I just love a pretentious lager that has less flavor than a cheap Grain Belt beer."

"Just go. Get ready for dinner. And take your bags upstairs. The only way I knew you'd come in was by tripping over your luggage in the front hall." She turned and started up the stairs.

In a casual murmur, I said, "Love you, too, Mom."

That caught her short on the second step. I saw tears welling in her eyes as she turned around and nearly bumped into me. I was following her onto the stairs, beer bottle in hand. She wrapped her arms around me and cried, "I'm so sorry, son. It's been such a hectic day, and you come sneaking in without a word. Welcome home." She kissed me on the cheek, and then dashed up the stairs. Next thing I heard, she was hassling a caterer about dinner preparations.

The Bradford family gathered around the big dining table, sisters Linda and Char with their husbands, Linda's eighteen month old son in a high chair, with a plastic tarp protecting the carpet under him, brother Bryan, gramp (Senior) and gram (Charlotte). Mom (Kat) sat at the end nearest the kitchen door and Dad (Junior) at the other end.

"Where'd you go on spring break, Trey?" Linda asked.

Before I could answer, Dad added brusquely, "We know where he didn't go. You couldn't even call your mother? Tell her where you were going instead of home?"

"I went camping. As if you care."

"Yeah, I bet. Camping on the beach at Fort Lauderdale, prob'ly," said Bryan, who had one more week as a sophomore at New Trier High, "with some babe — not."

"One good day's drive or a couple hours flying and you couldn't come home even for a few days?" Mom whined.

"I'm here now." I reached my fork across Char to spear another slice of beef.

"So, where did you go?" Char sounded as if she really wanted to hear my answer.

"Camping, like I said. I was gonna try kayaking, but the lake was still frozen over."

"You mean 'as I said,' not 'like'." Gram took pleasure in correcting my grammar, but she also sounded interested, repeating Char's question, "Where did you do this camping, Trey."

"In the frozen north of Minnesota. Another student needed a ride to Bemidji, so we drove her home and then tried some cold weather camping out there."

"It's affected you. You haven't warmed up yet, to treat your family so coldly," Dad grumbled.

"'As' you say, Dad. Or is it, 'like you'? As in a family trait."

Junior glared at me. He put his fork down on his plate, pointed his finger at me, and said, "You start at the company tomorrow. You will learn and work with us until fall term begins. If there is to be a fall term for you." With that, he stood, glared at me a moment more and went downstairs to his liquor cabinet.

I took that as permission to be excused and stood, too. Before I got away from the table one of my brothers-in-law said, "It'll be great to have you working with us, Trey." The other husband added, "Super."

Without responding I went upstairs. Bryan followed, talking to my back about his tennis trophies and the high school team. I went into my room and opened my journal notebook. Bryan may have followed and continued his boasting. If so, I ignored him and wrote.

**

Suit and tie, at least white shirt and tie, were required in the executive suites at Bradford and Son, even for an intern. I reluctantly dressed the part and rode with the family car pool into the Chicago Loop. Playing the part was more difficult, but with my journal I had found an outlet. Each evening I'd write pages of commentary, reactions to the corporate and family systems I was desperate to escape. The journal (and Sociology 101) helped me see that they were systems I was unlikely to change even if I cared enough to try. For that summer the journal would be my escape. I wrote down all the things I wanted to say but didn't dare, and all the things I wished I had said but didn't think of until journal writing time.

I wandered the office hallways, or sat at a desk in a room with five other desks where diligent employees read reports, talked on phones and bantered with one another. I read similar reports without caring what they meant. I answered the phone when it rang, but didn't have answers to the questions callers were asking. I tried not to ogle the other intern.

Fortunately her desk was behind mine. I'd been sliding into this rut for over three weeks when I was called to yet another meeting. I was expected to attend these executive staff sessions, keep quiet, watch, listen, and learn. Senior, as chairman of the board, led the meetings. Junior was now president and in charge of the day to day operation of the family owned corporation. Senior interfered, but only came into the city for board and staff meetings.

We all filed into the board room ahead of the announced time. One didn't want to arrive late and face Senior's glare. Down the center of the big table we found rows of several varieties of small potted plants. We looked but no one said anything about them until Junior arrived. He stopped in the doorway, eyeballed the table decoration and grunted, "What the hell? Whose idea is this crap?" He came in and dropped his stack of file folders on the table with a loud plop.

Senior slipped in behind him, shook his head and said in a monotone through gritted teeth, "Thank you for your support, son." He stood at his place beside Junior, watched the wall clock advance the last ten seconds to ten o'clock. At that instant he banged a gavel and called the meeting to order. "You have the agenda, but first, about the bedding plants. Everyone is invited to choose a plant or two. They'll all do well in your offices in pots if you follow the care instructions on the tags. Let's remember what business we're in. Are there changes or additions to the agenda?" The meeting began in earnest and my mind went wandering to a certain Yankton co-ed.

I stirred from my daydream to hear them discussing what to do about some underperforming stores in the mid-west chain of garden centers. The stores were a retail end of the Bradford corporate structure.

I listened as Senior suggested ways to pressure store managers and I watched Junior shake his head at Gramp's ideas. Junior argued that there's only one way left to boost profits. It was time cut losses, close a couple outlets, and get the attention of the rest. I desperately wanted my journal notebook, which I kept hidden in my room out in Winnetka. I wanted to write about what crap it is to use only punishment, only this one bullshit technique to run a business. Same as the way they forced me to be sitting useless at this conference table.

Then I hit on an idea. If my grandfather and father would go for it, I could get away from suits, offices and family for a few days. The only drawback was that I would have to do actual company work along the way. They'd expect a full report, one they could base decisions on. Decisions like blaming me for a stupid report while taking credit for my work. But I'd get out of town. Full of nervous energy, I cleared my throat and raised my hand. Those gestures suddenly made me feel like I was back in fifth grade at Crow Island School.

Junior brought me back, saying wearily, "What is it, Trey?"

"Umm, well sir…"

"Out with, son. We haven't got all day."

"Okay. Don't you think, sir, that maybe someone should go take a look? See what's really going on? Hear what the managers have to say?"

"Oh, come on, boy. Our regional men are out there all the time and they aren't giving us much hope. We need to shut down stores that won't keep up with the times. Don't be stupid."

I was getting irritated with the insults. I'd had enough, but there was no escape if I wanted to stay in college. It wasn't that I wanted to stay in college, but the alternative was too frightening to consider. So I pressed my point. "The district guys are in the same situation, aren't they? Feeling pressure from you, from headquarters I mean, but… Well, anyway, like this. Umm, nobody knows me out at the retail stores. I could go incognito like, show up looking like a customer and find out where the profit's getting lost. You know, instead of telling them what Bradford wants, find out what they need to grow their stores?"

Senior interrupted as Junior was about to argue more. In fact, Junior had a finger pointed straight at me when Senior said, "Slow down, Wallace. The kid may have a point. And … what have you got to lose? He's supposed to be learning the business." He pointed to the potted plants. "What better way? Get him out there. Let him bring back a full report with some recommendations. We might save a store or two; or possibly close even more than you're suggesting. Like the kid … like Trey said. Find out what they need."

Relaxed now, I couldn't resist, "'As' the kid, Gramp, er, sir, Senior."

Senior laughed and I tried to hide my smile. One of my sisters' husbands said, "Great." The other said, "Super."

Junior glared at them both, then pointed at me again and said, "Just remember this, Trey. It's for the company. It's not about you. Got it?"

***

After the meeting, Gramp followed me to my desk. "I like your plan, Trey," he said. "You'll get to know the real business. We used to be about growing plants, not just profits." His eyes got big. He snapped his

23

fingers once and looked out the window, which was a long way from my desk.

"What? What is it, Gramp?"

"Nothing. Just a little idea. Never mind that, I was gonna give you an assignment. When you're back in the office and delivering memos or whatever, will you see what's happening to the potted plants? Just between you and me. See where they're being repotted, where they're left to die, or given to the secretaries to care for. No names, just tell me what you see."

"Sure thing, Senior. You're the boss. Sir."

(5)

I was pleased with myself. Of course it was about me. That was the whole point. Between the travel and the journal my summer internship was becoming almost tolerable. I went north in a company owned Ford station wagon into somewhat familiar territory. I had read Junior's revised plan, mumbled, "This is a pile of crap," initialed it, sent it back, and ignored my copy. Instead, I followed my plan to visit each store from Milwaukee to Duluth twice. On the way out I would browse, eavesdrop on conversations between customers and salespeople, and form an impression. On the return drive I'd introduce myself and talk with managers. I had no idea what we'd talk about, of course. The plan felt right; it meant the round trip could keep my away for three or four days more than Junior approved.

I left the house at dawn, which is incredibly early in June, and wandered around two of the three locations in Milwaukee suburbs. I skipped the third in order to reach Madison before closing time. All looked nearly alike, and the records that a vice-president (and sister's husband) sent with me indicated that they were all in about the same barely profitable condition.

I found my Bradford Garden Stores with a growing collection of local maps. I hated to ask directions. Again and again I found the same varieties of potted shrubs lined up in front of stores. Many, beginning to turn brown, were marked with price reductions. I copied the information about the plants into my 'Not the Journal', a pocket sized notebook. I kept to my plan to tour north and west first and ask questions on the way back to Chicago.

***

At about noon on day five I reached my turnaround point, the final destination north of Duluth, Minnesota. This store looked a little different. The parking lot size was reduced by an additional greenhouse. I looked around. The shrub varieties I'd seen in front of every other store were not in sight. Did they sell them all? Were they inside the extra pavilion?

The sales figures I had with me indicated a little better profit here, too. However, they also showed purchases outside the normal Bradford supply chain. Junior would not like to know that. No doubt some fine print in a contract was being violated here.

It was time to start talking to the managers. I couldn't put it off any longer. I really enjoyed silently looking around. Initiating contact with new people is not my thing at all. Maybe I could delay for an hour or two, so I did. I ate a leisurely lunch, found a motel, cleaned up and returned in blazer and tie.

The manager found me, betrayed by the logo nametag—with only my first name, Wally—attached to my breast pocket. "Good afternoon," the head honcho said, offering his hand. I read 'Ward Tinkle, Manager' embroidered on his windbreaker. "How can I help?"

I swallowed hard to avoid commenting on the name. I'm sure he'd heard it all before. "Nice to meet you, Mr. Tinkle. I'm Wally, summer intern at the Chicago office."

"Ah, that's why. A new face. Your regional rep was here just last week. He didn't say anything about visits from headquarters."

"I was here looking around a few hours ago. You know, Mr. Tinkle…"

"Please, Ward. Call me Ward. How did I miss you earlier?"

"Okay, Ward it is. I've been taking a little tour through Wisconsin and Minnesota. Just looking around."

"Sneaking around. Looking out for the bottom line. What kind of trouble was you looking for then? Did you find the restroom clean?"

"Oh no, oh no, it's not like that. Actually, and don't let this get back to the execs, I'm out looking for reasons to stir a little trouble back at h.q. You know, get them to listen to you guys trying to take care of your customers. Anyway, I am curious about a few things. The records show that you're doing a little better, profit-wise, than some stores. I'm new at this, so maybe you can help me out. At every other location there are tons of these shrubs in pots out front." I opened my not-journal pad, found the name of the shrubbery, and showed it to Ward. "I don't even know how to pronounce it. I looked all over out here, finally found a couple out back. It looked like they were dying."

"Ah, yeah, they're goners. I tried to refuse delivery of them bushes entirely, but we had to take a few. They can tolerate a cold snap, but not our deepfreeze winters. Have you done any snooping at your outfits in Missouri or downstate Illinois? Bet you don't see many of them shrubs sitting in tubs down there, turning brown, root bound from being too long still potted."

"I haven't been down there yet. This is my first trip. So, why won't I see them?"

"Oh, you might see 'em in folks' yards, just not in pots, unsold. They do great in that climate."

I was starting to suspect something about my family's company. I still had to ask about some purchasing outside the lines. We went into Ward's office where he taught me more than I wanted to learn. When we finished, I had reason to ask, "Do our stores even have public restrooms? Clean or otherwise?"

"That was just me being snide, Wally." Ward directed me to the men's room.

How could I report fully and convince Junior that Ward had a better approach? Over the next few days I talked to managers along the way, who mostly confirmed what I'd learned up in the Iron Range. Unfortunately, few had taken Ward Tinkle's initiative to do something about it.

(6)

I leaned back in my desk chair at the Chicago office, took another bite of doughnut and brushed powdered sugar off that hated tie and dress shirt. My suit coat hung over the back of the chair and who cares if it drags on the floor? I sat and stared at my notes, wishing I were still out there alone on the open road. I brushed more crumbs and sugar off my dark blue striped pants and thought of Mr. Wolfe, the high school math teacher we used to mock because he kept broken chalk in his pockets leaving white powder all over his pants. I wrote a reminiscence on company time to insert into my journal. Then I looked back at the travel notes.

No more procrastinating. A report was expected and I had to say it right. It must convince them to send me back out on the road. I had journaled and gazed into space. I'd mulled over my notes for close to an hour. Kim, the other summer intern saw all this from her desk in the other row and behind mine. I heard her coming and looked up, careful to focus on her face, not her ... um, you know, because they were ... yeah. Kim was a genuine intern, underpaid but gaining experience for her résumé. She was a University of Chicago spring grad on her way to grad school for an MBA.

"How's the report coming?" she asked as if it weren't obvious that it wasn't.

I just shook my head, wondering why she was suddenly interested in my work. She had turned down all my invitations, both of them, to go out for break time coffee.

"Start with a title. Say, for instance, 'What I did on my summer vacation,' and go from there."

"I think maybe that fits what I write every night. If only dad...er...Junior had enough sense of humor to find that amusing, I would do it. If you could give me a title that combines a dirty joke and golf, I'd have him."

She gave that a moment's thought and said, "Nope. I can't think of anything. So, what's the hold up? What's your stumbling block?"

"Do you really want to help?"

"If I help, you'll owe me."

"Owe you what?"

"We'll see." She wheeled the chair from her desk to the other side of mine and sat down. Kim asked a whole series of questions, gathering more detail as we went along. She occasionally wrote down a word or two, but didn't take real notes.

After she had run out of questions she made one more request, "Can I see your notes from the trip?"

I shoved them across the desk and she flipped through a few pages, struggling with my scrawled names of plants that I'd had questions about. She handed the little notebook back, said, "Interesting," and looked at the wall clock. She added one more word, "Coffee," and stood up.

"Hmm," I thought, "no time for coffee until it's her idea. Break time with a good looking, slightly older woman? Yes."

At a tiny coffee shop almost under the elevated track on Wabash, Kim didn't allow any talk about our report project. We talked about college experiences and the differences between Winnetka and Oak Park, where she grew up.

As soon as we were back at my desk, Kim said, "I see your problem, and maybe a way out. Your father will be super pissed, of course, but maybe you can make sure he's not just pissed at you alone."

"How?"

"Get Senior in your corner. Write what you found out. Go ahead and tell it. You know, tell how that guy in Minnesota is right and Junior's bulk buying exactly the same for every location is foolish. Maybe don't say foolish."

"I was thinking stupid, but ... no."

"Anyway, just tell what you found out, but take it to the old man first. Ask his advice. So, tell the truth, but with deference and more questions than answers. Like, not 'this is what I found out' but 'consider this possibility', or 'I noticed blah-blah; I wonder what it means.'"

"Wow. Thanks, Kim. Big help, yeah. I think I can do it, now. Deference to Senior, not to Junior. That should've been obvious all along. Senior still wants BS-Inc to be a nursery, so yeah."

Kim laughed and said, "Oh. I was certain I'd interned at a money shop." She paused, handed me the notes and added, "Now that I've heard all about your first journey, Wally, I know what you owe me."

"Oh? Okay, shoot."

"You're expecting to go to Iowa and down state next week, right?"

"I hope so. Or Missouri, if Junior doesn't cancel. He's gonna be mad, so who knows."

"Well, I'm coming along."

"Oh, god. You drive a hard bargain. They'll never go for that. If you were a guy, or I wasn't. Well, they won't."

"Yes they will. Just watch. I'm going and you'll be lucky to be going, too. Once they hear my pitch, they'll want me to replace you."

I groaned.

***

The following Monday, Kim and I were cruising down the Dan Ryan Expressway, southbound through the city. We would make stops in central Illinois and then head west to stores in Missouri and Iowa. A third trip, if approved, would take us to Indiana and Michigan, the eastern end the Bradford operation.

"Well, you sure convinced them, Kim. And you were right about that other thing, too. Thanks for salvaging my spot on the tour. I don't know how I'll survive the rest of the summer in that stinking office. It's making me sour on the whole Chicagoland Area. I actually miss Yankton. Getting away is the only thing that makes this job tolerable." I didn't mention the journal, my other sanity safety valve.

"A country boy from suburbia." Her eyes smiled as she shook her head. "Anyway, thank you, Trey. I thought you'd still be angry at me. You value your time alone, don't you?"

"Yeah, but it's okay as long as you don't expect this conversation to keep up the whole way."

"I'm cool with that. But hey, you gave me a compliment, here's one back. You really had them the way you pulled off that report. I don't know if you like the way Senior took credit for your proposals, but everyone has to take him seriously, so that slowed Junior down a little, didn't it."

"Gramp always takes credit. It pisses Junior off, so he tries to grab credit quicker. I knew all of that when I showed it to him. But I still don't know if it's working. Junior took my list of facts and Gramp's recommendations. Then he turned it all into a different question. He just wants this so he can decide which stores to close first. You heard that rant about bulk buying." I did a lame imitation of my father's heated tone, "Volume! You have to work the volume to run a chain. How do you advertise if every store has different stock? You don't. There's no profit and you die."

"I couldn't believe it when you spoke up after that," Kim said. "I've noticed that you try not to speak in those meetings even when you're asked a direct question. And when you started by agreeing, whoa."

"Well, it was the truth, wasn't it?"

"I nearly burst out laughing when you said it. 'Right, sir. That's true if we're talking about patio pavers, shovels and gnomes."

"Did I say that? Garden gnomes?"

"You did, and you made it clear about losing customers if the plants die because they don't belong in that zone."

"But he will never back down about anything."

"He didn't right then, anyway. The way I see it, this week our job is to find something that helps." Kim had arrived at her plan. "We'll trick him into something good he can take credit for."

I had to think about that. I drove in silence as we made our way out of suburbs into the flat prairie of corn and soybean farms.

After a long silence, Kim, gazing at the endless fields of corn, said, "Knee high by the fourth of July. It'll be right on schedule, I'd say." I nodded and tuned the radio to a top forty station.

***

Kim brought a more systematic, call it 'business-like', approach than I had used on my solo tour. The first day we wandered through a store, looking for any way it differed from all the others, went back to the car, compared notes and put on our company ID tags. We learned that the stores in Missouri were more profitable in part because plants for stores everywhere came from the Bradford nurseries in Missouri and Arkansas. Managers recognized us as the interns they'd learned about via the grapevine. I had only been asked for a business card in one store, but now they all knew the family connection of that summer-hire kid from headquarters.

On Tuesday we both looked around and listened as before. I was dressed in jeans and t-shirt while Kim kept the business look, ready to add jacket with nametag. She talked with managers alone.

By Wednesday evening we were ahead of schedule. The next stops were small cities in western Iowa. We had no idea whether stores would be open the next day, the Fourth of July. "They ought to be open," Kim observed. "People do yard work and projects on a holiday. They'd do a good business. But out here, what with local laws and traditions, who knows." Nothing in the material we had with us gave a clue.

"Maybe we deserve a holiday, too," I said after some thought. "We're making good time. But what do you do in Indianola, Iowa on the Fourth?"

"You're right. What the hell, let's take a holiday, Wally. We can make Indianola, and if they're open, hit another Des Moines area store tomorrow afternoon. It's not that far, really, even if we go back to KC tonight. That's only an hour or two."

We checked into adjacent rooms at a downtown Kansas City hotel and found a tiny table at the bar. The barmaid carded both of us and turned me away. Our two year difference in age and experience, a difference I'd all but forgotten, suddenly felt like a decade. At the restaurant, over Kansas City barbecue, Kim said, "I'll find a package store, or whatever Missouri's liquor laws allow. We can have a nip in the hotel before we join the KC nightlife, so unlock that door between the rooms."

"What door?"

"Didn't you notice that? Our rooms connect." I learned later that she had quietly arranged for those rooms with the desk clerk.

Kim brought a pint of rum through that door. I got three bottles of cola from the soda machine and filled the ice bucket. "This is a classy hotel – tumblers made of real glass."

"I only bought a pint because sometimes I tend to drink 'til it's gone, no matter, you see."

"I see. It's a good thing I'm here to help, then, isn't it." We lifted a toast to the rum. Then another and more until we were lying side by side on top of the bedspread. The TV was on, but we weren't watching. There was almost enough rum in the bottle for one more nip. "You want me to get another coke to finish this with?"

Kim answered by taking a swig from the bottle and handing it to me. I downed the last swallow and dropped back onto the pillow.

Kim turned, propped on an elbow, facing me and said in a slurred voice, "Hey. We were gonna go out? What happened to that?"

I looked at Kim without lifting my head from the pillow, giggled and said, "I think we got a little drunk instead." Our eyes stayed locked on each other. I had thought it, but would never have said it while sober, "I wanted to travel alone, you know. That was sure stupid, when I get to ride the highway with a beautiful lady."

"You're a strange guy, Mr. Bradford Trey." She leaned forward to give me a kiss and fell off her elbow into an embrace that worked its way out of clothes and under the bedcovers.

***

I opened my eyes to daylight and the sound of running water. I sat up and groaned. Sitting as still as I possibly could I reached for my glasses and watch. I put the watch on and looked without managing to bring its hands into focus. My glasses had fallen on the floor. Reaching that far made my head spin, but I managed to get them on and lie back on the pillow.

"Happy Fourth of July, Stud." Kim's voice was too cheerful for me to take.

"Oh, gawd. Have the fireworks started already, or is it just in my head?"

I pushed my glasses up my nose and cheered up immediately. Kim came out of the bathroom sort of wrapped in one towel while pulling another through her long, dark hair. She bent over, her wet hair dripping on my chest, and gave me a little kiss on the cheek and tried to keep the towel in place while I tried to pull it off.

"No time for that, Mister. We're pushing close to checkout time."

To the ragged looking kid in the bathroom mirror I said, "I think I'm in love." In the shower, when I closed my eyes for a moment it was not Kim in my lustful mind's eye. I saw Carolee, her hazel eyes and long blonde ponytail (no hairnet in my dream), smiling at me over the sneeze guard in the cafeteria line.

***

My expense report had three nights missing. When asked I said, "I camped." An alcohol fueled tryst turned into a week of passion in Iowa without much additional alcohol. Once back at the office, however, Kim became scrupulously distant. The first day back we each wrote a report, compared them, and submitted both. Hers would be more useful to con Junior into doing the right thing. I asked Kim if we could get together after work, but she refused and offered no reason.

Alone in my room that evening I opened my journal. The last entry – half a sentence – was an entry I'd just begun when Kim brought the rum. I'd made notes in the pocket not-journal as we visited the last stores, but nothing in my personal journal since Wednesday. Now I wrote about a Fourth of July with its fireworks between the sheets. It somehow seemed a fitting way to ignore the national holiday. I wrote then about the way the world was coming apart at the seams. First Martin Luther King was assassinated, then Bobby Kennedy last month. Now there was talk of major disruptions when the Democrats come to the city next month. I tried to write about how the events had affected my life. Except for the draft, they hadn't. I remained preoccupied with staying away from Viet Nam. To do so meant staying in college. To stay in college I couldn't quit the company job. I thought about that and wrote more questions to myself. Did I really care about those stores I'd visited? Did their employees and customers mean anything to me? Was it really about a fight with my father? Did any of it matter?

What had affected my life, what did matter, was the cold shoulder that Kim was giving me, so I wrote, filling three pages. I read what I had written and discovered the name Carolee appeared more often than Kim.

***

I kicked my feet up onto the desk and didn't try to look busy. Kim seemed to be quite busy. At 10:30 I stepped quietly behind her and asked with little hope of success, "Wanna go for coffee?"

"Now? Didn't you get the memo?"

"What memo?" I looked over at my desk and saw nothing new.

"From Junior, your dear father. He sent me a bunch of questions about our survey of stores. Are you sure he didn't send you the same thing? He wants answers by noon."

I went back to my desk and looked through everything there. Outbox – empty. Inbox – the carbon copy of my expense report. Otherwise the desk top held scratch paper, a few notes and a *Field & Stream* magazine.

"Guess he doesn't want to hear from me. I'm going to the doughnut shop. I'll bring you something."

"Just a black coffee is good, thanks." She hardly looked up from her writing.

"Stick to business," I mumbled to myself as I waited for the elevator. "I have to forget the rest." But no, I could not stop thinking about what I was trying not to think about. I breathed a sigh of relief as the doors slid open to an empty elevator.

(7)

We interns were included in the Friday meeting once again. I arrived early for no particular reason. Executive staff members filed in. Each had a similar reaction as they unloaded whatever paperwork they'd brought. Each in turn picked up the little paper cup from their place at the table, examined the contents and said some variation of, "What the hell is this?"

Kim was chatting with Becky, an administrative assistant, as they came through the door. They heard the question, giggled and gave each other knowing glances.

At 10:00 everyone was seated around the large conference table. Mr. Wallace M. Bradford, Sr. always began at exactly the announced hour, but Senior wasn't there. Mr. Wallace M. Bradford, Junior allowed the hum of quiet conversations to continue for a few more minutes before he banged the gavel. His first order of business was to announce that we shouldn't make too much of Senior's absence. "He's not ill. We're making a slight change. Senior remains board chairman, but he's further reducing in his role in executive operations."

Next he passed out a Xeroxed twenty page document labeled "Fact Sheet" that outlined revised plans for the fiscal year. I skimmed the pages. I might have been shaking my head along the way. I wonder if Junior noticed.

Junior spoke as the group flipped through the papers. "I think our young interns have done a good service with their travels. Doing it outside the usual channels brings some interesting results. And I don't mean the flak from regional reps about being left out. Miss Smith's feedback has shifted my thinking a little. It has prompted re-evaluation of a couple offers and plans we should pursue. She's accomplished the task such that a trip to the eastern region is unnecessary." He gave Kim the credit and he chose the meeting to inform me of the cancelation. "Here's the gist of it. We are negotiating with a Minnesota firm for the sale of our northern Wisconsin and all Minnesota sites. This will free us to move more aggressively in our other market areas. In addition, we see some promise in the purchase of a small chain of lumber yards in Indiana and Ohio that can help us reach into those markets adding Bradford garden centers into their existing trade. Questions?"

There were questions. Concerns about risk, concerns about abandoning market areas and adding product lines with the acquisitions would eventually be discussed. But first, Mr. Stevenson, head of one of those departments that moves numbers around on ledger sheets asked, "What are these cups of dry beans all about, Mr. Bradford?"

Junior shook his head and said, "I have no idea. Anyone have a clue where these came from or...?"

Becky, who'd been taking minutes, timidly raised a hand, no higher than her shoulder. When Junior gave her a nod, she answered, "Your father had me set them out that way, sir. I'm supposed to ask if anyone knows who has most, sir."

That sent the meeting into a moment of pandemonium as the gathered business leaders looked into one another's paper cups to see how full they were, with Junior banging his gavel and barking through it all.

They all saw who had most, but no one would say. As the meeting came back to order, Mr. Stevenson said, "I still don't know what the hell this little game is about. Are we supposed to plant these and water them like those damn potted ferns from a while back? Or what, Becky?"

Before Becky could try to answer, old man Widdington spoke up. Mr. Widdington had been with the company since the stone age and seldom said a single word at these meetings. "Stevenson, of all people you ought to understand how these count."

Trying to stifle and hide, Kim dropped her pen on the floor, but we all heard her laughter.

Widdington paid no attention to her and went on, "Before he dies Mr. Bradford Senior would like us to get back to the business we started in."

Junior had had enough. "He's not here. You have a proposal before you that warrants discussion."

After some back and forth, those who could vote rubber-stamped Junior's plan. Widdington announced his intention to retire and Junior looked surprised but not displeased.

After the meeting, despite how much fun as it was, I put a note on my desk and left for the weekend. I struggled with the note. I wanted to say, "Take this job and shove it." Instead I wrote, "Gone for the day."

I knew I couldn't trust my old man, but the way he praised Kim and disparaged both me and Gramp crapped me out. It was like a slap in the face in front of the whole damn company. I took the train to Winnetka and spent the afternoon at Tower Road Beach.

After a weekend of journal contemplation on business demands versus my desires, I knew the summer would finish my career at Bradford & Son. I would somehow finish the summer, so I planned a way to be at work while avoiding involvement in it. My lust for Kim and a deeper desire for the Myth of Carolee clung as a weight on my chest. No amount of journal writing or pushing from my mind could lighten it.

On Monday I hung my suit jacket on the back of my chair right on schedule. That couldn't be helped; I rode in a carpool with Junior and the Husbands.

At my desk, I looked quickly through the inter-office memo nonsense and the mail. Nothing looked important enough to open. I wrote a note that I placed at the center of the blotter. It said simply, "At the warehouse and loading dock." Leaving my coat on the chair, I took the 'L' to the Southside and carried a clipboard around the warehouse for the day, trying to stay out of the way of people doing actual work. As much as I could get away with, I would find places other than my desk for the remaining month of my intern summer.

***

I couldn't always get away with it. On the following Monday I was given an assignment that would keep me at the office for a day or two. I made the most of it. When Kim asked me to join her for lunch, I felt a strange mixture of anger and joy: Anger because I was finally beginning to get used to the idea that our affair was all in the past, joy because I could hope it wasn't. We hadn't spoken since the staff meeting with the bean melee. That still confused me, even as it firmed my conviction that this business was not for me. On the elevator I asked Kim, "Tell me about the beans at the meeting. Anybody give you crap about your guffaw under the table?"

"Only behind my back. What do you want to know?"

"What was Senior plotting with all that? That's all."

"Isn't it obvious? He's trying to show them how the bean counters have taken over and it's killing his dream and his life's work."

"Yeah. That's kinda what I thought. Too bad Junior doesn't get it. But hey, isn't bean counting or maximizing profits what you'll do with an MBA degree?"

The elevator doors opened and she ignored the question, saying only, "No business talk outside the building."

At the sidewalk café table Kim held her menu in such a way that I would have to notice. I did. Her left hand, on her ring finger, there it was – a large diamond glistening in the sunlight.

"Whoa! What's that about?" I could see what it was about, but couldn't believe I was seeing what I saw.

"Well, you see. I finally gave James my answer and we're getting married."

"You were going with this James person when we..."

"It was sweet, our little thing, but yeah. I'm more certain it's the right thing now, so I told him yes."

In spite of August heat I was shivering as if a blast of freezing wind had hit me. Trying desperately to keep calm, I asked, "Are you still going to grad school?"

"Yeah, at Wharton. James is an officer, a lawyer in the JAG Corps. He's stationed at Fort Dix."

A waitress approached. I'd lost my appetite and said so. "Enjoy your lunch. I'm going for a walk."

My journal entry that evening began in large angry print, "DUMPED! Betrayed again. In more normal script I began the longer entry, "Can anyone be trusted? Is the whole world out to crush me?"

***

My last weeks at Bradford & Son were marked by endless avoidance. I avoided Kim. I avoided my desk. I avoided assignments. Instead, with my clipboard I wandered through the warehouses and offices looking like the boss's son with hell to raise. At the staff meeting on August 23 I announced, "Goodbye, B&S. It's time to get back to Yankton and junior year." I did not mention that I still had a week and that I would visit Grant Park before leaving the city. Yippie!

(8)

I sat with my journal, pondering. The Bradford approach to politics was all about gaining influence with money and connections. If Junior ever fawned over me the way he did his Congressman friend? I wish. No, I don't. I'd still escape to one of my solitary hideouts. I didn't do politics or toadying and never really questioned the Republican assumptions I grew up with.

But now? Now this journal forced me to think. The company summer caused me to question. "Maybe I'll get arrested protesting the war. That'll tie Junior in knots. It might give him a heart attack, though." I concluded it'd be worth the risk.

On Monday I slept late and spent the day with the ring binder and the four spiral notebooks that contained three months of almost daily journal entries. I could only find three days on which I hadn't written, so I added these notes in the margin: July 4, holiday; July 5-6, more holiday. Still in blissville with Kim. See the crash ahead.

On Tuesday afternoon I stuffed my sleeping bag and a sack of trail mix into a sport duffle and took the train to the Loop. At Grant Park I found groups of hippies, yippies and other radicals milling about, getting stirred by bull horn speeches and preparing to march in protest to the Democratic Convention at the International Amphitheater. I found the streets near the park filled with more police, National Guard and their machinery than there were protesters with their signs and rants. My entire body twitched and vibrated as I stumbled along.

At the park, I heard a guy giving lessons on minimizing the effects of tear gas. Nearby, a veteran of Mississippi freedom rides was trying to get the kids to accept the techniques of non-violent resistance he and his group were demonstrating. Across the park others were shouting taunts at the police, but I found it difficult to tell who was threatening whom.

The cops were armed, protected by helmets, shields and the Guard's armored vehicles. As far as I could tell, the protesters had noise.

In my nervous state I wandered the walkways, aware that my 'clean-cut' appearance, even in jeans and t-shirt, made me stick out. I was stopped by a police officer anyway, who asked, "What's in the bag, kid?"

"Just my personal stuff, sir."

"Open it up. Let me see."

A voice behind the cop answered the order, "You got a search warrant?"

The cop pulled out his night stick as he swung around to face the interloper.

That scared me. I yelled, "It's okay." I unzipped the duffle, fumbling with my sweaty hands. "Here. This is all I got, officer."

The officer saw the sleeping bag and said, "You can't fuckin' camp here." That got a laugh from the search warrant questioner.

I surprised myself by having a good answer. "I only brought it with me in case the Guard make everybody stay in the park later. It might cool off when the sun goes down."

"Maybe you better just leave right now, then... Fuckin' punks."

"Maybe you should figure out who's so dangerous they need thousands of armed guards around them ... officer, sir."

I decided to leave as directed, which made me feel ashamed, but old Doc Graves might enjoy reading that in my journal, too. I started across the park, leaving the cop to argue with the hippie looking guy who defended me about the search order. It wasn't only the cops making me shaky nervous. I couldn't handle all those people. Unorganized. Was it because the scene appeared to be out of control? It was, at the least, beyond my control.

Along the way through the park I noticed a small group of people, guys and girls, sitting on the grass and passing around a joint. I looked around to see if any police were nearby. When I didn't see any, I approached the group. They all turned and gave me cagy, suspicious looks. The roach disappeared.

I approached them anyway and asked, "All these cops around. Aren't you taking an awful risk?"

"Hey, friend, I ain't saying there was anything going down here like what you're hinting at, but I gotta say, if you're goin' to jail anyway, might as well go in mellow, hey."

I gave an agreeing nod, "Yeah. You might have a point, at that."

They still didn't offer me a toke. I guess I looked like I might be a narc.

I started to walk on, but turned back, "Hey guys, I'm heading out, so I won't need this." I tossed them the plastic bag of trail mix from my duffle bag.

"Cool. Thanks, man. You gonna come back to march on the convention?"

"I don't know. I might."

By way of a farewell he said, "Don't trust anyone over thirty."

I replied, "I don't trust anyone." They all let me down.

***

I hardly slept that night as Buffalo Springfield played in my head. "Starts when you're always afraid," I heard Stephen Stills sing. I was afraid. All those armed men surrounding the ragtag thousands of so-called yippies. I eventually got enough sleep, mostly after sunrise. I packed my little car and drove to Yankton in one long afternoon and into the night. I cursed my cowardice the whole way. In my new apartment I turned on a television that I didn't recall seeing as part of the furnishings the one night I slept there. I watched as police rioted. Tear gas filled the air where I'd been the previous afternoon. I wanted to scream when I heard commentators try to blame the protesters for the violence. The pictures showed police instigating violence.

My journal attempts left me with big questions. How could I respond? What difference will it make for my life? Or: What's in it for Wally? After all the questions and feeble attempts at finding answers, I wrote three closing words before I lowered the Murphy bed: "Home. For now."

(9)

A registration line extended to the sidewalk when I shoved my way up the stairs. After a few minutes of pacing in the hallway while Dr. Graves met with another student, I plopped a filled three-ring binder and four wire-bound notebooks on the desk in front of her. "I did the assignment."

She looked at the stack of journals, then up at me, then back at the journals, her mouth metaphorically agape. She pushed her bifocals up her nose and opened the most recent notebook. Dr. Graves turned a few pages, deciphering a paragraph here and there, then handed it back saying, "This one's still half empty. You can keep using it." She pulled the loose leaf binder from the bottom of the pile and read, more intently now.

I stood watching until she eventually looked up while reaching for her tea cup. "You may sit down, Wallace."

I sat. "I just wrote what I needed to, Dr. Graves. For myself. Know what? It kept me from going completely bat-sh..., completely nuts working at the family business. I think I'd rather write than be a businessman." I hadn't thought of that until I said it to my adviser, and yet I knew it was true the moment I said it.

She asked more questions about my journal writing and its self-revelation. That's what she called it. I tried to answer but it felt like I mostly shrugged and nodded. She went back to reading for a moment. "This is an impressive, revealing set of documents, Mr. Bradford. Have you come to a conclusion about your major course of study?"

"Umm, well, English? Writing stuff? Or ... auto mechanics?"

"I think you're at the wrong school if fixing cars is your aim. It's a big change. You'll need a heavy course load to complete requirements in two years. Hmm." She indicated the journals, "May I keep these for the day? If you're serious, I'll hold an opening in my creative writing section for you. Also, you must take Mr. Morton's American Lit. Come back at four o'clock and tell me what you've decided."

"Today?"

"Yes, today. Your decision was due six months ago. Now go downstairs and register. Make those class changes before they're filled.

"Okay. Sign me up for that writing class. Definitely. Thanks for the help. The journal was powerful help. And, umm, if you're looking for sex scenes, they'd be in the red wire book." Those were days with no entries at all. Oh, well, she'll be curious.

I ran off to begin junior year with hopes that I'd find a reason to stay. I think the good professor may actually have opened volume two, with a red cover, and browsed during breaks between student advisory meetings as a new term began.

***

"Who in their right mind thinks creative writing can happen at eight o'clock in the morning?"

I looked up from the notebook in which I was writing and doodling, if not creatively, at least sleepily. Was she talking to me? I nearly fell off my chair—one of those weird chairs with the too small writing surface attached. I recovered enough to mumble, "Hi, Carolee."

She sat next to me and repeated her observation. "Hi, Wally. Seems awfully early in the day to be creative."

"Yeah, I guess. How'd you know my name?"

"It's a tiny college, Wally. You knew mine, right? So, are you making a jump from numbers to words, or just doing this for the hell of it."

"A jump, yeah. From equations all the way to sentences, possibly paragraphs, yeah."

"Well, I guess somebody can be clever at dawn."

"I do my best thinking in my sleep."

After class, I lingered as Carolee gathered up her belongings. We had already worked together in a small group sharing and critiquing each other's ten minute writing assignments.

44

"Want to go get coffee?" I was mumbling again.

"I have another class, but we could meet for lunch."

I was so giddy hearing her suggestion that I nearly fell off my chair again. And I was standing up. Lunch would soon become a daily meeting as a year with Carolee began.

***

One evening a month or so later, Carolee and I were sitting on the floor at my apartment, studying for American Literature. We both took that class, too.

I looked up from the dismal Theodore Dreiser novel as I realized that Carolee was dreamily gazing at me. "What?" I said with a nervous laugh.

"Oh. I'm sorry. Dreiser is putting me to sleep. But, you know something? The real guy is a lot more interesting that the Wally I had a crush on last year."

"No shit! You? You, the prettiest, most perfect girl on campus, had a crush on me when all the while I was scared to call you? God, we lost a whole year to shyness or something. Damn."

"Well, I smiled at you. Batted my eyelashes and everything," she said, batting her eyelashes and letting the "prettiest, most perfect" claim settle without further comment.

That led to a long kiss with some related petting. Coming up for air, Carolee looked at her watch. "I have to get back. Thanks for making supper."

I walked back to campus with her, my arm wrapped around her waist pulling her close.

Before we kissed good night, I recall saying, "You know something? The real Carolee is more intriguing than my fantasies of the Carolee I was too nervous to call."

"I think I heard something like that a little while ago." We kissed and Carolee dashed for the door before she gave in to my further advances in a prohibited 'public display of affection'.

***

Carolee and I were getting closer to it, but Carolee held us back from making love, 'all the way'. She said, "It's not time yet." She would not explain that any further. Carolee set her own curfew to leave my

45

apartment. The tight restrictions on female students were rapidly being relaxed with changing times, so she couldn't blame the dormitory matron.

As the fall term advanced we fell into a nightly routine that came easily. I like routine; I like knowing what to expect. I had bought a meal ticket in order to have lunch with Carolee, so we often had a cafeteria supper and then walked or drove to my pad. There we studied, talked and almost had sex, but not quite. "It's not time yet," she'd repeat and slap a misplaced hand that was allowed inside bra put not panties. I wanted all of her, now and for all time. 'Now' and 'all time' were in direct conflict in my emotions; lust versus love where love must be honored trusting that our time will come. For always. Trust. What or whom can I trust, really trust? All I could do was try to be worthy of her trust. Still, my desire for all of her was immediate every time we kissed. She seemed to want me, too, but had some extraordinary strength of will that put it off. She never said marriage must come first, only, "It's not time yet."

With her help, I managed to get 'B' grades in those sophomore English classes. Carolee got 'A's and had already declared a major in Elementary Education with an English minor. She loved the practicum experiences with young children and was anxious for the time, at least three semesters away, when she could be a student teacher.

While she managed to have a boyfriend, work hard for good grades, and hold down a part time job on campus (that year as a library aide), I was in a turmoil of love and internal conflict. "Does she hold back because she can't really commit? Every time I trust I get shot apart. Can I trust Carolee?" These thoughts weighed me down and then I'd get another letter from home that felt like somebody 'up there' was piling on. My father's demands were written in a way that always made me feel small, the family traitor - not just black sheep, but the lone goat among the sheep. Carolee tried to help, to assure me that I should make my own choices and not let Junior get to me. Of course, she had never met another Wallace M. Bradford. I read again as Dad denigrated my decision to major in English, "after all that math, how could you..." Junior wrote that it ought to be obvious, that the logical course is to use that gift with numbers for accounting and business. I could feel superior for a moment when I read that sentiment. "Dad is too stupid to see that calculus, real mathematics makes numbers in ledger columns feel like having to walk the dog in a blizzard—even the dog hates it.

Carolee's help got me through the English courses. I was starting to love the courses' subject matter. At the same time, my obsession with Carolee caused other grades to tumble.

***

With final exams completed, Carolee and I set out for the winter break. We had a plan. We would drive my VW to Chicago, where she would board the train for Altoona. We planned for a two day drive, given the season and the fact that a Karmann Ghia is not a great winter vehicle.

As we got underway the US20 pavement was dry and we were making good time. In the middle of the afternoon that first day, Carolee seemed twitchy, making odd nervous movements for a few minutes. She had been bouncing between the euphoria of a semester's end and irritation at little things for a day or two. She spotted a small town, possibly a large farmstead, a distance from the highway. "Go over to that town, Wally."

"Huh? We don't need gas. Are you okay?"

"Just find a gas station or someplace with a restroom. Please. Hurry."

I slowed and made the turn at the junction. We found a rundown gas station. I pulled in beside the cinder block building next to the restroom doors. "You're not gonna like it," I said, thinking of the filth she was dashing toward.

After a couple minutes she came out and tapped on the driver's side window. I was catching forty winks. My eyes popped open and I climbed out of the car. "Just checking my eyelids for holes."

"Can you grab my bag? The small one I'll carry on the train with me."

I pulled the suitcase from the cramped back seat. She opened it on the fender, pulled out a couple things and went back to the women's toilet. She returned more quickly this time and was looking around for me. I came out of the men's and said, "What kind of candy do you want? I'll get something so they don't hate us for using the head and not buying."

Back with candy, a pack of gum and two sodas, I told her, "I told the man we'd drink these here. That way we don't pay the bottle deposit. We're making good time anyway." Then I noticed. "What's the matter? How come you're crying, Curlybabe?"

Carolee wiped her eyes with the back of her hand and took a drink of grape Nehi before she answered. We were both shivering in the December wind while holding cold drinks. "Oh Wally, get in the car and I'll tell you." She gazed at the sky for a moment before she got in. "I had a plan for tonight." She grabbed my hand and made me look at her. "I had a nice plan. We'd stop at a nice motel and I'd surprise you and say, 'It's time now'."

I lit up like the Fourth of July. "Yeah? And?"

"And I got my period. Merry Christmas."

I stared out the windshield, took a long swig of my Grape Nehi thinking to myself, "Time to be understanding. Don't let your disappointment show. What does a real man say?" I turned back to Carolee and gave it my best shot. "Guess it just isn't time yet. Just knowing gives me goosebumps. It will be a merry Christmas." I'd convinced myself so I smiled. The smile was genuine and I reached over the gear shift to give her a kiss. "Let's finish these drinks and get on the road. I feel a night of cuddling coming up. We're pretty good at cuddling."

***

At the motel in Dubuque, I grabbed a wire bound notebook from my suitcase, found the next blank page and began to write.

"We're on break now, so what are you writing?"

"It's just my journal. I've been keeping it secret from you, so maybe it's time you know."

"Secret? Why? How long have you been doing this?" and other questions like that.

I tried to explain. "Dr. Graves gave me the assignment last spring. I had to write every day all summer. I guess she thought it might help me figure out where I'm headed. It became a real habit and I can't quit. I've only figured out where I am *not* headed so far."

"Has Elaine seen what you write?"

I couldn't understand how Carolee could refer to a full professor by first name. "I don't know how much Doctor Graves has actually read, but I turned in everything from the summer. She didn't correct much, so I don't know."

"And you still write every day?"

"Every night after you're back at the dorm."

"Can I see it?"

"Umm ... not yet." I had brought it out expecting to let her read and know my innermost thoughts. Now I couldn't bring myself to share it. It had something to do with trust, but it would take more journaling to work that out. "I'm sorry, Curlybabe. I was gonna hand it to you and now I can't. I don't know why, okay?" Now it was my turn for tears that day.

"Not time yet, huh?"

(10)

"You're not gonna lounge around and hide in your room for two damn weeks, Trey." Junior's rant began as soon as I sat down to supper with Mom, Dad and kid brother Bryan on the first Sunday evening of the new year, 1969. "You're coming to work for these two weeks. I have a project for you."

"What the hell, Dad. Don't I ever get a little vacation?"

"You had a week and a half. Holiday's over."

"During which I did school work. What use is two weeks to you, anyway? It's just to keep me under your everlasting thumb, isn't it. If I stay for your friggin' two weeks, will you still try to hold me hostage at that friggin' useless office next summer, too?"

"Don't you *ever* talk to your father that way, young man!" Mom interjected. "You'll apologize right now!"

"What, Mom? I didn't even use the word I was thinking of."

Mom drilled holes in my head with her glare. "Apologize."

"Okay. I'm sorry I've been taken hostage by your money. I'm sorry that I still feel stuck."

"That was no apology," Junior said through gritted teeth. "Just get the hell out of here. In the morning you will be ready to leave for the loop at 7:45. I don't want to see you until then."

I picked up my plate of food and climbed the stairs for some entertaining journal writing.

***

I swallowed my pride once again and rode into the city with Junior and the Husbands. I tried to get into the back seat of the enormous new

Lincoln Continental but Junior stopped me, "Nope. You're riding shotgun today, Trey. I want to talk to you."

It was snowing with a bitter cross-wind off the lake as we slowly eased into rush hour on an expressway that was beginning to ice over. I wondered, "Why are any of us going downtown in this mess?"

"Shut up, Trey," Junior muttered.

I guess I wondered out loud. I zipped my lip and my father went on to his prepared speech. I heard words and phrases like "I expect" and "responsibility" and "success or failure" and "commitment" and so on, but I wasn't really listening.

I did not notice any mention of my two week assignment, but I might have missed it. No doubt my sisters' husbands in the back seat paid attention and heard the entire speech. Finally, as the car sat idling behind a long row of stopped cars and trucks, I spoke up again, making sure I was using my impertinent voice, "Why don't you bring Bryan to your damn office? He'd like it."

"He's at school. And yes, he *does* like it. He'll most likely take your place this summer, after you flunk out of college."

"I'm not failing. If you didn't have me hostage on this frozen expressway, I could be finishing my psych paper to clear the incomplete grade. The only one."

"Psychology. You're still taking that bullshit?"

"Psychology of Adolescence, Dad. I'm thinking I might like to teach junior high kids." I chose to say junior high in hopes that my father would react most bitterly to that.

He did. "Jesus Christ! Junior high teacher! How much have we thrown down the rat hole for you to come up with that crazy notion?" He sat shaking his head and honked the horn as if that would do any good.

"I don't think Jesus would mind," I murmured with a hidden smirk.

"Well, I do. My son." He shook his head again. "My son, junior high. We've got a good business. Can it be too much to expect of my first son?"

"Since you mention it," I turned around to make sure the Husbands were awake. "You have a first born daughter who'd be good at it and a second daughter who'd be great. But the chauvinist pig only hires the yes-men."

In that moment I could tell that Junior wanted to throw me out to the storm. The Husbands would say 'yes' if he asked them to help. Unable to be quite that harsh he sat and fumed. It was another twenty minutes before the jack-knifed semi was moved and traffic began to inch forward again. By a vote of three in favor and one silent abstention we took the first exit and drove slowly north on city streets. "So now we'll be at home. You can do your course work today and maybe not fail your 'ology of psycho punks class. Tomorrow you work for me." Having demanded two weeks, Junior did not let go.

***

At 6:15 the next morning a pounding on my bedroom door forced me into consciousness. "Channel Nine says the commute'll be better today. Up and at 'em."

I heard the radio go on in Bryan's room and let the disk jockey tell me when it really was time to get up. I was allowed the back seat for the commute driven by the Husband with the beginnings of a mustache on his upper lip. I spent the time in silence. I tried and failed to nap.

The old desk that had been my station for the summer had been gathering dust. Only three of the six desks in the big room looked like they were currently being used. I plopped in the chair and picked up the stack of paper from the inbox. It was all general to obsolete memos, nothing for me to care a damn about. Who drops memos at unused work stations? I spun my chair around and looked over at the vacant desk that Kim had graced in summer. To her empty chair I said, "You've been beautifully replaced, Ms. 'It was sweet.' I much prefer waiting with my Curlybabe for the right time."

After an hour of sitting and being greeted by workers passing by, Junior approached. "How's it coming? Are you getting anywhere with the calls?"

"What calls? I haven't heard what the assignment is. All you said was you have one."

"And you didn't ask. No commitment, no responsibility. You couldn't even take one little step forward."

So, it's always my fault. I should've known. He gave me the assignment. "Call all the store managers you visited last summer. A couple of them have been replaced, but call anyway."

I was to give them some sweet talk while bringing pressure to improve profits. I was uncomfortable with the entire corporation. Now Junior had found the part of his business that I found most distasteful. That's an understatement, by the way.

I thought about my approach to the task for the rest of the morning. After a vending machine lunch, I started at the top of the list. I chatted with a manager about our earlier meeting, how much I appreciated it, and the good time I had visiting all the stores. Then I announced that I had been assigned to put on a squeeze for better profits. I was thinking, "Let them curse Junior, not me."

After that first call it struck me that sitting with a telephone at my ear was the appearance expected of me. I propped my feet on the desk and called Carolee. And, I found her at home this time. My nightly calls since Christmas had been near midnight for two reasons. One, she was adamant about getting the lowest long distance rates. Two, if I called earlier her mother would say, "She's busy right now," and ask me to call later. When I called later, Carolee's explanation about being busy was that she was hanging out with some old high school friends. It ate at my heart. Why couldn't she make sure she'd be available for my calls? This time, this afternoon time, it was Carolee herself picking up the phone.

"Hey, Curlybabe, I miss you."

"Why are you calling now?"

"Don't worry about it. It's on the company dime. Dad finally gave me that assignment and it's all making long distance calls in the daytime. So, what's one more? But hey, if anyone comes near, I'll start talking like you're a store manager in some little Midwest burg."

"Maybe you should make your work calls while you're at work. I still can't figure out what you find so awful about working there for a few days. Sounds like a cushy job to me."

"Oh, yeah. There's some soft cushions under the old man's thumb. If he could just accept who I am. He goes on trying to mold me into what he thinks I have to be. ...Yes, that's great. Let's just see some better sales figures this quarter."

"What?"

"That? Just Jack Peterson wandering by. He's a back-stabber. Had to make it sound like work."

"Well, you better just make those calls for real while I do my laundry and read for the Shakespeare class. Are you getting into the Bard yet? That's gonna be a great class."

"Not yet. But hey, I finished my Psych paper. Got it right here, ready to mail as soon as I can sneak in and use the Xerox."

"You have to sneak to the office copier?"

"Yeah. The dutiful Becky J. guards that monster like it was her baby. I'm watching for her to go on a break."

"Well, get it in the mail. You said Dr. Schulte expects it before we get back."

"He'll have it in a flash."

"You know, Wally dear, sometimes you're not as clever as you think you are."

"I have an idea. How about I come and see you this weekend. We can read Shakespeare to each other... And stuff."

"Umm, it won't work, Wally. I have some plans."

"Can't you change them? For your Wally? What are you doing that's so important?"

"I can't. I'll see you a week from Saturday. We'll drive back to Dakota together. If my lady schedule is back on track, I'll have that Christmas present. I think starting on the pill threw it off or something. Saturday the twentieth, my train is supposed to be there at 10:15 in the a.m."

"Okay. I can't wait. But, your weekend plans. Why can't...?"

"Don't worry about it. It really is not about you, Wally. Now get to the calls you're supposed to be on. And send the damn psych paper!"

"Hey Curly, I love you."

"Love you, too. Bye." She hung up.

I sat there with the phone dangling in my hand for a few more seconds, "There's things she's not telling me. God, I want to trust her, but can I?" I slammed the receiver onto the phone. "Yes, it is too about me, damn it!"

(11)

Carolee and I found shelter from the snow and wind at a motel near Des Moines. Later I wrote in my journal, "We consummated our love."

As we lived into the new semester, our relationship was changing but not growing. Love making didn't solve it. I refuse to consider that it caused the problems. We kept doing the deed because we were young and ... you know ... hormones.

We began to argue over inconsequential things, and not only on those certain days. We always made up, holding on for dear life to what we had. If there was anything to my suspicions during winter break that there might be someone else, I didn't see evidence now that we were back together at college. Something had changed; it seemed as if Carolee found fault with anything, any event, meal, whatever I planned for us. She complained because they were my plans, I guess.

Then one day, near the time for mid-term exams, on our way to lunch together, we found ourselves both stopped at the bulletin board staring at the same announcement. "Well, that'd be something completely different from my life so far," I said when I saw that Carolee was reading the same notice.

"Do you want to go? I do, for sure."

"Well, if you're up for it, I'm game. Why do you want to? I mean, we haven't heard about it before this minute. You don't even need to think about it?"

"I just did think about it. We'd be helping people where it's really needed. We'll learn more about the real South Dakota. You say you're game. Is that just because that's where I'll be? You sure you wouldn't rather go camping by yourself. You always talk about that as the best ever way to spend spring break."

"It would've been even better with you."

"And bicker non-stop for a week in the woods."

"Hey, I'm not suggesting it." I was thinking let's go where she wants and I didn't plan. Go along to get along; anything to hold onto my Curlybabe. "Better yet, it's off to Cheyenne River to repair a community hall in some isolated village and paint houses for a week with the campus ministry group. You didn't say why you're so hip to this trip. Cuz I'm thinking maybe I want to do it for the wrong reasons. I mean, I've avoided the chaplain my whole time here. I even avoided him when I was in his class, the required one. Why would he even let me come? Do you know how hard it is to avoid the chaplain at a church related college with only four hundred students?"

"Reverend Small doesn't turn people away. He's probably desperate to get enough of us to make the trip. I just want to find out what it's like and give a week to something worthwhile." "You never know, I could end up teaching at some place like that. So, what are your wrong reasons?"

"You don't really want to know, do you?"

"You brought it up. Tell me."

"It'll be a middle finger in Dad's face."

I noticed the way she hesitated, how her shoulders slumped. The nod seemed to indicate that she understood.

"What, Carolee? What is it?"

"Nothing. It's not you. Let's go see the rev about the rez."

"After lunch."

***

I waited until the end of the last day of classes before spring break to call. "I won't be coming there for the break, Mom." I told her about my alternative plan. She made it clear that it frightened her and that I must cancel and come home. She put Junior on the phone.

"What the hell's going on? Are you going off in the woods alone again? You've got your mother all upset. When does it ever stop with you?"

"It's not about me, Dad." I had never said or even thought that before. As calmly as I could manage, I explained about the work camp, the storm damaged community center that we would repair, and the poverty on the reservation. After I finished, I waited. All I heard was my father's breathing into the phone and my mother's crying in the background. It felt like hours but was probably only a few seconds.

When Junior spoke again the rage was gone from his voice. "If you don't want to come home for the week, Trey, that's fine. I don't need the antagonism either. Instead of that hopeless excursion, how about this? A chain with the right kind of stores including Aberdeen and Watertown is looking for a buyer. Why don't you go check them out for us? Let us know if we can make anything of them."

"I'm going to the Cheyenne River Reservation, Dad. It's a different direction."

"I'm trying to compromise here, kid. Trying to be understanding. Just take a day or two for a side trip."

"All you ever think about is your business. I'm going a different direction. There's nothing to compromise." The double meaning of direction wasn't there the first time I used the phrase. Now I felt a smug sense of satisfaction because Junior apparently hadn't caught it.

***

As soon as our group of eight students and two advisers had climbed out of the van and sorted gear, I knew that I had better sort out my stereotypes, too. It was my third year at Yankton, where I didn't know of any native students and I hadn't even taken a half-day round trip through the Yankton Reservation.

I helped Carolee take her belongings into the church where the women would bunk. At the YMCA a few blocks away we set our men's camp and then returned to the church for supper and introduction with the local leaders guiding the project.

The week was busy, sweaty and dirty. The weather was quite warm for April on the plains and it only rained on the day we departed. We slept at Dupree and rode the van to an even more rural community with tools and paint. The painting we could do, with a little instruction and guidance. The repairs were more than a collection of young amateurs could accomplish in five days. Fortunately, another small group of more mature adults from Minneapolis was on hand. They were led by two brothers, one a nurse, the other a carpenter. The brothers were using this excuse to come home to the reservation, perhaps to stay. They came with skills and a willingness to help us non-Indian kids, who had a tendency to say and do asinine things as we became marginally acquainted with the local culture. We remained oblivious to any understanding of our white privilege or the many ways historic tensions define the present. I, solitary Wally who trusts no one, came to help and it didn't occur to me that others had reasonable cause to distrust us.

The local project leader, like the brothers, ignored our naiveté. He came across to us students as a tribal elder, though he couldn't have been more than thirty-five or forty. At break times he told stories. Stories continued in the evenings, with a campfire, a guitar and freedom songs. Carolee and I sat close, taking a brief outing into a different life.

On Wednesday evening, the local boys who'd often been shooting baskets at the asphalt court across the street were not around and some local girls were. We ate our fried chicken supper and watched for a while. I took our paper plates to the trash can and turned around to see Carolee sauntering over to the basketball court.

At first I was amazed. Carolee hadn't said anything that I could remember about being a fantastic basketball player. But here she was, making the long shots, keeping up with these other sharp athletes. I was in awe. Then I saw something more. The boys who'd been there every night had appeared, watching my girlfriend with her long swishing blonde ponytail and bright hazel eyes behind her wire-rim granny glasses. The boys watched Carolee, and started to show off some stuff with their basketball, though they didn't yet have access to the one and only hoop. I watched them, with a surge of adrenaline that I could never explain. The local girls watched the boys, too, and began to play more aggressively. It started to look like it was everybody against Carolee. She upped her game, too. Did she even notice what else was going on among those teenagers?

I stood immobilized, a burning sensation in my chest but no way to act. It wasn't long before the girls yielded the court to the boys. At Carolee's beckoning, they all came over to meet the college kids. The moment had passed, but it left an indelible mark in my psyche. I wanted Carolee all to myself. So much so that I didn't want other guys to see her at all. Maybe if we could have some time really alone together. Maybe I could figure it out.

On Friday evening the local community joined us at the partially repaired Community Center for a pot luck supper built around fry bread tacos and jokes. I still didn't know how to relate to these kind and generous folks. At least by then I knew that I didn't know. When I thought about it, I decided that I wasn't much good at relating to the people closest to me in the city and suburban culture, either. I didn't even have an answer to my internal question, "Do I want to?"

Carolee seemed to be quite at ease laughing and talking with the basketball girls, ever under the watchful eyes of the basketball boys. Then the two groups merged. With my second helping of fry bread I watched from across the big room. From that distance it looked like Carolee was flirting with these younger boys.

As the party wound down, I coaxed Carolee out the door. As soon as we were alone, I asked, "What was going on with those boys? It looked like you were flirting with them."

Carolee was taken aback and retorted, "You men can be so damn possessive. I can take care of myself."

"Men? Who are these men?"

"You see what I mean? You're doing it now." The conversation was over.

All the way back to Yankton I stewed in silence, fearful that much more than a conversation was over.

***

Monday at noon, I waited at the usual place for Carolee's class in Child Development to be dismissed. She didn't run away, so I asked, "Lunch?"

She frowned but nodded and walked with me. As we were finishing lunch I said, "Let's walk over to my pad. I have an idea I want to kick around with you." Neither of us had another class until Rhetorical Composition at three.

(12)

I got my current journal notebook out of its hiding place and handed it to Carolee with Sunday's page open and immediately began pitching my scheme. "I've been doing some research, Curlybabe."

"Will it help with the rhetoric assignment?"

"What assignment?"

"Geez, Wally. Don't you even look at a syllabus?" She was reading the journal now. "*To Altoona via ... alone together.* What does all this mean?"

"I'm trying to tell you. I was thinking how much it means and all; what you mean ... to me. Maybe with a special week or month this summer we'd be solid. And I'd learn not to be so possessive about it. So, I wondered. And then it hit me."

"Oh, this is gonna be good. You hear this neighbors? He won't be possessive while he arranges my life!"

"Come on, Carolee. Just listen for a minute. It's an idea for you to think about. Let's hike the Appalachian Trail, or part of it."

When she heard the actual idea a surprised, far-away look spread across Carolee's face. Her expression said it without words. This was something she really would like to try. I intended to prove our love with an intense shared experience. She, perhaps, simply wanted to do the hike.

She began to add up the good and bad about the idea. "I might see what life is really like for some Appalachian people we might encounter. Beyond Altoona, that is. I did grow up by the Allegheny Mountains, not far from the Trail. For some reason I don't think of it as Appalachia, not like you hear about on the news. Is it like what I read about poverty in America, or is it like my home town or Melissa's? She isn't like that at all." After a long pause, she asked, "How can I earn any money for school next year if I'm hiking instead of working?"

"I turn twenty-one in June and a little trust fund will start to kick in. Gramp set one up for all his grandkids the day we were born. We become part owners of that damned family corporation. It'll let me give you enough to cover the difference. And even if Junior cuts me off, I can take out a loan against it for my tuition. He can't touch the trust and Gramp won't."

"You've covered the angles. Okay, I'm thinking about it. Um, do you really want me along? Don't you really want to be alone with Wally?"

Carolee didn't let me walk with her to campus. "I'll see you in class later. And look at the darn syllabus, will you? We have essays due in a week. Don't expect Mr. Morton to take you by the hand and remind you. It's not junior high."

"I told Dad I want to become a junior high teacher. Did he ever come unglued! I loved it."

"I said I'm thinking about it." Carolee ran down the steps.

From the window, I watched her dash down the street. "She'll say yes. She wants to do it."

***

Among classes, study, writing and hoping to pass, Curlybabe and I perused maps, made plans, and talked endlessly of what the summer had in store for us. Argument gave way to debate. We listened and learned to compromise and yield to the better rationale. Carolee answered a few calls from Altoona during those weeks. She muttered about the calls but would never say who. If they were from her parents, she'd have said so. Worry over what they meant hit me at odd moments. I wanted answers and couldn't ask the questions.

(13)

"Are you ready for some 'We' time, Curlybabe?" I asked as we retrieved my backpack from baggage claim at the Asheville airport.

"Whee! Are you ready for some Appalachian spring?" Carolee asked in reply, bouncing on her toes.

In our negotiating through the last month at Yankton, we had agreed to start at the Great Smoky Mountains National Park and hike north to Pennsylvania, stopover for a week at Carolee's family home in Altoona, then either hike on to New York or renegotiate, depending. Depending how long this middle third of the trail took. Depending how we felt about going on. Depending how we felt about other stuff. Carolee knew what she meant, I guess.

"I'm ready. We better get out there and start walking north. Any minute now it'll be hot Appalachian summer."

The previous day Carolee had taken the bus from Altoona to Boone, North Carolina, where her friend Melissa lived. Melissa had volunteered to drive us to the trailhead. I was relieved that my plane was on time and so was my Curlybabe. We each grabbed hold of my pack's aluminum frame and carried it between us to the car where Melissa and a guy were waiting. The trunk was open with three packs in it. I gave Carolee a glance that said, "What?"

"I have a surprise for you, Wally," she said as she emerged from another hug and kiss, distracting me from the knapsack count. "Not only are Melissa and Jack going to drive us to the trailhead, they're going to hike with us the first day or so." Melissa, a fellow Yankton student, never hid her excitement when a letter from Jack arrived at the mailroom. The plan that both Jack and Melissa would join us for a few miles came as a happy surprise to Carolee.

I, however, didn't do well at hiding my feelings that they were interfering in my plans.

Carolee pulled me aside as Jack slammed the trunk lid, "It's for *one* day, Mr. B3. Just enjoy, and take things as they come for once. It won't hurt you."

I mumbled, "One day means two nights," and nodded glumly. I put on a courteous mask to say, "Good to have you aboard, Jack ... and Melissa. Hi, good to see you."

It was already late afternoon when we arrived at the Park boundary town of Cherokee. The hiking adventure began with drive-in food in town, another drive and a short, uphill, hike to a camp shelter. The next day we hiked another four miles before we reached the Appalachian Trail along the mountain ridge.

I wasn't sure I liked finding out that Carolee seemed to be in better shape for backpacking than I was. I knew that wouldn't last, but still. Carolee took the lead, with Melissa strolling behind or beside, chattering away, except where the trail was steep. Jack asked me questions, attempting to develop some rapport. I answered, with one word whenever I could, and asked nothing of Jack in return.

We ate a lunch of trail biscuits and summer sausage on the North Carolina – Tennessee border. At that point I re-arranged my load for better balance while the others enjoyed the view. Carolee took the first of many pictures along the trek.

Now on the Appalachian Trail for real, we got under way again. Carolee helped Jack finally get me out of my taciturn frostiness. I hadn't yet said anything about the restored '49 Chrysler we'd ridden to the trailhead, but she had seen me admiring it, inside and out. She asked me, "Where did you hide the Ghia for the summer? I just love that car of yours."

Before I could answer, Jack said, "A Karmann Ghia? That's a fun little car. Is it an old one? Have you been working it over?"

I could have answered all that the same way I'd been fending off questions all morning, with, "Yes. Uh-huh. Yes. Overhauling engines, mostly," but I didn't. I did say, "It's a few years old and the body is great. I overhaul engines and swap 'em in and out. I gave it to my brother last week. Did you do that fine restoration of the Chrysler?"

We walked and talked then; of cars, restorations versus hot rods, antiques and sports cars; talking autos while walking where there were no sounds or sights of motor vehicles.

"You gave your car away? To Bryan? The brother you're always bad mouthing?" Carolee gave me a sideways glance and added, "You do surprise me sometimes. That might have been a nice thing to do, though."

"He'll burn out the clutch before I get back. And he won't know what to do about it."

***

"Should we go on a little farther, do you think?" asked Carolee when we arrived earlier than expected at the campsite we had marked on the map.

I was feeling the aches of a first full day and was ready to stop. Not wanting to disagree with whatever Carolee wanted, I just shrugged.

Melissa saved me. "Jack and I have a longer walk tomorrow, you know. We have to go all the way back to the car."

She gave me the opening to remind Carolee, "We said we'd take our time, not try to go too far each day."

For the hell of it, Jack and I pitched my tent next to a shelter where many had camped before. With some dry brush Melissa and Carolee got a fire going in the concrete pit. They urged Jack and me to get firewood first, before the tent, if we wanted to eat. They cooked the real food from Melissa's pack. Soon the two of us, always carrying provisions for several days, would dine from the dehydrated, light weight supplies.

When I took my notebook and wandered twenty or thirty yards into the woods, Jack started to follow. "Wait, Jack," both Carolee and Melissa chorused. I heard Carolee explain, "Wally needs his alone time to write his daily journal." Twenty minutes later they dealt me into a rummy game I'd never played before.

I ached everywhere as I stretched out on our open sleeping bag. The sun had finally dropped below the western horizon. A long evening of emerging friendship, of talking and playing cards, had ended. It was time to sleep and I ached. I had been swimming every day to get in shape. I was in shape, but hiking up and down the hills uses muscles in a different way. Carolee snuggled up to me briefly, but only that, and we tried to sleep.

"You got any aspirin, Curlybabe?" I gave up the pretense that the day hadn't stressed my muscles.

Carolee dug in her pack in the dim light of dusk. By the time she found two aspirins and the canteen, I was sound asleep.

***

Carolee and I (yes, even 'It's about me and our alone time Wally') found it hard to say goodbye to Jack and Melissa the next morning. They said they'd like to hike on with us, but needed to get back to jobs. Not to mention that they hadn't carried food for more than this day. Jack gave me his deck of cards, saying with a gentle shoulder punch, "To remember me by."

As soon we could no longer see them when we looked back, I quickened my pace just a little and held my back with the forty-five pound pack a little straighter. It took me another quarter mile to realize the difference. The real hike had now begun. Just me and my Curlybabe, onward to Pennsylvania. And New York? Connecticut? Carolee matched my pace with so little difficulty that I asked, "Have I been holding you back? Am I walking too slow?"

"Don't worry about it. We'll really have our mountain legs in shape in another day or so. It's different now, isn't it; just us with a long trail ahead. What do you think, Wally-man? Will we meet up with some real mountain folk along the way? See another side of poverty in America? Like the reservation only different?"

"Just us, Carolee, with a trail to enjoy. 'Whose woods these are I think I know...'."

"The woods are lovely, dark and deep, But I have promises to keep, And miles to go before I sleep, And miles to go before I sleep.' Just us, but maybe? Anyhow, these aren't Robert Frost's snowy woods. Steamy woods by noon is more like it."

"And miles to go. How far did we figure we'd make today?"

"Well, we'll still be along the Smokies for a few more days unless we get real energetic. How's your pack riding?"

Our conversation settled into more of the mundane issues of this new thing called distance hiking as we traveled the ridges and valleys of the mountain range.

***

Soon we fell into a daily pattern. We liked a hot breakfast of oatmeal, unless we'd touched civilization the previous afternoon. Then breakfast would include eggs fried either over campfire or the little kerosene burner. We'd break camp leaving absolutely no hot coals, as little evidence as of our stay as we could manage, and hike. Some days we traveled up to twelve miles, seldom more. Some days we encountered more climbing or rock scrabble to traverse that slowed our progress. Carolee took pictures; I admired the big views. We spent many hours without talking to anyone but each other; often not even each other. We walked in silence listening to sounds of forest and mountain meadow. Other times we enjoyed visiting with other hikers along the way. When our mid-day cold meal was taken with these groups, I liked it best if the party was southbound. We could swap information about what to expect ahead.

We even made fair progress through three days of steady, warm rain during the fourth, or possibly fifth, week. We did as best we could to keep our belongings dry. By the second night it wasn't clear whether it was rain or sweat that had dampened our sleeping bag. The damp let the morning chill join us inside the bag. Those mornings were the two times, the only times, I thought the hike might have been a stupid idea.

On the afternoon of the third day after the rain began a patch of sky visible above the dense forest cleared to an intense blue. The trees were still heavy with moisture, but our spirits were lighter. I looked up, then down and around, and muttered, "Wow, look at that."

"At what?" Carolee was taking a close up picture of some wildflowers blooming among some ferns.

"How green it is here. Dark green ferns, bright green leaves, mossy-green moss."

"How long have you been walking with your eyes closed, Wally-man?"

"They've been open. I've just been looking at this beautiful lady instead of the trees."

"Keep it up, Fool. Haven't bathed for a week and that was in a campground shower that used my last dime before I'd rinsed. Now my hair is rain rinsed in snarls."

"And yet, radiant." I smiled; Carolee called it a smirk. We walked on. I was daydreaming in pleasure that my hopes for the journey seemed to be coming true. In my estimation we were building a comfortable partnership. The tasks of camping and hiking were being easily divided. We were dealing with each other and not worrying about the rest. I was patting myself on the back for investing in that double bag. She had little choice but to crawl into the sack with me.

A sign at a junction to a side trail indicated that we would be coming to a town in just a couple miles.

I made the suggestion that was occurring to Carolee at the same moment. "If there's a hotel, let's take a night to dry out and such."

The next day I learned that Carolee had other agenda.

(14)

"It won't be long and we'll be in Pennsylvania, and home. Can you afford another hotel night here?" Carolee asked when I was about to go the front desk of the old downtown hotel and check out.

"What do you have in mind? Last night's history tour wasn't enough?"

"That was good. And fun to be reminded that we're at the halfway point of the trail, even if we're at more than half of our plan."

"Our basic plan. I still hope we'll do more after your home town. I think we should hike into New York State." I didn't dare say what I was really thinking: "Massachusetts."

"We'll work that out when we get home. Today I want to poke around a little bit. Talk to some people. As close as it is to home, I've never been in West Virginia before. Not even Morgantown. We've seen some rural people on side trips in hollers along the way, even talked with a few, but that's all. I want to get a feel for the place. You know what I mean? Would teaching school in Virginia or West Virginia mountains be any different than in Altoona? Or in a small town mountain community in Penn?"

"So, is this what our five hundred mile walk is about? Scouting career locations?"

"Um, no. Well, today it is, yeah. Can we stay at Harpers Ferry one more night, huh Wally-man?"

I pondered. For a long twenty seconds I didn't answer. I wanted to say, "No, it's about our hike. It's about us." That thought caught me out. *Us*. I knew deep down that I wanted Carolee to be a partner, not an appendage, and it was hard for me to trust that. "Okay," I finally said, nodding, "we'll stay. You'll let me come along today, right?"

"Of course. You might notice things I don't."

***

I noticed things, but not in the way that Carolee had suggested. I noticed the way she connected with people. I noticed the questions she asked, her interest in the elementary schools of small communities like Harpers Ferry-Bolivar and in isolated rural mountain country. I noticed that her interests didn't seem to connect with mine, and that didn't seem to be on her mind at all. I noticed and it occurred to me that, for Carolee, the trail was another journey to Cheyenne River, or something like it.

Carolee led me here and there. She talked with storekeepers who catered to tourists visiting the Historical Park; she talked with anyone who seemed to be local. As we ate sandwiches at a picnic table, Carolee said, "I should have paid more attention to your maps, Wally. Who'd have thought that a trail that follows the length of a great mountain range, when it gets to the state that calls itself the Mountain State, I mean look at this. The trail only goes through a little corner of West Virginia, where it drops down to the river valley."

"Two rivers, actually, that come out of these mountains." I pointed out and around at the steep hillside town and beyond.

"Okay, but you see my point. I was thinking about all the stories about moonshiners in the hollers, growing corn on hillsides and pulling a shotgun on anybody who comes near; and kids going to one room schools where they might or might not be taught."

"Aha! It's all about that, really, isn't it. You want to be a teacher who goes where it's hardest to be the teacher."

"I want to go where I can learn the most about the way different people live, and what drives them. And, you know what? This place isn't much different from home. It doesn't feel like going to a foreign country the way the reservation, the way Lakota country did."

"It's all foreign. Everywhere, everybody. Did you even notice as you were chatting away how that one clerk told you whatever lie she thought you wanted to hear? We're outsiders, just tourists to these people. God a'mighty. People. Can anybody be trusted?"

"Well, there's…" I think Carolee was about to say that I could trust her. She had only hinted that her intention for our summer was not the same as my 'just us' plan and I hadn't picked up the hints. She hadn't challenged my plan directly, only details. For a moment her thoughts seemed to be far away. "Maybe no one can be, but trust what I'm about to say."

"What? What is it? Why so tense all of a sudden?" I tried to wrap Carolee in a hug but she brushed me off.

She daubed at her eyes with a paper napkin that left mustard on her cheek. I grabbed a clean napkin and wiped her face. That got her even more choked up but she finally blurted it out. "You can quit making plans to hike on to New York. Our trail ends at the point closest to Altoona."

"Curlybabe, what are you saying? 'Our trail.' You mean the hike? Or us? What's going on?"

"I don't know, Wally. The hike, yes. But... Oh, I don't know. Am I worthy of your trust? You have such need and it's so hard for you."

"Oh, Babe. Can't we work on it for, um, the next twenty, or sixty years?"

Carolee laughed, a single brief giggle, turned to me with a wan smile, and hugged me. I did not push her away.

***

That afternoon we didn't consciously decide to avoid having any more serious discussions, but apparently we needed to lighten up. We took a river walk, from the Potomac along the Shenandoah River. I broke into song, embarrassingly loud.

> "Oh Shenandoah, I long to see you,
> Away you rolling river.
> Oh Shenandoah, I long to hear you,
> Away, I'm bound away 'cross the wide Missouri."

Little did I know the way that last line would again figure into my travels. I sang it pretty well, so Carolee joined in as we repeated the only verse I knew. A dim memory of a second verse let me make one up.

> "Oh Mr. Siebert, I love your daughter
> Away you rolling river.
> That she'd be mine, with hope I sought her
> Away, in Yankton town beside the wide Missouri."

"That better not be a proposal, Mr. Bradford," Carolee murmured, almost inaudibly.

I heard, though. I hadn't given my line much thought, nor intended any import in it. Still, I felt kind of hurt at her whispered response. I said, "Only if you want it to be. Only when. Otherwise it's just a rhyme, okay?"

As we wandered again in the historical park with its markers describing the Harper's Ferry Raid, Carolee clapped a hand over my mouth when I started singing John Brown's Body.

"Hey! What's the matter with another rousing chorus?" I asked when she loosened her grip on my cheeks.

"You're just lucky that wasn't my fist."

Changing the subject, I suggested, "As long as we're living it up here, let's have a decadent dinner. We can go over to that other half of the town."

"To Bolivar. Sounds nice. First we better find a coin laundry."

In clean clothes, including long jeans instead of hiking shorts, we hitched a ride across to the Bolivar side of town, ate at a nice restaurant and walked back to the hotel with a thumb out as the occasional car passed us. My journal entry that evening was built around my Shenandoah verse. As I wrote, recalling my feeling on hearing what Carolee said after my verse, I brightened. I hadn't been thinking of the future when I sang, but she had heard it that way. She's thinking about us seriously for sure. I wrote that down. Later we snuggled, and more, in the comfortable bed for a second night.

Re-supplied and dry, we were ready to get back on the trail early the next morning. From our previous trail experience and the look of the map, Carolee figured we could easily reach Harrisburg within a week. I didn't argue the point, but I set out to make sure it would take ten days, even if I had to fake injury.

For two days Carolee won out when I wanted to stop in mid-afternoon. I complained of the heat, which wasn't nearly as bad as it had been the week before the rain. After an hour's rest, she insisted that we go on to our planned campsite. The third day, she gave in. The fourth day she picked up the pace and we arrived at our intended campsite before I had a chance.

The next day I resorted to subterfuge. After lunch of peanut butter, crackers and apples, I discovered an odd stiffness in my hip. I groaned as I lifted my pack and limped along beside Carolee for a quarter mile. With a sidelong look at me she resumed a more normal pace. Around a bend and out of sight, she stepped off the trail to wait behind a large tree. Sure enough, she caught me walking normally, if slowly, when I came into view.

"Aha!" she exclaimed as she stepped out behind me. "There's nothing wrong with your hip. What's the deal?"

"Hey, I walked it off. It was stiff and it loosened now."

"Bullshit. You've been trying to slow us down since Harpers Ferry. Tell me what's going on." I was pretty sure she knew but wanted to hear it from me.

"I don't want it to end, Curlybabe. I'm scared. It was all about pulling us together, solid, forever. I'm scared it hasn't. Now we're in Pennsylvania, and…"

"Uh-huh." There was a long pause before Carolee added, "Well, thank you for saying what's really on your mind, Wally-man." Then she laughed. She tried to suppress it, but the laugh would not be held in.

"What the hell? What's so funny? Come on, Carolee."

"The limp, Wally. I mean, did you really think…? Here you are, all worried about what or who you can ever trust and you pull a kid's stunt like that."

"Well, I'm desperate, Carolee. You said that one thing I can trust is the hike ends at Harrisburg. No more after your home visit. I'm trying to make the most of it and I'm scared."

"Oh, Wally, I am sorry. And, well, it's possible I could change my mind. I don't know. We'll cross that bridge and so on and so forth."

"Can we cross that bridge before you burn it?"

(15)

"Good morning, Poppy."

"Why, Carolee!" Harold Siebert turned away from the phone, shouting, "Maxine, it's Carolee." Back into the phone, he said, "Your mother's picking up downstairs. Are you all right? Is anything wrong?"

"No, Pop. Hi, Mom. Nothing's wrong. We're at a place called Pine Grove Furnace State Park. We should be at Boiling Springs sometime tomorrow afternoon. Can someone pick us up there?"

"You're so close," her mother said. "We've missed you. We had a postcard in the mail yesterday. Was it yesterday or the day before, Harold? Well, no matter. It had a picture from that Civil War place, in West Virginia. We didn't expect you to be this close yet."

"I forgot to mail it for a couple days. I'd think of it and then forget when we were near civilization the next time. That's why it's so crumpled. It was like that before the Post Office got it. Can someone get us at Boiling Springs?"

"Your dad can come get you where you are right now. His boss knows all about it. All he has to do is call and he'll have the day. How 'bout that?"

"Boiling Springs, Mom. Tomorrow afternoon. Tell your boss that, Dad. Our goal was Harrisburg, and we'll be pretty close. Wally'd rather keep walking to New York, you know. There's parking at the trail crossing where you can wait, or we can wait."

"'We.' You and Wally. Is he coming here, then? Or is he going on to New York?"

"We, Pop. Wally is coming for a week. Then maybe we'll both go on for a ways. Maybe he'll go home to Chicago. For a week, though, you should get acquainted."

"You remember when you were four? You told us you were going for an adventure. Put your stick horse over your shoulder and off went the little hobo to the corner and…"

"I'm on a pay phone, Pop. We'll talk tomorrow. Appalachian Trail parking at Boiling Springs. Love you, Bye."

"I can't wait to see you, Honeybunch. Are we still connected?"

"Bye, Mom." Carolee opened the phone booth and said to me, "Pop sounded like he hoped I was coming home alone and you'd go on right away."

***

Carolee recognized the car as we came off the trail into the parking area. She had never seen it before, but she was sure which one we'd find her father, or possibly both parents, waiting within. "Pop's here, Wally. The white car with the dark vinyl top."

"How do you know that? You said he'll be in a car you've never seen."

"Don't have to. The dealer cars they drive are always white." She broke into a trot, with a bouncing backpack making it awkward, toward the shiny Chevy.

Her father saw her coming, sprang out of the car and met her halfway. "Here. Gimme that load, so I can give my baby girl a proper hug."

Carolee let him lift it off her back. I stayed a couple yards behind, enviously watching their homecoming greeting.

"My gosh, you've been carrying that heavy load across half a dozen states?"

"It's not so heavy now. We ate half what was in there in the past four days." They hugged. "Wally, come meet my father. Poppy, this is Wally Bradford. And my Pop, Harold Siebert."

We shook hands while Harold looked me up and down with a sour, squinting expression. I could read the accusation in that look. It had me pondering, "He thinks I stole his daughter's innocence."

"Pop," Carolee cried, "don't be that way." She looked like she was about to say more, but held back. Instead, she said, "Mom didn't come with you."

"Well, you see, truth be told, she's home getting the surprise ready. But I'm not supposed to tell you that, so you didn't hear it from me." They

73

laughed. "Let's get you kids loaded up here and get us home to it." He popped the trunk open.

I pulled my pack off and started to put it in, then held back. "That's the cleanest trunk I've ever seen. I hate to soil it with this grungy pack frame, sir."

"Well, it's not going on the upholstery then, so shove it in there."

Carolee told stories about our trek as we rode along, three across the front seat with Carolee in the middle. Every now and then, when she started to lean against me, she'd jerk upright and equalize the distance between father and boyfriend again.

Carolee spun the events or our journey into entertaining yarns. As she reached a punch line, I made a wild stab at getting along with Harold. "I was there, and I don't remember it being that funny, Mr. Siebert. I think your daughter's 'A' grades in creative writing come naturally. Does she get it from you?"

"She's an original, Wally. And don't you forget it."

"Come on, Poppy. Of course it's from you." She turned and pinched my knee, "Wally, he comes home from a dull day at the car lot when there are only lookers and no buyers and he tells about it like the *Laugh In* cast took over the lot."

***

Harold's early mention did not make the party any less surprising. Carolee assumed it would be a special family dinner. Maybe her brother would be home on leave from the Navy. That'd be cool. As soon as the hugs, greetings, and cold lemonade at our arrival were done Maxine suggested a bubble bath to Carolee. "And put on the new dress I got you. I hung it on your bedroom door. For tonight, okay?"

"What's tonight?"

"The surprise. Your father told you there was a surprise, didn't he?"

"No comment. You want a quick shower first before I use up the hot water, Wally?"

"Yeah, great. And maybe I should go buy a decent pair of pants to keep up appearances."

"While you're at it, you can stop by Anderson Motors and buy a new muscled up Camaro to replace the VW you gave away." Carolee said it in jest, but I heard a bit of hinting that a big purchase might also buy her father's approval.

***

I wandered through the business district until I found the store that Maxine recommended. I was helped there by a man, younger than I, dressed in flared striped pants and a tight fitting shirt in a green that matched the pants stripes. I did not let the salesman convince me about loud stripes. I bought brown slacks with flared legs and a definite crease. The big collared shirt went well but I said no to the ascot. At the counter I noticed a poster, taped to the front at knee level. There was a yellow bird on a guitar neck and words large enough to read, "Days/Peace/Music. I stooped down to read the smaller print. "Woodstock Music and Art Fair. White Lake, NY. August 15, 16, 17. 3 Days of Peace and Music."

The young clerk was asking me about payment, so I stood up and pulled the Master Charge card from my wallet. The card had been accepted just a few days earlier, but I'd put two nights in a hotel on it. I had fingers crossed in hope that my overpayment before the hike had been enough. The clerk had me sign the slip with its carbon copies and didn't call for authorization.

With the transaction done, I mentioned the poster. "That's coming up real soon. I would love to go to that." I bent down again to read the list of scheduled performers. "Are tickets still available? It's probably sold out by now."

"Oh yeah, I think it is." I was suddenly a mark with a credit card. "But as a matter of fact..." He paused for effect, and found the envelope in a drawer under the cash register. "I have a couple tickets that a friend of mine is willing to part with. That's if he can get a little more for them than he paid."

"Oh?" I pictured my little tent pitched in a camp area with a stage in view and rock music blaring, Carolee lounging with me and grooving to the tunes. "How much?"

"I could let you have them for fifty ... each."

"A hundred dollars?! That's more than double."

"I already have an offer of eighty for them," the clerk lied. "Take it or leave it. I need cash, of course. No checks, no charge card."

"Okay, I guess. I don't have that kind of cash on me. Will you hold them for me while I visit a bank?"

"I'll keep them here for you – for a while. There's a bank around the corner, there." He pointed. "At the end of the block."

75

"Is it still open?"

The clerk checked his wristwatch. "Um, no."

"Hold the tickets and I'll be back here before noon tomorrow. Promise?"

"I'll have 'em. Just bring the money. And hey, so you know I take care of my customers," he glanced up at the window where the owner's office overlooked the sales floor and lowered his voice even though there was no one else in the store, "if you bring a hundred ten, I can let you take a lid of some good grass with you right now."

I considered the offer and considered what would happen if it was discovered by Carolee's parents. My fear prevailed and I refused the marijuana.

(16)

"Oh-wow, you do look great, Curlybabe." She bowled me over. I came into the kitchen and got an eyeful of mini-dress and makeup. I dropped my sack of new clothes on a chair and reached for Carolee.

She avoided the contact and said, "Except I don't dare lift my arms. It's too tight. I'm afraid the seams will rip."

"Too tight. She grew shoulders carrying that pack across the USA," her mother said. "And, it is way too short. You didn't grow taller on your hike, too, did you? I don't know why I even bought it. They only had ankle length or so short there's hardly a dress at all."

I leaned in close to Carolee and whispered, "Works for me," and gave her a little kiss on the cheek. "I like the eye stuff, too."

"Yeah? And I'm about to get rid of the lashes. They're smearing my glasses. See?" She peeked into my shopping bag. "What did you find? Maybe you should change. Did Pop show you where you're sleeping?"

"No. Unless that's why we came in through the garage earlier."

"Don't, Wally. Not a good joke. I'll show you."

At that moment I bumped into a reality. Carolee and I had been sleeping together in a little pup tent for nearly two months. Her parents had to be aware of that but it made no difference. I would be assigned her brother's basement room while she occupied the upstairs room that had been hers since she was six.

***

Pop Harold was squirting lighter on the charcoal with one hand and holding a wide mouth stubby of Rheingold beer in the other. He didn't offer me one. "You want some help with the grill, Mr. Siebert?" I asked.

"Nah. Stand back, kid." Harold struck a wooden match and the fluid exploded into flame. "Nice threads, kid. If you could've found a barber you'd look almost human."

"Well, um, thank you, sir. I guess." I looked around and took note of the group of people near my age standing near the back fence. I had assumed the surprise was really just a family barbecue. This looked like something more. Having just been shopping in order to dress better, I noticed the faded cutoff jeans and t-shirts worn by both sexes.

"Go on out and introduce yourself, kid." Then Harold shouted, "Hey you punks. This here kid's Wally, Carolee's friend from college."

I had no choice. I wandered out to the mixed group of Carolee's high school friends. After we'd exchanged names and they'd asked their polite questions about hiking the Appalachian Trail which I answered with shrugs and a few words, the conversation settled back into the usual routine. There was one guy, though, who kept staring at me, except when I returned the look. Then he'd look away for a second, all the while clenching and unclenching his fists. Another guy, a tall man of rugged good looks wearing long pants appeared to be a few years older than the rest of us. He didn't say anything as they talked of parties, summer jobs, relationships, break-ups, and cars.

The minute that Carolee came out the back door, the girls left the boys and went across the lawn to join her. She was dressed like the others now, explaining to her father that the dress had to be exchanged for one that fit. The clean cutoffs she'd found in her dresser had to be cinched with a belt. Her waist had shrunk. Always athletic, now she was tightly muscled, tanned and more attractive than the gawking guys around me remembered.

The tall guy came back from the beer cooler, looked across at the girls departing, noticed Carolee and said, "God, who's the babe?"

"She's why we're here, Jeff. That's Carolee." The guy speaking looked over at me. "She and this dude called Wally have been hiking together, you know."

"Well, she's damn gorgeous, Wally."

I blushed, the evil-eye guy clenching his fists added a bristling scowl and we all followed the girls.

***

"Rodney, why are you here?" Carolee approached him in disbelief. "I don't understand what would make you want to be here."

"Him. I had to see what kind of scuzoid you think is better than me."

"Well, now that you've seen him, you can leave."

I heard enough of this to move away. I was no good at fighting with my fists. The explanation for the clenching fists and intense stare made me afraid. It really looked like this Rodney person intended to pick a fight.

"And if I don't?"

"Wally and I will leave and you can explain to Pop."

"Is there a problem here, Rod?" Jeff had come up behind Carolee.

She turned and looked at the guest she didn't know. She turned back to Rod, then turned and looked at Jeff again.

"There's no problem, Jeff. I'm leaving," Rod growled. We watched as Rodney walked the narrow path between Siebert's and the house next door, pounding his right fist into his left palm.

"Are you okay?" Jeff asked after Rod was out of sight.

Looking at the ground she answered, "I'm fine. He has to face facts and get over it." She looked at Jeff again and asked, "Should I know you?"

"Not at all. Jeff Martin. I work with your dad; which means, of course, that I work for Rod's father and with Rod."

"You sell cars. Pop sells cars. Wally's happiest when he's rebuilding his car. My friend Melissa's boyfriend restores antique cars. Guys and cars. Is that what we're stuck with? Is that what life's about?"

"Well, actually. Don't tell your Mr. Anderson, but for me it's just a job right now. I'm getting my real estate license."

"I see. For you it's all about selling. 'A good salesman sells himself,' so they say. Do you agree with that?"

"Yeah, mostly. How am I doing so far?"

"Basically, pretty well."

I had been metaphorically circling. Now I stepped in. "Your Pop has the burgers about ready. Let's get something to eat, okay?"

Carolee nodded and went with me to the small patio. Jeff stayed put. When Carolee glanced back at him, he smiled at her. I thought, "What's going on?" and watched in utter confusion. Her expression reminded me of what I saw when I came through the cafeteria line while she worked but this had a sharper edge. I tried to read her face and it frightened me. Was this a more intense desire?

"Curlybabe! Are you there?" I fanned her face with a paper plate, trying to get her attention.

She looked at me, or through me. The look was a pain in my gut, a fear that I was losing Carolee. I suppressed the notion, and found it even harder to keep from telling her about the surprise I had planned for tomorrow. I intended to tell her after I had the tickets in my hand. But maybe now is the time. I compromised with myself. "You'll have another surprise coming, Carolee."

"Oh? What is it?" Carolee still wasn't giving full attention.

"Tomorrow. I can't tell you until tomorrow."

"O...kay. Is that my plate?"

I handed her the paper plate. We loaded them with salads and hamburgers and joined our peer group sitting on the grass. Carolee positioned herself where she could watch in a way that wouldn't make it too obvious if I tried to see what she was watching. Jeff had taken over the grill for a second burger round while Harold and Maxine sat at the patio table with Rod's parents and a new neighbor couple.

Carolee and I were still on trail time. When sundown beckoned others to a hangout where they could drink beer without a legal age test and smoke some weed, we went inside. It wasn't long before we headed to opposite corners of the old two story craftsman house, where I wrote five pages in my journal. Carolee was upstairs. I suppose she was contemplating her future.

(17)

The banker kept me waiting in suspense for forty-five minutes while he called my bank and allowed his well-known depositors to interrupt. Finally I was told to write the check for an additional $7.50 in transaction fees. With my $250 in hand, I visited the clothing store clerk. The creep tried to increase the price to $120. When a police cruiser drove slowly past the store windows, I had, for once, a ready response.

"I see Altoona's finest are on the scene, my man. Maybe I should go out there and mention a certain non-inventory product you have in stock. You know I really don't want to do that. On the other hand, we could talk about forty apiece?"

"That wasn't the deal."

"No? Then let's do the deal." He bared his teeth with an angry dog look, but two tickets for all three days at Woodstock were traded for one hundred dollars even.

***

The house was locked. No one answered. I'd been gone longer than expected, of course. Harold would be at the car dealership and Maxine at her new job, but Carolee should be home. I rang again. I tried the door again. That's when I found the note. It read, "I waited. You said it wouldn't take long. If I'm not at A. Motors, Pop can tell you where I am. – C."

"Well, more walking. I'll stay in shape, anyway. We might walk part way to White Lake, New York." I looked around when I realized that I had said this out loud. Harold had pointed out Anderson Motors when he brought us into town. Now I would find out if I remembered how to get there.

***

"Hey, Mr. Siebert, Carolee left a note that I'd find her here. Is she around?"

"Call me Harold, Kid. She was. Wait a sec. Lemme check." He went into the area behind a long counter and whispered something to a woman working the phones there.

Harold came back and said, "Liz'll get her. Meantime, there's something out here I gotta show you." He led me to the grass and dandelions out back. "We just got this in. It hasn't been cleaned or prepped yet, but I want you see it. Just the little car for a guy like you. Carolee told me you had a Karmann Ghia and gave it away. Is that right?"

"Not exactly. Well, I gave it, yeah, to my kid brother. If he hasn't totaled it yet, it's still in the family."

Harold pointed across the row of older cars, "See that? That's a sweet little road machine there."

I couldn't figure out which car he was talking about at first. Then I saw the white Saab Sonett. "Wow. That is sharp. It can't be more than a year old."

"That's right, a '68. Whataya think? I can make you a real nice deal if you want to drive that honey out to Dakota."

I knew how foolish that idea was, but it was hard to resist. I paused and looked across the lot of cars. In the distance I saw Carolee and that tall guy walking along the sidewalk. My mouth open, staring past them, I thought, "The tall guy, um, Jeff, yeah. Making moves on my girl. At least it looks that way, it sure does."

"You're thinking about it, aren't you." Harold, still admiring the car, interrupted my thoughts.

"What? Oh, yeah. Let me think about it, yeah. It wouldn't be the smartest thing to do, though, would it." With that, I tore myself away and walked briskly to catch up with Carolee. When she and Jeff saw me coming they immediately went separate ways, a move that made the goings-on look even more suspicious.

"I told you I had a surprise." I pulled the tickets out of my hip pocket. "Check this out. It's gonna be an amazing rock concert. Three days, incredible line-up."

"What?" She looked at the tickets. "But that's this weekend. In New York. Where's White Lake?"

"I don't know. I haven't had a chance to check that part out. Oh God, what if it's way upstate, by Lake Champlain or somewhere."

Carolee looked away and sighed. "That's your big surprise, huh." She wiped her eye where a tear had started to form. "Doesn't matter. I'm not going."

I was building toward a boil. "Not going. Not going. No ifs, ands or buts. Just 'not going.' Man, when I saw the poster I just knew it was right. I had to score these tickets. What a great cap to our summer. After all that time alone together, you'd get a weekend with crowds of people, enjoying loud music from some of the best rock and folk artists. It just seemed so right. 'Not going.' Just like that."

"Oh, Wally, please don't make this harder than it already is."

"It's not hard, just come to the Woodstock Festival with me."

"A surprise, you said. You couldn't ask, you just up and buy these damn tickets and tell me I have to tag along. Well, just go to your goddamn concert where you'd expect me to help settle the heeby-jeebies you get in crowds. I'm staying here. And, if you must know, I have an appointment on Thursday, anyway. I'm transferring to the Altoona campus for now, and finish at Penn State."

"Holy shit, it's that Jeff guy, isn't it. One look and we're history. All we've planned and ... pow."

"No. Why must you assume the only thing is some man? We planned? More like you planned. But, it's *my* life, dammit. You're as bad as Rodney."

"Rodney? That creepy guy who looked like he was gonna punch me?"

"Oh, Wally. I didn't mean that. It's just. Well, I have to figure things out for myself. I can't let anyone else decide my life right now, okay? It's not about you. Go to your rock and roll show. I can't take your money for college, so I have to live at home this year. It's that simple." The tears were flowing freely now, from both of us.

***

I didn't manage to write about how clever I'd been—for once in my life—with that ticket seller. Too many thoughts crowded my head and filled pages as I considered my next move with the journal on my lap. "Did she betray my trust? That knot ripping at my gut, what is that? Betrayal. Yeah. And cuckold. Yeah, that's the word. A cuckold, because of that tall handsome selling-himself-man. She says I shouldn't assume it's some man. But it damn sure is. It's not about me, though. Well, screw that. Do I have a life without Carolee? Hell, yeah. I'll just go it alone, like I did sophomore year. Shit, I spent that year in a dorm room pining for my fantasy of Carolee. Okay, really alone this time. By choice."

That afternoon I jammed everything into my backpack. I stowed necessary gear that had been shared by two packs; I left unnecessary items behind along with Curlybabe and my heart. I hiked away alone with my thumb out.

(18)

By the time I got to Woodstock it was clear that I would not be scalping the extra ticket. So much for clever "let's do the deal" repartee. I donated it to the guy who gave me my last ride. I managed to find a place to pitch the tent on an almost, but not quite, level spot near the torn back fence at the top of the hill. I had a decent view for the moment, but the stage was a long way from the tent camp. People kept pouring in, packing the large grounds; already milling about a day before the concert was scheduled to begin. I felt the same anxious rush I'd experienced a year before at Grant Park. As it had then, the feeling lingered as tension in my chest. Get busy. The crowd allergy will pass," I promised myself and tried to shake it off. "The music will fix it soon enough."

I got busy perfecting my little camp. The process took me from the anxiety to feeling sorry for myself, thinking how different making camp is without you-know-who. Carolee and I had set and broken so many campsites over recent weeks that we had a pattern we followed without thinking. The only difference one day to the next was whether we were in a lean-to shelter or this tent. Carolee would be arranging her transfer from Yankton now, leaving me all alone among these tens of thousands of people – gah, so many people – waiting to use the portable toilets. The radio news called us hippies. I was thinking, "Maybe by Sunday, I'll be a hippie, too; or a basket case."

With my camp ready, I sat on the ground, cleaned my glasses, opened my current journal and clicked a ball-point pen. Ready to write, suddenly alone in my notebook, lingering anxiety evaporated. I looked around, I thought about my summer and the last school year. I watched the crowd grow around me and thought of some people that Carolee had caused me to meet, people who lived with not much more than what I was seeing; not for three days of 'peace and music,' but their whole lives. I couldn't manage to put more than hints of these thoughts into the notebook. Sometimes when I'd write, the words on paper revealed thoughts I didn't know I was thinking. "Hmm, was that Dr. Graves' whole point when she assigned it?" Anyway, that's what happened then. I'd been feeling sad, missing my Curlybabe. Writing revealed a new truth. I was enjoying my melancholy. I had a peaceful sense at being alone in spite of the noise and smells from thousands around me; in spite of my despondent attitude; in spite of too many people too freaking close together.

I reached back into memory. "When was the last day that I didn't write anything in a journal?" It took a while, but then I remembered. Blanks were never because I couldn't think what to write. The only time I could recall was Kansas City with Kim. We were drunk or too busy in bed for any journaling. And she was using me the whole time. I was just some weird last wild oats fling. They all betray.

I began to write of betrayals. Then a disturbing thought found its way to the page. "What have I done that may have betrayed Carolee?" I had only wanted what's best for both of us. My plans were our plans, weren't they? She says her life isn't about me. What the hell was the last year? It was us. Thee and me.

***

"Hey man, I never thought I'd run into you again." The voice was vaguely familiar. When I looked up I saw that it came from the guy I'd hitched a ride with. He had his arm draped over the shoulders of a cute chubby girl and they were passing a joint between them. "Oh-wow man, like I wanna thank you for that ticket. I still got it. Nobody's paying, but thanks anyway. Hey, man. Me and Lindy here, we scored some nice pot." He passed the joint and I inhaled a hit.

When I eventually breathed out, I said, "Thanks. Nice to meet you Lindy," and went back to my journal.

The guy and Lindy whispered conspiratorially a few yards away, and then the guy sat down near me and passed the roach. I drew in as much as I could and passed the last little bit back.

"Wally, right? Did I remember it right, man? You don't remember my name. I can tell, man."

I nodded, still holding my breath, and grunted, "You?" while shaking my head.

"Oh-wow! Listen to that, man." There was a moment of feedback as they ran tests on the sound system at the base of the hill. "Yeah, man. They call me Gus." He tried to get another puff from the roach and it was nothing but Zig-Zag paper.

I breathed out and extended my hand, "Okay, Gus. Thanks. I'm gonna do a little more in my journal while I've got some mellow, thanks to you. So, I'll see you later, maybe."

"No, man, you gotta understand somethin'. Wow, man. See it's like this. You see." Gus might eventually get to his point if he remembered what it was. "That girl. Where the hell'd she go now? Shit. Anyways, that girl Lindy. She's coming back over here with a couple of friends, see man. We're gonna have another little toke with you, help you feel better. You understand me, man? Wally? Right, Wally?"

"Help me feel better, huh. What do you even know about how I feel?"

"Oh-wow. There they are. Hey, Lindy, what took you so long, man? Hey, where's the rest of 'em. Least you brung your girlfriend. Hey, man, Wally here's been telling me how he needs cheering up."

"The hell I have. I haven't told you a damn thing. You go prattling on with your 'hey man wow man'."

"No man, hey, don't crap on me, man. I didn't screw you over like somebody musta done."

"Would you guys cool it, please?" Lindy stepped in. "Peace, remember?" She held up a two finger V sign. "Hey, Mister, this is my friend Abigail."

"Hi, Abigail. I'm Gus and this guy Wally here is so sad or mad about something, man. Like he gotta punch something. Good thing I'm here for him. Hey, Wally, my man, on second thought, you can crap on me if it'll help."

"Could you just shut up for a minute and let me finish this journal note?"

The pause gave Lindy's friend a chance to correct her. "My name is Gail, just Gail, not Abigail, Linda. They'll be calling me the wrong name because of you."

I looked up at them in surprise. "Wrong name? How long have you two been friends?"

They looked at each other and answered together, "About two hours."

"And you all came to cheer me up because Gus the shrink said so. Is that right?" I was trying to understand how someone obviously dense could be so perceptive about me.

Gus said, "Where's the rest of the guys you was hangin' with?

"They went down there. They want to get close to the stage."

I stood up and looked over the crowd with them and said, "Well, good luck with that," and had a moment of crowd induced twitching. I decided I was stuck with Gus and his gal-pals so I might as well make the most of it. I closed my journal and put the pen in a pocket. "You guys can join me on the sofa if you want."

The girls giggled. Gus said, "Wow, man," and we sat on the ground. I did not want to be cheered up. The journal had already informed me that I fully intended to enjoy wallowing in despair for the rest of the day before the music. Damned if they didn't cheer me up anyway. That doesn't include the getting high part, either. When I wrote in my journal that evening I had another flash of insight that comforted, because it defied Gus's unspoken plan. I didn't know if Gus and Lindy had gone off at nightfall for some hanky-panky, but I deliberately fended off the small awkward advances from Not-Abi-just-Gail. I thought or hoped she was relieved and that she was only hinting out of peer pressure inspired by the setting. I even told her some of the reason I needed time alone. As I wrote I felt good about that, too. I had actually been considerate enough to make sure she understood that it wasn't anything about her. She did seem like a nice enough person, after all. Then there was Gus, who saw through me even in his marijuana haze. Then I pondered again. Gus talked like he was in a constant drug buzz, smoking the same mild grass that hardly affected others, who most likely had less experience with the stuff. Did he inhale better? Or was it mostly a put-on or pose?

I let that thought go and wrote two more words by the lights moving all around, 'music tomorrow,' closed the notebook and crawled into my tent, but not the oversized sleeping bag. The night was still comfortably warm. I closed my eyes and lay awake listening to the sounds of people everywhere, trying not to think about my own life. It seemed as if hours had passed before I slipped into a deep sleep.

(19)

I woke up sweating in a sun baked tent. New sounds filled the air; sounds of tuning amps and testing mikes. When I climbed out I saw lines of anxious people waiting at the privies. I used a nearby bush in full view of people crawling through the torn fence. When I got back to my tent I was handed a Styrofoam cup of coffee and a small bag of stale donuts. "Hey, thanks. And good morning, Not-Abi-just-Gail." Feeling as grubby as the clothes I'd slept and sweated in, I was stunned by how clean and fresh Gail appeared. With her wavy black hair, deep brown eyes and rich tan skin that could be from a summer at the beach or it could be her natural hue, she looked quite pretty. I hadn't noticed that the night before.

"I figured you might've advanced from munchies to definite hunger by now, Lonesome Wally."

"Well, it's real nice of you." I took a bite of sugary donut. "Thanks, but I'm not lonely, no. I do my thing. I'm okay. I mean, listen. Do you hear what's about to happen? The aroma of rock and roll is in the air today, huh. The Age of Aquarius, yeah."

"Yeah, right. I'm sorry you're still sad. Hope it gets better for you."

"Jesus H. Christ, is it so freaking obvious? I just want to enjoy today. I'm trying, Not-Abi-just-Gail, I'm trying?"

"Mm-hm."

***

The music revved to full power. The crowd was too massive, too dense; I shook nervously. People, music, fun. Forget everything else. Leave all the world's baggage behind and let the good times roll. I tried.

When a light rain began shortly after nightfall, I crawled into the tent to wait it out. The tent had kept me—oh, and Carolee, too—relatively dry all summer. I was trying not to think of her. I failed at not thinking of her every time I looked at that special sleeping bag. The tent and bag had been our home for two months. It didn't feel like home now.

I made sure my pack would stay dry and picked up my journal. Before I could open it, Gus, Lindy and Gail were in the two-person tent with me. That's two-person if the persons are intimately close, for instance with someone I was absolutely not thinking of.

I looked up. I saw and felt Gail, who was pushed against me, looking back. Apparently she caught my pained expression. I know she heard my low moaning because she nodded in recognition and put two fingers to her lips. Then she pressed them against my lips and held them there.

That quieted my groans. Her gesture reached me with understanding. I got the message, "It will be alright." In that moment I believed it.

We sat. It was impossible to avoid touching the fabric that I was certain would cause little leaks. The rain didn't cause too much problem—this time. As sitar music wafted up the hill to us, Gus pulled out a ready-rolled joint. I grabbed it before he could get it lit. "Not in here, Gus. Sorry."

Gus apologized and I returned it. I had taken the correct, quick action to protect my property, and yet I began to moan again, and even I noticed it. I caught Gail's eye and put my own fingers against my lips and heard myself say, "It'll be alright, Trey."

After the rain shower the girls and I followed Gus and his cannabis supply out where we sat on the damp ground to enjoy the night and more music.

***

I crawled out to the sunshine of the new day, intent on spending it alone writing observations in my journal and enjoying the music. I would watch the crowd but not join it, or so I thought. The friends arrived in early afternoon. I ignored them. They hung around anyway but gave me a little extra space. When I started to speak of a new plan, Gail and the others moved closer to hear what I was saying.

"I think I'm gonna pack up and head out in a little while."

"Really, Trey? The show's getting even better tonight, for sure," Gail responded.

"Where'd you come up with that name for me?"

"You said it. Last night. And there's the way you said it. When you worried about what we were doing to your precious tent."

"Oh, yeah." Everyone was quiet, watching, waiting to see if I was about to say more. There was even a pause from the stage, where Country Joe McDonald had just finished a set. "Oh, yeah," I eventually said again, "I think I'll go home for a few days. Home, huh. I mean, visit my parents. Haven't talked to them since, God, it was early in June, I guess; when they gave me shit about hiking all summer."

Gus had practical advice, "Wow, man. How the hell're you gonna get outa here today? There's still people packin' in."

"I don't know, Gus. It's just. I never thought I'd say this, or even think it. I guess I miss my family."

"That's who calls you Trey, isn't it," Not-Abi said. I didn't hear over the introduction blaring from the huge loud-speakers. She moved closer and repeated it.

"Yeah, that's who. I'm Wallace the Third. Two days with Junior and I'll be ready to run far and fast again. I don't know, maybe I'll stick around. I don't know." My next comment made me jumpy again. "So many people. Grr."

"You remember what Arlo said last night, man?" Gus nodded toward the distant stage. "The Thru-way is closed, he said. You are gonna stay and enjoy the scene, man, until we all drive outa here, if my wheels ain't impounded or stole by then. And looky here what I thought was lost or already smoked, man."

Gus passed the lost and found item around. It affected me more this time. Maybe it was better pot. Maybe it was my sorry condition.

Lindy spoke for all when she announced, "Is there anybody selling ice cream around here? God, I'd just die for a Dairy Queen right now."

I headed for the tent and my pack, "No ice cream, but I might still have some trail mix in here."

"Well man, beggars can't be choosers. Bring on the raisins and nuts, dude."

"That and better, Mr. Gus. I added a little extra since Carolee's not watching anymore."

"Is that who you been pining over all this time, some chick named Carol E?"

I ignored Gus's question and brought out my mix with both plain and peanut M&M's added to the raisins, cashews and more peanuts. We all munched until it was gone, listened as the music continued through the afternoon and night, talked, ate food we could locate to buy or acquire, and dozed. Gail fell sound asleep using my shoulder for a pillow. That felt good and neither of us tried to make it into anything more. My arm went to sleep first, keeping the rest of me awake. Moving would wake Gail, so I put it off as long as I could.

***

When I sat with my journal on Sunday morning my mind drifted to people I longed to see. But did I really miss any people? I wanted to see my family, knowing full well I'd soon leave in anger. At the same time I was desperate to plead my love to Carolee and win her back. My thoughts always come back to being thrown aside. People take my trust and smash it in my face every time. I wrote that down and crossed it out as too judgmental. Then I wrote it again, because I still believed it; it meant that much to me. I thought about Junior trying to control my life and decide my career for me. What career, anyway? I tried not to, but I thought again of Carolee, who accused me of trying to control her life. I simply could not see how that could be true. I turned my attention to some other females. That girl from high school; I followed her around like a puppy. I guess I was her boyfriend for promotional purposes only. I had no idea. What was her name? What did she look like? Where's my memory? Was it Nancy? Oh yeah, she was named Nancy and so was her best friend who always hated me. I thought again of Kansas City with Kim. The glorious start of something big and over in a fortnight. Popped like a balloon.

"Hey! Wow, man." Gus was prattling as he and the girls came into view. Although none had met until Woodstock, they seemed like settled, life-long friends in three days. "Yeah, man. We're gonna try to score some breakfast. You want anything, Trey?"

"Not you, too. I'm Wally."

"Hey, stay cool there, Walter."

"Wally! Yeah, breakfast sounds good. Whatever you can find." I dug in my wallet. The small bills had been spent. I gave Gus a twenty with an absolute promise. "Use that to get something for us all and bring me the change." I secretly hoped Gus would splurge on some more marijuana but I kept that to myself, reserving the right to be irritated at Gus if that happened.

"Wow. Will do, boss. Wally. You comin' Lindy sweetheart?" The two wandered away.

Gail sat down on the damp bare ground where rye grass had been growing three days earlier. "What are you writing this time, Wally?"

"If I tell you, everyone around here will call me by some other names, rude ones."

"What's that supposed to mean?"

"Trey. Gus called me Trey. Where do you suppose he got the idea he should do that?"

"Oh. Sorry. Like I'd know it's a big deal and you'd get pissed just because someone used the name your mama calls you because she loves you. Shit, everything's complicated with you. Gotta watch out. Wally has hurt feelings and the whole damn world better give him a wide circle. Because it's Wally the Third and he's the important one."

"Is that what you think? It's not, well hell..." I started again. "It's not that it's a big deal, it's just that blabbing about my family nickname is one more bit, see. I was thinking about how I get shot down whenever I trust somebody. And then Gus comes messing around. Well, you know. See?"

"Geez, Wally. You miss your folks. Isn't that what's important? It's not like you told me any big secrets or anything."

"I just now did. Not a big secret, but not for you to grab a microphone down there and announce to those half a million hippie-dippies, either."

"I don't know what you're talking about. Except for your stupid superior rich boy act. Hippie-dippies, like that's everybody else. Not Wally. Not Trey. He's too good for us. If you told me something private, I don't know what it is."

"So, that's that. I can't trust you, either."

"Is that it? In that case ... no, you can't."

After five minutes of stony silence Gail said, "I wonder what's keeping Lindy and Gus. I'm real hungry."

"They're probably having steak and eggs in Monticello on my twenty."

"Why didn't I think of that, man," Gus arrived behind us. "There's a helluva lot more hungry people than there's food down there. We got some coffee and shit, though."

The four of us shared the two cups of weak black coffee and handfuls of corn flakes from a box. "This here was trucked in for the refugee camp. That's what they think we are today. Maybe it's true." Lindy's commentary continued as Gail and I sat silently ignoring her.

The Saturday program had continued all night, ending not long before the search for breakfast had begun. We were now in a break before the Sunday lineup. Lindy, with extra effort, got our attention and said, "Let's go down and see what all's happening."

Gus and Gail agreed. I told them, "I think I'll stay here. I have some more stuff I want to write down."

"Are you scared somebody'll come and steal your tent or what?" Lindy asked.

"That's gotta be it," Gail said, glaring at me, our disagreement still unresolved. She undoubtedly was about to say something about my distrust, but she held back. "Let's leave him be."

***

The trio reappeared hours later, soaking wet, after the rain storm began that afternoon. They jammed themselves into the tent, shaking like wet dogs. Soon, three more people crowded in before I could say anything. It was impossible to move or to avoid rubbing against the sides of the tent. That or the hard wind and rain was causing leaks. I sat there hugging my belongings. I'd have rocked and moaned if there had been room to move. Gail repeated the two finger on lips 'it'll be alright' gesture that had helped on Friday night. I nodded in response. Gail smiled and our argument, though not resolved, was over.

The storm crashed around us. What little conversation took place was all about rain, mud and stage towers that reached up toward the crashing lightning. We were cramped up in the foul-smelling, increasingly damp tent for two hours that felt like two weeks.

When the rain eased to a light drizzle the unknown visitors decided to leave the stuffy, airless shelter. Two crawled out. The third caught his sandal in the zipper threshold, tearing out a long seam meant to seal the entry. That let more water in where some had already begun to collect. I opened my mouth to scream and curse. Two fingers pressed my lips.

The unknown guy untangled his sandal and provided the curse on my behalf, "Fuckin'-a. Sorry about your tent, man. I didn't mean to." With that, he joined his friends and they disappeared into the muddy crowd.

"Jesus, did those dudes even thank you for letting them in?" Gail needed the two-finger gesture returned. "Oops, by the way, thanks for letting us in, Wally."

"It'll be alright, Gail. I'm a superior acting rich kid. I can buy a whole new tent, can't I?"

"I suppose you can, inferior as you may seem at times. Thank you for using my name, and not that snotty Not-Abi-just-Gail nonsense. Which I never said word one about before, you must realize."

"Set and match to Miss Gail."

***

Jimi Hendrix was still playing when they helped me pack my torn tent and start walking the couple miles to Gus's car. He'd left it by a road among thousands of other badly parked vehicles. Gus stopped worrying when he saw that it was pretty much as he'd left it, with only a few other cars still abandoned and waiting beside the country lane.

"What's that under the wiper, Gus?" I asked.

"Shit, man. Did they give me a damn ticket?" He pulled the folded paper out and took a quick look at it. "Wow man, at least it ain't a ticket. Wow." He passed it to Lindy.

She read aloud, "Where will you be five minutes after you die?"

We all chuckled at the religious tract's strange question.

"I'll be dead and I won't give a shit," Gus said. After a pause he went on, "It's where I'm gonna be five minutes before I die is what scares the hell outa me. Setting in the jungle waiting for the next VC round to take me out."

"The war? You? What?" The questions came for us all.

"One more week. 'Bout this time next week I'll be inducted into the U.S. Army, like it or don't."

"Jesus H Christ singing Purple Haze, Gus. You never said a word about it."

"What's to say? Nothing I can do about it but-cept show up." That was all he would say. The news had us all replaying Gus's part in our Woodstock weekend.

Gus drove. Lindy made sure he didn't fall asleep. Gail and I rode in the back seat of the old Ford Galaxie. Gus would drop us all at a bus station somewhere.

I was thinking about Gus and how the draft suddenly became a personal issue again. I'd only thought about it while Country Joe sang, and it hadn't affected me personally then. Now it did. It had me thinking, "I can't even trust a guy to trust me. He sees right through me and I don't have a clue about him." Gail was dozing off, or at least closing her eyes. I tried to rest, too. I was incredibly tired but sleep would have to come later.

When an intersection stop woke her, I said, "Hey, while I think of it. Can I have your address, to maybe write to you?"

Gail gave this a moment's thought before she answered, "No. I don't think you should. Trust this: I won't write back. Today we go back to the real world. I think I'll leave Woodstock and Max Yasgur's farm to memories.

"I see. I guess I see. Memories? I remember meeting myself here and learning that I never want to see this many people in one place ever again. How's that strike you?"

"Whatever you want. I think you and yourself should go live in a cabin in the woods somewhere with no people nearby at all."

"Exactly. What a cool idea! Maybe I will."

"Does yourself agree?"

(20)

Train, plane or bus? I quickly ruled out more bus travel; they had been packed the day after Woodstock, of course. There would be a wait for a seat to New York City or Altoona. Why did I even think that? I didn't want to go back into Pennsylvania, with no cause for hope to win Carolee back. I rode by bus all the way from Monticello to Rochester. From there I could fly and be in Chicago by supper if a flight was available. Train would take a little longer, but also give me time to think things over.

At the depot, I wandered over to a row of telephone booths, thinking, "I should call, let them know I'm coming. There's plenty of time before the train comes, maybe later." I sat on the bench, pulled out a new journal notebook, put it away again and wandered back to the phones. This time I stepped in and closed the glass door, keeping a close eye on my backpack that wouldn't quite fit in with me. I put my finger at zero to start a collect call and began to turn the dial. Instead, I hung the receiver back in its cradle and went back to the bench. "Maybe I'll be ready in a few more minutes."

***

Writing in my journal on a moving train made for interesting penmanship. On this day I was determined to focus my notes on the future. I listed plans. "Will I go back to Yankton for my senior year? If not, what happens to draft status and that whole can of worms? A hideout in the Rocky Mountains of Colorado? Far from the Appalachians? Was Gail onto something? And wasn't she a good friend for three days? Why won't she let me write to her?"

Those thoughts led me to fill a page and a half before I realized I was sidetracked. I turned the page and started to write down my struggles about facing the future again.

***

The house was locked. No one answered the doorbell. The hiding place held only the gate key to the fenced backyard overlooking the Lake Michigan shore. It took a minute before I remembered exactly what had happened to my house key. Then it came to me. My ring of keys was hanging from the ignition when I gave the VW to Bryan. If he totaled the car, I hope he didn't lose the key to my pad in Yankton. I had walked from the commuter rail depot. I still hadn't called to warn them. Now I sat in Senior's white Adirondack chair and looked out at the lake, trying to relax. I took out my journal, thought about what to write and fell asleep.

***

"Trey! Well I never. When did you get here? Why didn't you call?"

My eyes popped open. I slowly came to, and said, "Hi, mom." She was leaning over me, so I reached up and we hugged for the first time in ... who knows. It had been a long time.

"We've been expecting a call for weeks, Trey. Where have you been? We've been so worried, your father's been playing detective. He tracked down the folks in Pennsylvania. They said you were angry at Carolee and left. That's all."

"Angry, yeah. Because she told me to leave, yeah," I muttered. Then a little louder, "They didn't say where I was going?"

"No. So tell me." She sat in the green Adirondack, Junior's favorite.

"I went to Woodstock. I wanted to take Carolee. It was for her. I went anyway. Too many people in one place. I hate that. Everybody all happy and 'wow, half a million,' and I kept trying to be alone while Gail and Gus and Lindy kept trying to cheer me up. Like I was their pet project. And, you know what? On the way out, after three or four days with him, that's when Gus tells us he's about to be inducted in the army, drafted." I stopped chattering, then blurted out, "Can anyone ever be trusted?"

This was my most open sharing of personal feelings with Mom since grade school and she must have tuned out most of it.

"Woodstock? You were in that mess? Hippies and dope?"

Deep down, I suspect if a weekend like it had been available when she was young and enduring rationing; when Junior was on a Navy ship somewhere; she'd have been in the middle of it — a three day escape from worry.

"Did you hear my question, Mom?"

"What? About that Woodstock whoop-de-do?"

"Never mind."

**

"Trey, bring us up to date," Junior said as he passed around the platter of steaks he'd just removed from the brick barbecue grill.

"Well, sir, I hiked the Appalachian Trail from North Carolina into Pennsylvania."

"Got that out of your system, then. Now it's time to think about your senior year and finishing up ready to make your mark in the business. You did okay out talking to the store managers, when you weren't leering at Miss Smith. We could work you in as regional rep for starters. Think you can handle that? You're good at the mathematics, so you might yet use it for finance, for something more practical than that Boolean mystical stuff you used to bore us with."

"It wouldn't be boring if you... Oh, what's the use. My major is English, anyway." I cut into my meat and shoved a big chunk into my mouth. "That's good T-bone, Dad," I said while chewing.

Mom shook her head at this. She was all ready to criticize my manners. Instead she took my cue and mumbled, "What's the use."

"You aren't going to avoid the subject, young man. We'll settle this now. Will you or will you not be ready to take your rightful position at the company next year?

"Good. Let's settle it. I will not."

Bryan, who'd been quietly eating at the opposite end of the terrace, smirked. He never could understand my resistance to the prosperous life handed to us. Because he liked the country club lifestyle that the business made possible, my attitude confounded him.

"I've tried and tried. I'm done with you, Trey." Junior thumped the small tray table with his fist, as if he were gaveling the meeting to a close.

"Please, Wallace. He's your son," Mom pleaded.

"There's my son." Junior pointed with his fork toward Bryan.

"Thanks for letting me tell you all about my summer." Sarcasm was the best I could do. I took my plate down the sloping lawn to the Adirondack chairs.

***

I had expected to spend a week with family before traveling on to Yankton. The previous evening's settlement convinced me to leave sooner. This day I met with Mr. Boyer, trust fund manager. We went over the records of summer expenses. We noted the available trust balance after I paid off a credit card, and so on. I was most concerned about what Junior's declaration might do to the fund from Gramp. Could he interfere?

Mr. Boyer gave his assurances. "It looks iron clad but it is possible that your grandfather could revoke. Unlikely and difficult, but…" He shook his head and shrugged.

In the detailed report, I noticed that there were two separate deductions for management of the account. "You'll be taking a cut twice. What's that about?"

Mr. Boyer hemmed and hawed. I wasn't supposed to notice that detail, I guess. "Ah well, son, it has to be that way for honest clarity. The first is by contract with Mr. Bradford, Senior. The other little monthly fee is something you agreed to a few minutes ago after we talked about the extras you're getting. You say that you may not be at college, and could be hard to contact. That adds certain complicating factors. There's that unusual storage deal. You must understand."

"Did you have your thumb hiding that line? You make it sound like we needed it in writing to hold you to account, not to pad your wallet."

"Be that as it may, Mr. Bradford, it is in the agreement if you want these services."

"Yeah. Pretty good pay for writing a monthly check and tossing a couple fat envelopes in a box."

I arranged to move some funds to a separate account. I picked up the box of journal notebooks I'd already mailed to myself in care of Mr. Boyer. On the way through the lobby, I said loudly for bank customers to hear, "People. You can't trust any of them."

Then, ignoring Mr. Boyer's advice, I borrowed against a coming deposit. It was money I'd intended for help with Carolee's after-scholarship expenses. I bought another Volkswagen instead: A brand new 1969 Westfalia camper.

Mom convinced me to stay until the next morning and all the family gathered that evening. As soon as I'd promised to stay, Mom said it was to be my night. Over dinner and for another half hour, Junior and the

Husbands talked business. Senior didn't have much to say until Junior started bemoaning my refusal to support the family enterprise. At that point he said, "I get the impression that maybe, just maybe, Trey knows his own mind by now. Why not let him live his own life with your blessing." He turned to me and said, "How about it, Trey. Tell us about your walk in the park."

I sighed in relief at my grandfather's support. "Thanks, Gramp. It was a little more than that, but not much. We trekked northward for weeks. Had some rainy days." I talked about the hike for ten minutes while Junior stared at his own knees.

Mom sat on the edge of her chair waiting for a break to have her say. When she got her chance, she said, "He went to Woodstock, too."

Junior jumped to his feet at this news, pointed an accusing finger at me, his namesake son, and opened his mouth. Nothing came out. He turned and pointed the same way at Gramp and stomped out of the room.

Bryan had been observing all this. After watching Junior's angry departure, he moved closer to me and said in little more than an awed whisper, "Cool. What was it like?"

"People, crowds of people and mud. The music was great when it happened. I don't like people much. Too many of 'em. I did make a couple friends that I'll never see or hear from again. So, what's the use?"

"Wasn't your girlfriend there, too?"

I shook my head.

**

I wrote in my journal that night about leaving what I used to call home. And about deciding whether there would be a senior year at Yankton or not. If not, where? What?

(21)

I drove slowly around the campus naming each of the buildings, old and nearly old, of the small college. I had reached a decision as I drove through the corn fields of Iowa. I would not change my mind now.

With my box of summer journals I stepped into the office. Old Doc Graves came around her desk, ushered me to a chair and sat in the other side chair with a small round table between us. I handed her a large manila envelope from the box. "I like your new table and chairs, Elaine."

"This is sealed and addressed to you, Wally. Am I to open it?"

I nodded. "They're just some journals from summer. I mailed them to myself. Carolee and I hiked on the Appalachian Trail. For all the good it did. Now she's transferring to Penn."

"Oh dear. I shall miss her — such a bright, promising young woman. The journal was last year's assignment. Has it become such a habit for you?"

"Yeah, I guess it has. I write every night, pretty much. Even at Woodstock I wrote every day."

"Woodstock, hmm. I'd be interested to hear — or read, I suppose — your take on that."

"It's in there. Wait, no it isn't. I haven't filled that book but another one is started. I'm not very organized lately. I hope those smaller books are okay. They stuffed better in my pack."

Dr. Graves mused, "Such a habit," then asked, "Since you have taken so zealously to writing these daily observations, would you be interested in a senior independent study? My thought is that you turn as much as possible into a coherent narrative. With a little guidance, you may come up with a book or a number of stories worth reading."

"You'd like that, would you, Dr. Graves? To be my editor along with writing coach, I mean teacher?"

"Yes, I would. What do you think?"

"I'm not coming back to school this year. Maybe next year, if I don't get drafted and killed in Nam."

"Oh, my word. You say that flippantly when you ought to be seriously concerned about it. Are you ready and willing to go to war?"

"No."

"Then, if you aren't in school, how will you avoid it?"

"If I am in school, there's a chance I might graduate." I knocked on the little wooden table. "And I'll end up drafted next year anyway."

"I see. Is there no way that I can persuade you to stay and complete your studies?"

"None. I just came to clear out my apartment and such."

She tossed the journal she was holding back into the box. I took the box and started to leave, turned back and said, "If you promise to send it back, I can put the book with Woodstock in the mail when it's full."

"Most assuredly. Where will you be?"

"I'm heading west. I'll be camping out to start with. I'll have to let you know ... when ... where."

***

I began at the brick and board book shelf, making three piles: books to keep, those to sell or give away and undecided. It was there I found, on top of the required books for Western Culture, a small ring binder with four by seven inch pages. It looked sort of familiar but I couldn't think why or where. I opened it and saw Carolee's handwriting.

"Did she become a secret diarist, too?" I wondered as I began to read.

I opened a random page she labeled "an attempt at verbatim recollection", memory practice before an education class requirement.

> I said goodbye to Mama and hung up the dorm phone. Before I could get ten steps away the phone rang, so I answered and, damn, it was for me. Mother had immediately told him I wasn't coming home for break. His tone was angry. "I thought we were getting back together? What's it about?"

"It's about a great opportunity to do something useful and completely different for one week, Rod." I was beginning to feed off his anger and tried to suppress it.

"Well, I had some good ideas about that week, too. I thought we could talk about it. But, no. You have to play missionary or some such."

"Ideas like the way you dropped out?"

"Hey! What's that got to do with this? Penn State or no, I'd still be back at Pa's dealership and with my bunged-up knee I can't play ball. This way I'm making good money right now. But you wouldn't care about that. You just throw insults at me when we WERE talking about you coming home for break week."

"I'll be in the Cheyenne River Sioux nation. Call me again when you've calmed down." I hung up the phone. Did I even say goodbye? Why oh why. I love Wally but I hate his clingy jealousy and demands. And Rodney. I still like him too and hate his short temper and controlling. I should dump them both. Should get a handle on my own life. But I can't.

I closed the book and my eyes. "God, if only I had known how Carolee really felt. What would I have done? I was so involved in my own feelings, wanting to keep Carolee, that I didn't pay real attention. I knew it was different between us. I worried it but I didn't deal with it. I just ran with my big idea how to fix it in summer. If I'd known about Rod sooner, would my plan have been any different? At least I might have realized something about planning Carolee's life for her. But I didn't know."

I tried to go back to sorting books. As if. "Why was it left here?" I wondered. "Was it lost for me to find? Did she assume I had found it? I opened it again, skimmed until I found this:

I told Rod about the hike. He lost the cool he'd been posing. Any future with Wally is far from certain. If he'd just forget about how everything affects him for one minute. One thing is certain; Rodney is all past and no future.

"Shit. It is about me." She was ready to be swept up by handsome Jeff because I was an ignorant fool in love.

***

It took a few more days to leave Yankton. Trying to let go, I kept busy. Replacing the temporary Illinois license with real South Dakota tags on the VW required two extended visits at the courthouse, a lie about my permanent address and a false promise about my driver's license when the examiner came to town. While the real students were going through fall registration, I parked my microbus on campus. I sat beside the car holding a cardboard sign marked, "Wally's Big Sale," in large sloppy letters. Boxes of stuff, mostly books, surrounded me. An hour later I made a new sign, "Wally's Give Away." My load lightened quickly then, but not enough. After trips to a thrift store all my remaining worldly goods were fitted into the microbus.

***

After a drive across Nebraska on US 20, I turned north at the junction in Lusk, Wyoming and parked in front of a small café. A youngish woman wearing a waitress' pocketed apron stubbed out a cigarette on the brick wall and followed me in. The only other customers were two men drinking at the bar.

"You're from over to South Dakota. I seen it on the license tag," she said as she handed me a menu. "Lemme guess. You live in Rapid and you're on your way home from Denver."

"Nope. I've never been to Rapid City or Denver. I've been in Yankton for a few years." I was pleased that I'd accomplished the neutral South Dakota over suspicious Illinois plates. People do notice. "Maybe you can do better at guessing what I want for supper."

"Hmm, you want today's special – the ten ounce sirloin, on the rare side of medium rare, with fries and a Bud in the long neck."

"Perfect. I get a salad with that, right?"

"Thousand Island dressing, right?"

"Oh, you were doing so well. Blue cheese."

Setting beer and salad before me, she said, "You've never been to Rapid? In Dakota for — what did you say? — two or three years, and you haven't been to the Black Hills?"

"No. Should I go?"

"Oh, yeah. We love to camp up there. Me and the hubby and kids. We don't have no fancy outfit like you drove up in. We rough it with a tent and the little guys have a great time."

A shout from the opening to the kitchen said, "Order up, Patty." An empty beer can was waving above a bar patron, too.

"Be right with ya, Dave." She brought my steak, pulled bottles of ketchup and steak sauce from her apron and went to take care of the guys at the bar.

"Is there a good place to camp around here?" I asked as Patty put the check on the table.

"You want a good place or a place around here?" Dave, at the bar, heard this and turned around scowling. Undeterred, Patty plowed on, "A good place would take you a couple hours over to Hot Springs in Dakota. But there's a coupla private campgrounds closer."

Dave was off his stool and on his way over. "Get him another of them long necks, Patty." He slid into the booth with his can of Coors. "Patty's just goadin' me. I happen to know a nice cozy little park, which I and the wife own." He pulled a napkin from the dispenser and began to draw a map while explaining the directions. "Got electric and water for ya. Just head on out and the wife'll getcha all fixed up there."

I wrote a short journal entry that night. "Friendly folks. Bleak campground," it began. Three years in SoDak. Now time to see the place. Onward to the Black Hills, Mt. Rushmore even."

***

Swimming twice across Sylvan Lake and poking a campfire in solitude made for a relaxing few days. I played tourist at Mt. Rushmore, admired the huge carving of the granite mountain, but was uninspired. I could check that off as done. A climb to the highest point in South Dakota convinced me that I would not look for a secluded place to spend the winter in the Black Hills. I did my journal writing on the third evening with a road atlas on my knee and set a new destination: Glacier National Park.

(22)

I took an immediate liking to Sam Doakes, my new landlord, for three reasons. He didn't sugarcoat, he loaned me tools, and he introduced me to Cracker. It's not that I trusted him or anything, but I liked him.

"Soon be winter, kid. If you ain't drafted or on the lam you need more firewood if you don't wanna freeze."

"The place has electricity. Can't I get heat that way?"

"Yup. Got electric. Until you really need it and—bam. Lights out for hours or days."

With Sam's help I got a salvage permit from the Forest Service. With Sam's chain saw and ancient pickup I grew the woodpile. When I returned it, Sam was so pleased to find his truck running better than it had in years that he counted it fair exchange. The saw was sharpened as Sam had taught me and tuned, too.

Winter's warning came early and with a vengeance just as Sam had predicted. The snowstorm drifted over the narrow trail from county road to cabin. There was no way the VW could get to the road. Electricity did as Sam said. It was only out for ten hours, but the snow and wind storm had lasted less than a day. It wasn't yet October and a warm week followed the wintry blast. Heeding the warning, I loaded in provisions to keep myself fed. To break in my new insulated boots, I cleared a spot to park the microbus down near the graded road. I tried to think what else was needed to be ready for the next storm.

By the third day after the storm there were only a few drifts remaining and the trail was nearly dry. At about noon I heard a vehicle chugging up the hill. "That sounds like Sam's truck in four wheel." I talked aloud to myself a lot in that solitary place. Sam brought another man with him who looked about my age, but he could have been ten years older. His brown skin and way of hiding behind the brim of his hat shouted true Montanan to me. His black hair hung loose to his shoulders under the hat.

"This here's Cracker. I want you two to get acquainted. There's a reason, might relate to whatever mail it is makes DeDe at the post office wants so bad for you to come get."

I shook my head a couple quick shakes. "What are you talking about? I'm not following."

"Well, that's just it, ain't it, Wally. I don't know nothing. Just DeDe's asking for you to get some mail she can't let me bring ya. And you and Cracker gonna talk after I leave. I still won't know nothing and it's gonna stay like that." Sam adjusted his hat and wandered a few yards into the woods.

Cracker pulled a ragged old canvas knapsack and a paper grocery sack out of the truck box while Sam was watering the bear grass. He leaned the pack against the cabin wall and sat down on the big log near the outdoor fire pit.

Sam returned, tipped his hat to us and left in the pickup. I watched him go before I sat down at the opposite end of the log. I looked at the man and was about to speak, but hesitated, watching Cracker stir the cold ashes with a long stick. We sat in silence that way for a long time. I was watching and wondering but didn't know where to start. He kept on calmly poking where sometime in the past there had been campfires.

Cracker finally looked up. He still didn't speak right away, just gazed at my hands, which were in constant motion. Still nervously watching the stranger at my fire pit, I clasped my hands together, suddenly conscious (and self-conscious) that I'd been flexing them open and closed or drumming fingers on the log. After another long moment, without looking up, Cracker muttered, "Well go ahead then. Just ask."

I was caught off guard and thoughtlessly asked the question that really was on my mind, "How long you gonna stay here?"

"You came out here to be alone, didn't you? Don't worry. Won't be long. It's about that old pack I dropped there, innit."

I nodded sheepishly.

"The pack's mostly for tomorrow. While the weather holds."

"Tomorrow? What about tomorrow?

"Wally, do you know my people at all? And hey, is that your real name? Wally?"

"Yeah, it's my name, short for Wallace. The third. Why am I telling you this? Is Cracker your real name, then?"

"Depends."

"Do you have a real name?"

"Yep."

"And...?"

"Just between you and me, do you need to know what name is real? I was about to tell you a little about my people, since you don't seem to know anything."

"Still no name. Still you don't tell me about tomorrow and the canvas bag. Seems like you're here to make sure I don't know anything."

"Do you know what's waiting at the post office?"

"No."

"Any ideas? You can prob'bly guess if you give it half a thought. Might be a stretch for you. Give it a whole thought, then?"

"Screw you. It's a draft notice and I don't want to know. Okay?"

"You're smarter than you look. Let's go back. I was gonna tell you. Do you know anything about my people?"

"I have no idea who 'Your People' are." I signed the quotes in the air.

"A great nation, innit. We are warriors. From way back. We stood strong against the invaders, your people, until all our strength was torn out of us. I got cousins over in Nam right now. Warriors. My daddy and granddaddy and uncles all been to Korea or in the big one against the Nazis and Japan. We're proud of our warriors. We honor them—the men who walked on and the men who come home to us—they lead us proudly."

"So you're gonna tell me to go get that notice and sign up to proudly get myself killed for LBJ's and Tricky Dick's egos. Is that it?"

Cracker, not answering, stirred the dead ashes some more. Eventually he looked up at the sky and said, "We should get a little fire going here, so we can have good coals for the steaks. I brought some deer meat from my freezer for us." He stood up and walked slowly across the clearing around the cabin and disappeared into the forest.

I got up, too, and brought a couple chunks from the woodpile, logs I'd split the day before, still learning to swing the axe. I put them next to the ring of rocks that marked the fire pit, found some paper trash and other kindling, and sat back down and stared blankly at the spot where Cracker had entered the woods.

I had a small fire started by the time he returned with an armload of kindling and fallen branches. "That's good; small like that. We'll feed a little fire until we have some nice hot coals in there. Don't want a big fire, just a hot one."

"I know how to build a cooking fire." I was getting defensive. "I just spent my summer walking the Appalachian Trail. I don't mess with bonfires."

Cracker nodded and said, almost under his breath but I heard, "You do look like a white man, so my mistake." At normal volume, he continued, "You been hiking. That's good. You'll be ready to go into what 'your people' have started calling the Bob Marshall Wilderness tomorrow morning, then." He mockingly imitated my air quotes.

"Okay, I may be a white kid from the 'burbs, but you're the one wants to be called Cracker." We laughed the tension away as if it were truly funny.

"The name does sound kinda white, don't it."

"We're hiking into the Bob tomorrow? You've decided that for me, have you?"

"That I have. We gotta work on what you have to decide for yourself, if you're gonna let the Selective Service decide your life or not."

"Why should you care?"

"Tomorrow. The wilderness, the Bob. Just for the day—morning up and in, afternoon back down and out the same way. We'll see where the snow's gonna stick around while we're at it."

We passed the time poking the fire. Cracker talked of earlier times when his ancestors tried to defend their home territories and way of life against the unrelenting advance of the Euro-Americans and the diseases my forefathers brought. He spoke of genocide and the reservation and resilient people still here. Mostly we sat without speaking. During one long silence, I went inside and got my journal. Cracker watched as I wrote, sensing, I suspect, that this was an important activity for me.

When he'd decided that the fire was ready, he put the venison on a rusty grill we'd found leaning against the big fir tree close to the building.

***

"You want a beer, Cracker?" We had retreated from the evening chill into the cabin.

"I really like beer. Oh, yes I do. I like it a lot. I never touch it. If you make some coffee, I'll help you drink it."

I took a sip of the bitter brew and asked, "Are you a warrior? You said your people are, but are you?"

"Tomorrow. On the trail. We are gonna find out if you're a warrior or just a egotistical entitled rich white son of a bitch."

"Maybe you're taking me into the wilderness to kill me and call it counting coup. I need an answer."

Cracker put down the coffee that he was about to sip and possibly choke on. He was shaking with inaudible laughter before he answered. "I am. Warrior, that is. Not with guns, though. Not even with slings and arrows of outrageous fortune. I'm trying to work out who the real enemy is. And how we can beat him. Counting coup, huh. Where'd you hear that?"

I shrugged. "Not with guns, you say. Are you a politician, then? Is that it?"

"God a'mighty. If it comes to that we're sunk. ...Hmm, it might even come to that. That's a horrible thought, innit."

***

We left in darkness the next morning. Cracker had it timed to reach the trailhead just at sunrise, and he was only off by a few minutes because he didn't account for the gutless VW engine chugging the steep upgrades in second gear.

"I don't know why we couldn't take a trail that starts closer to where I'm living. Why are we driving away from the wilderness to get to the wilderness?" Short sleep was affecting my mood.

"Because I know the trail and it'll take us up high and still give us time to get back before dark. If it don't snow." The sky was clear and full of stars as Cracker spoke. "Three deer in the barrow pit on your right."

"Good deer spotting, man. I didn't see them at all. Barrow pit. Never heard that one. Is that what you call a ditch out here?"

"A ditch is for running your white man's irrigation water, innit."

***

We bundled up against the morning chill and hiked for a couple miles without saying much. After an hour on the trail, as the sun and exertion warmed us, we stopped to rest along the mountainside and remove a layer or two of outerwear.

"It's too bad you couldn't get to town when the post office is open before we come up here," Cracker said, watching me closely for a reaction.

"Incredible view already right here. And we're going up there?" I pointed upward to a snow field as I asked, though it wasn't really a question.

"You don't want to talk about it. That's fine, innit. But soon, my friend, very soon you're gonna hafta choose. And you do have a choice."

"Yeah? Gimme a hint. What's to choose?"

"You can take that step forward when they call your name. Maybe end up in Viet Nam. But you're a rich college boy, so you prob'bly spend two years in Germany driving some general around in his Mercedes, which you keep fine-tuned like Sam's old pickup."

I chuckled at the thought. "That wouldn't be so bad, except for the general."

"Or. Now listen up for a sec. Or, you could stand on moral and religious principles and apply for conscientious objector status. If a draft notice is waiting for you down in Bynum, it might be too late for that. Or, and this is where the Cracker man comes in, you could take an extended Canadian vacation."

"Canada, hmm. Are you for real?" I made a big show of pinching my own arm. "I'm awake." I repeated the question, "Are you for real?"

"I am, and that's not an easy claim for a Blackfeet man living in your world, innit. I am a warrior, one who foolishly believes I found the real enemy."

"Yeah? Who's the real enemy then?"

"I believe, and it's just me, you understand. I believe the enemy today is the wrong war in the wrong place at the wrong time."

"Nixon? LBJ?"

"Only what I said. Whoever. Whatever. Mount Rushmore. Great White Father in Washington. It don't need a face to be wrong."

"I see."

"Do you? I doubt it. Anyway, first thing you gotta do is consider your choices and make a decision. Once you make your choice, ain't no turning back."

I closed my eyes for a moment and nodded.

"Day's gettin' on. Let's take the trail a little farther up."

***

"I never thought about Canada. As a way out, I mean. I came here to get away from ... well, some situations. Maybe I came this far north for a reason and didn't know it." I took another big bite out of my squashed peanut butter sandwich.

"Now don't you go all mountain spiritual on me. You go stealing my stereotypes, I won't like it one bit."

"Just saying. These mountains are a little different from the ones Carolee and I walked through all summer. I love this place. There more of it in Canada?"

"How ignorant are you? You never heard of the Canadian Rockies?"

"Well, yeah, now you mention it."

"Anyways, I was about to give you a little heads up, see. If you decide to go north, I can prob'bly get you across safe. What I can't do is get that little three room house you drive around in over the border, though."

"Why not? Can't I just get a thirty day pass, like we used to get on fishing trips to Kenora? That's in Ontario."

"You might could. If you ain't on the list. Lemme see your draft card." Cracker put his sandwich on a rock and held out his hand. He kept it there, palm up, while I shifted around and pulled my wallet out of my back pocket.

"Still a '2-S'. Not expired yet. How can they be sending you a draft notice? Hmm, maybe that mail you gotta sign for is just the change to '1-A'. Maybe you still got some time after all. You could even have time to petition for C.O. That'd stall 'em at worst and might get you two years at something doesn't kill ya, put you in jail or expatriate you for life."

"See O?"

"God damn, for somebody whose life depends on this stuff you are mighty ignorant, rich boy. You want me to define expatriate for you, too?"

"Come on. Don't give me that shit. I know expatriate is about living the rest of my life in Canada. Just tell me what C.O. stands for, please."

"Conscientious objector, like I said about your choices this morning. You got a religion that tells you don't go to war, maybe?"

"Huh, not freaking likely. I got confirmed at Winnetka Congregational Church when I was fourteen. I got C grades in the religion classes at a college founded by Germans whose forebears took their religious scruples against war to Russia. That's Gram's heritage, not mine."

"You could make it yours. Or, how about a philosophy of life that you can sell in two-hundred words."

"Like, for instance, 'I don't want to get killed in the jungle'?"

"Not a C.O. then. I could ask, 'why not?' But I won't bother. You got another ten years of growing up to do and get a conscience to object with."

"That's harsh."

"Truth can be, innit, my friend."

"So, why do you want to help me?"

"Good question. I don't know. Have to think about it some. For now, eat your lunch and we'll wander back down the mountain."

"We're not going any further?

"Darkness won't wait for us to get back. Sun don't care if we're ready, so I have to."

***

While we were stowing our packs in the van and emptying the last of the canteen water down our throats. Cracker said, "I thought about it. Conscience. I got one. And my warrior spirit."

"What are you talking about?"

"God you have a short attention span. Shee-it. That's why I'm willing to help a self-centered fool like you, innit."

(23)

I pulled two weeks' accumulation of mail from my new post office box and signed for the large item Postmaster DeDe was getting ready to return to sender. It was not a draft notice, yay. My trust fund manager explained it in the letter that accompanied the detailed fund report. It was certified mail only because Mr. Boyer wasn't convinced it would find me out in the Wild West, especially when I had informed him about the designated wilderness area so near.

I read mail. Nothing from Carolee. "Why do I even take note of that? She doesn't even know where I am. Why do I care?" My mother had written, only because I had no telephone. The letter was several pages in her tight script that started out asking why I want to hurt her, quitting and going away like this. That one I stuffed back into the envelope to read and rant at later. I drove on to Choteau. The Bynum general store didn't stock enough variety. In the larger town I bought more supplies to keep me fed and secure even if I got snowed in for a long time. It was hard to know how many cans, how much flour, and so on, that I really needed, so I bought more.

On the way back I stopped at landlord Sam's ranch. "If you see Cracker anytime soon," I asked, "could you give him a message for me?"

"Hold it right there, son. Before you tell me some story I gotta pass along, just don't. I will call Cracker and tell him you want to talk to him. That's it."

"Okay. That's good. Thanks. You see nothing, huh. Like Sergeant Shultz?"

"Damn straight. I don't know nothing about no schemes you and Cracker's cooking up." I turned to go, but Sam added something more. "As long as you come by, though. You ever work on a diesel tractor?"

"What've you got? I never have, but there's a first time for everything ... innit."

Sam squinted at me with a deep frown. I figured that was a reaction to that last borrowed expression.

We jumped into his pickup to ride the short distance to the ranch machine shop. Sam turned the key and said, "Listen to that baby purr. All her grunts is gone. You got a magic touch with them engines, kid." The shop was a large sheet metal pole barn with an oil-stained concrete floor and a hangar door across one end large enough for a combine harvester.

Sam showed me the big tractor. He explained the maintenance he was trying to accomplish and the problem he was having. "So whataya think, kid?"

"Like I said, I never messed with this kind before. Do you need to use it soon?"

"Yeah, I like to get the barley seeded when the ground's froze with snow cover." Sam said it with a one sided smile.

"Well, next question then. Do you have the service manual, so I can read up on it first?"

Sam dug through a stack of ragged books and magazines on a work bench and sent the manual along with me. "I'll call Cracker. I expect he'll come see you in a day or three."

"If you give me his number, I can call him. Maybe take care of it on the phone."

"You got no phone up there."

"I could call from here. Or the pay phone at the Bynum store."

"I said I'll call him. He'll come see ya."

As I drove away with my big load of groceries, I shook my head and murmured to myself, "He doesn't want to know anything about it, but still insists on being the go-between."

***

Before long I fell into a winter routine of daily chores and weekly projects. There were only a few days when snow and ice made traveling the roads difficult, fewer still when I was thoroughly snowbound. I studied the manual and worked on Sam's diesel tractor until it was reconditioned. That paid some rent. I wrote in my journal as always. Sam came to see me every two weeks when rent was due and always stayed for half a day. It had stumped me when he insisted on bi-weekly instead of monthly payment. He may have had some other reason, but an opportunity to hang out with the kid for part of a day was a good enough explanation. He didn't seem to notice the aroma or recognize my houseplant. That might be a problem when the wood stove wasn't mingling its odor through the cabin.

Cracker came to see me, too. He brought snow shoes one day and we made our way to some back country in the cold. I discovered that day that splitting wood, feeding the fire and writing my journal hadn't kept me in shape for the workout. Cracker and I made plans for a border crossing in early spring, whether or not the Selective Service was on my trail. We hoped it wouldn't have to happen in mid-winter.

Some weeks, when no one came around and there was no good reason to go to town, I did get lonesome. To fight it, I visited the only bar in that desolate little village with its constant stiff winds a few times. A couple beers and conversation with the wintertime drunks made the loneliness worse every time. I'd hurry back to the little cabin to talk it out with a journal.

I tried to talk to the neighbor when he visited his land bordering Sam's cabin plot. I heard a chain saw one November day and went to investigate. I found the man near the fence line, cutting up some fallen timber.

I started to crawl between the strands of barbed wire. The guy spotted me, shut off the saw and yelled, "That's far enough. You're on my land and I want you off. I don't need anybody connected to that Sam Doakes fucker coming near. You hear me? That fence is gonna move to the real line soon, so back off." He pulled the starter cord and let the saw chew into another log.

I left quickly. I did not want to be involved with a property dispute that wasn't mine. Hell, I didn't want to be in a dispute if it *was* mine. The next time Sam came for the rent he mentioned that he was being threatened with a nonsense lawsuit. If he said the neighbor's name, I missed it. I referred to him in my journal as 'the mean bastard'.

Sometimes it was lonely as the thermometer dropped and the snow piled up. Other weeks without human contact had an opposite effect. At those times I did my chores and sat by the fire in the pot belly stove enjoying a blissful solitude and didn't pine for Carolee at all. It's true.

***

On the day that spring announced itself with snowmelt runoff and crocuses poking through, I sat in the sun and read a winter's worth of my diary. The enjoyment of solitude, a feeling of settled quietude, clearly prevailed over the times of loneliness. The lonely entries seemed rare after about mid-January, giving way to a tone of dreamy solitude. I sat on the damp log by the fire pit and stared into the trees. I tried to figure out why. It was a puzzlement. The potted plants under the special light couldn't explain it. That wasn't a change in habit, just a more convenient way to feed it, and hence, more frequent.

Nevertheless, springtime meant change. There might be more traffic at my door. Sam might figure out what I was growing and take offense. I didn't think Sam would report me but he'd likely get angry and possibly evict me. So, risking their loss to a late freeze, I took my two potted pot plants and made a hidden garden out back among the trees near the mean bastard's fence.

(24)

"Your truck's starting to sing its old chugga-chugga song, Sam. It might need a head gasket. I could use a little break on the rent about now, so I could check 'er over." I had come out to meet Sam while he was still behind the wheel. He shut off the engine and we both heard a chain saw.

"You figured I was coming for the rent, did ya. Well, you'd be right and there's more. Are you expecting to stay the summer?"

"I have another possibility that you don't want to know about, if that's what you mean."

"What I mean is—this here is our little getaway place not so far from home. The daughter and her kids like to come out from Billings and use it for a couple weeks of a summer and at harvest. But if you need to stay, we can..."

I cut him off and told him, "I'll be out. Is three or four weeks soon enough?"

"Stick around a little longer is okay by me. Your call, though. It's been good to have you taking care of the place. I got some diesel engine work needs done. That's more needful than this old beater. I can forgive the rest of your rent for a few days of mechanical work."

"By a few days, you mean it's enough work to take at least a week, right?"

Sam nodded. "Yeah, well, I got some other business to take care of, so I'll be seeing you at the shop. Tomorrow too soon?"

"See you tomorrow."

I listened as he pulled down the path. The pickup was really growling in first gear. I mumbled, "Guess I won't work on that one. It's not just a blown gasket and I don't want to mess with a gearbox when I might not have much time." I started back up to the cabin and heard the same old truck noises coming from the same direction as the earlier chain saw noise.

"Maybe Sam and the mean bastard will work something out." I went inside, grabbed a can of Oly, cranked the country music up loud from the only radio station with a clear signal during daytime and wrote in my journal. Before I got around to writing down my worry about the next move, I wrote, "How far I've fallen! I'm actually enjoying that hillbilly music."

***

The next morning I drove out of the forested canyon, some graded road, some blacktop, through the open farmland for thirty miles to Sam's ranch as promised. I was heading through the farmyard toward the shop when Sam's wife came running out of the house flagging me down. I had never talked to her before; I didn't even know her name. Anyway, she stopped me, crying something I couldn't understand, she was so excited. I shut off the ignition. She was closer now, so I heard better.

"He's not with you?" she screamed. "Oh, Sam. He said he was going to your place and he never came back. Is he behind you? Coming?"

I tried to calm her down so I could get a grip. "When? This morning? When did he leave?"

"No. Yesterday. Afternoon. He went for rent and talk about summer. Did you see him? Eighteen years of sobriety. Eighteen years with AA and everything copacetic. Or so I thought. He must've fell off the wagon. On a bender. Oh, sweet Jesus, no."

She was sobbing and I didn't know what to say or do. I just stood there lost for a long time; it seems like a long time the way I remember it. Finally my brain started working a little better. "I heard his truck going into the neighbor's; at least it sounded like it. It was after he left the cabin."

"The neighbor?"

"I don't know his name. I just call him the mean bastard. Sorry, ma'am."

"The property line, oh dear. I told him, 'Let the lawyers handle it.' The lawyer told him that too. But good ol' Sam. He didn't say he was going there, of course, but I imagine he thought he could patch things up and avoid all the expense and headache. Probably pushed him over the edge 'til he…" Her sobs made it so I couldn't understand any more.

"Did you call the sheriff?"

"I thought, you know, oh, Sam. Where?"

"Let's go call him." I forgot for the moment that I didn't want local law enforcement to know anything about me.

***

The sheriff himself, not a deputy, was at the farm in forty-five minutes. He got our statements, when and where and all that. He mentioned drinking with Sam in the old days. He radioed the Choteau police and had them checking all the bars while he was asking us the questions. Sheriff didn't say where he was going when he left there, but as soon as he'd gone a big old Roadmaster Buick pulled into the yard. The car must have been fifteen years old, but still had a new look about it. A woman jumped out and almost ran to the door.

With the two farm women hugging and commiserating, I excused myself. "Tell the cop guys if they need me I'm at the cabin. And ask them to tell me when they find him."

As I drove home, I tried to remember if I had heard the truck leave the mean bastard's. I'd stayed inside long enough that I couldn't be sure. Then I remembered my planting. I was within a half mile of the turnoff to the cabin path when the sheriff's cruiser came past trailing a cloud of dust, headed back down. I watched in my rearview as he braked hard and did a U-turn, which required a back-up across the narrow road. So, I pulled over and waited.

"You got a license and registration you want to show me, Mr. Bradford?"

"C'mon, I showed you my ID back at the Doakes' place."

"Humor me, then." He held out his hand waiting for the documents.

While he looked at the South Dakota registration and the Illinois driver's license, he said, "I was at your neighbor's. Must be another out-of-stater like you. Never met him. Is there more than just him? Nobody around now. Place wide open. Pickup sitting there. Minnesota plates, which let me find a name. Sawdust all kicked around by the woodpile. Nobody anywhere near. How long have you been living out here?"

His way of changing subjects without even looking up caught me off guard. "Since fall, is all. So, what's the guy's name?"

"Name of Mean Bastard. I should ticket you for no Montana licenses. You've been a resident here for a whole winter. How'd you get away with this?" He was comparing the documents from two states. He didn't wait for an answer. Instead, he changed the subject again. "I might need your help. Have you wandered around in this area to know the woods pretty good?"

"Yeah. I've toured where I can get to. Not the mean bastard's place, though. Do you think Sam went over there and didn't find anyone, then?"

He ignored the question. "Did you hear Sam leave over there?"

"No. I went inside. I had the radio on. I did hear the mean guy's chain saw earlier yesterday, come to think of it."

"How do you know that? A chain saw could echo from anywhere in this canyon."

"They don't all sound the same, now, do they."

"I'll keep it in mind. Earlier, you said. How much earlier?"

"Oh, man. I couldn't say. Wait a sec, it was when Sam came by. We both heard it."

"Okay. I don't want to stand out here on the road all day, so I'll let you go for now. It'll help if we can find you at Sam's cabin tomorrow."

"You'll tell me if you find him, I hope. I'm getting worried."

"Sure will, kid. Nothing has turned up so far. We're checking with the bars from here to Great Falls, Shelby, Valier, you name it. That's about all I can tell you."

Tomorrow. Before then I knew I had to do something about my garden. Why are there always complications? Can't even enjoy a little grass without it turning into one more way to screw up my life.

***

I didn't do it, though. Not that afternoon. I was beginning to get really worried. They didn't seem to have a lead. Sam was about the easiest landlord a guy could wish for. Ready to bargain mechanical work for the rent. Loaned tools without a second thought.

I went for a drive to think it over and calm myself. I drove up the canyon about as far as the microbus could manage as the road petered out. Then I had a grand time getting it turned around on the wheel-rutted trail without getting high centered or hung up on a boulder. I drove slowly toward home. My mind churned, trying to come up with some possible answer. Where could Sam be? Is he really on a binge? Or, has something worse happened?

I was back on the graded road with less than a mile to the cabin path when I saw someone walking between the road and the creek. Could it be Sam? The hat looked right. I slowed to a crawl. He walked with his head down and didn't look in my direction, so I had a hard time trying to recognize. I'd slowed almost to a stop, ready to offer a ride and he suddenly was moving away from the road, down into the aspens near the creek. He moved pretty well for an big old guy. Was he old? Was he big? It was a fleeting glimpse. What I did see was tan coat and big hat; dressed the same as half the men in the county. Could it have been Sam? Or did he move more like the mean bastard stomping away when I tried to say hello? I stopped. I scanned the creek and trees but didn't see him. I called out, "Sam. Is it you?" No answer.

I shoved the stick into first gear, hit the accelerator and killed the engine pulling the clutch too fast. I had to find a phone.

Sheriff's deputies, Search and Rescue volunteers, and more of us combed that area until full dark and found no sign beyond boot prints where I saw him. We might as well have been looking for Big Foot. Whoever he was, he didn't want to be found.

I was still so shaken up by everything that I went into the cabin and sat. It was too dark and I was too tired to deal with the illegal plants. I told myself I could get up early and remove them before the sheriff could come around. I liked him. He seemed like a good hearted lawman. And could he ever organize a search within minutes! I wanted him to like me, too. Not that it would help if Selective Service came asking where to find me.

(25)

Loud pounding jolted me out of deep sleep. "Oh, crap. I shouldn't have put it off. That's cops knocking like they're about to break down the door." I stumbled to the door in my undershorts, ready to be caught with what they'd found while looking for something else.

"Hey, kid. You gonna sleep all day?" Cracker asked as he pushed through the door.

"Geez Louise, am I glad it's you and not —"

"Hey, it's only me. I left Jeez and Louise out in the wagon."

"Oh man, it's just. You heard about Sam."

"What about Sam?"

"He's missing. Or did he turn up after we searched all evening?"

"This is first I heard anything. I come to see what you're gonna do. Might could be time to move on, innit."

"Ah, shit. There's no way I can sneak off before that Law man comes visiting." I was pulling on my pants, getting ready for the next thing. "And before he shows up, I have a little garden to tend." I pulled on my boots and headed for the door. "How about it? Can you stay here and keep him occupied while I get rid of the cannabis?"

"No guarantees, kid. And you didn't say nothing to me about, what'd you say, 'rhubarb'?"

"Yeah, transplant some rhubarb."

"Okay, I'll stick around. We gotta settle up how we gonna get you north. If you still wanna go."

"I do. Yeah, but I'm getting scared about Sam. He's a good guy. Best landlord I ever had." I thought about how silly that claim was, so I added, "And I've had two, not counting the Yankton dorm."

I grabbed the long handled shovel leaning against the big tree; then changed my mind about it. All I had to do was pull them and get them to a place they wouldn't be found or at least hard to connect to me. The plants had only been in the ground a few days, so they pulled right out. I kicked the dirt around to stir it. It still didn't look natural. The plants were looking kind of sickly, too. I headed deeper into the wooded back part of the property. Not sure what to do, I ended up throwing them over the barbed wire fence. Might've been into mean bastard's. Might've been Forest Service.

I headed back down the slope and nearly stumbled in some softer ground covered over with leaves and needles. Curious. I tested the soft area here and there with my foot. Then I saw it.

(26)

I pushed the pine needles away a little bit, still using the toe of my boot. It wasn't a worm. Oh shit. A finger. And another. A hand, half buried. I raced back to the cabin, shouting all the way. Cracker said I screamed and wouldn't stop.

When he finally got me settled down, I said, "I think I found Sam. There's a body out there, half buried. We have to call the cops."

"Well man, you're right. You can't leave now. They'd pin it on you, for sure. Hey, you wouldn't be just an everyday draft dodger; you'd be a fugitive felon. Alleged."

"It isn't funny, Cracker. Sam was a friend of yours, too."

"Don't I know it. Oh, man ... I'm just trying to keep my head on straight, here. You see, I hate to do this to you, but I don't work well with all your white sheriffs and police and such as them. I'll be on the rez and come see you when things settle down again."

Stunned, I stood there watching as Cracker drove away in his beat up old black Ford Falcon.

***

With Cracker gone, I stood frozen for another long moment before the memory jerked me into action. I took to the road heading eastward for a telephone. I vaguely recalled seeing a pay phone in front of the dude ranch main building. That'll be closest. I pulled in there and discovered I didn't have a dime or my wallet on me. Back where I grew up we always kept change in the car for the tollway, but not out here. I had to get the rancher guy's help.

"Sam? You think somebody killed Sam. Oh my God."

He didn't give me the phone; he made the call. Then he told me the sheriff wanted me to go home and wait for him. The rancher dude (dude rancher?) wanted to come with me. I didn't like that idea. "The sheriff knows you're ready to help."

***

Of course, earlier I had run hollering all the way from the body to my cabin in mindless terror. I wasn't sure I could find the place again and it did take too long. The searchers were calling me crazy, that I must've dreamed it up. Then a deputy stepped right on him. And immediately upchucked. I guess you don't get many opportunities to trip over homicide victims in Teton County. That deputy was too shook up to be of any help after that.

I kept back while they brushed the leaves and dirt away. I was ready to throw up at any moment, too. Whoever put him there had done a half-assed attempt at burial. I was away in the trees trying not to barf when I heard the Sheriff calling me.

"It ain't Sam. Do you know this guy? This is somebody I've seen but I can't say where or how."

I took one step closer. The sheriff waved me over to get a close look at the body, "You know who this man is? It sure ain't Sam like you thought."

"Not Sam. That's good." It was like I was only half there, in some kind of bad dream, numb. I looked. I couldn't hold it back. There was blood all over him and looked like the gun shot hit him under the chin. I turned around and heaved, just missing the deputy's shoes. They waited. "I don't know his name, but that's my mean neighbor. The guy who has, er, who had the trailer and a half-built house over there." I pointed toward the fence row to the west.

"Anybody else live there with him?"

"I never saw anyone else. He didn't want anything to do with me, so I really don't know."

***

Suddenly my alone and silent Montana life had been dropped into a TV cop show, or so it seemed. The FBI cane to help, scouring the forest around the scene. Sam was still missing and they wanted him for questioning. If they were looking for him it didn't show. The traffic was constant through my yard. I hardly had a chance to write it down in my journal.

About the third or fourth day after I found the body—oh man—things changed and not for the better. Sheriff Whatshisname came for me. I remember the name now. It wasn't journaling shorthand after all. His name really was 'Law'. Law said he needed to ask some questions and would I ride with him to his office. He put me in the back of the patrol car where there are no door handles or window cranks. He wouldn't talk or answer a question or anything all the way to Choteau. He just drove and hummed. About to drive me nuts. And I thought he liked me, too. I thought I liked him.

He sat me down in a little room with a table and two chairs and left me there. After about twenty minutes he came back with two big mugs of coffee. He set them down and asked, "You want anything in this?"

I guess I answered or shook my head or something, because he sat down on the other side of the table and started to talk.

"We have a problem, Mr. Bradford. Maybe you can help us figure it out. We found a couple interesting things out there. Do you know anything about a couple plants, not natural to this area? Uprooted and tossed out there?"

How could I answer that? I could lie or I could incriminate myself. I just stared at the table and the coffee mug I was too shaky to pick up.

When I didn't answer, Sheriff Law went on. "You see, Wally, there's also a little patch where the soil's been turned over. Turns out they were planted in that plot not so long ago. That FBI technical guy can find things the rest of us don't have a clue to even look for. Whose plants do you think those were, Wallace?"

I looked at him for a second. "What kind of plants? Do you think the mean bastard was growing something on Sam's land?"

"It's possible. By 'mean bastard' you mean Mr. Olson, the murder victim?"

"Yeah."

"Are you saying you don't know anything about the plants?"

I was about to cry. I couldn't answer and if I said I wanted a lawyer, he'd assume I was guilty. They'd probably offer a plea deal where I end up in the military for four years instead of two. A death sentence for a little weed.

"There's another possibility we have to consider here, you know," the sheriff said. He'd read my silence and let it go. "It could be that Mr. Olson was threatening to turn you in for the marijuana. You knew that's what kind of plant we're talking about, right? Maybe you got into an argument with him and you shot him. Now, I'm not saying that's what happened, but we have to consider all the angles. We're dealing with homicide, here. Serious, serious deal."

"No. I didn't. After one shot at being neighborly – um, bad choice of words – after one try, I always stayed away from him." The sheriff's idea scared me enough that I broke down. "Yeah, I did have those plants. And I got rid of them when I thought we'd be searching for Sam out there. Honest to God. I just had them for myself. I never sold so much as a leaf. Never even shared a toke, matter of fact. Nobody knew about them but me."

"Did you toss anything else out there with the plants?"

"No. Was there something else out there?"

"You know I kinda like you, kid. But I can't deny it. Too much points in your direction. I'm gonna hafta keep you here for now and get some word from the county attorney."

"Are you charging me? With murder?"

"We're still gathering things together on that one. For now, there's a drug charge I can use. Or, you can just agree not to leave, so I won't have to start all that paper work. Until we need to."

I agreed to stay.

***

I was never charged with murder. Or drug possession, for that matter. When Law admitted he hadn't informed me of my rights, the County Attorney dropped it. The sheriff's wink told me all I needed to know about that. I digress. I wasn't charged with murder but the press thought I had been. It made for some touchy moments but if it hadn't been for the false report in the papers, Sam wouldn't have heard about it.

The guy I saw by the road that day was Sam. After that, what happened next, he took off, went a long way. He got the news sitting in a bar, drunk for days, in Coeur D'Alene, Idaho. The way he told it, he set his beer down on the bar, went to a phone and called an AA partner, who brought him home. He turned himself in; said it was self-defense.

Law wanted to believe it. Everybody liked Sam and couldn't imagine that he could kill another man. At least not since the war, and Sam didn't talk about that. Law had no choice but to place him under arrest. I was there, being cleared of any wrongdoing, and saw it—the moment that turned the tables, from murder to justifiable homicide.

Sheriff Law and a deputy were guiding Sam through processing. They took mug shots and were trying to get him to the counter where they did the fingerprints. Sam was still kind of fuzzy after the binge of alcohol poisoning. The deputy grabbed Sam's upper arm and Sam winced in pain. Everybody noticed.

The local doctor examined his shoulder. Sam said Olson shot him but almost missed. Doc said it was highly likely caused by a small caliber bullet. That was enough for Law and the county attorney. Finger prints on the .22 pistol found under the body were too smudged to tell them much.

There was still one big problem for Sam. He had tried to hide evidence. He didn't report. He ran off and all. He admitted guilt but that didn't settle it. Sam wanted to serve his time and get it over with. So did Sheriff Law and the County Attorney. The press was doing its job which meant there'd be an outcry of sweeping it under the rug if they didn't keep investigating. Sweeping it away was exactly what we all wanted. My draft board back in Illinois now knew where I was, but since I was a witness, they had to wait.

The Doakes family were relieved to have me stuck at the cabin through summer. None of them wanted to spend much time so near the scene of the incident.

After harvest, Sam's guilty plea finally sent him into lock up for the winter. His neighbors (and good behavior) convinced the system to parole him early enough to plant spring wheat. I heard that he got to be pals with a probation officer, and dutifully served his required visits to an alcohol and drug counsellor in Great Falls and he's staying sober as far as I know.

Even Olson's ex-wife was satisfied until she had the new survey done in preparation to sell the property. Despite divorce, she was still the beneficiary. It turned out Olson was right. Sam's fence was nearly a foot onto the mean bastard's land. Sam bought the foot width on his side and kept the fence.

(27)

Cracker spotted the envelope as soon as he walked in. He picked it up. "Still sealed. From US Government Selective Service. You gonna open it or what?"

"Naw, just leave it. I hear Canada's lovely this time of year."

"Let's go then. You got everything you need so you can carry it on your back?"

I picked up the overloaded pack. "Yup. I hate to leave my Rocky Mountain home. And I'd sure rather drive the VW across. I really like that outfit."

"You bet, Rich Kid, the cops are already waiting for you to try, innit. You've been in the papers. Your lawman Law had to tell the draft where you been hiding out."

I didn't argue the point. I just nodded and gave Cracker the car keys. He had a plan and a promise. I figured even if he got me a good price for it that he'd deduct a high enough payment for his services. I gave him the title we'd have notarized on our way through Browning. Cracker assured me that he'd either find a way to buy it or he'd sell and send me the money. I was too anxious to think straight and didn't ask, "How will you know where to send the money?"

We hiked a couple miles through the woods to a logging road and a vehicle I'd never seen before. "Neither has Mr. Law," he told me. A Chevy Bel-Air like half the cars on the road in those days, much nicer than Cracker's Ford.

The escape went easier than I could ever have hoped. I was scared out of my mind, always looking for the trap. We arrived at Babb in the Blackfeet Nation during the afternoon and hung out with friends of his until evening. Those friends and cousins revealed the secret. Cracker's

131

real name is Graham. We swapped to an old Jeep pickup for the rest of the way. Cracker explained, "Looks like rain coming, innit. We might need to lock the hubs."

I didn't know where the hell we were, half the night creeping along some wheel rut trail, the only light coming from the dim old headlights and stars. The moon was down, letting the darkness swallow the starlight. Cracker seemed to know exactly where we were and where we were going.

Bouncing along the rough track I kind of fell into a daze. I was still too keyed up to sleep, as if anyone could sleep in that truck on that road. Anyway, I was still worrying and imagining about what I was getting into when we stopped. Cracker flashed the headlights off and on three times and left them off.

"Well, this is it, my friend," he said, without taking his eyes off the darkness ahead. "We should get an answer soon. What time is it?"

I couldn't read my watch in the dark. Neither of us could find a switch for the dome light, so he lit a match. "3:50," I said.

"Whoa. We're in good time. A mere ten minutes early, innit." Cracker started telling a story then, about the Trickster and Coyote and winning a fight without actually fighting. He flashed the lights three times again and an answering flash came from a half mile or more ahead. I soon discovered that it wasn't that far away. It came from a flashlight, not vehicle lights.

I reached out to shake Cracker's hand and say thank you. He grabbed my shoulder, pulled me closer and gave me a sloppy kiss on the cheek. I did not know what to think about that, so I opened the door. The dome light came on and we both laughed at our stupidity. The light ahead stayed on. With my pack secured, I walked toward the light. With a last three-flash signal we heard the Jeep turning around. I waved a good-bye in the dark and turned to meet my escort.

(28)

"You warm enough? We should wait here 'til there's a little daylight if you can get down with that. It won't be too awful long." My guide was saying all this before we'd even introduced ourselves.

"I have warm layers, so yeah, whatever." I stuck out my gloved hand. "I'm Wally Bradford. Wallace the third, my family claims."

"I'm glad you've got the same name as a guy I came out here for. I'm Keith. Keith Kawahara. I came over about three months ago. Where're you from, Wally?"

For the next hour or two we talked about our lives: Chicago, Yankton, Hilo, Cal Tech, women, and coming to Alberta. Sitting there in the dark, shivering, we covered this topic and that, eventually getting to things I might expect in my new situation of zero legal status. As dawn began to beat back the dark, I looked back at the way I'd come, where a line would appear on a map but the reality was unbroken forest and meadow. Keith watched me and said, "Don't look back, man. The future is north."

We hiked for a couple up and down miles along a horse trail—too narrow for the jeep that delivered me to the border. We came to a small, low cabin. Keith caught my expression as I looked it over.

"Yeah," he said, "it started out as a lean-to built from the scrap of an old prospector's hovel. It'd be enough back home on the Big Island. But here? With grizzlies and all?"

"Have you had any bear encounters?"

"No. Just tracks and scat, which those who should know say was black bear. As if a black bear couldn't kill you just as dead as a grizzly. I did my best to make the place a little more secure. No place to spend the winter, though."

"No. It'd take more than chinking to keep out the wind and snow. We've had some freezing days and a little snow over where I've been staying in Montana. Must've had some here, too. You got a warm enough sleeping bag?"

"Warm enough so far, but I intend to be in Vancouver damn soon."

"So, what happens in the winter? Does anybody come across this way?"

"I don't know. I came back out four days ago to get you. And one more who's even later, it seems. It feels like I been out here for years, what with nobody to talk to. I only let Preach and those guys talk me into coming out to keep from being considered a low life by the other ex-pats. Which brings us back to you, Mr. Wally i-i-i. I'm going to Vancouver. Do you have a warm enough sleeping bag?"

"What are you telling me?"

"Welcome to your new home away from home." He waved his arm in a sweeping motion across the more-than-lean-to but less-than-cabin. "A guy name of Steve Van Cleeve should be making the 4:00 AM walk within two or three days. You get to meet him."

"This sure wasn't in my plan. Nobody said…"

"I heard you like to be alone. This'll be great."

"You heard. Okay, I wait here? Is Cracker bringing him?"

"Who's Cracker?"

"Shit, man. This gets crazier by the minute. He's the guy dropped me off, helped me with the whole thing."

"Your escort out of country was the native guy, Graham?"

"That's him. I go back to the border and wait for him every night in the wee hours until Cracker and this Van what's name show?

"Van Cleeve, yeah. And you guys will go from there. Use the same signals. It won't be Graham, though.

"Does the trail get clear enough to follow? It's kind of obscure from what I've seen."

"Tell you what, I'll leave word and you'll have a guide bring you down. But if you go downhill you get to a jeep trail. Go east; make sure you don't go back south."

"Let me get this straight. I wait for Van Cleeve. Steve, right? I go back and wait in the night and then he and I wait right here for a guide who'll drive us down?

"He'll be walking. Word is, and it might be total bullshit, but word is the FBI is watching and if a vehicle came out here from Cardston, they'd have someone standing on the line to arrest the man the vehicle's coming for; and they watch this side because they figure the rez is too much hassle. They'd be spotted and the word would get out before their boots get muddy. Of course, sometimes it's a bit vague, like with you. Vague about time, and the FBI'd be vague about the legal border. Preach said a guy name of Wallace the third'll be coming and told me the week. Not the night, mind you. Four or five A.M. on any night this week. I sat out there in the dark on four nights. And glad it wasn't seven."

"Sorry about that. It was hard to schedule, what with the neighbor guy who got killed and all. Who's Preach?"

"Killed? As in murdered? What?"

"I'll tell you all about it after I get a little nap, okay? Who's Preach?"

"Don't know his real name. That's what they call him. He'll come sneaking in here to get your man Steve and you. Go on in there and get some rest. I'll just sit out here and worry you're gonna kill me, too."

"Hey, I didn't kill anybody. I came here so I won't have to. Anyway, they thought it was murder, but it wasn't after all. It was self-defense. Might've been necessary. Or bad luck. I was only a suspect for a few days. Long enough for the draft sons o' bitches to find out where I was and keep me on edge all summer. I had to stay there to testify so the draft had to wait."

***

It took a long time to tell Keith about Sam and the mean bastard. He wanted to hear all about it, but mostly he needed to talk. He was the kind of guy who had to interrupt with stories of his own all along the way. I guess that comes with being alone for some guys. Even for a solitary like me, only it takes longer to kick in.

When the sun was high we ate crackers and hard cheese. As soon as we were done, Keith announced, "I'm outa here." He was already organizing his belongings for stuffing into his backpack. "I'll let Preach and them know you're here. You'll get a visit soon. Make sure you're at the boundary with a flashlight tonight."

"Are you leaving me anything to eat?"

"There's plenty in that box, there. All dried trail food that won't bring the bears until you start cooking it."

I was familiar with trail food, tasteless but filling, so that was okay. I had my new tent and one person bag, so I set up a hidden camp near the drop off spot and waited. I hunkered down with my flashlight from 3:30 to daylight—for six nights. No Van Cleeve. I was getting hungry for real food. I rigged together some fishing string and managed to catch a little trout. Good for flavor, but I burned more calories catching than I gained eating. "I gave it a week," I decided, "Van Cleeve isn't coming and there's no sign of that Preach person either." I packed up my tent and wandered back to the shelter that Keith had used. A tall, skinny man with long tousled hair over his shoulders and a beard to match was looking around and combing his beard with his fingers.

***

"Who're you?" he asked before I could say hello. That put me on edge.

I wondered, "Is this my contact, Preach? Or is it an undercover cop? Under a lot of hairy cover." After I decided there was nothing to be gained by not answering, I spoke up. "I'm Wally. Who're you?"

"Preach. Where's Keith?" For a guy with that nickname, he sure was terse.

"Didn't he tell you? He's off to Vancouver and left me to meet a guy who never showed. He said he'd tell you."

"I haven't heard a thing. We've been expecting him to bring one Wallace Bradford and one Steven Van Cleeve to Cardston. Kawahara couldn't take it, eh."

"He said he was going to Vancouver and would tell you to guide us. He left as soon as he could pack up."

"At any rate, it's time to shut down the wilderness road for winter. Snow is on the way. We need to get down the trail."

I packed up and we set out. Preach really seemed to be in a hurry to get down to 'civilization'. I was thinking about this latest betrayal of trust. I learned that day that I couldn't trust an ex-pat just for being one. Or the weather. You can't trust Canadian weather.

***

The snow came too soon. The wind blew hard. Preach had been right to hurry, but we couldn't move fast enough.

"I've heard it said that freezing is an easy way to die. That'd be relative to other ways, I suppose," said Preach.

He wasn't helping. Freezing might not hurt as much as falling off a cliff, but dead is still dead. And I didn't want to die. Oh sure, for ten minutes after Carolee dumped me I thought I did, but I got over it. I sometimes wonder why, when people keep on proving their untrustworthiness. Deserted by that Hawaiian. Well, what should I expect? We're both deserters from army or draft, why should abandoning duty stop there!

Preach soon shifted into survival mode and he knew what he was doing. We battled against the wind to pitch my tent. I guess we were trying to take our minds off the weather as we talked. One question I remember because I wasn't so sure about my answer, which one would expect to be obvious.

"Where's home, Wally?"

I gave that some thought and eventually answered in questions, "Montana? Canada?" I went on to say where I grew up, where I'd been at college and how comfortable I'd been at the wilderness cabin in spite of the mean bastard neighbor and all that had happened there recently.

Preach insisted that we take turns sleeping and keeping watch in case the snow buried us. "We don't want to run out of oxygen," he warned.

In the end there was no real danger of that, the snow eased after a few hours. We still slept in shifts, but the sky cleared. The sun was blinding in reflection off the snow the next morning. The drifts, up to two feet deep, made for slow progress, some confusing moments looking for the trail, and aching legs. But we got down. Preach taught a good lesson in what to do and what not to do in a sudden storm.

The lesson has served me well a few times since. I always seem to wake up cold and hungry but not dead. So far.

(29)

More than six years after that snowy hike, most of that time at Hy-Pru Farm as hired hand and mechanic, I was told it's time to move on. Hiram and Prudence were selling out. "Go home," they were saying on that January day. The snow was beginning to blow as it had that night that welcomed me down the mountain north of the border in the autumn of 1970. Except this time it was twenty degrees colder; that's degrees Celsius (we're Canadian).

***

"Today's one of them times, boys. If you was caught out this evening, you probably would wake up dead tomorrow," Pru said. She got up and passed around the cookies.

We all looked out the window then. For hours we, mostly I, had been talking to the fire in the hearth.

"Weather like this we expect in January. It's the way it is out here. Makes me glad I cut back on cattle and rely on the grain for the cash crop. Iffy as that is between drought and hail." Hy listed more 'farm life' observations, but I had quit paying attention and nearly dozed off. He'd slept through some of my long storytelling. Fair is fair.

Pru insisted that I phone as soon as I got to the trailer where I made my home, fifty yards away plus the short side trip. I broke bales for the few cattle, the last remnant of Hy's herd, huddled against the barn wall. I did call Pru to let her know that I'd made it safely across the farmyard and the steers were fed. That night I wrote as usual. I also dug into the stack of old journals. Up to that day Hy had never challenged my claim that Kamloops was my home. Was Kamloops home? "Go home," they said, "to Chicago." To the family I renounced. Is that home? Not so much.

I dug out the books labeled '70 and '71. I had a need to refresh my memories of British Columbia. I read and remembered things I

138

pretended to have forgotten; things I'd truly and deeply repressed. At least, I try to believe so. Women. Crap. People, especially women. Crap.

***

It was still too cold to work in the shop, so conversation near the fireplace resumed the next morning after breaking more bales. I was loaded with firewood on one arm and journals under the other when I knocked on Hy and Pru's back door with my boot.

I've worked so hard to repress any thought of her, doing my best to forget what kept me in Kamloops those several months. Always there down deep, my secret heartache became an overwhelming pain in my gut that morning. I thought Hiram would believe me that Kamloops was my home town while I tried to forget. I do remember Kamloops, a boom town with logging and the pulp mills working overtime. New people, many from India, were growing the city. I tried to blend in, well not with the Punjabi, with the native Canadians. Oops, not them either. I mean the other white people, eh.

I remember the city, and enough about it to think I could get away with claiming it as home. I carefully constructed a home town story with schools and activities, on and on. But there was this one thing, the most important while I was there. Bonnie, whom I never mentioned, was reason to stay and reason to leave Kamloops. She was my secret disgrace, my stupidity exposed. Now I missed her more than ever.

"Hy, did I ever mention Bonnie?"

"Is that her name? Break up brought you our way is all you ever said. Do tell, Solitary Wallace. A feller needs a good woman to give him a daily dope slap and knock some human reality into ya," said Hiram with a smirk.

"Back when I was in high school I didn't give a girl a second glance if she was the least bit overweight according to some juvenile standard I held. Of course, that meant I never got to know some fine young women; lovely in the fullest sense of that word. I got to Kamloops after a year when my entire sex life had come from magazines like *Playboy* and, you know what I mean."

"No. I don't. What do you mean?"

"Huh? Um," and then I looked up from the journal I was thumbing through in search of the right page and saw the big grin across Hy's face. "Okay. Maybe I need a little more caffeine."

Hy took our mugs to the kitchen while I located the journal entries. On his way he poked me with an elbow. "Just like at your hermitage across the yard, eh?"

I found the journal entries and gulped some warm coffee.

***

I was looking for work. My trust fund wasn't helping since I didn't have an address and I hadn't yet contacted Mr. Boyer. Before I left Montana I asked him to hold the payments and I didn't dare say where I was going.

Good jobs and also the dreaded Bradford & Son, Inc. had always fallen in my lap before. I first had to learn how to look for work. As I walked around, getting acquainted with the city, I happened upon the local history museum. I went in, thinking I'd have a look around. There she was, sitting at a small desk, greeting visitors, answering questions, fielding phone calls. I stood there in the entrance staring like a fool. I was smitten. Her pretty face, her manner with the few people who approached the desk, was so pleasant as I watched from a distance.

Then she saw me. I must have blushed, staring like that. She stood up and started toward me. She wasn't much taller standing up than she'd been sitting behind that desk.

"Can I help you, sir?" Even her voice had a pleasing lilt. Even in that routine offer of service.

"Huh? Oh, I dunno. Um..." I stammered.

"Is there something in the archives you're looking for?"

"Uh, no. I'm new in town. Just, um..." Then something came over me and the words spilled out before I knew I'd thought them. "Can I take you to dinner, or something, or... Oh, I'm sorry. It's just." I stammered on.

Now she was at a loss for words. She was shaking her head, about to speak; and then she closed her mouth again. I noticed her hands—no special ring, that's good—at her sides rubbing up and down on the polyester pants she was wearing.

I tried again. "I'm so sorry, Miss. I don't know what came over me."

Then she answered, "I have a break coming. You can buy me a coffee," and dashed off to check with another staff person.

She guided me to a little café nearby. When she ordered chocolate pie I noticed that she was chubbier than any girl I'd dated before. And I didn't care. She was beautiful. I was finally ready to forget that I was still in love with Carolee, whom I hated passionately. No sooner had we begun to talk, or so it seemed, than she jumped up in a panic because she'd taken much too long on break. It had been forty minutes and we were just getting started. She was so interested in my story, and seemed supportive of my decision to leave the USA. We ran back to the museum, where she would give me the grand tour and accept my original request for a dinner date.

***

If it weren't for Bonnie, I could never have presumed to claim her city as my home town. She showed me the sights, where kids did what kids do, taught me local history at the museum. My interest in local history, of course, was mostly the excuse to be near during her working hours.

I hoped to find work as a mechanic, but the shops all expected me to provide my own tools and a Social Insurance Number. I'd had to let go of the few tools I still had when I crossed the border. Some employers may have turned me away because I looked or smelled like a draft dodger. The Illinois driver's license and my 'student visa' that was always at home in my other jacket would confirm anyone's suspicions. When I was offered a job as a yard man at a nursery and garden store, and took it, I figured I'd hit bottom. God must have a sick sense of humor.

Bonnie was quite sympathetic and that helped. In fact, her expressions of understanding and love sent her rating up several notches when I explained why that brought me so low. As I told her about my background, of suburban North Shore Chicago, Bradford & Son, Inc., and my need to escape that scene as much as the war, she listened with caring concern.

"It'll be okay, Wally. You'll soon find something better." She paused, trying to figure something out. Then she said, "So how is it a rich guy like you would bother about a fat working girl who still lives in her parents' home?"

All I managed to say to that was, "You're not fat," and changed the subject. "Next I need to find a place to settle for a while. I don't want to tap the trust fund until I can give Mr. Boyer an address and phone number."

"Trust fund?"

"Yeah, it'll let me live a little higher on the hog than I can on transplanting geraniums."

Her face lit up. "Gramma's little house sits empty. Mama doesn't really want to rent it out because she won't admit that Gramma'll have to stay at the rest home. I think I could convince her if you rented week by week; with the understanding that you'd have to move if Gramma actually does come home."

I nodded. "Where is this house?"

"It's right next to ours. On the same lot, more or less. And Gramma's not getting better. She had a stroke and she's not like herself."

I reached over and, with my thumb, wiped the single tear running down her cheek. Which turned out to be a cool move because then we kissed. Deeply.

***

Living in that mother-in-law cottage was like staying an extra week in the guest room. It was full of old lady stuff that I wasn't allowed to disturb, just in case. But once her folks got used to the idea that Bonnie would spend evenings with me there, whether they liked it or not, I could tolerate the knick-knacks. I'd become a boarder, too. The Coughlan family included me in supper night after night. Her dad would force seconds on me while eyeing me as if he were looking down the barrel of the shotgun; a look that said, "First you marry our Bonnie. Then and only then will we be ready for grandbabies."

Bonnie's mom, on the other hand, would tsk-tsk in a way that said, "Get married, you two. I want grandbabies." Both her folks could see that we were a good fit and in love. Her dad gave those shotgun looks, but he also helped me get my papers in order to stay in Canada.

Bonnie's little brother and I shot hoops in the driveway. He was really good at shooting long, but he'd never be tall enough even for high school varsity. No one in the family reached five foot six (1.7 meters — we were still 'going metric' at that time).

It was a pretty good life, except for the job. I couldn't quit it, now that I had a work visa. But that got better, too, when they discovered that I could tune a tiller so that anyone could start it in two pulls of the cord. Then I was maintaining engines in the rental department. I was in my comfort zone, daydreaming while doing something I loved to do.

***

Life was going great there in home town Kamloops. Then I blew it. God, I wish I could shove those five words back into my mouth and down my throat. So stupid.

(30)

I was stretched out, propped on all the pillows, in her grandmother's narrow bed. Bonnie was in the bathroom. I was thinking about asking her; wondering what might be the best way to propose. Should I just suggest the plan when she crawled in with me? Or should I wait and get down on one knee in some special setting?

While I was considering all this, she came from the bathroom wearing only a long tank top that kind of hugged her body. She slid in under the sheet and out of my mouth came the destruction. "You could lose some weight."

She burst into tears and ran back into the bathroom. All the while, I, of course, was crying out my apologies, trying to take it all back. "You're so pretty. It doesn't matter. I'm sorry, sorry, sorry." On and on I pleaded, to no avail. She was too hurt and I could not mend it or make those five words disappear. I must have said other stupid things before and this was the proverbial straw dropped on a most sensitive spot.

Dressed again, she ran past me and out the door, with tears still streaming down her face.

***

The next morning, when Bonnie still wouldn't talk to me, I packed. Once more, I wrote to Mr. Boyer, saying, "Hold the checks again." I knew he'd be irritated at my frequent changes and threaten again to increase the fee. Maybe he would do it this time. I suspected that the real source of his antagonism was that I was a draft dodger.

I paid a little more rent and loaded up the old Dodge pickup truck I'd bought cheap and overhauled. I threw in my few possessions and hit the road. After a few blocks, in a deep funk, I pulled over to the curb to look at the map and decide. First I sat behind the wheel sobbing for ten or twenty minutes. "I'm the one who can't be trusted. What a shitty thing to find out about myself. What if other people just had a stupid moment and I called it betrayal?" Pulling myself back to the moment, I considered. "North to wilderness? Southwest to Vancouver? East to... There's lots of east."

I pulled onto Trans-Canada One, eastbound. I had enough money in my pocket. I could see the sights. I might be broke before the Maritimes and I'd vacationed in Ontario as a kid, but there was much more to see for the first time.

PART TWO

(31)

After a cold Canadian Rockies night of camping in the truck bed, I came down the east slopes. Signs announced the distance to Calgary. I had been there for a day and I'd had enough of cities just then. So, I tossed a coin. North would take me to Edmonton, another city, so I tossed it again and headed south. I was enjoying the uncertainty of the back roads, putting troubles out of mind, when I spotted a pickup much like mine alongside the road, out on the open prairie, a few miles from a town so small its one horse moved away, where I'd just taken a coffee and piss break. Those were separate activities, by the way.

The hood was up and a weather beaten man sitting halfway out the open door was smoking a cigarette. I slowed as I passed, and pulled off just ahead of him. The cigarette looked like a roll-your-own. Maybe it was one of those smokes like I hadn't touched since Sheriff Law let me off with a warning. It turned out to be Bull Durham, so I stayed clean.

It looked like he could use some mechanical help. That was right up my alley so I had him try the starter while I poked around. Neither of us had the right tools, of course, but often it doesn't take much.

I tapped here and there, twisted wires and had him try again. It cranked but didn't start. "How's your gas?"

"Got half a tank. It ain't that." His speech was slurred, which may be just the way the old cowboy talked, but it caused me to watch him more closely.

I tried to adjust the carburetor a little. The set screw was stuck, so it moved too far when it finally gave. I had him try again. The engine started and died. I was reaching the screwdriver to adjust some more when I had an idea. I stepped over to the driver's window and said, "I think I might've found one problem, sir. Come here and take a look." This was the idea—watch him walk and get a sniff of his breath before adjusting again. I saw the half empty pint of cheap bourbon on the seat, so I already knew the answer.

He came around, keeping one hand on the truck for balance. I tapped the side of the carburetor with the screwdriver and said, "I think something's plugged up in there. Gonna take a little more effort and tools that aren't so worn out, too. Where you headed?"

"Bash to the farm, o'coursh," he said, as if I were a fool not to know.

"How far? I can run you over there. Your outfit can wait."

He nodded, inched back to the cab, grabbed a heavy coat and rolled up the window but didn't lock. He stumbled and nearly fell about half way to my pickup, so I helped him through the loose gravel on the road's sloping shoulder and got him into the seat. I spotted the booze and said, "I don't mind you keeping the bottle with you, but no nips at it 'til we get to the ranch.

"It's moshly farm. Wheat. I work for Hy Magelshon. I'm quittin' though. Soon as…" He paused. "Soon as … sumpin." He nodded off.

"Hey!" I shouted, "You can't go to sleep. You gotta tell me how to get there."

He came to with my jabbing at his ribs. "Can't mish it. Hiram Magels…shon, right on the mailbox."

"So it's on this road, then?"

"Nah. Down here about two miles, turn there."

"Which way?"

"Which way we going now?"

"East, I think."

"Yeah, from town, righ'?"

"From that one horse burg with just a bar and café where you've been drinking, no doubt."

"Shit, you givin' me a bad time about it? Jus' toss me off here, shithead."

I tried to calm the outburst and keep him in the jocose stage; don't let him go to bellicose. "What else would anybody be doing there? That's all there is."

"Maybe thash why I gotta quit. Nothin' better'n drinkin' and stretchin' wire. Friggin' hell of a life out here."

Our road came to an end. North or south were our only choices. "Which way now?"

"Huh?"

"Come on, man. Give me some direction here."

"Oh," he said, looking around. "Go that way." He pointed to the right, southward. Another five or six miles down the road, I was beginning to think we'd gone too far. In his half stupor the cowboy wasn't helping. I was about ready to turn around when I spotted the big mailbox marked 'Hy-Pru Farms, Inc.' and 'Magelsson' in large white letters. We turned into the long drive. I saw in the distance a large house, two bigger barns, elevator silos, big machinery, and a single wide mobile home.

I pulled up to the house with its wide porch and yard surrounded by rabbit wire fence. My rider looked up again as I turned the ignition and the engine quieted. "No, kid," he said, "over to the trailer there, eh."

Before I could restart—he was in no shape to walk the short distance across the farmyard—a man came out of the house with a big dog jumping ahead of him. I got out to greet and explain. Before I could he was at the other side with the door open, ordering and pulling. "Where've you been, Jack? It doesn't take seven hours to pick up one part that's setting on the counter waiting for you."

"I got waylaid a bit, Hy. And the outfit broke down on the way back. I got yer damn part, though."

"Well, let's have it then."

Jack looked on the cab floor, then at the topper over the truck box. "This ain't the truck. Mus' be back up..." He waved his arm around, possibly in the general direction of the broken down truck.

"Who's your pal, then?" Hy said, becoming more fully aware of me. I was staying inconspicuous on the other side behind the topper.

"Huh? Who?"

"Your driver. Who brought you back?"

"The smartass there? I dunno. He just helpin' out, you know." Jack blinked and stumbled against the fender.

"You're so drunk you can't even stand up. Or have any idea what the hell's going on. And you were driving my outfit in that condition. I oughta fire you right now."

"You cain't, cuz I jus' quit." He stomped off toward the trailer. He made it about six steps before he dropped down on his knees and threw up.

I started toward him. Hy stopped me, saying, "Let him wretch it out of him for bit. Then we can haul him to his bunk." He approached me then, with his calloused hand out to shake. "Hiram Magelsson. Is my outfit really out on the road, or did you bring him from the bar?"

"It's beside the road. My name's Wally Bradford, Mr. Magelsson. I could've got it running easy enough, but I figured it was better to leave it than let him drive."

"There any chance you'd take me out and help get it going?"

"Sure. No problem. I'm not on a schedule today."

"I'll just ask Pru to set another plate for supper and we'll get Jack inside. Then we'll go."

"Dinner? You don't have to."

"'Have to' got nothing to do with it."

We dropped Jack onto his battered sofa to sleep it off. Hiram didn't want to see the bedroom mess or drag him down the narrow hallway.

**

As we backtracked to the breakdown, in answer to Hiram's questions, I described what I thought was wrong with his pickup. We brought better tools and a tow chain along, just in case.

Hiram asked, "You heard Jack say he quit, right?" I nodded in reply. "He won't remember, but I have to hold him to it. You're witness. I feel like I'm throwing the poor guy in the gutter, but I just can't take it anymore. His wife left. God, he probably should be in jail for what he did to her. At least she got away."

I looked over at Mr. Magelsson, curious, but not wanting to ask.

He shook his head at his thoughts and changed the subject. "Where you headed?"

"Nowhere in particular. Someplace new."

"What're you running from? The law?"

That gave me a start, because I had been and I almost said so; but not now. "Break up," I said and left it at that.

"I see." Hiram didn't try to coax details from me. "You're headed nowhere certain. Where're you going there from?"

"Kamloops."

"And before that?"

"Kamloops is where I'm from. Got people there from way back."

Hiram gave me a funny look, but didn't say anything because we'd reached his truck.

***

During the promised supper, Hiram couldn't stop praising my mechanic skills. "Pru," he said more than once, "that young man is a wizard with the internal combustion. Spotted the problem right off, and took care of it right there and then."

While Prudence dished up a dessert of rhubarb cobbler and ice cream, Hy asked me, "Do you know diesel mechanics, too?"

"More than I know about quantum mechanics, yeah. I learned by working on Sam's equipment." I almost said too much before I remembered that I came only from Kamloops. "A farmer-rancher I used to know. He showed me stuff and then claimed I was better at it than him."

"Can you string fence wire?"

I shook my head. "I know less about that than I know of quantum theory. I painted a board fence once, though. Why are you asking?" I had a feeling I knew what was coming. I knew my answer, too.

"You know, Mr. Bradford, that I'm currently in need of a farm hand. It pays crap, but you'll get a filthy, stinky trailer house. I just need a man until harvest is in. Of course, if you're willing to give it a try, I'll want you to stay long enough for some extra maintaining of the combine. All the engines, really."

"If you're really offering me a job, I guess I'll take it. I can go on to Nova Scotia anytime."

"Don't you want to know how much the crap wages are?"

I shrugged, just to confuse him. If I could trust him to be fair about the money without a contract, maybe he wouldn't betray my trust too soon. But everyone does.

(32)

I'd been working for Hiram Magelsson for something like five years, waiting for him to let me down. In the end the best he could come up with was Jimmy Carter's amnesty. Not much of a betrayal. Or, was his retirement plan a betrayal? He approached that as a trusted friend, too. There was the secret, of course. He'd let me get away with my lie about home town Kamloops. He didn't believe it for a minute but he left my secret untouched.

***

"It's right there in the journal. See that, Hiram? 'If I could take back those five words.'"

"Do you still love her? ...eh?"

I stared at the fireplace, searching for answer.

Likely trying to lighten the mood, Hy said, "Must be. Lord knows love hasn't blown in on the prairie wind. I've never seen such a guy for never having a second date."

"I had some second dates."

"Damn little more than that. Pru goes to town and the gals ask after you, eh. 'How's Wally?' they say, and tell about a nice but kind of standoffish guy who never called again. 'He's still pining for the one that got away,' she could've told them." After a pause he asked again, "Do you still love her?"

I looked up from the fire and stared at the ceiling.

"It's been a few years, of course. She's like as not married with a couple ankle-biters by now, or maybe not. You could find out, you know. If she's a single lady, you can show her your journal. You might yet be able to eat those words. It's unlikely as a tsunami in Saskatoon and maybe you don't have that kind of courage. Yeah, you'd be walking straight at incoming fire, eh. Unless it works. Then you have a reason to get over your solitary ways.

After mid-day dinner with Hy and Pru I took my journals to the trailer. The sun was bright on the snow, the sky deep blue from horizon to horizon. There was no wind. That was rare indeed. I went to the shop, fired up the heater, and finished repairing the engine I'd been working on when Hy told me to go home.

I had a lot to consider. "Do I have enough courage to face Bonnie? She'll be right to tell me to get lost, even if she doesn't have a husband or boyfriend." I concluded it wasn't worth the pain. Then I decided I had to try. She says boo, I leave. I'm good at living alone. She says yes, I learn how to live with, well really I might learn how to live. Period. Full stop.

"On the other hand, is this finally some advice from Hiram that I cannot trust? Nah, he didn't make any promise. And he was careful to say so – that it'll probably backfire on me."

In the evening I wrote a long letter in the journal. More like a transcript for my speech. Then I packed and figured out how much I should offer Mr. Magelsson for the Dodge pickup that contained many parts including a topper from the one I arrived in and later crunched on a bull elk.

***

Hy took a dollar for the truck, just enough to transfer the title. He taped the dollar coin onto the kitchen bulletin board. "To remember you by," he said.

"Looks more like remembering the Queen to me."

He re-taped it showing tails: the canoe voyageurs. "There, for our traveler who put up with me longer than any other hired man."

Travel was pretty clear winter driving to a few miles beyond Calgary. I'd have stopped for the night in the city if I'd paid attention to weather forecasts. As it was, it took two more days west of the Rockies due to snow, ice and jackknifed semi-trailers.

(33)

"Bonnie Coughlan is long gone from here, I'm afraid," the museum director said after I had been passed through three other employees who had no idea. "She went off to Vancouver to complete her degree, or so she said. I've completely lost touch with Ms. Coughlan. I think her folks are still in town, although I'm not certain of that, either."

I had wanted to avoid Agnes and Ed. With my museum plan at a dead end, I couldn't come up with another option. I rang the bell, half expecting a new homeowner and total stranger to answer.

Bonnie's mother came to the door, stared at me for a long moment with an expression of "should I know you?" Recognition clicked, "Wally? Wally Bradford? Is that you?"

"Yes, ma'am." We stood there in the open door.

"Well, you best come in from the cold before you let it all into the house."

I followed her to the kitchen where she put a cup of coffee pumped up with cream and sugar on the table. "Sit. What brings you back this way? And why come to my door?"

"It's a long story, Mrs. Coughlan. I've been a farm hand in Alberta ever since I left here. Now Hy and Pru are retiring, and Carter... Well, long story short, I was remembering your sweet Bonnie and what a stupid fool I was. I just had to know. Is she married now? Do you have grandchildren? Or..."

"Oh, Wally, you are a sorry lot, aren't you. Carter, you said. You must mean your U.S. president. You can go home now, go back to your real place."

"For five years I've been claiming that Kamloops is my home town. Yeah, only a few months and it did feel more like home than Winnetka.

154

Please, can you tell me? I don't want to intrude but I really would like to see Bonnie if that's at all possible. At the museum they said she went to college."

"She did, yes. She went off to Simon Fraser where she studied in education and history. Now she teaches."

"Wow. Good for her. Where? Is she still single like me?"

Mrs. Coughlan opened a bag of store-bought cookies and dropped it on the table. She looked at the wall clock and said, "Take your coffee and cookies out front. I may be able to reach her at home. I won't tell you more without her say-so. She's a grown up professional woman, dontcha know. Trust her to make her own choices."

"I'll be glad to pay you if it's long distance."

I had a feeling that she hoped Bonnie would say, "Tell him to get lost." I dunked a cookie in my coffee confection and listened, trying to hear one side of the phone conversation from the other room.

The door was open and I could see her at the wall phone. Listening took effort; it was a long way from the front room through the dining room to the kitchen. She dialed and looked my way, lifting fingers: one, two, three. Then she said, loudly enough, "Oh, good. I found you at home. ... I had to call now. No, don't worry. It'll be paid for. ... News? Just this. Someone has come to our door. Someone from your past. ... Oh, my. That was quick. And you guessed right, too. He's sitting in the front room right now. Straining his ears to hear us. ... Well, that's just it. What do I tell him?"

She said something more at a volume too low to hear. In her normal voice again, I heard, "No? Well, all right then. I'll tell him what you said. ... Not that? What then? ... Okay, I will. ... Living out there next to nowhere will cause you to gain. Believe me. ... I'll call again Sunday, when the rates are cheaper. ... Oh, and you call me just as soon as you can when he gets there. Understand? ... Yes, I love you too, dear. We'll talk again soon." She hung up and beckoned me to come back. "Bring your cup. We'll have another."

"Did she say I should get lost?"

"She probably should, but no. I'm to tell you this. Bonnie is teaching history and social at Port Hardy Secondary School. That's nearly the end of the road on Vancouver Island; way north from Victoria. She told me you can come and visit her there. 'If he really cares,' she said."

I was jumping up and down ready to give Mrs. Coughlan a big hug. She resisted. "Thank you, thank you. Oh, I will. Port Hardy. I've never heard of it."

"You'll need a map then. It'll be a long drive and ferry ride in January weather."

"I'm ready. I've been driving through some real winter so far. Isn't it milder on the coast?"

"Wally, I must tell you. And don't you dare tell Bonnie I said this. She said I should only tell you to come. Nothing else. Am I a bad mother if I tell you?"

"I don't know, but now you have to say it or I'll go totally nuts right here."

"More than you are already? Bonnie said she hadn't thought about you, she'd put you out of her mind is what she said."

I nodded at that. "It's what I tried to do, too. Strange." Maybe she was more successful.

"Anyway, she said she's trying to diet. Teaching out there, she's a little heavier than you remember her. So, don't you dare say anything! Or even think it. If you care…"

"Oh, Agnes, I learned that lesson. I've done a lot of stupid things, said too much rude and dumb stuff. I guess you know what I said. That was the worst, stupidest, unbelievably wrong thing I ever said. I knew she was touchy about it, too. So stupid. I was planning… I just have to see her. Just in case. If there's still anything for us, I have to know. Is that wrong of me?"

"Maybe, maybe not. It is unusual, I'll say that. After five years. She's quite an independent woman. Can you handle that? If you crowd her, you'll be sorry."

(34)

As I filled my plate at the buffet I felt the judgmental stare of an older woman. I watched as she pointed and whispered with her friend. It pissed me off, but also made me take inventory. My jeans were dirty, but not ragged. They were my best flannel lined pair. I ate my chicken and considered the contents of the clothing box under the pickup topper: Overalls, heavy coveralls, t-shirts, sweats. Maybe a new outfit could make a better impression with my Bonnie. Well, not mine ... yet. Shit, never mine, ours together? How will this work? I shook my head and tried to quit thinking about it. But I stopped at a shopping center in a Vancouver suburb and left with a leisure suit and a couple sport shirts in bright solid colors despite the salesman's urgings about patterns or stripes. He reminded me of a guy in Altoona. So did my new clothes.

***

The ferry ride through choppy water to Departure Bay gave me time to journal hopes and worries. Recent entries had been fairly short, retracing the same questions over and over. Now I sat with pen and paper, pondering a longer diary. I imagined what our meeting might be like. What should I say? What will she say? Will the old spark return? Question after question rolled in my mind. The page stayed blank. Instead, I wrote a letter, intended to be a short note, to Hiram and Prudence, telling what had happened on the journey through Kamloops.

Dear Hy and Pru,

It has been a slow journey. Ice and snow from the pass on down the west side. Semi-trucks jackknifed. But at Kamloops my hopes were lifted. I talked to Bonnie's mother. She's still doubtful about me, but she did call her daughter. Guess where? In Port Hardy on Vancouver Island. I'm on my way there now, cruising on the ferry from Horseshoe Bay on the Straits of Georgia. ...

The letter was never sent, never torn from the journal. After that newsy part I descended into private details — a journal entry after all.

A ferry ride gives one time to re-read and consider. By the second page the entry had slipped into my expectations. I discovered there the me-first, last and always problem that I thought the Magelssons had helped me outgrow out there where critters and crop come first. Well, at least now I can sometimes notice when I do it. Mrs. Coughlan had laid it on the line. Bonnie is an independent woman, making her own decisions. I cannot control her life. I sat with my journal, closed my eyes, and there was Carolee, left hand on her hip, slim and athletic as ever, right hand pointing at me in accusation. I opened my eyes hoping to shut away the memory.

***

The map made it look like the drive along the east side of the island could be slow in the steady rain. I didn't want to arrive late and weary, so I got a room in Nanaimo. I wrote many words of little consequence in my journal that night.

In the morning the rain had eased to a light, cold drizzle as I found my way up the coast. Later the sun even made half-baked attempts to peek through from time to time. I told myself, "It's a good day," thought about it and nearly ran off the road in anxiety, fear and excitement at what's to come.

***

"What time does school let out?" I asked the guy with scruffy gray whiskers pumping gas into the Dodge. I knew I had some time to kill before I could appear at Bonnie's classroom.

"Why you want to know? You some kind of pervert?" His retort came while getting a good look at my Alberta license plates.

"No way. Nothing like that. I'm supposed to meet with a teacher after the students have left, is all."

"You come all the way from Alberta for a teacher conference and you don't know what time? I should call the cops right now."

"Okay. I'm a stranger here. Don't you think if I was gonna abduct some kid, would I ask you? Especially you - where you get a good look at my old vehicle and the license number and all?"

"Yeah, well ... I'm still takin' it down. You gonna pay with a credit card, so I can get your name down, too?"

I had planned to use cash. "Sure, why not?" and pulled out my Esso card. "You want to see a driver's license, too?" I followed him into the station before I gave him the card.

I signed the receipt and he handed back the card, saying as he did, "Long about quarter to four buses'll go by here."

"Thanks," I said, and sarcastically added, "Is everyone in Port Hardy as friendly as you?"

"Welcome to North Vancouver Island, Mr. Bradford. If you stick around long enough, you can call me Butch."

We shook hands, as if that covered all suspicions. "Pleased to meetcha, Butch."

"You ain't stuck around, yet." He laughed, but I think he was serious.

I found the school. It would only be half an hour, but I knew I couldn't park and wait. Not if Butch the pump jockey was telling the police about me. I found a little coffee shop and bided my time over a slice of apple pie.

***

At exactly 3:50 I tapped at the open classroom door under the gaze of the vice-principal who guided me. The teacher stepped down from a footstool and turned from the chalkboard where she was writing Monday's assignments as I said, "Hi, Bonnie. I mean, Miss Coughlan."

I read her look as hesitant and questioning. She nodded an okay at my escort and he left us. We stumbled among the student desks toward each other—our clumsy version of a slow motion run through flowery meadow. She took both my hands in hers, felt their roughness, looked at my calloused palms and said, "A working man. Good for you, Wally."

My heart was pounding. It was that first meeting at the museum all over again. "A professional educator. And beautiful as ever. Good for you, Bonnie."

"Five years. It feels like a lifetime ago, another life entirely." She paused, looked more earnestly at my grinning face. "And it feels like only yesterday. God, it feels like... Let me finish up here and we'll talk."

I asked, "How can I help?" She answered me with a shake of her head, a movement that swished her long brown hair in a way that struck me as alluring, maybe even seductive. I sat at a student desk and watched her work.

***

159

We started walking toward her house in a trailer park near the school. I tried to take her hand. She pulled away, then gave me a sideways glance and slipped her hand into mine. I floated the rest of the way. I'm not ashamed to say it, though at the time, it was said only to my private journal.

The 12-wide trailer house was cold. She turned up the thermostat and we shared her lap blanket in the meantime. "You can't stay here, you know."

"You've already decided? I can't stay in Part Hardy and try to win you back?"

"Oh! No, that's not what I meant. I mean you can't stay here, at my house ... overnight. It's a small town and appearances matter. You know what I mean. Gossip could cost me a job that I love. I won't take that chance."

"Whoa. You really had me going there for a minute. It's a fine Friday evening. Would you care to step out on a dinner date, Miss Coughlan?"

"Why, Mr. Bradford, I shall quite enjoy such an outing. Who will chaperone?"

"I know a Dodge pickup truck with a long shift lever that's always in the way."

***

There was so much I wanted to tell Bonnie. It was hard to hold back, but I managed. I wanted to know all she had to say, too. Still, it took extra effort to avoid dominating our conversation. And I certainly didn't want to blurt out some stupid remark. Now the danger was that I again wanted to propose marriage and that subject must wait until she'd be ready to hear it.

After she had told all about going back to college, her student teaching and coming to this town at the end of the highway, she said something, said it in such a matter-of-fact tone, as if it was just like an observation of the weather. It sent my hopes sky high. "The school district has an opening for a part-time support person in special ed."

She went on to tell more of her current assignment, about the kids who kept her excited or horribly frustrated or both at once. All the while, that bit of news about a local job opening stayed on my mind.

We left the restaurant, climbed into the chaperone where I asked, "Where do the kids go to park and make out?

"You really want to keep me from a second year in North Vancouver Island, don't you."

"No, I tease. I just want to hold you and kiss your face. It's been so long, and everything I felt before is coming back."

Bonnie had tears running down her face.

"What's wrong? Did I say something stupid and wrong again?"

"I wish I could let you stay with me. At my house, I mean. Still, it's probably for the best that we not rush in. What if we're fooling ourselves?"

"Speaking of which, I better find a hotel room. I plumb forgot."

"That shouldn't be a problem in winter."

We said good night with a long hug and kiss, and a plan for Saturday. We'd take a drive and see the sights of the island's forest and north shore.

Into the night at the hotel I wrote page after page. At the top of the third page I wrote, "I came from suburban Chicago's North Shore and found myself on another north shore where nothing is the same beyond name and water. 'Found myself'? Hmm…"

***

Life soon settled into a comfortable routine of meals and whatever time Bonnie and I could be together. She was burdened with a first year teacher's lesson planning and the overcoming of times when the plan didn't work. I was getting adjusted to a job like none I'd ever had before: half time resource room aide to school kids with disabilities that kept them from fitting into some regular class routines. I also enrolled in a couple classes through the new North Island Community College. With no real campus and a distance learning experimental model I was pretty much able to create my own program. With my transcript from three mediocre years at Yankton, all I needed was to fill in some blanks to get certified for the position I already held. Both my tutoring with special needs kids one or two at a time and my college work via phone, mobile unit and mail were a perfect fit for solitary Wally. Even though it wasn't about me, it worked well for me and I did a good job. So, there.

***

On the first of June 1977, wearing suit and tie with dessert about to be served after a nice restaurant dinner, I got down on one knee. Bonnie agreed to marry me and we made plans for an engagement announcement trip to Kamloops and Winnetka at end of term. I was finally ready to face my family. I thought, "With a future bride at my side they'll surely be happy for me. Even Bradfords can handle that, right? Eh?"

(35)

We arrived two hours behind schedule. We had carefully arranged our travel to be at the Coughlan's house by five o'clock, in time to make our big announcement before supper; Mrs. Coughlan was expecting us at that time. It was after seven when we pulled up to the curb. All because of the jewelry store tussle.

This was not my fault. As a politician or business leader might say, "I take full responsibility, but it was not my fault." Port Hardy had a nice little jewelry store. I had picked out nice rings. I nearly bought them, but for once I remembered. I reminded myself, "You're not the decider, Trey. She will wear them. She should have a say." Still, I almost bought, encouraged by the jeweler, looking at a big sale, as he gave assurances about his return policy.

Bonnie wouldn't even go to the store with me. I asked, "Why?"

Her only explanation was, "We're going through Vancouver. We can get a better deal there with more choices."

I didn't care about better deals. I wanted to see that big diamond on my beloved's ring finger. I wanted to watch as she drew everyone's attention to it. I wanted it now where her friends would see before summer break. I wanted tangible evidence that she wouldn't betray me or our relationship.

***

We shopped in Vancouver on the way. I spotted an even larger stone at the same price I had almost paid on the Island. Bonnie's practical nature came out full bore. I admired large stones and rings with many small stones. She shook her head.

After a half hour of wrangling we went to lunch. Before the waitress brought menus we agreed that we would not discuss jewelry until after we had eaten. It was a quiet lunch. As soon as we were out the door, Bonnie asked, "Do you want to stay at Port Hardy? I mean, how long do we want to live on the Island?"

"I'd like to say, if you do. I just want to live where you are."

"I don't want to change too soon after I get permanent status, at least. And I like the atmosphere of our school. But you know it's typical for the woman to follow where the man's work takes him."

"We're not typical then. Come on," I gave her arm a light tug, "the light changed. We can cross."

"Okay, so let's get a nice little set of rings. You can wear a gold band when you're not working on motors. Just remember to take it off when you are doing that risky work. Let's get something reasonable so we can put together a down payment on a house. A real house with a foundation. No more trailer."

"Is that what this is about? Do you have any idea how easy I can make that down payment? And more?"

"Easily—I like adverbs. You certainly seemed anxious to get that job at the school."

"Yeah. Part time, pay the rent, and a wallet fat with bills. We've talked about this. You just can't wrap your head around it, can you?"

"I guess not. But I'm still not going to wear the biggest engagement ring in Port Hardy history. So, give up that idea." We were standing in front of the jewelry store. I looked in and saw the jeweler watching us, waiting for his sale.

Inside, Bonnie chose. I settled up with the man. It was a tasteful, attractive, not ostentatious setting. We went back to wandering and another café for coffee while the rings were given a hurry-up resizing.

We were hours behind our promised schedule, but Bonnie could now flash our announcement for family and friends in Kamloops.

*****

She didn't have a chance. Agnes watched us pull to the curb. "Oh, Bonnie honey, let me look at you," she shouted as she dashed to meet us as we clambered out of Bonnie's little Toyota. Keeping her eyes on Bonnie's face, Mrs. Coughlan took both Bonnie's hands in hers. I watched closely as she probed at fingers with her thumb until she felt what she was searching for while looking eye to eye with Bonnie. Smiles spread across both faces and they turned to look at me. I smiled, too.

"I'm sorry we're so late, Mrs. Coughlan," I said.

"Don't worry about it, Mr. Bradford. Ed said, he did, 'Don't expect them that early. It's a slow trip with the ferry and all.' I made chili in the crock pot so it's ready any time."

"Crock pot? Is that something new, Mom?"

"My-my, you do live at the end of the world, don't you." Then, in a stage whisper, she said, "Tell Wally he can still call us Agnes and Ed. Or he can call us Mom and Dad. No need for all this 'Mrs. Coughlan'."

"Thank you, Agnes." I let her know that the whisper was heard.

She was saying, "Congratulations, you two," as Edward came down the front steps with an old Brownie camera in his hand.

"Are they? Were you right, Aggie?" he asked.

"Just look at them, Ed. You can see the sparkle without you seeing the ring."

It took me a moment to recognize the bearded young man sauntering out of the house. Bonnie confirmed that this was her brother fully grown by shouting, "Ben! I was worried you couldn't come." She ran to greet him and wave her left hand in his face.

"About time, Sis."

"Oh? Did you think you'd beat your old sister to the altar?"

"Possibly."

"Is there someone? Is she here?"

"She's in Prince George. She couldn't get time off work. In fact, I'm heading back up there tomorrow. I have a big project proposal to finish up for my senior independent study."

With hugs all around, examination of the engagement ring resulting in exclamations about the grand size of the small diamond and more hugs, we went in for supper. Bonnie and Ben made the most of their one evening. They talked. I listened and tried to figure out the inside jokes.

***

We had a happy few days sharing the news with Bonnie's friends. Agnes pushed us to prepare an announcement for the newspaper. That meant setting a wedding date. We, at least I, hadn't given any thought to when the ceremony and party should take place, or how. Bonnie brought out her resolute practicality again. We decided to be married the first

Saturday of September in Kamloops. We'd have just a week for honeymoon before beginning the school term. I gave no thought to the pressure Bonnie would be under, no matter how simple our plan.

Details of those few days are in the journal, book 117, June 26 and following. There's just one more little thing I must mention here. I came in for breakfast that first morning at Coughlan's and stopped to listen just short of the kitchen where Bonnie and Agnes were talking. I heard Agnes say, "You've lost weight since Christmas, haven't you."

"I'm trying, Mom. I do so want to fit into a nice wedding dress. I know Wally would like me to slim down. I don't think he's even noticed. At least he hasn't said anything."

"Well, don't expect him to say a word. Not after what happened."

"Her mother absolutely knows all about it." With that thought I backed up a few steps and made a noisier approach. Ben had caught me, but he didn't say anything.

(36)

We drove the Trans-Canada through the mountains. Bonnie didn't complain about the way I managed to do almost all the driving in her car.

At Calgary she did *not* ask, "Why aren't we turning south to the USA." I could tell she wanted to, but may have heard me mention something about Medicine Hat. I deeply desired to find Hiram and Prudence. I wanted to thank Hy in person for encouraging me. 'Encourage': That's a good word. He inspired me to be 'in courage' to find my Bonnie.

It took two calls to get directions and find the house. Pru put the iced tea in our hands as soon as the hugs and introduction were done. A full meal was nearly ready even though it was mid-afternoon. Bonnie understood then why we hadn't stopped closer to noon. Hiram pulled us out the back door to tour his fenced back yard. He was still farming. A garden of tomatoes, sweet corn, pumpkins, string beans that required a climbing trellis, and more filled the lot. The tour took us to every vegetable. Hiram carried a hoe to attack any new weeds, but mostly to point and brag. We enjoyed some early raspberries at the back fence.

On the road again, Bonnie asked, "We could head south now and see your Montana mountain haunts I've heard about so often."

"On the way back." My answer was terse. I didn't want to admit that I was putting off the border crossing. At that point I didn't know where that would be. At Regina she asked, "Can we head for the border now?" At Winnipeg she asked again. When I didn't answer, she asked real questions. "Are you afraid of something? Is it the amnesty you don't trust? Or is it about facing your father? Please, Wally, talk to me. Whatever it is, I'll understand."

That was just it. I wasn't sure I trusted her to understand. I wasn't even sure what was making me avoid the international boundary. "I've been in Canada a long time and I never travelled this far east. I wanted to see some more of the country."

"That's not the reason. We both know it."

"Yeah, you're right. I don't know what the real reason is. Maybe it's because I won't be able to explain myself to Junior. But then, I never could. Not so he'd ever pay attention, not to the real me. It was always about what he wanted me to be, or do. So what the hell."

Bonnie gently laid her hand on my forearm and inched a little closer to me, belted in her bucket seat with gear shift and parking brake between us. "I'm sorry. I guess to truly understand I have to meet your people."

"Yeah, well, we have to be careful they don't eat you alive."

Bonnie gave that a thoughtful nod and turned to her highway map. "It looks like your last chance is Fort Frances; unless you intend to go clear to Montreal or something."

"No. Fort Frances it is. Or, as we U.S. Americans call that border station, International Falls, Minnesota."

"Wallace Bradford, you are a Canadian. By choice and betrothal, and Port Hardy, BC is your home at the end of the road. Born and raised in Kamloops, same as me. Your friend Hiram told me so."

"Amen. I love you, you know. Wherever you are is close enough to call it home for this ex-patriate."

***

At the bridge that connects Fort Frances and International Falls an American border agent looked hard at me, then at Bonnie. We gave him identification with BC driver licenses which he read letter by letter moving his lips. He leaned over a big gut hanging over his belt into the open window, pushed his cap back on his head revealing a gray crewcut, pointed to a parking area and said, "Pull on over there. I got a couple more things to check out wit yuz."

Hearing his accent, I said, "You're not from Minnesota, are you."

He pointed to the lot again, "Don't be holdin' up dese good folks behindja."

We got out of the car, as requested; and waited, as ordered, while he went into the office. He brought a clipboard and asked, "Anyting to declare?"

I told him about the new diamond that would go back with us.

He shook his head, "Don't be shittin' wid me, kid. Any outstanding warrants?"

Now we were getting into his real motives. "I left the United States in 1970 after I was sent a draft notice. Yeah, there might be a warrant, but it's covered in the amnesty."

"How 'bout you, Missy? Any warrants? Bringing in drugs or whatnot?"

"No, sir; no to all that," Bonnie said. She was starting to shiver, warm as it was.

"Come with me, Mister. You can if you want, Miss."

Bonnie locked the car and followed us into the building. The agent had us sit on a bench, told us to wait there. Then he disappeared. After a half hour or more, a younger uniformed agent approached. He looked about my age.

"Sorry to keep you waiting," he said. "What can I do for you?"

"What can you do? Give us a thirty day ticket to visit my American family. You can do that." I was getting testy.

"I'll be right back." He turned to leave. I noted the time.

He did come right back with our thirty day pass. As he handed it to me, he said, "There weren't any warrants on you. Enjoy your stay, Miss; and welcome home, Sir. Oh, and congratulations. Agent Miller said you just got engaged." Then he moved closer to me and said in a much softer voice, "I hope you can forgive him. He saw some rough combat in Korea. He doesn't have much use for draft dodgers ... or should I say avoiders."

Bonnie noticed something in this, and said, "And you're cool with it, even though you were in Nam, eh. Am I right?"

He nodded a slow nod and turned to find either his next task or an opportunity to flirt with the only female staff member in sight. Over his shoulder he said, "Get outa here."

Bonnie seemed to be studying my face as we got back in the car. She clearly wanted to say something, but my expression must have alerted her to keep silent for now. I hardly breathed until we stopped at a red light. I let out a long breath, said, "Welcome to America," and forced myself to smile.

(37)

"This is it." I pulled the key and opened the driver door.

"Just a sec." Bonnie grabbed my arm and held me in the seat.

"What? Are you praying or something?"

"Or something. Just give me a moment, okay? Let's get the right picture in mind. What do we see when the door opens?" She looked across the wide lawn to the big front entry at the huge house – higher and wider than my memory of it.

"I've been thinking about that ever since we cruised through Kenora. We used to go on fishing vacations up there, so it's been on my mind. If you don't believe me, just take a look at my last couple-three journal entries."

"Okay, I'm ready. Are you?"

"Never. Nope. So ... ready or not, here we come." In the same instant we both hopped out of the car.

***

"Hmm, no answer." I pushed the doorbell button again. "Somebody's always here at this time of day."

"Wally, it's been like seven or eight years. Things change. You did send that letter, didn't you? They are expecting you, right?"

"Yeah. I sent it. I wasn't sure we'd get here today, though. Maybe somebody's out back." I led Bonnie around the house. We didn't have to scale the tall fence because the gate key was still hidden in the same old place.

"Whoa! There's something new."

"What's new?"

"The swimming pool. Pretty weird. The lake's right there. It's an easy walk to a nice public beach, even with the uphill climb to get home."

"Would you have said that back when you were a kid here?" Bonnie, teacher of teenagers, saw through me.

"You know me too well. I just said what Junior told me when I argued for building a pool. Maybe I'm pissed because they did it after I left."

"No. Be fair to yourself, Sweetie. You don't think like a rich kid anymore, and," she took a slow, deep breath. "And that might be why you're so apprehensive about seeing your father."

I nodded, heaved a giant sigh, and, aware that she was right, changed the subject. "No one's around at all, so we have a choice. We can wait on the terrace, or take a little tour, see the local sights, and check back later."

"Let's walk down to the beach."

"We'll have to pay. Is that practical?" I took the gentle shoulder punch and we went for a walk.

When no one answered the door two hours later, we found a pay phone, found the listing and dialed Senior's number. Gram answered after several rings. "Wally? Really? Oh, it has been so long. Where are you? Still in Canada?"

"I'm in Winnetka, Gram. There's nobody at the house."

"Oh, dear. You're here and your parents are in Europe somewhere. I think they're on the way home soon. Char can tell you."

"Can you give me her number, Gram?"

"Oh, Wally, just come over. I sold the house, you know. I'm in a nice village for old folks in Lake Forest now." She gave me the address. I had her repeat it a couple times.

"Bonnie, we're going to see Gram in Lake Forest," I said as I hung up. "She said Junior and Mom are in Europe.

"So I heard. What'd she say about Senior?"

"Nothing. In fact, she said 'I' not 'we'. Like he died and no one told me."

"You haven't been easy for them to find, so don't be too hard on them."

"As if they'd even try. I can always trust my family to be not worth trusting, you know."

"Wallace Bradford three, I'm about to say something right now. I hope it isn't a deal breaker, but if it is, I'll let you return the rings."

"No way! Nothing can break, no-no-no. We are together forever."

"Good, because here it is, Wally." She paused, struggling to get it out. Then in a rush of words, said, "You could lose some weight."

The words left me speechless. Bonnie finally broke the silence. "The weight on your mind, you must see that. It isn't about you. Your family grieved when Senior died. Assuming he did and that's why Gram used a singular pronoun. You have to grieve now. So, you blame. It's okay."

She was about to say more, but I stopped her. "I see. I've been tossing off these weights ever since I ... since I don't know when. And it all piles back in an instant. Thank you, my love. I could lose some weight, all right. Dieting's hard, ain't it?"

"How would I know?"

"Aw come now, I'm not in a complete fog. I have noticed. But what's there to say? I love you every which way." I was about to mention the way I puffed up when I saw other guys' heads turn. I caught myself in time, wondering whether or not that had always happened.

Bonnie gave my hand a squeeze and we let the rest go.

***

A brown woman in a white uniform showed us into a modest sitting room in Gram's suite. It took a moment for my eyes to adjust to the bright and shadow. The only light was a glare from a foot wide opening between the heavy drapes covering a large window. When she spoke I spotted Gram sitting in the glare.

"Where've you been, Trey? It has been a long, long time." Gram started in without saying hello or even reaching out from her chair.

I edged over to take her hand. "Hi, Gram. It's good to see you after so long. I've been in Canada, you know. Oh, there's someone I want you to meet." Bonnie was hanging back in the doorway. I motioned to her to come closer. "This is Bonnie, my fiancée. Bonnie Coughlan. We're getting married in September."

"Fiancée, my my. Come closer, dear, my eyes are failing." Bonnie bent next to Gram. "Where're you from, Miss Coughlan? Is your family nearby?"

"Not near at all, Mrs. Bradford. I come from Kamloops, British Columbia. Wally and I both live in Port Hardy, now." Bonnie stood up from her uncomfortable squat.

"Fort Harvey, Cameraloops. I've never heard of these places."

"Nor have I, I whispered in Bonnie's ear."

"What's that, Trey? Why do you want to go and marry a Canadian girl from the frozen wastes way out west?"

"That's easy to answer, Gram. I love her and she said yes when I asked."

"Huh. When's the baby due, then?"

Bonnie stiffened, glared at Gram and said through clenched teeth. "Mrs. Bradford, really! I would expect when we conceive a child it'll take about nine more months."

The question and her tone made it time for us to leave, so I asked, "Can you give me Linda and Char's phone numbers, please, Gram?"

"They are all in my datebook there." She lifted her arm and flicked her fingers toward the little desk beside the bedroom door. I found the book, copied all the family numbers. Bryan had his own number now, too. I had no idea where, or if, he was in college. Maybe he'd already graduated. While his older brother is working and still messing around with community college.

"We have to go, Gram. I'll look in again tomorrow."

"Just a moment, Trey. I'm sorry for saying that." She said this with a smirk. "But, you know, why else would you." It wasn't a question and she continued before I had a chance to react. "It got Linda stuck with that dull man of hers, you know. I suppose you're finally ready to join the company and take care of your little chub-deb."

"No. Bonnie is a professional educator and I am going into my own business in Port—with a 'P'—Hardy with a 'd'. Where we live. Good night, Grandmother."

"There's another thing you owe me an apology for. Where were you when Wallace died, my husband?"

"No one told me. I didn't know until right now."

"Hiding out in the wilds of Canada, how could they?"

"Mr. Boyer knew." I stomped out the door, tugging Bonnie along.

Once outside the building, I paused to catch my breath and said, "I'm sorry, Bonnie. And to think—she's the nice one. Used to be, at any rate."

38

"What was that you said about starting a business?" Bonnie wanted to know.

"It's just an idea. Nothing solid. Although I might have to pretend it's so real that I'm about to sign papers. That might keep Junior and company off my case."

"Okay, but what's your idea?"

"Auto repair. My friend Butch, the pump jockey who once pegged me as a creepy pervert, wants to retire. I could buy or lease and make the Esso station a go-to shop for honest, quality repair work. There's a couple of our slow guys I tutored last year that I think I could train to work the pumps and do routine jobs."

"You've been giving this some thought. Why haven't you said anything before?"

"Well, you see, I hear there's a wedding coming up and the bride would like a house where the winter wind doesn't blow through the floor. Priorities, maybe? Priority one this minute is to find a phone and call Char or, if I have to, Linda. I was gonna call from Gram's, but I had to get out."

"Me, too; you say she's the nice one, eh. Has being widowed made her bitter?"

"Or she's been part of the Bradford world too long. You always find a reason or some way to be understanding when people are being asses, don't you."

"It's something my students are teaching me, yeah. Doesn't mean it's acceptable, just that it won't ever change if you don't try to understand what's behind it."

***

"Hullo," the Husband answered the phone in a hurried, abrupt tone.

"Hey, um, is Char there?"

"Who's calling?"

"It's Wally, er, Trey, her brother. Can I talk to her?"

"Well, I'll be damned. We thought you were gone forever. Are you still in Canada?"

"Not at the moment. We're at a gas station on the Skokie Highway. Can I talk to Char, please?"

"In town, I'll be damned. You better not have designs on my office. I'm the only one keeping the company going. Your old dad is about to destroy it."

A voice in the background asked, "Who is it, hon?"

"It's your brother Trey. He's in town."

Suddenly Char was on the line and I sighed in relief. I much preferred to connect with Char, the family mediator, over Linda, the know-it-all. I certainly didn't want to hear any more of the Husband's complaining about Junior when he'd never say anything of the sort to the man's face.

Char cut our phone talk short with directions to their new house in Deerfield. She invited me to stay there for two days until Junior and Kat, that is Dad and Mom, returned from their travels. I let her know that I wasn't alone. She said, "Bring your friend. We have lots of room."

When we got back into the car, I wondered aloud, "Will my sister have a separate beds rule like your folks?" I quickly added, "Nothing against them. We expect that from parents, even when they happily send us off together on a long road trip. But Char? I don't know. It has been so long."

Char was pointing upstairs, ready to guide me to an upstairs room with my bag. She'd send 'my friend' to the guest or nanny suite beyond the kitchen. When she saw the ring and we told her our plans she guided both of us to the suite and sent the Husband to the wine cellar to find something for celebrating. She put their two little boys to bed before we opened the wine.

"Enjoy it while you can, Trey and Bonnie," Char said as she lifted her glass in a warning toast. She took a sip and added, "I'll be surprised if Dad celebrates."

***

The next morning, while we were getting dressed, Bonnie and I were considering the day ahead and rehashing the previous day. "Well, now you've met both Charlottes," I said. "Do you see any difference?"

Bonnie considered the question for a moment before she answered. "Yes and no. There are big differences in the way they treated us, of course. Your Gram is old enough that she doesn't give a shit. If she even noticed, I don't think she cared that we went away angry. Char's careful. Keep things calm. No waves. If she'd been with us at your Gram's, she'd have left in tears. She'd have failed to keep the peace, and she'd blame herself."

"I see. That's the yes. What's the 'no'?"

"I'm overanalyzing, aren't I."

"Yeah, but go on."

"Okay. There's a lot she keeps hidden. I'd guess she sees the family and company as one and the same, if what you say about them is accurate. I wasn't so sure, but I'm starting to see it. She probably resents that she's expected to stand behind her husband as company man when she'd do the job better."

"I'm a male chauvinist pig and even I resent it. Do you think Char would do better?"

"I have no idea, but I'd lay odds that she thinks so."

***

We had another day and a half before Junior, Kat and Bryan were due at O'Hare. On our way to a tourist outing we stopped at Rosehill Cemetery and put flowers on my maternal grandparents' graves. I don't remember them and I'd never visited the cemetery before, but Bonnie had asked about them.

Then we spent the afternoon at the Field Museum. It was a wonderful day. Touring a natural history museum with a history and social teacher is a marvel of an experience. At least my tour with that certain teacher and former museum guide beside me was. Details, as always, are in the journal.

***

Linda absolutely refused to allow us to meet the plane with them. Char explained, "It wouldn't be fair to them, Wally. Learning you're engaged and going back to Canada while we're standing at the baggage claim? No way."

"I will not let you make the public spectacle that would be," Linda added. She hadn't heard the part about returning to Canada before this. "How can you even consider going back? The company could really use some fresh ideas. You've been seeing the world from a different point of view. You might be the guy to bring some new life to Bradford and Son."

I just shook my head. I had no good answer until that night when I wrote one in my journal. It was rude.

***

Bonnie picked up Char's home telephone because it was ringing. I was too late saying, "Let the answering machine pick up." Bonnie was right. The call was from Char at the airport.

"Okay," I heard Bonnie say. "We'll head that way now and meet you all there."

She hung up and turned to me, "Char says the plane finally arrived, late. She told your folks that you're here. We're supposed to go to the Winnetka house and meet them."

"That I'm here. Not that we're here. Not even Trey and his girlfriend. Figures."

"You can't expect your sisters to be answering questions about me right away. Let them talk about the trip first. It really is not about you."

"It will be soon enough."

"Yes. And you're in charge of that part." She paused and added while grabbing me into a hug, "And I'll do my utmost to look worthy of their son."

"And if half your best doesn't get 'em, they're not worthy of you. Of course, I'm not either, but we can have that discussion later."

Bonnie took the bait without words. The hug grew more intense, making me even hornier.

***

"How did you get in?" Junior greeted us as he found us waiting on the terrace. We were absorbed in watching the sailboats out on Lake Michigan and didn't hear them arrive.

177

I jumped up. "Dad, hey. How was the European vacation? I want you to meet Bonnie." She was standing now. I noticed that she was keeping her left hand out of sight. "This is Bonnie Coughlan, my fiancée."

"No, really, Trey. How did you get in the yard?"

I did not punch him. I mentally backed away. We hadn't talked for five years and at that time he hung up on me. "Through the gate, Junior." I had long thought of him as Wallace Junior, not Dad. Now I said it to his face.

"The gate was locked, Son."

Ah, he noticed. "The key's been hidden in the same place for at least fifteen years that I know of. We, meaning Bonnie and I, soon to be my wife, who I'm trying to introduce to you, let ourselves in."

"Let's go in the house. We have to talk."

I shrugged and followed. Bonnie grabbed my hand and held it tight. We squeezed through the patio door side by side. As we entered we heard Junior angrily say to Linda, "I don't give a damn. Just order me something."

She was sitting on a stool at the breakfast bar writing on a torn envelope. Mom was peering into the open refrigerator, writing a list. Linda beckoned to us, "Trey, come here. You too, um, Brenda."

"Bonnie. Her name is Bonnie." We obeyed her call.

"What do you kids want? I'm about to order some Chinese."

The conversation pulled Mom's attention away from her grocery list. "Oh, Trey! They said you were here, but I didn't know you were here here — at the house. Come here, son. And who's this?"

Junior was grumbling something under his breath. I strained to hear. Don't ask me why. I heard, "Kid can't remember to call his mother, but he can still break into the yard."

We let Mom lead us out to the room that she called the TV room and Junior called the library. We slid onto the love seat. Mom pushed Junior out and pulled an armless straight back chair around to face us from a higher position. Before Mom could take control of an interview, I asked, "What's with Junior? Picking a fight about the gate key and he won't even acknowledge Bonnie."

"Is that an engagement ring I see?"

"I'm pleased to meet you, Mrs. Bradford." Bonnie extended her right hand. The hand shake was limp, but it happened. "I'm Bonnie Coughlan. Wally and I will be married the third of September. I hope you all can come." Now she displayed the ring.

Mom took Bonnie's extended fingers, carefully examined the stone and said, "Hmpf." She let go of Bonnie's hand and added, "That's less than two months away. How can you possibly be ready? There's so much to prepare. Why, the church may not even be available for the ceremony. Have you done anything?"

"The wedding will be in Kamloops, Mom. Bonnie likes to keep things simple, as best she can. She has a mother of the bride to do the worrying for us."

"Kam Loops? What is that? Where is it?"

"In British Columbia, Mom. It's a pretty good sized town. Bonnie grew up there. Now we both live in Port Hardy. That's on Vancouver Island. It's a beautiful place. You'll love it when you come for a visit."

"But you'll be moving here. You must take your place in the company. All will be forgiven. Just give your father a little time."

"Forgiven? I can try to forgive, but I can't live here. I cannot work at Bradford and Son."

Mom gave me a bitter stare and shook her head, then turned to Bonnie with a phony smile. "Do you have any idea what you're getting into with my ungrateful son? You might want to think about it long and hard, missy."

"I have a fair idea, ma'am."

"If you only knew, Mom. If you only knew."

"Knew what, Trey?"

I shook my head and stood to go. I didn't know where, but someplace other than this room.

Bonnie tried to say enough, which caused me to stop and turn around. "What Wally can't tell you, Mrs. Bradford, is that we both have had much time apart to consider other options. Finding each other again, at least for me, is finding the rest of myself. So, I'll take my chances with your son."

***

"Chinese is here. We're out on the terrace," Char announced from the doorway.

"How long have you been standing there?" It was Mom who asked, but we all thought the question.

Char didn't answer. Instead she reiterated, "Come out back and have some sweet and sour before it gets cold. That would make it fit the mood too, too well."

***

Bonnie tried for understanding, as her students taught her. "You must be exhausted, Mrs. Bradford. It has to be difficult with us bringing our news when you've just stepped off a long flight across many time zones."

Kat nodded and gave Bonnie's hand a little squeeze as we shuffled through the kitchen.

"Where's Bryan?" When we were all gathered on the terrace I realized that I hadn't seen my younger brother.

"He stayed in Germany, Trey. He's doing a year abroad, holding onto student status at Perdue. He's becoming a perennial—maybe I should say professional—student." Linda often added commentary to a simple answer.

"Well, he's getting a real education. He's already showing himself to be a great asset to the company," Junior countered, and turned it into criticism of his other son. "So Trey, did you ever finish college while you were hiding out? Or are those three years and thousands just dumped down the drain?"

I glared at Junior with a tight lipped refusal to give any answer. Why let the fight start? I forked in a mouthful of fried rice and chewed.

Bonnie tried to smooth things over. "Wally has been working with some of our most difficult students in the Port Hardy schools. Plus he's been adding some coursework in that area through North Island College."

"North Island? Sounds like a junior college. Is that what you're down to, boy? The liberal arts dropout moves up to glorified high school?"

Bonnie was about to try again. I said, "Don't bother, Bonnie. It isn't worth it."

She insisted. "Think what you like, Mr. Bradford, but your son is doing much good work. With or without that degree. He may soon have his own business, too. So, you see, your guidance bringing him up isn't lost."

"Your own business? What? Like a dope pusher?"

"See, Bonnie? Why bother."

"He plans to own a gas station and add quality car repairs with it. He intends to train some of his special education students, too. They'll have real jobs helping customers because of your son, Mr. Bradford."

"No college degree so they have you teach the retards. Is that how it works?"

Bonnie could not be dissuaded. "Have you ever seen any of Wally's writing? He keeps a journal every day. He's a natural writer. Someday, he'll put his journals aside and write a book, a best seller. You will not be a hero in that story."

I sat there, shoveling in the fried rice, sampling tasty dishes from all the little boxes, and waiting. How will Junior react to that? I couldn't remember it ever happening before, but he had nothing more to say. Soon nieces and nephews, an increase from a single toddler to five cousins since I last saw my family, were released to play or TV. After a few minutes Mom began to tell about sights and events from their three weeks in Europe. Junior still sat looking stunned. The Husbands looked over at him with worried glances. I resisted the urge to give him a final push. Remembering the activities during high school he kept hidden from Junior and Kay, I pictured Bryan in Germany, going from brewery to brewery tasting and guzzling. But I didn't say it.

When supper began I was sure I had no appetite, expecting the argument to commence. Now I was stuffed and the food was gone. I gave Bonnie a signal and we stood to make our escape. I tried for a civil goodbye, "I'm glad you got to meet my Bonnie. We need to make it an early night. We're expected in Sioux Falls tomorrow. Don't forget to mark your calendars and make your plans. September third, Kamloops, British Columbia, Canada. The wedding of the year. But please leave all shoulder chips in Illinois. For Bonnie's sake, okay?"

When Char started to loan us a house key the Husband intervened. He was glad for an excuse to go home to his television sports and rode with us to Deerfield. Bonnie crammed herself into the little Corolla's back seat pushing our belongings into a tighter pile.

39

We'd followed the by-pass around Rockford and I relaxed a bit as we entered truly rural regions. "Next stop Sac City, Iowa for a farmer's dinner."

"Umm, I think your bladder will be full and the gas tank empty before then, Dearest."

"You know what I mean."

Slowed by construction, it was mid-afternoon when we reached Pete's house and met his wife and children. His parents arrived right behind us, loaded with casserole and cherry pie.

"Everybody lives in town now, eh?"

"Yeah, it's easier with all the kids activities, don'tcha know," Pete said. "And you tell me you've been working on a farm. Aren't you the guy who couldn't imagine that life when we were sophomores?"

"Okay, Pete, you won that one. I'm still ahead, though."

"Baloney."

After dinner, as we were looking at wristwatches ready to get back on the road, I made an impulsive pitch. "How'd you like to stand up with me. Be my best man, Peter."

"When's the wedding again?"

"September third."

"Okay, Mr. Farmhand, I know you're joking."

"Why? No, I'm serious. I think I understand, though. Harvesting something, right?"

"Or so close to it to be damn busy. Thanks for the offer, though. I didn't think we were that close."

I nodded and didn't admit that I didn't have many male friends, or that I'd already asked Garret—fisherman, friend and husband of Gretchen, the special education teacher I assisted.

***

"Why Sioux Falls? I thought we were going to Yankton to visit your college." Bonnie asked as we got back on the highway.

"Didn't I tell you? I called the college and they said Dr. Graves retired to the city. She's expecting us tomorrow morning."

"So we are going to Yankton, too, right?"

"Yeah. Of course hardly anybody'll be around in the middle of summer."

***

Dr. Graves met us at the main door and showed us around. The building wasn't an old peoples' home but it catered to retired people and had a central dining room. As we rode the elevator to her third floor apartment, she asked me, "Did you bring me some reading material, Wallace?"

"You still want to look at my weird journals?"

"I take it you're still writing; wonderful. If you're willing, I would like to see a few samples. I'm curious to see how your writing has grown."

I followed Bonnie's gaze as she perused the desk under the window. Next to an electric typewriter were stacks of paper. A wastebasket beside the desk overflowed with crumpled typed pages. Bonnie turned back to the conversation as I was telling Elaine that I had my most recent journals in the car. Bonnie asked the professor, "Are you writing a book?"

"I wrote a novel forty years ago. It was never published, of course. I'm trying again. As you can see by the mess, it isn't going well. I never believed that old adage, 'Those who can, do. Those who can't, teach.' But, here I am, struggling with words in rows after all those years teaching literature and creative writing."

"So, you have an ulterior motive, perhaps? Maybe you'd like to read some of Wally's personal diaries to get some ideas for your story."

183

I blurted, "Bonnie, I don't think…" Dr. Graves interrupted me before I finished.

"I was not thinking along those lines, dear. Are Wally's notes that interesting, do you think? If that is so, I hope I'll be allowed to see what he has. I could use a spark to get my novel off dead center."

After three or four cups of instant coffee, she went down with us. I handed her three journal notebooks from the car. "Can we take you to breakfast tomorrow and retrieve the books, Elaine?"

"Excellent. Eight o'clock. I'll be waiting here."

Bonnie and I decided to take a day trip to Yankton and stay at Sioux Falls another night. To be honest, I decided and Bonnie didn't disagree.

***

We were having lunch at a sandwich shop within sight of the campus in Vermillion. "Are you sure it was a good idea to leave all the journals with the prof?" Bonnie asked.

"Why not? She got me started. She was a mentor and guide all along."

"Well, now she's desperate to write a novel. She liked the notion of stealing material or ideas from your work."

"Is it stealing? If something I wrote helps her, it'll be fiction and changed to fit her experiences or imagination."

"I don't know why, but it bothers me. It's so personal. And … and if anybody uses those notes to write a novel, it should be you."

"If that ever happens…" I stopped, sipped at my Pepsi, pulled a slice of green pepper out of my sandwich and gnawed at it. Bonnie ate her pickle and waited (impatiently, I could see). Finally I said, and Bonnie understood in spite of my talking around a mouthful of ham, cheese and sourdough bread, "When that happens, it will be nothing like whatever the good Doc Graves comes up with." I swallowed and added with a smile, "She'll enjoy grading my assignment today, too. We can expect to see some red pencil nasties about lack of clarity and odd constructions in the morning."

"And you look forward to that?"

"Of course. Don't your students like it when the corrections you give help them see that they're learning something useful?"

"I tend to do that verbally. I sit down with each of them and go over their essays. That way I can tell if I'm getting through."

"That's beautiful. They're young and you're willing to take that extra time. You should be paid more."

"Tell it to the Legislative Assembly."

"So, tell me. Say a student of yours writes a paper that includes some historical facts or insights that teach you something new. You can't tell me you don't use that knowledge because that would be stealing their work."

"Good point. Let's go to Yankton."

***

As expected, the campus was deserted. We walked around town and I showed Bonnie the apartment building where someone she wasn't to know about and I worked on creative writing assignments and other things. I stood there on the sidewalk, staring at the window I'd often gazed through from the other direction.

Bonnie poked me in the ribs to yank me out of my reverie. "Whoever she was, Wally, she's entirely in the past."

"What? Oh, yeah, betrayals of the past." I pulled Bonnie closer, forcing my gaze from the window to her face.

"I'd rather not know any more, Wally. Let's go."

"Is this your practical side again? Sparing me? Because, you should know this: the present is bliss. I don't want to screw it up when the future looks real bright."

"You are a weird guy. It's not about you, though. I worry I'd dwell on the past. Mine is enough."

I didn't have anything to add to that. There are things we don't ask about, just because. I gazed, admiring this amazing woman beside me.

Bonnie looked around, then back at me and said, "Are you just gonna stare at my nose, or are you gonna kiss me."

***

Back on campus we spotted a guy with a fat briefcase locking his car. He looked familiar, and young even in the heavy framed eyeglasses with thick lenses. Well, nothing ventured... I approached, "You look familiar somehow. I was a student here in the late sixties."

"Wally? Are you Wally Bradford?"

185

I nodded, "I am. And this is my fiancée Bonnie. Sorry, but I don't remember your name."

"Kermit Schneider. You roomed across the hall from me. You were a year ahead of me. I'm working in admissions now. Don't quote me, but it's becoming a hopeless task."

"Is it really that bad? I heard something similar already today."

"Oh? Where? There's hardly anyone around."

We didn't answer the question. I said, "Yeah, the place is deserted. Is anything open?"

Kermit had some access and took time to tour with us. He lapsed into his prospective student guide persona, forgetting that I was familiar with every nook and cranny.

Along the way, he asked, "Did you ever graduate? You were always kind of a loner back then. But it seems like you just disappeared."

"That's what I did. I was always intending to come back and finish, but I ended up in Canada when the draft was blowing down my neck."

"Canada. Wow. Good for you. My eyesight kept me out, so I never had to face it."

"I think it was the way a couple profs here approached those required religion courses. They gave me the courage to say no. Even though, when Cracker asked me about going conscientious objector, I had to admit it was only about saving my own neck." I was lapsing into dreamy reminiscing.

Bonnie brought me back. "I didn't know that. About your college, I mean. Isn't there some way to keep this school open?"

"We keep trying to find it. Thanks for the encouragement. Maybe if you'd come back and graduate, Mr. Bradford?"

I thought about that statement before I replied. Or was it a question? I shook my head, "No, I'll be in Canada, but it's not about me, is it."

***

"Thank you for letting me into your life story once again, Wallace," Dr. Graves said to begin our conversation as we settled into the booth for a pancake house breakfast. "Or should I say your lives, but from Wally's point of view."

"Oh? What's he say about me?" Bonnie asked without looking up from the menu.

"He's quite enamored of you, Miss Coughlan. I'm surprised. You really haven't read any of it? Does he lock them away?"

"No. I just don't. It's personal. And I'm Bonnie."

I was surprised, too. I wrote honestly about our ups and downs, but was always careful not to leave blame for anything on Bonnie, a discipline that was helping me 'get over myself'. I left the notebooks out, assuming she took peeks at them.

Dr. Graves let it go at that and turned back to me. "I find a much more mature man in your writing now, Wallace. When you turn some of your story into a book, try to use complete sentences more often." She said it with a smile and a twinkle in her eye.

She shifted her attention again. "Do you keep a journal, too, Bonnie?"

"No, I write lesson plans and then keep notes on how I have to adapt them, And I try to record some self-evaluation at the end of the day, so I don't make the same mistakes next year."

"Excellent. What do you teach, dear?"

"History and Social in the secondary school. Those extra nightly notes to myself always seem to be dominated by grade nine Canadian history."

"Well, well. Imagine that, Wally. A person can be in love and still do one's job."

Bonnie gave me a quizzical look, so I said, "It's not about me. Mustn't dwell on the past."

"No, it's about your Gram, of course. This trip through your past is a bit of a test that way."

"Yes, dear," said Dr. Graves, "but won't it be best in the long run to know where your man comes from, how he got to the place where he's ready to make a life with you?"

We had all finished our eggs and refused the offer of yet another cup of coffee. "Let's go to Montana, find Sam and look for Cracker."

(40)

"Is anyone staying at the old cabin, Sam?" Bonnie and I had been drinking their coffee and trying to tell Sam and Mary Doakes everything that had happened in the years since I absconded to Canada. At the same time, Sam was itching to tell me about defeats and a new victory that all started with the shooting. He'd been cleared of the most serious charge, served his time and I assumed he'd stayed dry. I thought that was the end of it. It ended for me, once I'd crossed that northern border.

Instead of answering our question, Sam used it as a way to begin his story. "It's hard to spend much time over to the cabin, Wally. It all comes crashing over me any time I step onto that piece of ground."

I had to ponder what Sam said for a moment. When it hit me, I had no words.

"I couldn't sleep after. Every time I closed my eyes I seen that guy Olson, the one you always called the mean bastard. For months when I'd shut my eyes there he'd be, keeling over in a puddle of blood and sawdust. It was self-defense, true enough. But what the hell made me grab the varmint shooter off the rack before I got out of the pickup? I went there to negotiate; it was to keep it out of court. I saw his pistol in the holster. Is that why? To even us up so we could talk? Maybe I wanted a gunfight."

I shook my head, fumbling for something understanding to say.

Sam looked at Bonnie who was gripping the edge of the table, then at me, and went on. "He pulled the handgun. He was about to get a better shot at me. We all know that. But was he? All through the war and I never killed nobody. Come close enough and lost three buddies in it. Which made me into a drunk, or maybe I was going that way regardless. I never figured I'd ever see combat after the war was done. I shut my eyes and I seen him bleeding to death in front of me. I had to do

188

something, get it away somehow, so I hid him. I crawled back inside of a bottle one more time after you disappeared. They sprung me from the hoosegow and my probation included the alcohol counselor. I maintained through those months. When that was done I went out to seal up the cabin. I seen it all in my mind again and I needed a drink so bad."

Mrs. Doakes was nodding. I didn't need to react to that word 'disappear', but I did. "Come on, Sam. You knew where I was going all along."

"Yeah, that's right. But, don'tcha see? I needed to talk it out with somebody who already knew all about it, kinda like I done just now. That was you or Sheriff Law. And I didn't feel like I could say too much to him. He might misconstrue me back into being a murderer if I said something the wrong way. You see how it is? So, I made my peace with help from Jim and Johnny."

Bonnie had been listening attentively to all this, without saying so much as an 'um-hm'. Now she looked at me, then at Sam, relaxed her grip on the table, and asked, "Jim and Johnny?"

Sam answered simply, "Beam and Walker, the whiskey boys."

"Oh, but they've been sent packing since, right?" Bonnie said, with hope in her voice, and then fell silent again.

"Oh yes, thank God," Mary chimed in. "I got my husband back."

"Thank God and AA. I go to meetings regular and I been blessed to help some other fellers along through the steps. Twice I thought I graduated from AA. Now I know better. One day at..."

"I'm sure glad to hear that, Sam," I interrupted, still fumbling for the right words, but settled for those.

"Anyway, kids. The cabin is setting empty and waiting for you. But you ain't on no honeymoon yet. You said the wedding's in September? That right?"

"Yeah. September third. So be there." Bonnie gave my hand squeeze when I said the date.

"Jumping the gun a little then, ain'tcha."

"Oh, Sam, get over yourself. Course you wouldn't wanna remember back when we got hitched. So long ago. I can't forget it, what with morning sickness on my wedding day, but you didn't know about that, I guess." Mary laughed at a memory that wasn't a bit funny at the time.

Sam laughed, too. Bonnie and I looked at each other and squeezed hands a little more. More at ease for having told his story, Sam said, "Purdy girl come into our lives that year. Growed up and married a Billings businessman just to get off the farm. Right, Mary?"

"Not at all, Sam. She married a fine man who happens to have a good little business. So they live out toward Molt where they keep a couple horses. She took a piece of the ranch to the city with her."

***

Sam handed me some keys as we went out to the yard and asked, "You still know how to get there?"

"Where? Molt? Oh, the cabin. I think so, but now you mention it." Of course I knew, but I sensed a way to get a little more time with Sam.

"I'll guide you out then. You can help me keep my wits out there. That okay by you, Mary?" he called back to Mrs. Doakes in the screen porch. "Just follow me. There's a locked gate installed since, so the turn off looks a little different anyhow."

I called to her, too. Or, maybe it was Bonnie who said, "Thanks for everything, Mary."

I turned to Bonnie, "How about I ride with Sam and you keep up with us. Would you mind too much?"

"Oh, I get to drive my own car for a few miles. How generous." Until her sarcastic reply it hadn't occurred to me that I'd been hogging the wheel since Chicago.

Riding with Sam seemed like a good idea at the time; a chance to ask him about Cracker and have a little guy talk. What I didn't consider was how noisy the pickup was and the way Sam's hearing had diminished in the years since we parted. I shouted the name for a third time, "Cracker! Do you know where Cracker is? How can I find Cracker? Graham what's-his-face."

It still took Sam a quarter mile before he replied. "Oh, Cracker, yeah. He don't come this way no more. Ain't seen him in years," he shouted louder than I had. "He might be working for the tribe. Seems like I heard something like that."

I shouted once more, "Too bad I don't have time to tune up this outfit, get it running a little quieter."

Sam said, "What?"

I gave up trying to talk in the moving truck. We picked up the subject sitting on the log beside the fire pit in the yard while Bonnie went on inspecting the cabin's rustic features. "You said Cracker might have a job, what, in the tribal government?"

"I don't know for sure. Seems like sometime back I read something on that. Whatever, he shouldn't be too hard to find if he's still on the reservation."

"Yeah? Do you know his full name? I know the Graham part. I don't recall whether that's first, last, or what."

"Hell. Just go over to Browning and ask around for Cracker. You'll be more likely to find him that way than you ever could with his real name."

With a big wad of plastic tarp under her arm, Bonnie shouted from the steps, "This place really is rustic. I believe you now. Is there running water?"

Sam got up and grabbed a jug of water from the truck box. "Will be soon, little lady. Real soon."

I had to hide the silly expression on my face when I heard him address her, "little lady." I hadn't thought about how short Bonnie and all her family were for a long time. "She's just the right height for Bonnie, and a lady for as long as I've known her," I thought. All the same, I loved hearing my old friend and landlord use that expression. I could tell he meant it, too.

I helped prime the pump, which had Sam recalling my mechanical abilities. "So, you worked as a farm hand for a few years up there, huh. Why don'tcha come back this way? I got a ranch about ready for the highest bidder." He went to the fuse box, started the electrical service, then checked water lines for leaks. "You and Bonnie could make a good life out here, you know."

"I'm sure we could, Sam. But she's teaching school and Port Hardy is our home now. We can make a good life there, too. And we will."

I may have heard Bonnie murmur under her breath, "For now. Port Hardy is our home now. For now."

"We hope you and Mary can come out to Kamloops for the wedding." I kept inviting people to an occasion that we intended to keep small. Ah, well. Bonnie's mother was undoubtedly growing it at her end, too.

(41)

We stood in front of the desk waiting until she hung up the phone. Then I asked the young receptionist at the Blackfeet Tribal office, "Do you know where I can find a guy they call Cracker?"

The laugh could not be stifled. "I'm sorry, sir, but," she let out another little giggle, "I don't know anyone by that name. Just a sec. Maybe Geraldine can help." She went into an office. I overheard, "There's a cracker out there asking for somebody named Cracker. He-hee."

The other voice, presumably Geraldine, said, "You don't know Cracker? I'm surprised." They both came out.

"You're looking for Cracker. Is that right?" Geraldine (I guess) asked.

"Yeah. I'm Wally Bradford and I'd like to find him, yeah."

"Can I ask what it's about?"

"Well, he helped me out years ago. I just want to catch up. For old time's sake. Thank him."

"Uh-huh. Do you think he wants to see you?"

I was taken aback by the question. "The way I remember him, I think we'll know real quick if he doesn't."

"Don't matter anyways. I can't help you find him today."

"Do you know where he lives? Or works?"

"I'm sorry." She went back into her office. The giggly young woman shrugged and was relieved by a ringing telephone.

When we were back in the car, Bonnie said, "Well. That was interesting."

***

192

"We should check out the college." In the office we'd just left a bulletin board announcement about course offerings had caught my eye.

"Yeah, I saw a poster in there. It's something new here. I hope it works out."

"I was only thinking someone might give a lead to Cracker. But yeah, it'd be interesting to hear how they're doing it. It must be something like North Island's experiments at bringing college to the people. Here it'll be almost exclusively for a first nation people, not so much both/and like ours."

When I asked after my friend Cracker at the college office located in a double-wide trailer, it was as if the man was expecting me. The one person on hand in mid-summer was as evasive as those at the tribal office. He was happy to talk about Blackfeet Community College and his hopes for the future. The partnership with another junior college made the mission look quite similar to my experience with North Island, but with different methods.

Still looking for Cracker, I suggested to Bonnie, "There's one more place. You'll enjoy this." I drove there without answering Bonnie's query.

After forty-five minutes perusing the exhibits at the Museum of the Plains Indian, I was ready to give it up and head back to Sam's cabin. Bonnie, on the other hand, was just getting started. She was in her element. That this museum was so different in scale and presentation from Chicago's Field Museum seemed to make no difference to her.

While Bonnie went on studying and taking notes, I turned around to look first for the men's room and then for a bench. A familiar face under a broad flat hat brim was looking me in the knee from a chair near the entry. Cracker was chuckling under his breath with a grin so wide it stretched from West Glacier to Cut Bank. His black hair, no longer hanging loose, was now in long neat braids and speckled with a bit of gray. Above his blue jeans he wore a white western cut shirt with a beaded string tie.

"I hear you been looking for me, Rich Boy. Is the cute little white chick with you?"

"Bonnie, come here," I shouted as I trotted over to shake Cracker's hand or hug him or something. "He found us. And he's cleaned up his act."

"You come to pick up the car, innit?"

"Car? No way. The microbus camper? Do you still have it?"

"Pleased to meetcha, Bonnie."

"Same here, Mr. Cracker. Wally speaks of you fondly. I hope I'm not being impertinent, I'm just curious. Is that a local idiom, saying 'innit' where completely different words belong? Back home I hear the expression, but only where is fits better. Don't you see?"

I answered before Cracker had a chance. "I think that's so local it's only Cracker who does that. And he didn't used to, innit."

"The rich kid's right. I'm just trying to sound inyan for you. If I knew more of my Blackfeet language I'd be forcing that on you, too. Now, here's the thing, purty Bonnie. You can call me Cracker, but if you add mister, it's Mister Stands Alone or Mr. Monroe or Mister Stands Alone Monroe."

I pulled a slip of paper and pen from my pocket and wrote, "Graham Stands Alone Monroe." Before I finished writing down his real name, I asked, "Do you know any Piegan language?" I hoped that we'd eventually get back to the status of the camper vehicle.

"Some. We'll have a course with good teaching elders at the college this fall. I might sign up. I grew up in Missoula, so that's a disadvantage, innit." Cracker put a hand on each of our backs to usher us toward the exit. "There's not much left of it, Wally."

"Of what? Piegan?" Bonnie chimed in.

"Every now and then I screw up bad enough that I stay in it for a couple nights 'til the wife cools off."

"Does it run? I don't want it or anything. I just wonder; I did love that outfit."

"It doesn't run. I got it back after some cousins used it up, innit. It's setting out behind my house on blocks with rotten tires still on it. We gave the engine to a mechanical kid like you. If I can't sound inyan enough for you, at least my yard's an indigenous stereotype."

***

Sitting at a picnic table outside the café, I'd told enough about my life in Canada before Bonnie and after (or between) and with her. Now I was stuffing more fry bread into my mouth, so it was Cracker's turn.

He watched me devouring the bread, smiling with that inaudible laugh of his. He didn't say anything for a long time. Bonnie seemed to sense that she should not try to fill a conversation void. She kept looking back and forth, to me and then to Cracker.

"I ran for tribal council last year."

"You what?" I garbled with my mouth still full of delicious fry bread.

"Didn't win, though. They did put me on an advisory board for the college, so that's something, innit. Sent me to Washington to help make our case for funding. Ours and for the other tribes trying to help the kids get educated at home where they can be their own selves."

I swallowed and said, "What did you once say about being a politician? It was when Sam first brought you to the cabin and we went hiking. We're staying there now for a few days, by the way."

"I don't remember. What did I say?"

"Something like, 'If it comes to that, we're sunk.' Is your new college sunk? With you politicking for it?"

Cracker looked at his plate and mumbled to himself, "Never say what you won't never do." He rubbed his eyes and looked up at the sky. "Did I really say I'd never do politics?" Then with a dramatic scowl and added loudly, "Innit." We sat nodding in silence for a minute before he said, "Hell, Rich Kid, we were doing politics all the time. When I helped you across, that was politics."

"Speaking of that," I said, "how come we did that back woods, middle of the night skulking. Most dodgers I've met went across without all that cloak and dagger stuff. Even Keith and Preach acted like they were play acting a paranoia game. Was all that really necessary?"

"It was for me, considering where you come from. You had to show us your real self, didn't you … innit. Prove you're a warrior peacenik, not just some pampered playboy too good for 'em."

"And?"

"And, nothing. You're here. Musta passed the test … innit."

***

By the time Bonnie got back from talking to her mother on the pay phone, Cracker had gone. I answered the question in her look, "He said he had an important meeting at one o'clock."

"One? It's nearly three."

"What? You never heard of …" I didn't need to finish. We did live in the native northern regions of the Island where fish movements set the clocks.

"Well, yeah, but. Let's head back to your cabin. Mom's in a state, I gotta tell you."

"Cracker said he's coming to the wedding and he'll raise holy hell, ruin everything until he gets deported. But he won't."

"Won't raise hell? Or come? What?"

"Won't come. I think. Maybe."

"Meaning, you don't know anything."

"That's another thing he told me the day we met." I tried and failed to imitate Cracker's accent, "'You don't know anything, do you, Rich Kid.' It's in a journal somewhere."

(42)

As we got up to speed on Highway 89, Bonnie was in constant motion. I could tell she had something to say, but wasn't getting it out. I was impatient, so I started, "Cracker's become a company man. Looking good in his braids. He used to just let his hair hang loose and slap a big hat on his head. It never occurred to me that going native could make a guy look more respectable."

"Don't you start sounding like a company man. 'More respectable,' says the white man with his superior ideas of what that means for everybody."

"Damn, Bonnie. Did I say all that? I was just noticing how Cracker's using his good skills for the tribe; for the Blackfeet Nation."

"What you should do is shut up and listen to me. Mom's having a fit about the wedding. Jumping down my throat about leaving it all to her; there's not enough time; the dress; no clear plans; get invitations out; talk to the preacher; the dress; on and on. And did I mention the dress? We have to head for Kamloops right away."

"Right away? Wednesday is our plan. Can we at least have one day to relax at the old cabin? I've been looking forward to kicking back in my old Montana home for a day or two."

"Tomorrow. Early start. Wally, it can't be helped."

I pouted and didn't answer. As we were whizzing along the narrow two lane blacktop I read the sign, Speed Limit 55. I glanced at the speedometer. It read 85. I eased off the foot feed. 'Foot feed' – where? Oh yeah. I got that from Sam, a Sam-ism for accelerator. Something hit my head just above the right ear. I brushed at it and she snapped her forefinger at my ear this time. "What?"

"Did you hear anything I said?"

"Yeah, Sweets. Your mom's in a snit, the dress, gotta leave Wednesday."

"No, Wally. Tuesday. Tomorrow. Early. And you haven't been listening."

"Sorry. We were speeding. Had to focus on the road."

"Oh? This is Montana, remember. It's not speeding. It's wasting a resource. Five dollars U.S."

"Yeah well, we were wasting gas. Dangerously."

"Can we talk about the wedding now? And please, Wallace, don't sulk just because we have to leave right away. It's not about you."

"There's another reason not to speed. I got a lady I love who's fool enough to love me back. No time to drive reckless…ly, innit."

We discussed wedding plans and preparations. She talked. I agreed.

***

"Thanks for letting me take the Going-to-the-Sun road. Incredible!" We were drinking coffee outside a little general store at West Glacier, noting that it really did take longer than avoiding Glacier and Waterton Parks.

"Oh? Was that for you? I thought it was for me. I did want to go through the Park on the U.S. side. Magnificent!"

I started to stand up. Bonnie urged me back to the bench. She said, "There's an idea I've been mulling over. Let's see what you think. After we have another meeting with the minister, what if you were to go on home to Port Hardy until a few days before the big one? It might make the preparations with Mommy go a little easier."

I nodded a non-committal nod. "I guess maybe. But I could just go camping and get out of the way for a while."

"Just a sec. There's more to it. You know that house we both liked but I thought was too high priced?"

"I think so. The old remodeled two story?"

"No way. That IS too pricey. And too big. I mean the split level. You liked it, especially the big garage."

"Oh, yeah. It's good 'til the third kid comes along."

"Third? Um, I think we have something else we need to discuss, Mr. B. But not now. A house, big enough for a SMALL family. Small enough to keep up when we're both working. Solid enough to hold its re-sale value. You can go to Hardy and make them an offer while Mom and I scream at each other."

"That sounds like a good plan. Except for the screaming. I hope you don't have to do that."

Back on the road, Bonnie didn't mention family size, but the subject was hiding in what she did say. "With house payments we both need to keep working. And if you start into a car repair business, that's another mortgage. We can't be in a rush to have a baby."

"You still can't wrap your beautiful mind around the rich kid's trust fund. Is that what they call middle class values?"

"Like you can plunk down $40,000 all at once."

"Well, no. Two-thirds down and the rest in six months. Is forty grand their asking price? If we use the trust as collateral there's less hassle and we can get if for thirty-five."

Bonnie gave me a cross-ways look and started laughing.

"What's so funny?"

"You. Listen to yourself." She imitated my low voice but didn't quite get the accent. "We can get it for thirty-five."

"Damn it to hell. That was Junior talking. My father's biz-speak out of my own mouth. Holy crap and shame on me."

***

The rest of our drive into Idaho and across the border to British Columbia involved frequent driver switching, almost but not quite hitting a couple of deer, and a flat tire. That caused much swearing and grumbling, but you've all been there. My journal note is just a few, mostly naughty, words.

With the spare tire on and our cargo re-packed I was in a sour mood until the stop to get the tire patched. We got quick service in some little BC town. The man grudgingly accepted my American money. His hesitation surprised me, so close to the border and all. Anyway, I determined to get a better attitude. Bonnie drove and I thought about the friends I'd invited to our party. After a few minutes with only the radio and road noise, I said, "It'll be great to have my American friends come out for the wedding, won't it."

"Oh? Who's coming for sure?" Bonnie was being realistic as usual, I hoped, and not just questioning my take on things.

"They all promised, right? Sam and Mary, my sisters and folks, even Cracker."

"Where was I when they made these promises?"

"Hell, Bonnie. You were right there. They said, 'Yeah. We'll see you there,' right?"

"If you were watching, you'd see that there was a lot less promise than there was avoidance of letting us down."

"What does that even mean? I heard what they said."

"You didn't notice anyone calling their travel agent, though, did you."

"Junior has people for that stuff."

"Junior. You don't even call him Father or Dad. You say Junior, his company nickname. And he hardly looks at you as a son. At least that's the way it appeared to me. I'm still trying to figure out your family. They're a different crowd than any I ever dealt with."

"You got that right. Junior can't be trusted and besides, we rich are different from you and me."

Bonnie laughed at my paraphrased quote. "All I'm saying is you shouldn't get your hopes up about anyone actually coming. If you do, you'll set yourself up to see everyone betraying your trust again. I really don't want that to happen. Okay?"

"So you think the groom's side'll be empty benches and I'll be pissed."

"It's harder than you realize for people to consider. That line on the map is easy to cross, but it is a definite line for lots of folks. And besides, your side of the church will have our Hardy friends. Our attendants will have family along. For instance, your best man Garret, Gretchen and their kids including Charlie the terrible-two will be there. Love that little Charlie. He moves so fast and loud he can fill the space of six adults."

Kidding around and talking about the wedding pulled me out of that sour mood. Then I just felt deflated. Can you trust anyone to do what they say? I slouched in the passenger seat and didn't speak.

Bonnie glanced over to see me sulking. "Wally, it'll be great. If people don't come, they have their own reasons. It isn't about us. They really do like you. I saw that, especially in Montana."

"I think Mom still likes me a little."

"She's not the only member of your family who cares. I do think Char will come and probably bring your mother with her. And Char's husband will come to keep an eye on her."

"Whatever, it'll be okay. Besides, I hate crowds, after all. If I run from the reception in terror, just remember this. It's not about me. It's about relatives."

"Sure thing, Wally dear. I'm pulling over. It's your turn to drive."

***

We drove through the night and completed the trip without a motel stop. At Coughlan's house I went over to her late grandma's still-vacant house to sleep while Bonnie listened to her mother frantically list all the things that need to be done yesterday. Agnes was still ranting when Bonnie fell asleep in the chair. She ranted to me about that as soon as I returned from my nap.

(43)

Hiram and Prudence Magelsson came to the wedding. Bonnie was mostly right about my family. Mom, both sisters and the Husbands came, but not their children. Mom didn't even try to make excuses for Junior. Gram sent a long letter with neither apology nor meanness. Bonnie was right. Friends, mostly teacher families, from Port Hardy made the trip. The father of one of my students from the special class brought his son and a friend. Both were young men I had in mind to train and employ for customer service if I should buy the gas station. Their presence made up for a host of no-shows.

Bonnie told me about her refrain while I was off buying a house. She said it so often her mother started saying it with her until they both relaxed and laid out the simple plan. "Let it go. There's no time for all that."

For some reason I didn't write in my journal on our wedding day. Back in Port Hardy two days later I wrote: "I met many of Bonnie's extended family that day. Not only are names a mystery, I have no idea who they are at all."

It was good that we had a pre-nuptial honeymoon. Once back at home Bonnie was preoccupied with preparation for the school year. I was busy consolidating rented trailer households into our new split-level cottage and also making plans for an auto repair service station. I had assumed that I could take my time and let things fall into place. Now there was this new complication. Yes, I had accumulated enough trust money by living frugally and having some work income that we could buy a house without a long-term mortgage. And yes, I did plan on buying the station, but I hadn't considered that it might take some time before it showed any profit. With Bonnie's teaching we had income. But, you see, you were right in your assumption about one reason I didn't journal on our wedding night. Obviously. But there was another when Bonnie whispered to me after that activity, "Do you remember what Mary Doakes said about her wedding day?"

"I'm not sure. What did she say?"

"If you don't remember, that's okay. The doctor thinks I'm about four or five weeks along."

I didn't understand at first. She had to spell it out. "I'm pregnant, Wally. We're going to have a baby sooner than we expected or planned."

"I thought you were on the, you know, the pill and stuff."

"Well, yeah. But, along the way there was some confusion. I sort of slipped up and here we are. Can you be happy about it?"

That question grabbed me by the throat. I was scared shitless and Bonnie could see it. Pregnant. Baby. Parents. That's for grownups. A baby! Wow! Incredible! She asked me 'are you happy?' It forced me to take another look, from a different angle, which I did. Yeah, scared out of my wits and ecstatic at the same time. Now, looking back at that journal entry, I know something else: It's a near universal jumble of emotions for new parents.

An unbidden smile stretched itself across my face. Bonnie pinched my cheek and kissed the smile. Into the kiss, I said, "You can't say it's not about me."

"I *can* say it's about *us*, you *and* me always." And she wrapped herself around me again, even though we were both spent and sleepy.

***

Oh, by the way, did I mention? About the wedding? Well, if not, Bonnie was stunning in the dress. I mean she was even more beautiful than usual. Just so everyone knows, because it is true. Lovely Bonnie in the classy gown saved me. Whenever I started to get into my crowd panic from 150 people crammed into that little church social hall, all I had to do was look at my bride and I'd glide into dreamy bliss.

"If I can survive period one, I'll be okay for the rest of the day," Bonnie muttered as she dropped the big canvas bag and dashed back to the bathroom to lose her breakfast.

I felt for her, I really did, but I was discovering that there could be no correct way to respond to her morning condition. With her, I hoped this part of pregnancy would be over soon. Fortunately her first hour was a small group of bright grade twelves studying world history. Group work with class presentations was always in the plan. Unfortunately, bright seniors were adept at manipulation during their teacher's sudden brief absences from the classroom. Bonnie toughed it out, wanting to save up her leave time for after, and the nausea phase soon passed.

In December she was feeling wonderful and I was feeling soggy. The constant rain that winter had me questioning everything. Why didn't I start a little shop for repairs only? What made me think I should deal with gas pumps, too? My part time helpers, slow learners, still needed lots of supervision. All of us were in and out of the rain so much that my engine work was slowed. Delays would mean unhappy customers and that would kill my business before it got off the ground. It would soon be Christmas, our first together in marriage, and I was being a grump. Bonnie wanted to spend the holidays with family at Kamloops. So did I, actually, but how could I possibly close a full service gas station for a whole week.

Then I caught a break that gave us our Christmas break. As soon as school let out for the holiday, we would drive to Kamloops and stay with Bonnie's folks through Boxing Day, thanks to Butch, Campbell who sold me the station.

I had just unlocked the door on the morning when rain turned to wet snow and everyone wanted help with winter tires. Butch was on his way in before I'd pocketed the keys. He plopped down in the squeaky armless swivel chair that once was his, let out a long sigh and said, "It's useless. I'm useless." He looked up at me. "She pushed me out the door, Wally. I was all ready to start painting the spare bedroom and she pushed me out the door."

I wasn't sure what this was all about, but it must have to do with adjusting to retirement. "Your wife isn't used to having you around all the time. Is that it?"

"She ain't used to me being home at all. I was just the guy in the greasy coverall what came for late supper and a place to sleep. Now it's all 'fix this, fix that' but 'don't get in my way' and shit."

Just then a car pulled up to the bay door and another to the pumps. My pump helper wasn't expected until after school. "Which do you want, Butch," I asked, "tires or gas?"

Butch headed for the gas pump without answering. I was left with the heavy grunt work of swapping summer for winter tires. By the end of the day I had learned to be grateful for customers like that early arrival, who had snow tires mounted on an extra set of wheels. Butch and I had worked out a deal. He would cover the days we needed to be open around Christmas. He even grudgingly agreed to supervise the guys still learning routine tasks. I worried that despite assurances, he'd be harsh with them.

***

Christmas with the Coughlans will never become a movie; it was much too relaxed and uneventful. All the tightness of our winter drive left my body soon after we entered the warm house with aromas of beef roast and fresh bread from the kitchen mixed with fir tree from the front room. Ben and Ed were stringing lights on a small tree that Ben had cut and hauled from his home up north.

The only moment of new tension came when Bonnie asked Ben, "Are you here by yourself? We thought you might be with Monica's family."

Agnes was sending out all kinds of signals and jumped in to change the subject, but Ben stopped her and answered simply, "We broke up." To Bonnie's pouty expression he added, "I'm fine, Sis. It just wasn't right." He turned away to check another string of lights for dead bulbs and ended any further discussion.

As the family's newest member I sat and watched, not certain whether I'd be welcome to help with decorating the tree, or anything else for that matter. My thoughts drifted to comparisons of this heartwarming present with remembered events of joy and pain. I pulled a journal book from my luggage to work through memories and be reassured that this present, so warm and comfortable, was real.

Ben's break-up brought Carolee to mind, the good times we had at college and walking the long trail and the pain of the ending that seemed so sudden. There were signals, and yet it hit me unprepared and stunned. I wrote my questions, uncertain that I could do any better if something changed between Bonnie and me.

So I watched this family. Ed, Ben, and Bonnie were decorating a tree with ornaments that held meaning and memories for each of them. I listened to Agnes humming carol tunes as she put finishing touches on a family dinner. I thought about my family of origin, of Junior ordering me to company work just because college didn't resume until mid-January. Will I do better with my son, growing in Bonnie's womb? He could be a girl, hmm. I surprised myself as I realized that while there is a definite difference, son or daughter, I really didn't care which. Healthy, please. That's all.

"Are you writing your journal now, Wally dearest?" Bonnie pulled me back to wakefulness.

"Mostly falling asleep, Sweets. I was thinking about whether I can be a better father than Junior."

"Mom's calling us to supper." She pulled me out of the deep comfy chair, put her arms around me and whispered, "You'll be great. Still a Bradford, you can't help that. We both know enough not to expect that our son will love to do exactly what you love."

"She might be a girl. Pretty and smart like her mother."

"The same rule applies."

"Come on, love birds. The potatoes are getting cold." Edward hurried us to the table.

A conversation began during the meal that would continue until Ed's death. "Are you looking at openings in our Kamloops schools, Bonnie?"

"If all goes well I'll have permanent status at Port Hardy next year, Pops. We'll see how it goes."

I chimed in, "And I just took on a business, after all. It could take until the baby goes to kindergarten for me to establish a reputation and be accepted as a local."

"Well, keep it in mind, you two. Our city is growing. Be needing teachers and mechanics both."

I looked at Bonnie, trying to read her reaction to her father's suggestion. I couldn't get a clear answer. While we were getting ready for bed I asked Bonnie about it. Still noncommittal, she said, "It's not about you, Wally. That's a Pops and his little girl thing."

***

For the rest of our Christmas visit I was determined to live in the moment and not allow worries to interfere. Aunts, uncles, cousins and their children whom I had seen at our wedding were now met as real people and more than faces in the crowd. I promptly forgot names again, but I had heard them. Even when two cousins argued about Prime Minister Trudeau's policies it was a courteous disagreement. They saw me as an American, only allowed opinions about Carter and U.S. politics. That was fine by me. Pierre Trudeau had been PM as long as I'd been in the country. I didn't know what any alternative might be. In a journal note I suggested to myself that I should pay more attention to Bonnie's Canadian History class preparations.

(45)

After two months of my nagging, Bonnie finally relented and began a leave of absence at spring break. We left church early on Palm Sunday because she couldn't sit in the pew through the long service. She spent the break week, Holy Week, fidgeting, arranging and rearranging the nursery bedroom. The following Sunday, Easter day, she was all ready to try church again. That plan changed quickly just after breakfast. Cynthia was born just before midnight on Easter 1978.

It goes without saying that our amazing baby immediately became the center of our attention, so I'll attend to other issues. During the summer Bonnie and I had our first real disagreement. Well, other than those five stupid words, but that's ancient history. My trust fund wasn't growing in value because Bradford and Son was into a long decline. The quarterly payments were still enough that Bonnie could take an extended leave with Cynthi in her formative early years. Bonnie countered that she needed to stay current in her career, with points in her argument too numerous to remember. She said that if she weren't teaching, her parents would push harder to move us to Kamloops, and she held my devotion to the auto shop over my head. Two things occurred that fall. While they didn't settle the argument, they did settle it down for the time being. Bonnie went back half time, sharing the position with her department mentor. He had expected to retire and do research for a local history book with the indigenous peoples of the Island. The partnership meant that Bonnie taught only her least favorite younger grades.

The other issue was also a compromise. I was able to hire a young man who shared my love of putting engines back into working order. With an assistant mechanic-manager I reduced my hours, too. Except—customers expected a quicker turn around, because there were two of us. We'd held out with full service gas long enough and went to self-serve. Chuck, my one remaining special employee was now well trained and able to do routine oil changes and watch for those few customers who really needed full service. Chuck was great at that. He had such compassion and empathy for others with disabilities and the aging. I mostly kept my word about shorter hours, but Bonnie might have had another perspective.

After Cynthi was put to bed on her first birthday, Bonnie opened her baby book to write about it and paste in the Polaroid pictures. I grabbed my journal of the year. It was all in one book. Who has time to write at length when there's a baby in the house? I sat on the sofa next to Bonnie and we compared notes from the baby book and the journal. They were remarkably similar. That day I determined that I would simply live the family life and note only brief highlights. I would write more from the odd encounters with customers at the shop. I had begun sketching those as a matter of course. My favorites were the tourists who must have it done in time to drive to Nanaimo before the ferry departs.

***

Curtis arrived two years later. He was a big baby but it didn't last. He inherited the Coughlan short stature. He was still a toddler when both kids began spending time with a wonderful day care provider. Bonnie had to return to full time or give up the position entirely. "There might be some less-than-full time opportunities in a larger system, Wally. Like Kamloops, perhaps."

"But Bonnie, we've made our home here. Think about it. The school faculty, your church friends — it's like the whole town is caring for us and our kids. Yeah, there's a distinction between us and the North Island born and bred, but still ..."

"And that fence will always be there. It's in the nature of small towns. How much effort is it worth?"

"If anybody can knock that fence down, you can. Your interest in local history, the way you capture the meanings in the stories the traditional elders tell, the way you connect with the young people. Love for Ms. Bradford sends me customers, you know. This is Cynthi and Curt's home. That makes it ours, too."

"Come on, Wally. They're not even in school yet. That's your feeblest argument yet."

"Yeah, but you really do want to stay in Port Hardy, don't you."

"As in, 'I don't want to fight about it' and the path of least resistance works for me in most situations, okay. I did not expect my off-hand comment to get you so worked up."

We stayed on the Island. As I said, my journal changed focus, such that we'll set aside the telling of conventional family time for now. I wrote those words: 'conventional family', and immediately thought of times that were far from ordinary and want to tell about them. But no, there are more recent events I'm compelled to write first.

***

Bonnie taught there for thirty years. When she retired I expected to continue our ordinary, conventional ways in our empty nest. Bonnie longed for something. It escaped my notice. Even when she said it in clear and blunt terms, I dismissed it as unimportant. I did not, could not hear.

PART THREE

(46)

"Pop! We're here! Where are you?" The front door slammed.

Then a child's voice sang out, "Poppy! He's not home, Mommy."

"Oh, he's here somewhere, Megan."

Why does she assume I'm always at the house? "I'm up here, Cynthi. In the attic. I'll be right down. How was the drive from Victoria? Is Jared still enjoying government work?"

My daughter Cynthia came up to the hall on the bedroom floor and looked up at me from the bottom of the fold-out attic stair while preventing Megan, her four-year old, from climbing up. Brad, the toddler, was on her arm. I'm glad they named him Bradford and not Wallace. I hoped to be the last Wallace, but my brother Bryan gave the name to his firstborn son. I digress. I started down the ladder-like stairs and pulled along the box of old journals I'd been digging through.

"Wait Pop. Let me take that." Cynthia put Brad down. "Don't let him get on the stairs, Megan. Okay?"

***

"What should I do with all these old diaries – the famous Wally B3 Journals? I can't toss them, but nobody wants to read them but me."

"We could scan them into computer files. Then you'd have them with your newer entries."

"What do you know about those?"

"Oh, come on, Poppy. Do you think this thing you've been doing my whole life is some big secret? You tell about 'the old days' and when you're done you'll say, 'It's all in the journal somewhere.'"

"What have you read?"

213

"Aha! See, you know that you're not really the only one who's interested. So, there. Not yet, Meggie."

Megan won. We turned our attention to the children's hunger. Later, after the kids were bedded down in Curtis's former room, our talk picked up where we'd left it.

Settled on the sofa, I opened the box of old journals and said, "I ask it again. What have you read? And what have you discovered?"

"God, it's been years. I was maybe twelve or thirteen the first time I poked my nose in. I looked up the day I was born. I seem to recall some excitement in your notes that week; like you were happy to see me or something."

"I suppose you compared that to the day Curt was born next, huh."

"Not right away, but yeah. You were impressed with him, too. Of course, I also noticed your concern that a jealous almost-three-year-old should get attention, too."

"Hey, that entry was not about you, Cynthi."

"Touché, Pop. Of course. It's about you, as always, right? I have read enough to see your bitching about that line. I have to tell you—the last time I looked was on your computer. I got curious about how you were coping with Mom's death because I was barely coping. Was, am. The minute I walk into this house I feel her by her absence. There are so many things I want to tell Mom, … and only Mom."

Her talk brought me to tears, which caused her to cry, too.

A voice from the top of the half-flight of stairs made us jump. "Why are you crying, Mommy? Why's Poppy crying?"

"We miss your Grandmother, Meggie."

"Me, too," Megan said.

"Do you remember her?" I found it unlikely. She was only two and a couple months when Bonnie had the fatal heart attack.

Megan shrugged. The question stumped her. She disappeared into a bedroom for a moment, then came carefully down the steps holding the eight by ten framed photo from my nightstand. Without speaking, she handed me the picture of Bonnie and me on our twenty-fifth anniversary. In itself, seeing the picture didn't help, but the thoughtfulness of my little granddaughter sure did. After hugs all around and expressions of gratitude to Megan, Cynthia took her back to bed and I dug into my box of ancient journals once more.

***

I was looking for entries about meeting Bonnie, but they were in another box. Instead, because of our shared sobs a few minutes earlier, I turned on my computer. While it booted up on my lap, I sat with my eyes closed, waiting. I found the journal file for the week that Bonnie died, reached for a tissue to wipe my eyes and read.

I've often been told that an event that affects me profoundly isn't really about me; but is it not reasonable and just that my entries that week were all about what this sudden loss meant for ME? My partner and love for thirty years of marriage was gone. Just like that. Of course I was angry and hurt. How could she do that? How could she die on me without a warning or a fare-thee-well. I was angry at her for being gone and at God or fate or the universe or nature or something for taking her from us. And I was left to help my young adult children, Cynthia and Curtis, in their grief. All the while I wanted to curl up and disappear with Bonnie.

I found the description in my writing that I was most curious about. I had drawn a word sketch describing a tripod made of Curt, Cynthi and me holding each other through the days following her death. When one of us collapsed the others collapsed, too, until we could find some little thing to grab hold of and support each other like a three legged stool again.

I dug back in the digital files to the time Bonnie retired from teaching. We all thought that she would turn her attention to increased volunteer efforts with the museum's local history projects. Instead, she told me she needed to just rest up for a bit. Later I learned what she'd refused to explain to me. Somehow, she got crosswise with some of the First Peoples leaders in the project and she dropped out. So, she sat in her recliner and snacked. She was depressed and I didn't have a clue how to help. She ballooned up in weight. The only thing that ever brightened her was an infrequent visit from baby Megan. If I suggested that we visit them in Victoria, she was too tired to make the drive.

Here's the injustice, don't you see. Finally after nearly a year of letting herself go, she was fighting back for her life. She started exercising and was beginning to look and feel more alive again. Then, while she was out walking alone, making the big effort, she keeled over dead. I'm telling you, you can't even trust the universe to make sense.

I closed the computer. Cynthia was leafing through a really old journal and I hadn't been aware that she'd come back into the room, or that she'd been to the attic for that older collection.

"Did you ever tell us about hiking in the Appalachians? Hmm, Carolee, huh. You were smitten. As your daughter, I can't get my head around it. My dad, college boy, in love with someone before my Mom."

"Which is why you didn't hear much about those days."

"It's no big deal, Pop. We all have pasts. I think it's hormonal. Mom told me about a couple boyfriends she had. When she was trying to help me cope with a break up, I think. Of course, I mostly tuned her out because I couldn't think of her with anyone but you. Same deal."

"She told you, mother to daughter. She did not tell me. There's the difference. If I started telling stories about hiking the trail, pretty soon I'd be reminiscing — wistfully I might add — about a cafeteria serving line or about Harpers Ferry, West Virginia. Your Mom didn't want to know about that any more than I wanted to hear about her boyfriends in Kamloops."

"Did she ever even say why you couldn't buy the wedding ring here?"

"She was looking for a big city bargain. Is there more?"

"Uh-oh. Cat's out of the bag. A month or two before you arrived the jeweler proposed to her."

"And?" I took the risk to ask.

"She turned him down. That's all I know."

"Before or after I showed up?"

Cynthia shrugged.

"He never let on when I visited his store. How about that."

***

That night I slept soundly but not for long. I was up early looking into those journals that Cynthia had opened. I even started scanning pages into digital files before I went over to the shop. I only stayed for a few minutes, just to see that Skip had things under control while I took a few grandpa days. I told Skip not to accept any new jobs unless they could be completed in less than an hour, with locally available parts.

He responded to that, "So we're retiring soon. Good. I'm ready."

"Good. I thought you were ready, but it worried me a little. I hate to see this turned into a C-store with pumps, but that's the way it is now."

***

"I'm thinking about taking a trip." I casually mentioned this to Cynthia over breakfast as she and the kids were about to return home to husband/daddy and job in Victoria. She gave me a sidelong look, so I added. "A long trip."

"Who'll run the station?"

"I'm tired and I've run out of pride. I'm ready to give up and take the offer. Let the corporate critters turn it into yet another convenience store. I'm down to one mechanic and Skip's ready to retire, too. Joe already left for a job in Nanaimo."

"So, you're off to Europe or what?"

"Nope, the old U.S. of A. Looking at those old journals we started to scan the other night made me itchy. There's places your mother and I visited the year we got married, places we all visited on that family trip, and there's some other places. I want to retrace some old steps."

"And your sisters and brother?"

"Yeah, seems like I only go there for funerals. They all look at me like 'Who the heck are you?'"

Cynthia's eyebrow arched in that cute way of hers and she asked, "Road trip?" I nodded. "Alone?"

I nodded again. "You know I like to be alone. But not here. This house without my Bonnie, without your mom … it isn't solitude, it's vacant. Lonesome. If I get out on my own adventure, maybe Solitary Wally can still get onto something new in this life."

Megan had been trying to follow our talk while her waffle got cold. "You can trip to our house, Poppy. It's not lonesome."

"For sure, Meggie. My first stop, and the last when I come home." I paused, rubbing my temples. "When I come back." I directed the next to Cynthia, "Should I put the house on the market, too?"

"NO! Just a sec, Pop." She dealt with Megan's mostly uneaten breakfast and sent her to potty and wash while she gave Curtis and his highchair tray a wash up. "She's becoming so independent. That's what good day care does. Anyway, Pop, go slow about the house. You asked about Jared's work when we first arrived. Well, he's looking at a change — and one possibility is with North Island College. So, don't burn your bridges out here, please."

(47)

After a couple frustrations with computer mapping sites, I bought a new road atlas. At the kitchen table I circled the places that I had taken Bonnie to meet my friends and relatives before our marriage. The next evening I highlighted a Wally and Bonnie route in yellow and a family route in pink where they were different. I pored over my maps every night for another week while I typed a few thoughts in a journal. Memories crowded out records of current activities. I was amazed again that Bonnie was still willing to marry me after meeting my family. I remembered people we'd visited who had since died or with whom I'd lost contact and assumed they had passed on.

I started off carefully following routes that connected to our pre-marriage journey and seeking my lost Bonnie travel. After a week in Victoria with Cynthia's family I backtracked to take the ferry from Departure Bay. I needed to stay in Canada for the first leg not out of fear but to visit Curt. This time I drove a fancier camper than the old micro-bus outfit, and much more than Bonnie's little Toyota that had eventually become Cynthia's and then Curt's first car. The RV was old but sturdy. And I love to tinker with diesel engines. A woman, recently widowed, wanted me to put her 1985 Winnebago LeSharo on consignment at my shop. First I told her I didn't run a used car lot, despite what she saw behind the shop. Next I bought it and rebuilt the engine. Now a drive to Chicago would give it a road test.

The plan was to stay loose, with a destination but no daily goals; loose but with two rules for travel days: 1 - No more than eight hours on the road each day (don't rush, stop early, exercise and get plenty of rest); 2 - Each night along the way journal on the laptop and read the old books of earlier events as I passed their locations. Guesswork at finding the correct dates would let me browse through many entries about long forgotten events.

I stayed a day at Kamloops. I walked the neighborhood that Bonnie had introduced to me and visited the museum where we first met, noting the many changes. At the nursing home I apprehensively approached Bonnie's elderly mother. She didn't recognize me but when I mentioned Bonnie her face lit up, but soon teared up.

"Where is Bonnie?" She looked all around with her fading vision. "I don't see her?"

"Bonnie died, Mrs. Coughlan." Having tried before, I knew that there was no gentle way to tell her again.

"It should've been me." She began shaking her head back and forth and kept it up through the rest of our visit. "I'm ready to go. Why did she die before me? It makes no sense."

I couldn't dispute that.

"Ed's gone. Bonnie's gone. My only daughter and here I sit."

I tried to change the subject. "Are they taking good care of you here?"

"Here? Where am I?"

"Gemstone Care. This is where you live now."

"Who're you?"

We'd been around the memory loop. "I'm Wally. It's good to see you again, Agnes." I attempted to give her a gentle hug and made my exit. I guess I don't have the patience to go around the same tree too many times in one visit.

Curtis, at Calgary, was my next stop of more than a night, on the map's pink line. Curt and Bill — what do I call him? Fiancé, partner, husband by common law? — his significant other, talk about getting married, but don't seem to get any closer to a solid plan. They've been together long enough for me to get used to the idea, if not completely comfortable about it yet. They live like an old married couple, better at bickering toward agreement than his mother and I ever were. I have had to dope slap myself out of old prejudices and misunderstandings, reminding myself that Junior couldn't mold me. I worked at keeping my vow to love and encourage my children to be fully their own selves, even a gay accountant. Boy did I struggle with it, though. I didn't know how prejudiced I was. I love math, but for years I looked down on bookkeeping. Through Curt's teen years I was angry at the bullies, worried that they might be right about my son, angry at myself for wanting Curt to be different than he is, which made me angry at Junior again because I saw myself in him — and I hated that. When Curt came out to us, a huge sense of relief came, too. By then I wasn't surprised by the news, only relieved at knowing for certain.

**

Curt and Bill kept me jumping through our two day visit. We played tourist in their adopted city, visiting sights that needed the excuse of an out-of-town visitor to take time to see. My kids had turned me into an admirer of zoos. Bonnie and I always took the kids to the Wildlife Park when we visited the grandparents in Kamloops. Curt and his old Pop at the zoo had a fun afternoon being kids. The sky was clear and bright. A cool breeze made the sunshine enjoyable. The air was dry! I hadn't realized how habituated to the damp along the straits I had become. The animals did their animal things.

We talked long into the evening, remembering and arguing about any and everything. My son had become an Alberta oil patch conservative. I am more self-aware than self-absorbed now. I like to claim so, anyway. Just to egg him on I had to say it this way, "How could you do this to me, Curt? You've become a Chicago Bradford just to spite me, haven't you."

He started to respond, "It's not about..." and stopped, realizing I was setting him up for that line. He changed tactics, "Well you see, Pop, coming out and introducing you to Bill didn't work. Thank God. But I had to do something. You boomers think yours is the only generation gap that counts."

"But it's true. The generation gap isn't about you, is it?"

He nodded along with the gentle laughter all around.

Our sharing of grief, of missing Bonnie, was quite different with Curt, unlike the tears with Cynthia. I find no words to describe it, but it helped. I was trying and failing to remember at what point the screaming terror had given way to a dull ache that sneaks up and grabs my chest at odd moments. I had a small epiphany as Curt talked about Mom. I'd been driving along, living into the journey along roads that Bonnie and I roamed together on that summer before journey. I had this feeling that she was there in that empty passenger seat. I'd start to say something to her, much like what happens in bed during some of those half-awake times. What was new was that it was a pleasant sensation. Not missing her so much as having the memory of her along for the ride. I don't care what they say, that's about me. It's about Solitary Wally.

**

I was packing up the camper. Curt was preparing a special last blast breakfast. Bill came out, admired my twenty-five year old Winnebago motor home and asked a favor.

"This is a great outfit, Wally. Is it a trust fund benefit like Curt told me about?"

"Thank you. It's a benefit of having a buyer for the shop and it has nearly 150k on the odometer. It needed work and I still love to work on old diesels. The fund Curt's told you about dried up quite a while ago. It was dependent on Bradford and Son earnings when the company went under."

"Can I ask you something?" It became clear that he had something more pressing on his mind. I nodded and he went on. "I sure appreciate the way you accept us. Um, you know?"

"I do know. It hasn't been easy for me. It scared me when Curt was growing up and the hints were there and I hoped and prayed he wasn't. But he's my boy. I had to help him through the abuse he got from his classmates. You know all about how that is."

"Well, it's this, Mr. B. My father is still back there. He can't face the truth. I was wondering ... could you, maybe, stop and see my folks? They're in Lethbridge. Maybe you knew that."

"I didn't. Wow. I don't know how much help I can be. But, geez." I knew I had to try, but I don't easily change course when I have my map in mind. I was heading down the Trans-Canada to Medicine Hat, even though Hiram and Prudence had both died.

"If it's too much out of the way...I understand."

"No you don't. How can anywhere be out of the way? I don't have any deadlines or a tight budget." We checked the map together and I realized I had absolutely no excuse not to try. It wasn't going to add much distance. I'd be off the Bonnie and Wally trail for half a day. The problem was the fear that I'd say the wrong thing and make their relationship worse instead of better.

"Should I call first? Or just bang on the door."

"I'll call." Bill fished in his empty pocket and went in to find his phone and make the call.

Curt came out. He found me rearranging and securing items. "Bill said you wanted something."

It only took a second to get that Bill didn't want Curt to know about my errand for him. "Yeah, um, I hope you can find some time to visit your grandma. Senile as she is, she's still your granny."

"Was that it? It's hard, though. All day on the road for a ten minute visit in a town where I don't know anyone else. Yeah. But, hey Pop, what about your family? I had an idea that it might be cool to fly to Chicago when you're there, so I can meet aunts and uncle and cousins. What do you think?"

"Can you get away for that sort of thing? You and Bill have both taken time from your work this week."

Bill called from the door, "Breakfast is ready and getting cold."

We started toward the house. "We've been connected to work more than you realize. We can keep the books in order and make the payroll transfers for our clients from just about anywhere. And Bill will be here, anyway."

***

All the way to Lethbridge I fretted and rehearsed. I don't mind meeting new people as much as I used to. I'm easy with it when I'm in control. I can give a new customer an estimate of the work needed, no problem. But this? I was supposed to...what? The whole idea was giving me Woodstock levels of crowd twitches with a hundred more km yet to travel in solitude.

(48)

"Thanks for allowing me to come. I know this is hard for all of us." I said this while spooning macaroni salad onto my plate after Mr. Coe had led us through a long, winding table blessing that included a plea for Bill to see the error of his ways and enter the light, and so on. Nothing was included on Curt's behalf.

"If it's so hard, why're you here?" he asked.

"Bill asked me to and I couldn't come up with a good excuse. Same as you don't have to feed me this delicious dinner. But here we are and I thank you for it." Mrs. Coe (I'd been introduced, but in my nervousness promptly forgot their first names.) nodded. Neither of them tried to fill the tense silence as they ate and waited for me to say more.

I chewed on a bite of pork chop, swallowed and picked up my knife. I put it back down and said, "Bill asked me because he needs you. He needs some acceptance from his parents. He loves you and needs to know you still love him." Mrs. Coe looked away, dropped her fork and ran to the kitchen.

Mr. Coe, still chewing, watched her go. "It's abomination. The way he's living. And your son. You come here stirring trouble, acting like the way they live is just wonderful. You'll rot in hell with 'em. God will not be mocked."

He was awfully strident, but hearing his absolute conviction got me to thinking. Now, I'm no kind of biblical scholar. If it weren't for required courses at Yankton, and occasionally paying attention in church while my kids went to Sunday school, I'd know none at all. I knew that our United Church of Canada pastor at St. Columba's was more open minded than Mr. Coe. I remembered hearing her point out many things prohibited in the Old Testament, mostly in Leviticus. I think that's the book. I wasn't so sure about her claims that those laws made sense for the time. But I sure agreed that they don't now. I gobbled some salad and beans to stall while I thought about a way to respond without mocking God or Mr. Coe.

Finally, in a voice loud enough that Mrs. Coe would have to make an effort not to hear from the kitchen, I said, "You know that this tasty dinner we're enjoying is an abomination." I lifted pork chop with my fork, and then fished in the salad until I found a tiny shrimp. "Pork, shrimp. Both are forbidden in the ancient law. Won't that condemn us all?"

"Jesus, the New Testament, Peter at Joppa, God changed all that. But in Romans…"

I wasn't ready for his next argument, so I interrupted. "I don't know about all that. It just seems like we do better to pay attention to our own sins and try to make them right, instead of worrying so much about judging others. Our sons did not choose to be gay. Bill would really like to be able to honor his mother and father, I think. But if you condemn him for being who he is and can't possibly change … Well, he's wired that way so there's nothing wrong to fix. You know what we say at the auto shop: 'If it ain't broke, don't fix it.'"

"I thought auto mechanics said: 'If it ain't broke, you ain't trying hard enough.'"

Mr. Coe had snapped the tension, God bless him. We laughed and nodded and then he went on, "It just isn't right. I love my son, I really do. But the way those boys are living, I cannot abide. God's word …"

"Tell you what. Wouldn't it be better to let your boy know you love him? Isn't that first and always? Tell him so. Why not pray whatever you're moved to pray, but let God handle it from there?"

Coe pulled his paper napkin from his lap, placed it carefully beside his plate, slowly stood and walked out to the kitchen. I waited. After about five minutes Mr. and Mrs. Coe came back to the dining table holding hands.

"I can't say what I will or will not do, Mr. Bradford. We pray and God expects us to act on his Word. That's still part of praying. Even so, I can't fault everything you say. Will you pray with us right now?"

He spoke many words to his God then, still with an appeal for change in his son, but I also heard a plea for forgiveness all around. When he stopped speaking I waited, hands folded, eyes down, for an 'Amen'. And I waited. Then there came a gentle touch to my forearm. I caught the meaning and made the attempt. I prayed for healing and acceptance and family. And added the 'Amen' with an eye to ending before he could correct my petition.

Mrs. Coe wiped her red, teary eyes and mentioned dessert. Over apple pie, trying to lighten the mood before I left, I said, "Do you know that Curt and Bill bicker? And it's over the same things that used to get me angry and yell at Curt. Bill likes things to be put away where they belong and he can find them. Curt drops whatever tool wherever he last used it. You can imagine how that used to upset things in my auto shop."

"They bicker," Mrs. Coe mused. "What goes around comes around. Bill used to come home from college and find us picking at each other over some useless trifle and he'd laugh at us until we were all laughing at the foolishness of it. Marv, let's go see them. It would mean so much to me."

"I don't know, Sheila. Let's don't be hasty. Going into a house where they do what those people do. Turns my stomach. That's no place to be."

"Ah! So there's a bit of what some call 'the ick factor' going down here." I should have kept that to myself. "It's about love, Marv. Sex is just one part of it. Not so different from us guys who love our wives, I think. Try to think of the love, and forget the other."

"Easy said." He shook his head and seemed to be lost in thought. I thanked and gave them the token gift – an advertising ice cream scoop with the slogan, "Here's a scoop from Wally's Esso. We fix it right. We don't just guess so." Old Doc Graves would have pulled me out of her class and booted me down the back stairs for that bit of 'creative' writing.

***

I stopped at the edge of the city and punched up Bill's cell number. I tried to be honest. The visit had gone better than I expected, and Bill needed to know it. "Your father loves you. He said so. He still thinks we're all going to hell, but he might be willing to keep you in the family anyway. Your mother wants to visit you and Curt. Your dad's still having a hard time with that."

"Maybe we should visit them. Would they let us in?"

"It might be better for you to go alone and pave the way. Avoid the ick factor for now."

(49)

I ended the call feeling pretty good about the visit on Bill's behalf. Bonnie would've been proud of me. I do tend to overthink things. It's a diarist's hazard. I drove along toward Medicine Hat gradually coming to the conclusion that Marv Coe might soon be pulled back to his hard-hearted ways by his fundamentalist friends.

Suddenly, out of the blue (the sky was pure blue and enormous that afternoon) I heard a voice in my head, a female voice that I couldn't immediately place, saying, "It's not about you, Wally. A seed is planted. At the right moment, if or when Marv and Sheila are ready, it takes root." The voice burst my conceit, but I still felt good about the visit, especially Sheila's macaroni salad.

I was anxious to get back to the yellow marker route. I don't know why, but I needed to travel the old routes. Medicine Hat had been on our eastward trip and I couldn't recall Magelsson's address. We'd had trouble finding it when we knew it. I had no fears about the border crossing this time, but I was already east of Glacier Park. I stared at my map shaking my head and talking to myself. "Heading for the border; should I stay on main routes and take highway 2 west from Shelby to Browning? Or find my way along the back roads in Montana? Considering my oversize vehicle, I opted for the interstate. The places I intended to visit no longer included the old friends. I'd been in touch just enough to know that deaths and departures had removed friends from the old locales. Still, I had to look, even though it would be several days of talking to myself behind the wheel and to my journal at every stop. Even without those special people, the drive through Montana was a journey of love. Love of the place and the companionship of Bonnie's memory occupying the passenger seat were enough to keep me chugging along.

A couple of journal highlights will suffice for the first leg of the journey on the U.S. side of the line. Entries always started with current weather.

- Temperature 26°C (79°F); Humidity – dry and dusty; light high clouds and sun. If it weren't for the wind off the mountains to the west it would be hot.
- Browning, Montana. Museum of the Plains Indian is more run down than I remember it. On the other hand, the tribal college is a real thing now. Did not find Cracker. Phone number I have no longer in service, gave up on finding anyone who would admit to a Canadian stranger that they knew him — maybe too soon.
- The cabin between Bynam and the Bob. Locked gate, vehicle path overgrown with grass and weeds. Climbed over and walked in. Looks as if no one has come near since the day Bonnie's mother pulled us away two days ahead of my plan — a plan I was sure we had carved in stone. If I could give it a year of tender care it might be livable again. (I dog-eared the page.)
- Choteau, Montana. Stop at the courthouse — learned who the current (California) owners of the cabin property are.
- Parked overnight at Gates of the Mountains on my much-loved Missouri River.
- It's a long way from the Rocky Mountains to Yankton. Drive was shorter with living Bonnie's company.
- Ghost image I've dreamed up — Bonnie at my side for the ride — starting to fade. No longer the serenity in solitude that I felt as trip began.

I held to my daily rule, driving no more than three or four hundred miles. My age, no one to share the driving, and no reason to hurry made me cautious that way. I didn't want to fall asleep at the wheel. At a rest area somewhere not long after I'd hit the Interstate I ate the last of provisions on hand. A voice inside me that sounded a lot like Bonnie's said it might be better to take at least one café meal each day where there are people around. Loneliness was beginning to intrude upon my solitude. "People, okay. But not too many. Gotta love Montana."

***

With groceries replenished at Billings I drove through the hills of Crow country. I'd just broken my four hundred mile limit when I parked the RV overnight near a reservoir called Lake DeSmet; a lake surrounded by an astonishing lack of trees. I guess that makes no difference for the boaters and water skiers, but I was ready to leave at daybreak. I decided to let someone else fix my breakfast at the next town.

It was still early morning when I pulled into Buffalo, Wyoming and found a parking lot near the center of town that called out a grand welcome to tourists' oversized vehicles. I expected to walk enough for exercise, but found a diner only a block or so down the street. I took a stool at the end of the long counter and looked around.

In a booth just across the narrow room from me were a man and woman talking with animated gestures. I noticed the woman first. Her graying hair said my age group and she held herself in a way that revealed a strikingly beautiful lady. Her casual attire—blue jeans and a hooded sweatshirt—couldn't hide it. Then I noticed the man across the table from her. He looked strangely familiar and kind of oriental, part Japanese possibly, but not clearly so. I continued to gaze at him, trying to figure. Where had I seen him? Or, whom did I know that he looked like?

He caught me staring. I looked away in embarrassment. When I glanced back he was staring at me with the same sort of questioning in his eyes.

My breakfast arrived and I dug into a meal that I knew as biscuits and gravy. This diner called it a half mudslide. I guess a whole mudslide could take down a mountain. I scalded my tongue on the first sip of rich black coffee and the man was suddenly at my side.

"Excuse me, sir," he said, "but I can't help it. You look familiar somehow. Did we know each other when I worked around here? Maybe it's just my imagination."

"Well, you look familiar, too. That's what had me rudely staring. I'm sorry about that. I can't place where, but yeah, I should know you, I guess. I'm not from here though; just passing through."

"No need to apologize. At least you weren't staring to place my race," and he was increasing the volume and looking at the man working the grill as he finished, "like some people in this joint."

The cook waved his large pancake and egg turner at us without looking up and went back to stirring some frying potatoes.

I was, but said, "I hope not. I'm Wally, Wallace Bradford. Ring any bells for you?"

"Wally! Wally Bradford," he paused and nodded, "the third, right?"

"The third, yes. Aha! I think I remember now. Keith, right? Keith…" I snapped my fingers repeatedly trying to remember. "Starts with 'K' but it's not Kamikaze. Kawasaki?"

Keith was grinning and grabbing my hand to shake. "Kawahara." We shook and he grabbed my plate and took it to the booth. I followed with my coffee and fork. "Jan, meet Wally. We were dodgers in the borderland forest together. Wally, this is my wife Janet."

We had a good old time bouncing memories of freezing in the night and getting by on tasteless little fish and dehydrated trail food. We laughed about the briefest of meetings as if it had been one big party. Keith and I kept interrupting each other to tell Jan tales from the correct point of view, of my murderous intent, of his waiting for me and my waiting for the no show after he'd gone.

After several more coffee refills, I wanted to ask Keith about his current life. "I've been fixing cars in Port Hardy, BC for thirty years. Bonnie, my late wife taught in the secondary school there. But … my kids are in Victoria and Calgary now and I sold the shop. What have you been up to?"

"Believe it or not, Wally, I recently retired from the Bureau of Reclamation."

"The US government? How did you finagle that?"

Keith shrugged. Jan giggled. "Carter's amnesty. He really meant it. With my engineering background I managed to do all right. I came home for a visit. I met Jan and couldn't leave. Home is where the heart is and the heart is where Janet is."

"Good for you," I said while wiping my eyes with a flimsy diner napkin. I was suddenly grieving again. I had never used the phrase 'late wife' before. I envied what Keith and Janet seemed to have in retirement.

As I was recovering from my moment, Keith went on, "We've moved back home now. Back on the Big Island —Hawaii."

"How is it we've stumbled on each other in Wyoming? Seems we're all just passing through."

"Not quite. As I said, we lived in Wyoming. Only for a couple years. My first assignment with Bu Rec was in Casper many years ago and Buffalo was always a rest stop between there and Yellowtail Dam."

Jan added, "You know, Wally, when you live in Hawaii? Where do you go for a vacation?"

I nodded, "Right. Wyoming, of course. And Montana?"

"Yes. We're headed for Yellowstone today, then to Glacier Park and some old stomping grounds in Canada," Keith pointed out.

***

Out on the sidewalk, the Kawaharas started downhill on Main Street. My outfit was up the other way. "Just a second, Keith. There's something else I have to ask," I said.

Keith sensed that the question was for him alone. "I'll catch up in a minute, Jan." She nodded and walked on. He looked at me with raised eyebrows.

"When you left me out there in the woods. You know. You were heading out to Vancouver, you said. Why didn't you tell Preach like you promised? I sat out there for a week waiting for the new guy who never arrived. Preach didn't know you'd gone. He'd been watching for us in Cardston."

"Wow! Is that right? For real? I tried to reach him, Wally. I couldn't locate him, so I left word with—I can't remember her name—but I did leave the message. It never occurred to me that he wouldn't get it. She assured me and she knew it was important. I am so sorry."

"It's been too many years to sweat it now. We survived, didn't we. I'm glad I asked, though. I've felt betrayed so often I just figured one more— even by a fellow outlaw. Thanks for clearing it up. You're off the hook. We were both let down by what's-her-name, then, I guess."

We parted from our brief renewal of a brief friendship. I was left wondering how many on my scoresheet of betrayals also had simple answers to exonerate them. A pair of voices in my head said, "Once again, Wally-dearest/Wally-man, it wasn't about you." I let those thoughts go as I marveled at the unlikely encounter. "What are the odds," I thought, "of meeting someone from so long ago. I never expected to see him again, even from the moment he walked off down the trail leaving me 'in charge'."

(50)

I journaled about a chance meeting and pondered my next destination. What will I find in the Missouri River town that once hosted my college, a college now relegated to history? I looked at my road map and remembered my rule. Yankton was a reasonable day's drive, but I was determined to keep to a daily goal by hours traveled, not by destination reached.

I sat staring blankly at the map of South Dakota. Then I reached over and turned the key; the idling engine quieted. I closed my eyes and remembered. Today's stopping point would not be an in-between night after all. How could I let that slip my mind? I'd been there three times already. I'd enjoyed the place when I was pointed that way by a waitress in another Wyoming town. Should I retrace that trip by way of Lusk? No, stick with the route Bonnie and I had taken through the Black Hills, driving from Yankton to the Cabin-by-the-Bob. Our one American road vacation with the kids had also included a stop at Mount Rushmore on the way to Chicago.

I sipped some already cooling coffee from the go cup to jolt myself alert, restarted the engine and struck out for the Black Hills of Dakota with a song playing in my head that made me try to remember all the lyrics to the Beatles' "Rocky Raccoon".

***

Campgrounds near Sylvan Lake were completely full. Times had changed. Demand now meant spots were reserved months in advance. I ended up at an overpriced private RV park near Hill City, which wasn't too bad. I could hold the site for a couple nights and spend a day poking around, see the sights, hike a trail that Cynthia and Curtis had led me along. Hiking, I imagined the presence of the children, running ahead and waiting for me while they caught their breath. I did not feel Bonnie's

231

presence. Where was she? It wasn't until I turned for the return walk and recalled the aroma. Bonnie was in camp preparing her signature fish chowder. At home it would be salmon. Here she had substituted trout caught by neighboring campers who enjoyed the chowder feast with us.

Return to a place became return to a past once again. By mid-afternoon I had fallen into that odd sadness, that embrace of sad serenity. Back at the trailer camp I took a long nap, then I sat in the shade with a beer near at hand and dug into old journals to compare what I'd written at the remembered times. I wrote a chapter in the current journal, too.

The next morning I was ready to roll once more.

***

I parked on the street near the campus. I looked at the sign and wanted to scream. I pounded the steering wheel until my anger gave way to the pain in my hands. A jail. "Yankton Federal Prison Camp," the sign said. It had been over a quarter century since the news had come. When I received the letter back then, that the college had closed, my only thought was that I'd never get the degree I did not intend to seek. Bonnie and I were settling into a good life with our two little children then. We both had fulfilling work. So, why should I care? It had been pretty clear when I was a student that Senior and Gram's endowments, along with other big donors weren't going to be enough without a major change.

Now it hit me. Hard. I did care. This institution had changed me for the better. Dr. Graves and her journal test, pushing me to grow from self-centered to self-aware. Mr. Schneider, historian who loved Shakespeare so much that they let him teach it with historical context. He opened insights into literature and history that still surprise me. Why did I avoid Chaplain Small? Within the sectarian German-Russian pietism of the school's milieu, he lived and mentored wide open compassion for all, no matter what. And in the midst of all that, I loved and lost Carolee.

But I found Bonnie, so that worked out in the long run. The long run, yeah, I've lost her, too. And where my college once was now is a prison camp. I sat behind the wheel there on Pine Street, and bawled, letting all my griefs rise to the surface.

I was leaning back in the seat, eyes closed, tears still flowing, gently now, when I heard a tap on the side window. My eyes popped open. I wiped my face with my hand and saw a man in uniform and badge signaling me to open the window, or possibly the door. I lowered the window.

"Can I see some ID sir? License and registration."

I dug out my driver's license and vehicle documents. "Is there a problem? I'm parked legally, right?"

He looked at the license, nodded and said, "Canada, huh. What brings you here?"

"I'm just traveling, officer. Visiting old memories."

"You've been parked here a long time, just sitting here. Next to a federal facility. Don't you think that might look suspicious? Who do you know inside?"

"Inside? What does that mean?"

"Incarcerated within, sir. A relative, perhaps?"

"Oh. No, sir, officer. I went to college here, back when this was the Yankton College campus. A long time ago."

"Well, it's time to move along."

"Can I walk around a bit? Touch base a little with the old place?"

"Nope. Time to dry your tears. Stay put. I'll be right back."

I watched in the mirror as he took my license and registration to a patrol car I hadn't noticed before. It was parked behind and the light bar was off—no spinning red and blue lights. I stepped out of the RV. As soon as my feet hit the pavement he was out too, hollering for me to get back in. I followed the order without trying to make sense of it.

After about fifteen minutes he came back, handed me the records and said, "You're free to go, Mr. Bradford. Now do it."

I drove away, found a café, washed my face and went in for a cheeseburger lunch. As I munched fries dipped in ketchup, I thought about college days and a friend I hadn't heard from in nearly twenty years, and my next stop.

I dreamily pondered, "I wonder if Pete is still in that little town." The last time we heard from them was a card about the next Christmas, maybe second, after they came to the North Island. Their big vacation trip let our location become an opportunity to see a different place and the Port Hardy Whalers' way of life. I remember Pete bringing up my best man request and accusing me of setting him up to make a commitment and then turn him into an extra attendant. He knew I already had a best man. He never did think we were close friends, which says something about me, I guess.

***

In Sac City I found the house with a carved wooden sign next to the front door that said "Ted & Mary Cook". No phone listing for Peter Schmitz, now this. What are my options? For want of a better idea, I rang the bell.

"No, sir. I don't have any idea. Ted and I've been here for years, more than ten anyhow. You might could find some of the old timers down at Hutch's." She looked at her watch and murmured, "You'd have better luck there in the morning. If you're hungry, try the pork tenderloin."

I enjoyed the pork chop, and learned the sad news from a gray haired couple who were ready to chat all evening. After talk about running gas stations, which we had in common, I eventually found that Pete's widow was in Minnesota near their daughter. She said Mankato, her husband was sure she was in Owatonna. They argued about that for a while.

"What happened to Pete?"

"He held on longer than some other of the small operations but the bank got the farm. Musta been back in the nineties. Broke Pete's heart. His Pop couldn't just give it to him. They had to finagle a sale, don'tcha know. Piled up the debt. Broke Pete's heart. He loved that farm."

"Don't I know it. Bonnie and I visited them once. Pete gave me a hard time because I once said farming didn't look like much of a life and then I spent five years as farm and ranch hand. Perfect life for the loner I was then. ... But, what happened?"

"Busted him. I got nothing more to tell you than that." The two of them both shook their heads.

***

I found a place to park for the night and poured my low mood into the journal. "Sounds like suicide they don't want to talk about. Maybe I wasn't much of a friend to Pete." Guilt feelings about something long ago and far away brought up a deeper shame about my lack of attention in Bonnie's desperate time. I wrote it all down, which helped, but not enough. Sleep was fitful. I did not want to think about what's next, either.

(51)

I finished yet another hamburger lunch sitting at an outdoor table at a chain fast food joint in Galena, Illinois, dumped my trash and sat back down to warn the family. First I tried Bryan's number. As I kind of expected, voicemail picked up. He still worked for a living, after all. I left a message and tried Linda's. One ring. Geez, she's over seventy now. Two ... Seven rings and no answer.

My last hope, on Char's line I heard two rings, then a click and more rings at lower volume. "Oh good, she's picking up."

"What? Hello?" said a voice I'd recognize anywhere.

"Hi, Char. Wally here. I'm at Galena now. I should be to your place in a few hours."

"Oh, for crying out loud, Trey. I tried to call you but I lost your cell number when my phone broke drowned in the lake. We're at the summer cottage. Come on up. We'll all be here. Bryan's coming tomorrow."

"How about Linda? Are they home?"

"They're here, too. Grandkids piled three deep." I shuddered at my mental picture of that. "It's great. You won't find anybody in the city." An empty city picture replaced the imagined dense family crowd, calming my anxiety.

She gave me directions to the address at Powers Lake, Wisconsin. Since I could bypass the worst of urban traffic, I could be to the summer place in about the same time as to the north shore suburbs.

I still intended to wander through the old place back home. Long ago, when I was trying to escape and didn't want to think of Winnetka as home, it still was home in my mind. Now my home was on the north end of Vancouver Island ... or was it? Without family or business, where was the home at that place? But there was no 'back home Winnetka', and yet it had now become an important stop on the remembrance tour.

***

"I should've called you sooner, Curt. But I've been taking it as it comes, never sure quite how far down the road I'll be one day to the next. I took an extra day in the Black Hills."

"What are you telling me, Pop?"

"I thought I'd be getting to Char's in Deerfield tonight. Turns out they're all over in Wisconsin. Linda and Char, the Husbands and hundreds of grandchildren. They apparently own a cottage together at a place called Powers Lake. So that's where I'm headed this afternoon. Do you still want to fly in? And can you afford a hurry-up ticket? I can reimburse you."

"Um, no. It turns out the timings all wrong, Dad. We're backed up with some complications on one of our clients. It should all be worked out soon, but Bill and I have to tough this one out together for now. I guess there's some work I can't do from any ol' where."

"I see. Yeah, stuff happens. Maybe someday we can come down together and give the Bradford clan a lesson in family."

"Yeah, stuff. I'd have used another word for this mess. But, hey, when are you heading back home? Are you going anywhere else after that lake cottage?"

"I'm having a fine solitary time, Curt. I think I'll be driving on east. So, yeah. If you're freed up by then, we could still meet in Chicago on my way home and go up to this Powers Lake place if need be." I used that word 'home' again, and wondered, "Is home a Winnebago motor 'home'?"

As I drove to Wisconsin, I didn't worry in anticipation of a Bradford family visit, I was too busy worrying about Curt and Bill and what kind of unscrupulous clients they might be dealing with.

***

They called it a cottage. The house a few blocks up from the lake was a little larger than mine in Port Hardy. On the other hand, it was much smaller than houses closer to the boat docks. And those were smaller than my sisters' homes where I'd last visited them.

"Great!" Char said as she pulled me into the house with a hug. "Did you have any trouble finding us? Have you eaten?"

236

It was too late to expect supper. "No and no, but I have everything I need in the RV." Char led me to a screen porch and deck at the back of the cottage where the Husbands were grilling kabobs and vying for control of the barbecue tools.

"Just in time for food. Good timing, Trey," Linda said and we hugged. The Husbands suspended their tussle long enough to shake my hand. "Bryan will be here tomorrow night. You'll be here through the weekend, right?"

"I haven't planned that far ahead. Junior's not here to throw me out, so … yeah, I guess I will, eh."

"Trey Bradford," Linda scolded, "not with us two minutes and speaking ill of our poor dead father. Way off in Canada, 'eh', you didn't see how he suffered those last weeks."

I opened my mouth to protest, closed it again and eventually muttered under my breath, "He may toss me out yet."

The younger generations came streaming in wearing bathing suits wrapped in wet towels. The chatter was all about water skiing and an end of day adventure when the outboard motor on one of the family's two boats died. They told of using the skier tow ropes from the working craft to pull the boat to the dock. I didn't say anything, but I knew that the next morning I had a great opportunity to become popular with some young grandnieces and grandnephews, even if I'd never remember any of their names.

With the older generation, I waited for the second round to come off the gas grill. The Husbands had abandoned their tussle for head chef ranking. They had both lost interest in cooking and a son-in-law of some sort quietly took over. I found a corner where I watched and avoided saying much. Saying the wrong thing was worrisome enough to keep me quiet. It felt better to listen and fill up on a salads and chips. Watching the family dynamic, I tried to figure out how many generations there were in the room. If I asked if any kids are great-grandchildren, would it annoy Linda or Char? I let it go.

***

It had been years since I'd worked on a small outboard. I had, of course, supervised engine maintenance on plenty of diesel fishing trawlers. The small engine wasn't a great challenge, but I sure missed my shop and its array of the correct tools for the job. With a trip to a marine parts counter we did get it purring and the young folks learned some things that might help them keep it running better. I joined them for a test run and we made it back to dock under power. I was beginning to enjoy myself, even with my family around. If there just weren't so many of them all in the same screen porch.

I missed my own two grandchildren and considered that they might like to meet their cousins someday. After a buffet of salads left over from the previous evening I retreated to my camper for some serious journal writing and reading plus a little nap. The sounds of a boisterous welcome to Bryan woke me. It was after five o'clock. I had slept the whole afternoon with an old journal dropped on my chest. It was a chronicle of repartee, nasty cracks really, words I should have said to Junior if only I'd thought of them during the arguments. I still hadn't written in the current diary since I arrived the previous evening. So I wrote. Greeting Bryan could wait a few more minutes.

An hour later I found my way around the yard to enter the screen porch without going through the kitchen. It was just as well. I found Bryan and the Husbands sitting in some old Adirondack chairs out on the sloping lawn. The chairs must have come from the Winnetka mansion. They were admiring the activity out on the little lake, the sailboats, the power boats pulling skiers, and in a cove across the lake, barely visible, a fisherman in a rowboat.

Bryan heard me coming, turned and jumped up. He slapped me on the back and said, "Grab a beer from the cooler there. Good to see you, big brother."

I swallowed hard before I could respond. I felt as if I were watching this scene instead of standing in the middle of it. It was Junior with a prospective supplier he intended to take to the cleaners. Bryan playing our father with me in the role of client sucker.

Bryan didn't wait for my reply. He ran off to find another chair. I got a beer, and one for each of the Husbands who didn't seem inclined to move out of their seats. I took Bryan's chair.

The Husbands resumed their conversation. "We should get a sailboat. Look at 'em skimming the waves out there. Powered by the breeze instead of that noisy motor."

"If we're gonna live out here year round like the girls want, an ice boat is more like it, am I right?"

"Nah. Get a snowmobile for winter."

"There's your noise again. And another engine to stall out on you in the middle of nowhere."

I broke in, "Haven't you ever been sailing? It isn't nearly as quiet as it looks from up here. There's noise from the wind in the sails and waves slapping the hull. That's good noise, though; feel good noise. You should get a sailboat."

I got a dubious look from both of them, but then I heard the one with the gray mustache say, "I've been sailing. Years ago. Kinda forgot what it's like. Makes me want one even more."

"Go for it, then."

"Kids won't take kindly to me trading their speedboat for a boat with no vroom-vroom."

Bryan came back; the bottle of light beer he'd just opened was half empty. "So, Trey, how's the family? Sorry to hear about your wife. Must've been an awful shock. You got grandkids now, right?"

My answer was brief, but I did want my family of origin to know how close I was to my real family. "Cynthia and Jared are at Victoria. She's a medical lab technician and he works in the provincial education ministry. Two kids. Megan is four and Brad is, oh, what? A year and a half. Curtis lives in Calgary with his partner. He and Bill have a two man company in financial services for oil field contractors."

A Husband perked up. It was the other one, the even balder one with a clean shaven upper lip. He said, "Lives with his partner. Business partner? Or what? Is he one of those, you know…?"

"Those, you know? I don't follow. What are you asking?" I was getting better at having the repartee ready on time.

"Shit, man. You know what I mean. All right, I'll just say it. Is he some kind of faggot?"

"Curt is my son, and he is gay. He and Bill talk about getting married, but they haven't set a date. They live as husband and husband, though. Does that answer your snide question?"

"Sorry, Trey, but it's just wrong. You, of all people, ought to see that."

The other Husband interjected, "We can blame Canada, allowing that gay marriage everywhere. Now America. Think that'll spread all over the USA?"

"In Canada we just call it marriage." I returned to the other provocation. "What I see, of all people, that my son is happy and living a full life. After all the crap he endured in secondary school while his mother was teaching in that same building. Boy howdy, I'm thankful he's past that.

I'm thankful for his loving partner. And I don't want to hear another word about it, unless you can tell me how wrong you are."

Both Husbands got up and took their beers into the screen porch. I took a deep breath and shifted the talk another way. "What about your family, Bry? Are any of them here with you?"

Bryan looked like he was about to cry. "No, Trey. I'm alone. Since not long after you were with us for Mom's funeral."

"What are you saying, my brother?"

"Peggy left me. Turned the boys against me, too. I got two grandbabies I've never met."

"Oh, man. That's a damn shame."

"Yeah, well, I'll tell you about it sometime. Not now, though. Too nice of a day." He stood up, teetered a little, and added, "You want another beer?" He was already twisting the cap off another bottle.

"No, I'm fine." I took another swig from my half-full bottle.

"Company went down the toilet. But you know that. I've been scrambling ever since. Real estate now. I even managed the garden department in a Home Depot store for a while. But, hey, I closed on a nice property this week. So, I'll be flush for a bit. Live it up while you can, huh." He lifted his bottle to clink against mine, but missed, and emptied it down his throat.

***

After a pizza delivery supper that was my treat, Bryan switched bottles. He had one last beer with the food, then he opened a fifth of bourbon.

At 9:30 I slipped out to the RV and converted the table and bench into the extra bed. Then I helped Bryan, who couldn't quite walk on his own, to that bed. As soon he was settled he seemed to force himself to be more alert again.

"Hey, bro," he slurred, "go get the bag outa my car. Got sumpin' you like."

I found keys in a pocket of the pants I'd helped him out of and wondered if I could tell which car. I got outside, looked at the ring of keys under the porch light and said to myself, "Dummy, of course," and I punched the unlock button on the key fob. Lights flashed and I found a soft leather overnight bag on the back seat.

I dropped the bag next to Bryan. With much fumbling he managed to get it open and rummage through it until he pulled out a smaller leather bag with a string closure. He reached out for me to take it. "Some good shit in there. You'll like it, Trey bro." I think that's what he said in his barely audible slurring of words. I couldn't figure out why he still hadn't passed out.

I took the bag. The smell as I brought it closer told me everything without opening it. "I haven't smoked grass in many years, Bry. Not my thing anymore." I laid the bag on the counter.

Bryan jolted, trying to lift himself to a sitting position. He gave up and lay back again. "Just load that pipe. Man, you are in for a... Ish better'n that crap back in your day. Jus' light it up. C'mon, a'ready."

I opened windows and complied, not ready to fight with him. He got one hit from the pipe, barely held it and lapsed into a drunken coma.

I crawled into my bed and lay awake in the dark for a long time thinking about this family of my birth and its troubles. With all the privileges we had, and still have, I worried about my younger brother, trust funds, and wealth — enough to assume we could always have everything. Did losing some of that send Bryan into this misery? And was this day's drinking from alcoholism, or just a getaway day let down? If I'd been alone in the RV I'd have turned on a light, sat at my table and written in the journal, then slept better. I'm sure a light wouldn't stir Bryan, but I wasn't entirely sure where I'd stowed the laptop when I set up his bed. I stewed in the dark about that, too.

(52)

I woke up early to the smell of marijuana. Bryan was sitting on the edge of his makeshift bed, one hand holding his head, the other the pipe. I rolled out saying, "What the hell?"

"Good day to you. You don't want me to puke on your nice rug, do you?" He offered me the pipe. "This helps me with that little problem."

I shook off his offer. "Well, you're not gonna burn that crap inside my outfit. That's it." I opened all the windows. While I did that, I was considering what to say next.

He said, "Oo, when did you get so righteous? The first pot I ever smoked came from you."

"When did I ever give you...?"

"I didn't say you gave it to me. It was out of your stash, though."

It was time to get tough, or so I thought. "You had a lot to drink yesterday. Do you get wasted like that every day? Or, what?"

"No. What's it to you, anyway?"

"So, it's not just on vacation. You do drink a lot, right?" I cringed at what I'd just asked. This trip was turning into a Dear Abby tour. Here I was trying to fix what wasn't my business. Again. But he's my brother. But we were never close, at least that was my assumption. But...but.

"I told you. Didn't I tell you? Peggy left me. My sons hate me. What's the use." The last wasn't a question.

"Did your drinking get bad after she left? Or did she leave because of it?" I was in a hole and digging myself deeper.

242

Bryan didn't answer. He glared first at me, then at a small rip in the flooring vinyl in front of him. He twisted the 'nice' throw rug around with his feet, pushed it over the tear and slumped back on the bed.

I watched and waited for a long moment and then said, "I'm gonna get into some clean clothes and find some breakfast. You with me?"

***

Maybe I was being too hardhearted. Bryan ate a good breakfast without any noticeable ill effect. I guessed maybe the pot was responsible. If so, credit where credit is due. The conversation with an officer of the law at Yankton made me certain that I did not want the aroma permeating my traveler's lodgings.

After breakfast my brother seemed to be moving toward the beer cooler behind the porch. "Don't interfere," I thought. "The problem isn't going to be solved this weekend, so why stir it." Then I had another thought; a way to delay him for a while, without confrontation.

"Bryan, let's us take a walk. Get a look around this village of second homes." I turned him around and hauled him out to the street.

"What are you pushing me for? Where're we going, anyway?"

"I just figured walking around a little couldn't hurt. If I go alone, I might forget how to find the cottage. All these streets and houses look alike."

"Bullshit. This is some kind of set-up. Are you gonna jerk me into another of those intervention games?"

That hadn't occurred to me. It sounded like a good idea. All I said was, "Not today, no." I had him walking briskly with me. We walked without speaking for a few blocks, and then slowed our pace. The fact that we were both winded after such a short distance without running should have told us something.

"Look at that, Trey." Beside a driveway where it meets the street was a sailboat on a trailer. It looked old, but well cared for, and longer than five meters. The sign taped to the mast that was tied flat on the boat said, "For Sale" with a phone number. I pulled my phone from the case on my belt, flipped it open, and a gray-bearded man came bounding out of the house with dickering a sale written all over his face.

"That's a helluva lot more sailboat than the Husbands were talking about. Their kids would love that," I murmured to Bryan.

"Were they talking about the dinghy?"

The man joined us and began to tell us all about his sloop. He made sure we knew the single mast, two sail vessel's correct name. He seemed to be ready to tell us about every sailing adventure the boat had ever taken him on. Lakes Michigan and Superior were mentioned several times. Finally I asked the obvious question. "How much?"

He gave us a price. I shook my head and with an outstretched arm pointed my forefinger down. I said, "We'll think about it. Meantime, you think about how much you really need for it." And I walked on up the street, leaving Bryan standing there shrugging his shoulders.

Half a block away I stopped and waited for Bryan to catch up. I was thinking it over. I could dip into my retirement savings that still included some unspent savings from back before the company trust went broke. It wouldn't change my lifestyle, I didn't think. A sailboat, that sloop, would assure me a fine legacy with Char's and Linda's grandkids.

Bryan caught up, took a couple gulps of air and asked, "What was that? You're a tough customer, Trey. Glad you're not in the market for one of my home listings."

"Not really, Bry. I'm gonna buy that bo … sloop for the kids.

"That boat's too big for this little lake, Trey. Wind fills the mainsail and you run aground across the lake before you know what happened. Probably why it's for sale."

"Yeah? Where'd you learn that sailor talk?" I had my heart set on it, but Bryan was right.

"I've been around. Been nice walking with you. Let's go get a beer."

***

All morning I stewed. I had a grand scheme for all of ten minutes. I was not comfortable abandoning a project. I had decided on a nice gift to the family. If not the sloop, what? After lunch I was on my way to the RV in hopes that journal writing could take the puzzle off my mind. Bryan called to me from a hidden spot between my outfit and the large maple tree it was parked under. He relit his pipe as I approached.

"What's up, Bry?"

"Did I happen to mention anything about a storage lot and what I got?"

"Nope. I have some writing to do. See you later."

"Hold on there, Trey. Let me tell you. You want a boat, right? One that'll suit this lake. Okay, the property is still in a little tussle, but I'm stuck with the storage rent. Gotta get it out of there."

244

"Are you saying you have a smaller sailboat, or what?"

"That's what I'm trying to tell you. I have a nice dinghy. Simple little boat, one sail, eight foot. Me and the boys used to have some good times with it. … Hold up. Let me finish."

I waited while he took another hit from the pipe and held his breath. Then he went on, "Here's the deal. You want to give them a boat real bad. I saw that bubble bust when you saw I'm right. What you do, I'm saying, is buy mine. I'll haul it up here. I give the money to Peggy. Everybody's happy."

I nodded, thinking it over. We agreed on a price, much less than the sloop but more than the dinghy was worth, I'm sure. We shook hands and he mentioned the storage rent in arrears that I'd have to pay before it got auctioned.

"I thought you just closed a big sale." His response was a shrug and a smile. I wanted to punch him, but somehow I managed to let it go and accept my fate. Drunk and high, he was still Junior's boy working the deal.

I wrote a check to the storage company and was about to ask, "Should I write the other to Peggy?" I caught myself and didn't ask it. My responsibility could end as long as I had proof of purchase.

*****

After an hour of journaling I was on my way around the house to relax and gaze over the lake with the Husbands or whomever. As I reached the back of the house I heard Bryan's voice from the screen porch saying to Char and Linda, "Next weekend I'm bringing my sailboat out for the kids to enjoy."

"Well, thank you, Bryan. But didn't you say Peggy had some kind of claim on it?" Linda asked.

Char added, "That was the reason you had to leave it in storage. What you told us before."

"Yeah, well. I got it worked out. She'll get paid and you guys can keep the dinghy."

This time I didn't shrug it off. I stormed into the porch and laid a gut punch into Bryan before I had time to reconsider. "You little shit!" Bryan is an inch taller and twenty pounds heavier than I am, but I'm still big brother. He had it coming.

Bryan doubled over in pain, but mostly in surprise, "What the ... Why'd you slug me, Trey?"

Now I had time to reconsider. Nope. I was still angry as hell. "How could you? I bought that boat from you not two hours ago. I paid you too much so I could give it to my nieces and nephews. You already cheated me into paying the overdue rent, now this. All of Junior's worst traits live on in you, you little drunken shit."

"Wallace, sit down." I obeyed Char's order. "You too, Bryan." He also obeyed. Char looked like she was ready to scream. Instead she took a deep breath and sat down between us. Linda had disappeared, no doubt hiding in the kitchen.

Char took another long counting breath. I was starting to be angry with myself, and tried the slow breathing, too. Then she said, "For once can we be a loving family? We can't stay angry forever, can we?" She turned to Bryan. "Is it true, Bryan? What Trey said?"

"You know I've been wanting you to have it. Goes with this lake and everything."

"Is it true?"

"Well, yeah. He put some money into it. We both want it out here. Right, Trey?"

"Some money. I bought the damn thing outright. On your word — like that's worth anything. On your word that your ex would get what she's due."

"Hell, I was gonna tell you he bought it, Char. That's how we can give it. And before I can say so, Trey comes storming in and pounds on me. Calls me names like when we were kids."

I didn't believe him. He wasn't about to mention my participation, but my anger was used up. "How's your belly, Bry? Did I hurt you?"

"I'll be fine. You ain't so tough."

Char slapped her knees, signaling that she was ready to conclude the mediation. "If you two are ready to be grown-ups again, think about it. Everybody gets a good deal; it seems so to me, anyway. You both want to see the boat in use on the lake. Trey puts up the wherewithal. Bry kept the boat because he wants it enjoyed in the family. The kids can learn how to handle it. Win, win, win."

Linda reappeared with a plate of blueberry muffins and a pitcher of iced tea. She insisted that Bryan drink a whole glass of tea before he was allowed access to the beer cooler.

***

I wrote in my journal, "My lying brother. Steals the credit just like Dad and Gramp. Bradford men! Can't trust Bradford men. Oh well, we just have to get along regardless. Family. Sheesh. Betrayed again. Why am I surprised? I never could trust him."

(53)

Bryan wasn't ready for the Sunday morning chaos, nor was I. It helped us put yesterday aside, however. In my crowd-anxiety state I beckoned and Bryan followed me back to the RV for a bowl of cereal and a mug of coffee. Afterward, he slipped away for some more of his stomach settling weed. I steeled myself and went into the house, where things seemed to be settling down. I found Char and Linda in the kitchen, leaning against the counter sipping coffee. I poured myself some and sat down at the little kitchen table. Char quickly joined me, pushing accumulated groceries and utensils to the table's center.

Linda grumbled, "I guess I'll just go by myself then. It's not worth fighting them on vacation. I just wish it wasn't always this big argument every week."

"No, it's not worth arguing, Linda. Can I say what I really think?" Char didn't wait for an answer. "I think that the more you demand, the more you push them away."

I was hearing this, but not getting it. It looked too much like a Junior and Trey picture. I asked, "Where are you going by yourself, Lindy?"

"Why, church, of course. Somebody here has to pray for you and Bryan." And she launched into an invitation that was more of a sermon. She had become part of a Pentecostal church while I was long away. I declined the invitation with a somewhat (cough) exaggerated claim of my involvement in that mixture of Anglican and United Church of Canada where Cynthia and Curtis were guided through years of Sunday School before we drifted off on other weekend activities. Linda gave up on me, looked at the clock, and left us.

"How're you and Bry getting along?" Char asked. "I'm relieved that last night you didn't boot him out of your — what did I hear you call it? — unit or outfit. Anyway, good that he's crashing out there with you."

"You know, Char, yesterday morning, to distract him and get some air into our lungs before he slid into a beer bottle, I got him to go for that walk. We saw an old sloop for sale. That's what started the whole sailboat mess. Anyhow, Bryan accused me. Claimed getting him on the walk was a set-up, that we were about to do an intervention. He used that word."

"Been there, tried that. That's when Peggy had had enough, when he fell off the wagon right away."

"Think it might be worth trying again?"

At that moment Bryan came in, grabbed a mug, filled it facing the coffee maker and added a little cold water from the tap. His hands were shaking. He steadied the cup with both hands and turned from the sink, looked at Char and me, shook his head, took a gulp of coffee and said, "That's it. I'm heading out this morning."

"Heading out? Where? I thought you were with us for another day, Bry. Please stay." Char pleaded.

"I'm going home. Live my own life without you trying to fix me. You can go find somebody else to fix up your way."

I guess Char had decided there was no point in pleading. She looked at me and said, "He sounds like you, Trey."

"I can't argue with that. I can almost hear myself … and see Junior's reaction. I hope I'm not Junior now. That's Bry's role." I stood up, poured the last of the coffee, reached my right had to Bryan and said, "Live your life, Bryan. Sorry I brought it up. I should learn when to leave well enough alone."

"I still wish you wouldn't rush off, Bryan. The kids will all be heading home this afternoon and I was looking forward to a few hours of just us old folks."

"God damn. You hear her, Trey? You talk about your déjà vu all over again. Char can guilt a guy as good as Mom ever did."

Through a sheepish grin Char said, "So you'll stay?"

Bryan put his cup in the sink and went out the door leading to the screen porch shaking his head. Two minutes later he was back, with a beer in his hand. "Deal. You won't use that freaking 'I' word again and you won't count these." He waved the bottle. "Otherwise I'm off."

"Works for me, kid," I said, and Char nodded agreement. An evening of siblings and the Husbands would include at least one drunken member.

"And you'll be back next weekend with a certain aquatic vessel." Char started another pot of coffee. I went out to put my unit or outfit or whatever in order and do some early journal writing. He sounded like a younger me; and I came just this close to sounding like Junior, which made for a bizarre turn of events, I thought.

***

"Where's Bry?" I asked. I'd wandered through the yard and into the screen porch. "I expected to find him near the ice chest."

"He found only one beer left, drank it, and said he was going to get more ice." The bald on top Husband without the mustache, Linda's I think, looked at his wristwatch. "Whoa, it's been two hours or more. It can't take that long to Twin Lakes and back."

"He might've forgot it's Sunday. Do some stores close?"

"Nah. He was in a surly mood. He's probably at a bar falling off the stool by now."

"He's pretty pissed and touchy about the booze. He was ready to go home this morning because he overheard Char and me. I had to promise to let it go and Char guilted him into staying."

"All I said to him was how I noticed he was starting early."

"Geez, he's probably nearly home by now. He must carry a cell phone. All I have is his home number."

"Char's got his cell number. She's inside helping the grandkids pack."

No answer. I left a message, and went out to the RV and tried again. Still nothing. I heard activity at the driveway. Maybe he's back. I went out. The Husbands were organizing grandkids for one last turn on the water skis before they had to leave, and catching flak from their adult children about the delay that would cause and having to repack again, including wet swimsuits. Parents won and younger children pouted. "Next weekend, " a Husband promised.

***

I punched redial and waited, half expecting to go directly to voicemail. After three rings, wow, an answer. "Wha'? Who's thi'?" Bryan slurred.

"Your brother. Where are you, Bry?"

"Who wants to know?" It sounded like he was making a real effort to sound less inebriated.

"They said you were bringing some ice and beer. It's been a long time so I just wondered. Thought maybe you'd changed your mind and gone on home after all."

"Nah. I'm at nice little inn at Twin Lakes, as if you cared."

"I do, Bry. What's the name of it? I'll come and ge... join you. We're out of beer here."

"Uh-huh. What the hell." Without pulling the phone away, he yelled, "What's the name o' this place?"

"I heard another voice answer, "Beach Bar." Then Bryan repeated the news.

"Sit tight. I'll be there soon and you're buying my first round."

I grabbed my wallet and was about to look for Char when a car turned into the drive. Linda arrived from her hours of churchgoing, so I asked her, though I worried, with all that Holy Spirit built up in her, if doing her Christian duty to retrieve her brother from the den of iniquity might go wrong. "We need to get Bryan. He's at Twin Lakes, the Beach Bar. Not in shape to drive."

"I just went past there. Oh, here's Char. Better tell her what's up."

Char joined us on the driveway. "Glad you're back, Linda. The kids have most of their stuff gathered up. They're itching to get on the way before the children start begging for one more day. Where are the guys?"

I answered, "The Husbands are down at the lake, without kids." Yes, I used the term 'Husbands' out loud.

"And Bryan? Did he really go home? Did you ever reach him?"

"Yeah, he's next. We have to get him. He's drinking at the Beach Bar. He needs a ride, and someone to drive his car. I told him I wanted to join him because we're out of beer. I plan to keep my word before I wrestle him for car keys."

***

I reviewed my day as I wrote the journal late that evening. I wrote about bribing Bryan with the promise of a boilermaker to get him to hand me the keys. I wrote about missing the goodbye time while we were rescuing the prodigal. The younger folks had Monday home and work routines calling them back to Chicago. I wrote more about Saturday's dispute with Bryan; of still feeling abused and betrayed; of hiding resentments under a mask of pleasantries.

My final paragraph for the night said that I had nothing to say about the banal evening conversation with my siblings. The family had lost so much in corporate consolidations and yet they held firm in their belief that business is all and needs no regulation. Phooey. I didn't argue. What's the use? Of course, I don't know what Bryan thinks. He spent the evening emptying and refilling his glass and mumbling. He could barely walk, but I still made him sit outside for his toke.

(54)

On Monday morning I was ready to go. I had to roust Bryan out of the dinette bunk so that I could put things in order for travel. He hesitated. He came back in from a morning after settling of the stomach, held his aching head between his palms and said, "Only thing worse than staying around here with the Wives..." He lifted his head out of his hands and looked at me with the wry grin his word choice inspired.

I laughed, "I was hoping no one noticed that I still refuse to learn the Husbands by name. Some kind of crazy, huh. What's worse?"

"Going back to crap city and trying to find two beans to rub together until they make soup. You're lucky about one thing."

"What? That I got to retire young enough to enjoy it? That I get to go where I want when I want?

"Okay, you're lucky about lots of things. I go back to that crap condo; the wife who isn't there still calls and nags me about all my screw-ups. You don't have to take that kind of crap."

"That was really low, Bryan." To think I was getting over his Saturday lies. "Get outa my house."

"What'd I say?"

"You think I don't have to face ... Hell, Bonnie DIED. Yes. You think after thirty plus years together that I don't love her or need her anymore? I miss her every day and I see the crap I put her through every day. Take it back or get out."

"God, I'm sorry, Trey. It's not...I wasn't thinking about...It's just...My life is a mess. I mean, it's not about you, Brother."

"You were doing better up to that. It's not about me? I don't want to hear it. Get out."

***

I really didn't want to get on the highway filled with anger. I watched Bryan gather up his few items and stuff them in the zippered case. He kept his pouch separate. The leather bag looked like an oversized version of the medicine pouch that often hung by a bootlace under Cracker's shirt. All of a sudden I was missing Cracker, too, and the forest cabin where we'd sit watching the fire in silence until there was something that needed words to say.

Bryan's feet hit the ground. He turned back in the doorway, hesitated, and closed the door without saying whatever was on his mind. When I heard him rev into forward motion on the roadway, I walked to the house. Maybe I crawled. It sure felt like I was bending that low.

***

"Welcome to Illinois," the sign read. "Used to be home … so to speak," I muttered. I was staying away from the expressways. I was in no hurry. I'd spend my day poking around on the old turf. Char's coffee and concern had calmed some of my latest anger before I left. I still have sibling family after all. I was musing as I drove along. Bryan and I had never been close, or so I always thought. Now I'd punched him and booted him away in bitter anger. I wouldn't have been so angry if we weren't close—brothers after all. It was a troubling discovery because it raised new questions. What must I do next with Bryan simply because he's my brother? And he's hurting.

Aloud in my solo driver's seat I said, "Well, I can't fix it. I can't fix him. Not today. I'll call him in a day or two, just to let him know where I am and what I'm doing. And that I'm no longer mad at him. Unless I am."

***

Solitude slid into loneliness as I wandered the streets, schoolyards and beach at Winnetka. The old mansion was still there, but changed in odd, confusing ways. Where another huge old estate had been nearby, there were now two large facades of the sort often called McMansions.

I must have covered several miles in my meanderings. In lonely melancholy I wished for my lady at my side. I imagined Bonnie's hand in mine, what she might ask about my childhood as we strolled past the schools I attended, the beach where I played, or the corner taco café in what was once the Pure Oil Station where I did my first engine rebuild.

I sat on a park bench to rest. With my eyes closed I turned my head to the side hoping to gaze at my remembrance of Bonnie, to enjoy her company in a moment of imagining. I looked through mind's eye and saw pretty Bonnie for a second, but then the vision changed. I saw instead, standing behind the bench, a tall, athletic young woman with long, straight blonde hair. With that description one might expect a sexual fantasy, and yes, there was a bit of that, but this was a particular memory. Bonnie was not alone in my longing, Carolee 'Curlybabe' had come, too.

The memory image came as surprise, and yet it wasn't so surprising. I had been contemplating my next destination for several days. I was moving beyond the retracing of steps with Bonnie. Re-connecting with siblings and their offspring at a new place convinced me that I would definitely go further east.

Before that could happen I had to remember the way back to the Monday-vacant church parking lot where I'd left the Winnebago.

***

I nibbled around a mid-afternoon lunch alone in the RV and opened my laptop for some journal writing of sadness, surprises, visions and hope. I tried to nap, but the achy legs of an old out-of-shape guy kept me awake. I took an ibuprofen and drove across northern Indiana. By the time I reached Ohio it was time to find a place to stop. I drove on, thinking, "There must be some place to camp for a short night."

An exit sign said, 'Middle Point' and I turned off thinking, "There must be a place to park at least. And what better; call it half way from where I started the day to Altoona tomorrow evening. Then what? Who knows? But this is a middle point of some sort."

The small business district seemed to be closed, not just for the day, but forever. I saw no one. I drove along a street of well-kept little houses and found the park—a baseball park. The people of the town were enjoying softball games on two fields. I asked, and got directions to a pond west of town. "Follow Railroad Street. You can pull in amongst the trees over there and no one's likely to bother you for one night."

"Amongst the trees," he said. He really meant, "Amongst the mosquitos." I snacked inside, took another pill for the aches, turned in early, slept well for a several hours, and at four in the morning gave up on trying to get back to sleep. The gothic novel that had been putting me to sleep most nights didn't help. I got up, dug into some old journals to let myself fantasize about the unlikely prospect of finding Carolee again. One cup of coffee alerted me to reality. "She could be anywhere, with a

255

husband and grandchildren. If I find anything of her, it'll be stay away or hell to pay."

At daybreak, I drove on toward Pennsylvania, disappointment and doom.

(55)

I was so close—so close to Altoona. I'd gone by way of Pittsburgh; don't ask me why. I could have stayed to the north and avoided the city. The Steel City, great as it is, held no interest. I just wanted to get to my destination and find out if there was anything to find out. And I was so close when I was jolted to alertness by a honking horn. I popped up from the noise to discover that the Winnebago and I were drifting left into the fast lane. Close or not, it was beyond time for a break. I pulled off at the next exit. Not only was I asleep for a moment, I was oblivious for a longer time. Coming out of a big cloverleaf a few miles back, I discovered I'd been driving away from Altoona. Now I was at Duncanville looking for lunch and a place to park for a nap. I passed the Dairy Queen and Pizza Hut. Pizza sounded good, but that meant turning left where traffic was backed up at the light. Eventually I spotted another pizzeria. Rosie's looked local, probably a one store independent. "Yeah, avoid the chain stores."

At the entrance I spotted a rack of brochures and fliers about area attractions and businesses. Prominently displayed at top and center was a glossy magazine, probably not the most recent issue. Over a photograph of a courthouse square, the masthead read, *SW-PA: Your Town Too.* At first glance it reminded me of airplane seat pocket material. I took a copy to a table. A menu and a glass of ice water appeared in front of me. I sipped the water and opened the magazine to the table of contents. The list revealed an interesting concept. A regional booster book, each issue focused on one small town. It included the usual touristy sites along with the locals' favorites with poetry and stories by local writers, and a photo spread on local artists. I turned the page and found the editor's introduction. "Hot damn," I said, a little too loudly.

A voice at my side replied, "We're all out, sorry. We do have pepperoni or anchovy."

I looked up and stared, either sleepily or dreamily, I'm not sure which.

"Are you ready to order, sir?"

"Am I too late for the lunch buffet?"

"Yeah, but we didn't have any hot damn then, either."

"Oh. I'm a little slow on the uptake. I nearly crashed my motor home. Fell asleep at the wheel for a second out there. How about a small pie with everything except anchovies?"

"Got it. I'll make some fresh coffee for you. I see you found our magazine."

"Our? Well you sure look like her, Rosalee." I read her nametag.

"Who do I look like?"

"The editor-publisher." I pointed to the name at the bottom of the open page. "Carolee Siebert. Unless that's a common name around here, I used to know her."

"My grandma."

I was stunned. This can't be real. "Except for your lovely dark hair, you look an awful lot like she did the last time I saw her. Is she still beautiful, too?" I looked again at the magazine, found the editorial address in Duncanville, the town where I was about to eat a pizza. "Will I find her at this address?" I asked. "She edits by her maiden name, I see."

"Just a sec." She took my order to the kitchen. I watched over the wide arched pass-through counter as she talked with the cook. He looked like he might be her father.

She checked on the other two tables that were occupied in mid-afternoon and brought coffee to me. "By any chance is your name Jeff?"

"No ... no, it's Wally. Wally Bradford."

"Wally? For real? Appalachian Trail Wally?"

I nodded. "How much do you know about...?"

"Oh, for fuck's sake... Oops. Sorry." Rosalee did a zipping her lip gesture and looked around. If anyone else heard her language, they weren't reacting. "Don't tell Dad what I said."

"Oh? What did you say?" I said it with a sheepish smile.

"Never mind. Grandma loves to tell me stories. From the time I was little. I know lots more about her life than Dad ever heard. Oh, and

Siebert's her name; since the divorce, I guess. That's long before my time." She nodded toward the kitchen. "That's Dad. Her son." Looking that way reminded her of her job and she wandered over, ready to bring my order as soon as it came out of the oven.

I strained to hear what she told her father, but couldn't make out a word. I did see the Dad make a phone call while she brought my lunch.

"So, you help your father run the pizzeria and your grandmother writes a prize winning magazine. We studied creative writing together, you know." I took a bite, burned my mouth, but got a taste. "Excellent. Best pizza I've had since…"

She interrupted, "Since the last time you had pizza? Yeah, I help out in Mama and Dad's pizza joint. Mostly summers, and after school except during basketball."

"Your grandmother was great at b-ball, too. Back when girls had those phony rules to protect their delicate nature. I once watched her hold her own against the entire Sioux nation. Playing real aggressive basketball."

"Right. Excuse me." Rosalee suddenly dashed away. I dug into the pie. Then I heard part of the conversation behind me. "Do you know who that is?"

I turned around. Carolee had aged well. Not so curvy anymore, more handsome sturdy. Her hair was cut short, still blonde. I stood up. We hugged, and lingered in the hug until Rosalee revealed her discomfort by clearing her throat.

Carolee pulled away, grabbed my hand and pulled me toward the kitchen. "Come meet my son."

He stepped away from the work counter, wiped his hands on his apron and reached out. He shook my hand with a crushing grip as Carolee said, "Wally, my son, Mitch Martin." To her son she said, "Wally's a friend from long ago. More than friend," before this she had never winked at me, "old flame actually."

"Mitch?" I said to Carolee, a question conveyed in my raised eyebrows.

"I'll explain later."

"That's encouraging. Later and talk, I mean."

We sat in the booth, catching up on the easy parts before skirting around some histories with emotion. Her separation before Mitch was born. Bonnie's death. I'd save the ex-pat Canada story and we'd both have something to explain later.

(56)

She toured my rolling home and I tagged along for a walk to Carolee's office. It was a cluttered two room suite on the second floor in an old building with an auto parts store below. What had been a former tenant's reception area was the office, filled with two large desks, one on each side of the built in counter. Flat surfaces held computers and piles of papers, some in file folders, some scattered. Carolee directed me to the layout room, the same size and dominated by a netless ping-pong table where every two months a new magazine came to life from the clippings and pages spread over it.

"You do it the old way."

"Some old, some new. It's all digitized in the end. The old way is a comfort for this old news hack."

Carolee was handed several notes as we came back to the front office. She flipped through them. "I was hoping to leave it all to you, Wanda. Guess not. I'll be taking tomorrow morning off, so don't make any promises about return calls and open on time in the morning, okay?"

"I always do, don't I?"

Carolee didn't answer. She turned back to me. "Looks like I'm stuck for a little while. If you move your vehicle to the back, behind Rosie's, I'll be there in an hour or so."

***

Two hours later I was jolted awake by loud rapping. The open computer slid off my knee and bounced. I pushed it aside and called out, "Come on in, Curlybabe."

She had trouble working the odd latch but I got her in. In a rushed explanation, she said, "It'll mean some twelve hour days to get the next bi-monthly rag out on time, but I'm taking the rest of the week off. I'm not sure it's the right thing to do. Probably not, but whatever."

"And it's not about me, of course."

"Don't push it, Wally B3. You still seem to have some eerie power, but ... well, we'll see. Let's go in and meet Rosa, my daughter-in-law. She's the power over there. It was her family's business since she was a little girl."

"Rosie's Pizza is named for her, then?"

"Got it in one."

We got acquainted in short bursts between greeting diners, coaching a new server, and trying to speed up the kitchen crew. I thought my work running the auto shop was multi-tasking, but Rosa was a constant cyclone of activity. Carolee and I finished our beer and got out of the way. I drove; she navigated to her house a few blocks up a side street from her office.

The tiny house reminded me of Bonnie's grandma's, the house of the five stupid words. Carolee beckoned me into the kitchen. The small drop-leaf table was set with two plates and an enticing aroma emanated from the oven. I sat, as directed. Carolee filled stem glasses with white wine and pulled a pan of pork and sauerkraut from the oven.

"I see that you weren't at the office returning calls all afternoon. This looks and smells wonderful."

Carolee loaded my plate, then hers. "You've had our pizza, now try some real Pennsylvania cuisine."

I didn't tell her that my mother put a similar dish on the table when I was a kid. I had a mouth full and was ready to shovel in some more while Carolee carefully sliced her first small bite of pork loin. She ate that bite, put down her fork and took a tiny sip of wine. I watched and chewed. She had something to say, so I reluctantly put my fork down, too.

"I'm so glad you found me. I had no idea. Your father called a couple times, looking for you. Then we heard that you were gone forever into the wilds of Montana. I had no idea that I missed you."

I thought, "Wow!" Guarding against too high expectations, I said, "I was too tired to be driving, but I wanted to get to Altoona and look for you. I half expected—more than half—I fully expected to come up empty. I imagined you living in Florida with your husband in a house full of pictures of all the grandbabies. I was too tired. I went the wrong way and nearly fell asleep." I fudged; I didn't admit the whole of it. "So I pulled off, stumbled upon Rosie's, picked up that magazine and looked inside. 'Carolee Siebert, Editor/Publisher', jumped off the page. I looked up and there you were waiting tables. A living likeness of Curlybabe but with dark hair. I mean, is this some goddamn spiritual thing, or what?"

"I'm just glad you're here. We have so much catching up to do. I want to hear all about how you ended up living in Canada way out on Vancouver Island, and all."

I was thinking, and almost said but managed to hold back, "Hell, you don't need me for that. You can read my old journals and learn more about that than anyone wants to know." What I did say was, "Do I have this right? Jeff is Mitch's father, and the marriage ended. When Mitch was real young? Is that right?"

"You know that sales mantra? Sell yourself? You'd think I'd have been able to see through that. I was raised by a salesman. Well, Jeff was a little too literal about it. I was a conquest. We married and he moved on to the next cutie. Seven months pregnant and he disappeared. We'd get something now and then when the court threatened garnishment. He was always behind on the child support. I haven't had any idea where or if he's even alive since the day Mitch turned eighteen. So, that's my tale of woe."

"And you never remarried? Guys must've been falling over each other trying to snare you."

Dripping with sarcasm, she replied, "You're so sweet; such a way with words. You should be a writer. … Seriously, Wally, I did come close a couple times. But …" She shrugged. "Mitch and I had a pretty good time of it."

"Your dream was to teach in some godforsaken hellhole. Did you?"

"I had Mitch. I was so close, but never quite finished college. Got a job answering the phone at a three-employee weekly newspaper, and soon started committing journalism myself, bounced among some small town weeklies. I don't think I'd have had the patience for teaching anyway. I'm pretty good at reporting, at getting the story and writing it. I used to write poems, too. I had a few published in small literary journals. I saw many examples of gently worded rejection letters. With all that knowledge of how to say no to writers, I kind of slid gradually into the magazine gig. There's no money in it, as you can see by this palace I call home."

We were washing the dishes, moving into the conversation that would continue late into the night. Carolee abruptly shifted the topic. "I have a spare bed in the attic room. You're welcome to it, but then again, you brought your own house along, so maybe you'd just as soon stay there."

"You know quite well what I'd just as soon. I may be getting gray, but there's still a twenty-three year old in me trying to take over."

Carolee chuckled, tsk-tsked, and wagged her finger.

"Ah, well. Do you have an outside outlet for my power cord?"

I think she brought up sleeping arrangements early in the evening because she was also tempted and maybe a little frightened by what I'd 'just as soon'. I tried my best to calm the stirring waters. "Remember how it was when we were young and overloaded with hormones? How I was that privileged kid who assumed that I should always get my way and if I didn't it was an attack on me? Remember what I wanted and figured was my due? You said 'not yet' and I had to wait. And I did because I didn't want to lose you. I didn't understand you, or have any real idea what was important to you, but those hormones kept me trying."

"Oh, I remember. God, it was hard to say no." What she said next was barely a murmur. I think maybe she breathed, "Still is." Having a daughter firmed my attitude, learned a little late perhaps, that no does mean no. I'd sleep in the RV no matter what the evening and the wine might signal.

The Winnebago got electric power and my electronic devices began to recharge. I could read with good light later but by then I would be too tired to care. A stack of old journals was carried into the house. We sat on the sofa with the journals and Carolee's box of pictures taken at college and on our long hike and we reminisced. Carolee was still flipping through the notebooks when I finally collapsed into my RV bed musing about the possibilities. Lying on my back, eyes tightly shut, I asked Bonnie for some advice. She wasn't ready to give any, but I didn't feel any discouragement coming as I talked as if my beloved wife were listening.

***

"Why are your recent journals so sparse? You go weeks without an entry." Carolee had barely said good morning before the query. We were sitting down to breakfast, which I prepared and served in the Winnebago.

"I write on a keyboard now. The paper notebook is only when I have to get it written down and the 'puter isn't handy." I pointed at the

MacBook on the counter, which luckily had not been damaged when I knocked it off my lap the previous day.

"I thought that might be it; especially when I paid attention to the kind of entries here. They go back a few years in this one book." Carolee opened the wire bound volume. "But then there's this." She pulled off the big clip that bound the filled pages and marked the next blank page. She held the book up to show me the sealed envelope taped inside the front cover.

I tore the envelope out. "I don't know. I don't remember putting it there. I have no idea what that's about." I turned it over in my hands; held it up to the light; turned it over again. There were no markings on the envelope, and, by the weight of it, no more than one sheet of paper within.

"Are you gonna open it?" Ms. Siebert was fidgeting like a school girl who can't wait for her turn.

I tore the end and unfolded the page. "It's from Bonnie." I began to read. Stunned, I fell back on the dinette bench bumping my head against the wall. "Oof." The thought flashed through my mind that banging my head on the wall was an appropriate reaction.

I refolded the message and stuffed it back into the envelope. Closing my eyes I slid back in memory. I saw Bonnie in her recliner, nibbling and growing fatter by the day. She talked often of going to Kamloops. She mentioned helping her aging and failing mother. Did she ever state it as clearly as did this written message? Not as I remember it. She didn't seem to want to go anywhere. She more often turned down than accepted offers to take her to visit Cynthia and grandkids, without leaving the island. "Going to Kamloops." Every time I offered to take her to see her mother—and we went a couple times that year—did she ever say, "Moving back to Kamloops"? It wracked me with guilt. Did my neglect cause the depression and obesity and, by extension, her heart attack and death?

I opened my eyes, saw and remembered that I was not alone. Carolee seemed to be holding her breath, watching me warily. I clutched the envelope, thinking, "Do I let her read it? How can I talk about it otherwise? *Can* I talk about it?"

Carolee slid from across the table to the bench beside me. As she massaged the back of my neck I handed her the envelope. Sitting side by side I reread along with her.

I sit here, Wally. I sit on my fat ass with my popcorn and soda and cake, getting fatter and wondering how I can ever get out and move again. There's nothing for me here. Only you. And what do you have? Your precious auto shop. Tuning engines and changing tires and you come home and tell me about this customer and that. I sit. Yes, I retired from teaching. I had it all planned. I would volunteer more and make the museum into something special. I had it all worked out in my mind. Some others had different ideas. They tore me down and turned me into a nobody. Did I really act as if I know best and we could only do it my way? Well, you know all about that routine.

You think I'm satisfied to sit and watch the stupid television with my snacks? Can't you hear me? Not only would a move home to Kamloops let me take care of Mom, but it would put us between Curt and Cynthi. It wouldn't be much harder for Cynthi, Jared, Megan and Brad to visit and much easier for Curt and Bill. But no. Your precious business---and you have offers. You could sell it.

Please, I hope you find this soon. I can't talk to you about it anymore, but I cannot go without you. You are everything to me. Please, oh please. Take me home.

Love (I mean that),

She signed it, "Your Bonnie"

Carolee looked at me. I expected her to say something, but she apparently had no words. I suddenly felt urged to defend my wife, my Bonnie. "Please don't get the idea that this letter tells you anything about Bonnie, really. This is so unexpected. Why couldn't I hear what she was trying to tell me? Thirty years in that little town. I thought we'd finally been accepted as real North Islanders. How was I to know that without her job, that Kamloops was still the only home for her? How? Why? Oh, Bonnie! I'm so sorry!"

"Do you need some alone time, Wally?" That was the most understanding thing Carolee could possibly have said just then.

I nodded. She stood up and grabbed the cardigan she'd worn against the cool morning. Without forethought I spoke my true need of the moment. "Yes, I need some time with my thoughts. But, please stay here."

Now she nodded, "I'll be right back." Within two minutes she was back with the daily newspaper. She started on the puzzles, while I stared at my current journal document on the computer screen, puzzling about how to work through my distress.

(57)

I'd stared for such a long time drumming over the keyboard without typing any words that I was getting bleary eyed. I typed one sentence, slammed the laptop closed and said to Carolee, "I can't fix it. I can't let it go. ... I'll just have to live with it."

Carolee nodded, took my hand and said simply, "There's a lot of that in our lives, isn't there."

Now I nodded. "Yeah. You, too. Yeah." I got to thinking about life's rough spots she'd been sharing with me. "Let's take a walk."

"Good idea. Let's walk around my old neighborhood, where I grew up."

We moved the stacks of magazine materials and submissions to the back seat of her Chevy and Carolee drove us into Altoona. She drove with the familiarity of one who'd been driving these streets since she got her first license, or before, and parked on the block where she grew up. She opened the trunk, rummaged around and suddenly there was a basketball in my hands. Looking at her childhood home, she explained to me how a death, a stroke, and nursing home care meant the house was no longer in the family.

We dribbled the ball and pitched it back and forth along the way to the building that had once been the car dealership where her father worked. Part of the property was still a car lot, used only. I took Carolee out to the back lot where her father had shown me a sports car that had just come in. I couldn't remember if he'd seriously tried to sell it to me, or if that was some kind of fiscal responsibility test of a potential son-in-law.

From the lot with weeds growing around a few junk cars I pointed to the street. "This is where I was when I knew I'd lost you. I watched as you and Jeff walked up the sidewalk. My heart was pounding. Your dad was talking but I wasn't hearing. I knew you were no longer my Curlybabe. I still refused to believe it, but I knew it. At that moment I no longer had a home, not even in my own skin."

"More shit we have to live with. Crap."

"I still had tickets to Woodstock to present to you. That's when I believed it. … Is that men's shop still in business?"

"I don't know. There was more than one back then."

We found what looked like the location, relying on my foggy memory. It was an empty storefront with evidence that its last tenant was a video rental store. That convinced me to abandon one idea. My nostalgia tour would not include the Woodstock site.

After shooting hoops at her childhood schoolyard — she sank shot after shot and I occasionally hit the backboard — Carolee said, "Let's go to Harpers Ferry."

It was as if we were twenty again. I drifted back in time as the shopping cart cruised up and down the aisles. I filled the cart with wonderful ingredients for a week of meals. I was almost to the checkout line when reality paid a brief visit. This was an overnight, two at most and the little fridge could never hold half the perishables I had. I went back around until I was left with enough for two great breakfasts, snackies, and some good wine. Putting the steaks back I realized that I wanted to take a certain lady out to dinner every night.

Carolee was almost, but not quite, ready when I got back to her house. While she pondered some difficult clothing choices, I dug in the RV's clutter bins for a couple CDs of old rock music. For the life of me, I could not remember what Carolee liked best. I put The Doors into the player and put the Hendrix and Joni Mitchell discs out where she'd see them. Joni Mitchell. The name reminded me that I hadn't yet heard how my middle name became her son's first. Maybe it was really Joni's "Clouds" that inspired her. I switched and put that one in the Walkman connected to the old RV's cassette stereo.

At last, she came out lugging a heavy suitcase. She almost had it to the vehicle before I got out to help. "Are we going for a week, after all?"

"One night. I couldn't decide, so I threw it all in. I'm so rattled. Like I'm as young and foolish as we were that other time."

I grinned at the news that I wasn't the only one. "We'll just have to stay two or three days while you decide what to wear."

"Unlike some people in this fancy house boat, I do have a job to get back to."

We were on our way. I had taken one quick look at a map. All I learned was that it wasn't nearly as far away as I'd remembered. Of course, we were walking that time. "There's a road atlas there somewhere. Find us a route that stays away from turnpikes … and freeways."

Carolee studied the map. "Okay, but it might take longer."

"So what. We're revisiting our youth, right? Remember the Trail. The journey's the thing. The destination can take care of itself."

"How do you know when you get there that you've reached the destination? Or if that's even the right destination?"

"That there is a stumper. Hmm. You know because when you get there, it's home. I guess. Maybe." None of it made sense and I didn't understand her question. We rode without speaking until I turned on the music to push destination 'home to Kamloops' out of my mind.

"Oh Wally, you remember what I liked, back when we were a trek team. Aha! I've got your number. This is all part of your time travel scheme, isn't it."

"Yup. And it's working, too, isn't it. Hey, speaking of which, did you name your son while listening to 'Both Sides Now'? A girl would've been Joni?"

"If I say 'yes' will you drop the subject?"

"No, probably not. Is that your answer? Yes?" I glanced over at Carolee in the cushy passenger seat. It wasn't easy to pull my eyes back to road and mirrors.

"It's this way, Mr. B3. Jeff took off. I was seven months along and he split with the dolly he'd been making it with for months. I was pissed. I was angry at Jeff, angry at his girlfriend for taking my handsome man, and angry at myself for being a sucker to his phony charms. So what happens when you feel that way? I got a case of the what-ifs. What if I'd stayed with Wally? Would I ever get over my ambivalence? Would it have become the right thing and I'd know it? In that bluesy state of mind I borrowed a piece of your name."

"Thank you for telling me." We were approaching a town, and slowing. I pulled off the road into a business parking lot. "I just need a minute." I opened the door while trying to grab a couple Kleenexes without it being seen.

"Take your time, Wally," she said. In a softer voice, mostly to herself, she added, "That time it was about you. Sort of. Or not. Maybe wasn't about you, just my state of mind."

"Do you regret the name then?" I was still in my seat, with my feet out the driver's door, looking out.

"Never. His last name? Yeah, that one stirred troubled waters when he was young. Not Mitchell. That's just his name. He was always Mitch or Mitchie, of course."

"I'm all right. Let's get back on the road. I have lots of oldies in those CD pouches there in the bin." Carolee started looking through the titles. She put a John Denver album in the player and we sang along as we rolled southward, "Almost heaven, West Virginia..."

***

All those clothes and I didn't give Carolee opportunity to change for dinner. We arrived, made arrangements at an RV park and went right to a restaurant that the campground lady recommended. As we were finishing dessert, I asked, "Did you want to get a hotel room?"

"Why? We brought one with us, didn't we?"

"Well, yeah. I stay there, but I wondered ... you know."

"Damn, we really have stepped back forty years, haven't we. As I recall, at that time we maxed your credit card at a hotel. After days on the trail and nights in one sleeping bag, the hotel was for the bath and a night of decadent carousing. Tonight we'll have that in the comfort of your old but well-appointed Winnebago."

"Well, you know. I didn't know if it's time yet. Let's get to it." She slapped my butt.

Back at the RV park we nearly emptied the red wine, cuddled and recalled our young love. "Why," I wondered, "were we putting it off?" I know that I was feeling a little fear and anticipation. Carolee would call it 'What ifs'. I had actually been celibate ever since Bonnie lost interest. I was curious about Carolee's recent history, but, boy howdy, I did not ask.

We finally grew tired enough to jump in the sack. Not as literal a sack as in our encounters along the trail. It was good. It didn't last long, but it was pretty nice. To be intimate with this woman, well, the physical intimacy was great, but the deep friendship we'd rediscovered in our long talks, that was a real intimacy filling a void in my life that my cherished solitude couldn't begin to fill.

***

I looked out between the closed curtains at a steady, misty rain quietly making puddles in low spots and mud everywhere that wasn't paved. It didn't look like a morning for hiking. Our forty years of time travel was giving way to my true age again. What only slowed us down in 1969 would stop me now. I busied myself with preparations for a massive breakfast of coffee, bacon, pancakes, eggs, juice, and coffee. The mellow snoring had stopped, but Curlybabe's eyes were still closed. I think she was faking sleep to avoid involvement in my cooking.

Very soon, I was sure she'd been pretending. As soon as I added the platter of pancakes to the table setting and filled the mugs she was bouncing from bunk to head to galley.

I pulled the curtain aside to show Carolee the weather. Without looking outside, she pulled at her bathrobe and said, "Hey! Let a girl get herself together before you open us to the world."

"What? You look lovely as ever. Nice bathrobe, too. I just wanted to let you get a look at our hiking weather."

"Oh? Did we plan to go hiking today?"

"I assumed so. Isn't that part of our return to trail days?"

"Harpers Ferry was our step away from the trail to indulge in luxury for a day."

"That hotel wasn't exactly the Palmer House."

"That hotel was exactly NOT the tent on rocky ground."

"That hotel. What were we talking about?"

"Taking a walk. You're still the same old Wally. Wally has a plan and all around him must acquiesce."

"Damn straight. Just because it's never worked before doesn't mean jack."

"Seriously. When the rain lets up we can walk around in the town. We wouldn't get far on the muddy trail now."

"Even if it rains all day? Even if that means staying here another night?" I hinted.

She agreed with more enthusiasm than I could believe. "We'll stay another night regardless."

We spent most of the day cocooned in the RV playing cards, talking again about the people and events in our lives, and emptying both bottles of wine. By the time the rain let up our tipsy walk took us only to a little café where we enjoyed a nice supper. Without any discussion or decision, we returned directly to the Winnebago after the meal. The sex was better that night than the previous night's rehearsal.

It felt good to be alive. If I could hold onto the moment — I wanted to make it last into dotage with a long ago and present love.

***

The morning was clear, the sun already turning up the heat as it rose in the eastern rain washed sky. "It's gonna be a muggy day."

"The word is sultry, Wally. We pretend to be Southerners here," she drawled.

"Let's take our breakfast outside while it's still pleasant. Is that word acceptable?"

"It's congenial, I reckon."

"Was that agreement or a correction?"

Carolee took her eggs and coffee out to the damp picnic table at the campsite without offering a clarification. When I sat down, she said, "I've been thinking about my little bi-monthly tourist bait. The red ink has been worrisome for a couple years now. I give it another year, eighteen months at most, before we have to give it up. Now I'm thinking that will be acceptable, if not pleasant."

"Not congenial?"

"Don't interrupt. I have an idea about ending it well. What if we did something completely different? Instead of focusing the issue on yet another picturesque village of Western Pennsylvania, what if I did the usual format but on the other end of the continent?"

"You want to retire it in deep debt. Is that it?"

"I was hoping some benefactor might help me get to Vancouver Island and provide housing."

"I see. Yes, indeed. But, in a year? In the meantime?"

She shrugged and emptied her coffee mug. I waited for a word, but she took plates and her mug into the motor home. I sipped my coffee. Soon I heard the shower running.

I went in, refilled my mug, opened my computer and a new journal entry began to appear on the screen.

(59)

"You know, Curlybabe, I've been telling you about all the places I've lived. I got to thinking about it, how long I spent different places. Geez, let's see. Eighteen years in Winnetka. I couldn't get away quick enough, especially from Bradford and Son. Then those few years of college, better than home but not home, except for one thing. You were there. That was pretty good."

"Pretty good. Wow. I adore hyperbole."

"Most fantastic, awesome … Where was I? Oh, yeah. Then I spent a year as a hermit at a cabin in the Montana Rockies. I could walk from my door into the Bob Marshall Wilderness, and the hike was almost all within the Bob. Alone, except that my landlord, Sam, was a good friend and a father figure when I needed one. And then there's Cracker — what a great guy he was. Still is, I guess, but I couldn't find Graham Stands Alone Monroe on my way here."

"Uh-huh. You want some more coffee?" Carolee might have been losing interest.

I went on. I had to speak this timeline out loud to figure something out. "I'd take a warm up. Cracker got me into Canada. I found my way to Kamloops and met this wonderful woman at a little museum there. We hit it off. I found some work and I was just about to propose marriage when I said something so stupid, cruelly hitting a most sensitive spot, on top of the usual dumb stuff she'd already forgiven. I ended up working as a ranch hand in Alberta for something like five years with Hy and Pru. I really trusted those farmer-ranchers." I breathed out a long wistful sigh and sipped some warm coffee before I went on.

"That had to end when they sold and I tried once more. I'm pretty successful at finding unattached former girlfriends, ain't I. Bonnie was teaching in Port Hardy. We made a life together there. We made our

273

home there. We raised two wonderful kids there. I've lived in the same house for over three decades there."

"Okay. That's nice, Wally. We've been sharing these stories of the decades for five days now. The only thing different is you've put it in chronological order. And it seems really important to you." She took a sip of coffee and another nibble at the donut drying out on a plate in front of her. "Where's this leading?"

"Home, I think. Oh, I don't know." I stumbled along, but it was getting clearer in my mind as I spoke. "Yes. I want to go home. With these damn journals I can write a memoir that no one will read." I reached across the table to grab hold of Carolee's hand. "Come with me."

She was shaking her head, though I'm sure it wasn't from surprise. I'd been making all the moves that said I wanted us to be together. Damn, I was still thinking everything centers on what I want.

"You're asking me to leave my life and go with you to Port Hardy, British Columbia where you're well known as the car guy, widowed husband of Mrs. Bradford the beloved history teacher."

"When you say it like that. Shit. Yeah, well. Whatever happens, I've got to say it all. The reason I had to bore you with that list of places is I'm trying to understand where; how home doesn't depend on how long you stay or where you grow up. I'm thinking about Montana. The hermit cabin is still there and starting to fall apart. I didn't know why at the time, but when I came through, I checked on the ownership after I looked at it."

I paused. Carolee had a faraway look in her eyes, but I went on, "All my life, and I had no idea this was happening, but all my life I've been trying to figure out where home is. And it's the strangest, least likely place. So, what — ?"

Carolee reached up and held her open palm in front of my face to make me stop talking and wait. An interesting girl in a damp cramped tent on Yasgur's farm with two fingers pressed to my lips flashed across my memory.

"I'm having a hard time taking all this in, Mr. B. Let's go for a walk... And don't say a single word until we get back."

"I could delay, Curly. Stay here, help with the magazine's last year, then make us a mountain home." She pressed the open palm onto my mouth — an unmistakable "shut-up."

***

Carolee and I had been talking non-stop for five days. We walked in silence from the RV park. I had a hard time keeping quiet and when we reached the Appalachian Trail where it crosses the Shenandoah and we were walking the trail toward the bridge across the Potomac, a word came out before I could stop it, "Remember …"

Carolee glared and shook a forefinger at me. We reached the other bridge through the town and turned around. This time Carolee broke the silence, "I'm thirsty. Let's find an iced tea."

We sat at an outdoor table in front of the ice cream shop, Carolee with her tea and I with ice water and a large cone. I dared not be the first to speak.

"Okay, Wally my man, I think I have a plan. And no, that's not a sample of my poetry. But first, let me say this, because this is where both the problem and the solution come from."

I nodded and hurriedly finished my ice cream cone so that I could listen more intently than my usual.

"I still love you."

That brought a smile from me and a tut-tut and don't-say-anything-yet wag of the finger from Carolee.

"I love you but I'm not *in* love with you. Does that make sense?"

"No, but do go on."

"I enjoyed jumping in the sack with you again, don't get me wrong. And I did hope that I'd suddenly fall in love with you again." She shook her head and wiped a single tear. "You must see where my life is. I have these babies near and dear to me. Yeah, they're all grown up or near enough to think they are. I have the magazine, which is part of a dying breed, being pushed aside by the webzine. My son and his family are nearby. Why would I leave that? Rosalee and her brothers may move on, but not Grandma. I love my settled life, you see. And besides, they need to know which funeral home to call. There's too much baggage and no way to pack it. Listening to you and reading in those journals, it's clear that I can't replace Bonnie. Not when I don't have the energy to be 'In Love'."

"Too much baggage. Uh-huh. Not like our summer with a sleeping bag, pup tent and some dry noodles. Yep. I said I could stay in Pennsylvania for a while."

She shook her head. "Do you hear what I'm saying?"

"Not 'in' love." I was starting to understand and accept that the feeling might be mutual. "It was a real invitation, though. I guess I'm not surprised. You're making too much sense. I hate that, but I can't argue and I won't try to talk you into it. But hey, you can come and visit."

"I was just getting to that. If you're serious about gleaning a memoir from those journals, you'll need a good editor. I'd like the contract. Sure, we can do some with email, but not all. I predict at least two or three week long meetings will be necessary. We'll need enough time to talk the process through and through, take an old people hike in your wilderness. There are other communications that can't be done at long distance, too. Know what I mean? And don't forget that you agreed to be guide for that Vancouver Island farewell issue."

"I will be most pleased to welcome you to my hermitage for as many visits, long or short, as needed for whatever purpose. You speak too much damn truth and it's whacking me upside the head. If I were 'in love' with that youthful intensity we once knew, no question—I'd park my camper and stay here forever, whether you like it or not. As it is, I'll take you to Port Hardy, home of the Whalers, as agreed. When exactly did I agree to that?"

"Just now."

***

We had our separate lives to lead. They would intersect again, not entirely as planned, but close. For now, Carolee had a magazine deadline to meet. I had a small piece of Montana to purchase and a crumbling cabin to restore. Not to mention the book that I promised myself I would write. I had a brother in need of tough love, and grandchildren to watch growing up while they watch me grow old.

Carolee was anxious to get back to her work. I had stowed my things back into the motor home. We were hesitant anyway. Breakfast in her kitchen included one more cup of coffee until to pot was empty.

Not 'in love' she'd said. We were certainly more than friends. After one last lingering embrace, Carolee pushed me out the door and said, "It looks like you can go home now, Wally."

ABOUT THE AUTHOR

Against medical advice Kent Elliott can be found carrying a mug of black coffee nearly everywhere. His theory, and it is his alone, is that by alternating between lifting the mug to his face and pushing the computer mouse around its pad, he is preventing carpal tunnel syndrome. Kent took up a serious habit of story writing as a retirement hobby. With some small but happy success and with appreciative readers he's unable to quit.

Kent's first two novels are set (mostly) in Eastern Montana, a familiar part of the world that he moved away from when an opportunity came to return to the mountains. *It's Not About You, Wally: the traveling memoir of a solitary white man*, his third novel, goes to places he's never been, with characters who do things he's never done. And yet, these folks in their fictional settings and situations take us on a quest that will be familiar to many. Kent maintains that just because he's never been to Port Hardy, he has been to the end of a highway and has not entirely abandoned the dictum: Write what you know.